W9-DIJ-447

DESERT DARK

Sonja Stone

Holiday House / New York

Library of Congress Cataloging-in-Publication Data

Names: Stone, Sonja, author.
Title: Desert dark / by Sonja Stone.
Description: First edition. | New York : Holiday House, [2016] | Summary:
   Sixteen-year-old Nadia Riley enrolls at a prestigious boarding school, but
   finds Desert Mountain Academy a training ground for undercover CIA agents,
   so Nadia undergoes a punishing regimen of elite physical training, foreign
   diplomacy and target practice, but then a double agent is reported on
   campus . . . and Nadia is the number one suspect.
Identifiers: LCCN 2015022317 | ISBN 9780823435623 (hardcover)
Subjects: | CYAC: Boarding schools—Fiction. | Undercover
   operations—Fiction. | Spies—Fiction. | Schools—Fiction.
Classification: LCC PZ7.1.S755 De 2016 | DDC [Fic]—dc23 LC record available at
http://lccn.loc.gov/2015022317

To Morgan and Elizabeth

1 NADIA RILEY
SUNDAY, DECEMBER 11

Before she formulates a plausible lie, shots explode into the canyon. Splintered limestone sprays like shrapnel. Nadia drops behind a boulder.

Noah must have found us. She scans the walls for movement.

Another shot. Alan screams. He's down.

Nadia bolts across the riverbed. "Help me with him!" Damon rushes to her side. They drag Alan toward the cliff face.

She pulls her Beretta. "Alan, stop crying! It's a tranquilizer dart. It doesn't hurt that much." *What a baby. You didn't hear me screaming when I got shot.*

"No—look!" he shouts.

She turns back. Blood seeps through his torn pant leg. *Of course it wasn't a dart. Tranq guns are silent.* "Damon, on point." Nadia holsters her gun, applies pressure to the wound.

"Is it bad?" Alan's panicked eyes search her face. He grabs her shirt. "Answer me!"

"I need you to calm down." She forces a confident tone. "You're fine. It's just a scratch."

"Where is Jack?" Alan yells. "I need Jack!"

"I'm right here." Jack climbs down from an overhanging ledge. "Those shots weren't from Noah's team." He pushes Nadia's hands

1

away, wipes the blood with a square of cotton. "It's grazed, not deep at all. Wrap it up," he orders Nadia. "We need to move."

Her eyes meet Jack's. A sick fear crawls through her like fire ants on a dead coyote. She knows what he's thinking, because she's thinking the same thing.

Someone messed up. That bullet was meant for me.

THREE MONTHS EARLIER

2 NADIA
TUESDAY, SEPTEMBER 6

As requested, Nadia Riley waited for her calculus teacher in his classroom after the final bell. By the time Mr. Milligan arrived, she'd finished her chemistry homework and was halfway through history. He dropped a packet of papers on her desk: the extra-credit assignment she'd completed during lunch. A dark red zero covered her name.

"My answers were wrong?" Nadia asked. "I double-checked my work."

Milligan leaned on the edge of his desk. "I can't give you credit for this. I specifically instructed your class not to use online resources."

"I know. I didn't."

"That simply isn't possible. This was meant to be a month-long project. There's no way you finished it in one day without outside help."

One hour, actually, but that's nitpicking. "Mr. Milligan, I promise you: I solved the puzzle on my own."

"Nadia, cheating is a serious offense."

"I completely agree. I didn't cheat."

"You're telling me you finished this *by yourself* in one day?"

"Yes."

"How? How did you find the answers so quickly?"

"I don't know. I'm really good at puzzles. I've been doing them since I was a kid," she said. Milligan raised an eyebrow. "Do you have another one? I'll show you."

"All right." He pulled a worksheet from his briefcase. "Let's see what you've got."

Nadia took the paper. Mr. Milligan circled behind the desk, watching over her shoulder. She instantly recognized the formula. The problem looked like an algebraic equation, but she knew a Vigenère cipher when she saw one. "Give me a minute." She stared at the equation, calculating in her head.

"If you can't do it, just say so." He reached for the page.

Nadia slapped her hand onto the paper, pinning it to the desk. "I can do it." This particular code, designed to disguise letter frequencies, had been around for three centuries. *If I can't solve this, I deserve to be expelled.* She scribbled the final steps. "Earthworm," she said. "The answer is earthworm." She held up the worksheet.

Milligan took the paper from her hand and moved slowly toward his desk. "This is remarkable," he mumbled. "How . . . ?"

"It's your basic polyalphabetic cipher based on letter substitution. I solved for X, used modular arithmetic and found the remaining letters." She stood and grabbed her bag.

His eyes didn't leave the page. "It took me an entire semester at graduate school to solve this equation."

"Oh." Nadia heaved her backpack onto her shoulder. "Please don't feel bad. I really have been doing these all my life. It's kind of a hobby."

"And I was a *math* major."

Enough about me. "Mr. Milligan?"

"With a minor in engineering!"

"Mr. Milligan?"

"What?" Milligan looked up.

"Can I go?"

"Oh, yes. My apologies. You'll receive full credit for the assignment."

"Thank you." Nadia didn't care about the extra credit. But

being called a cheater? She earned her grades; she didn't steal them.

"Listen," Mr. Milligan began, "have you considered supplementing your education at the university level? Or maybe joining the math club?"

She nodded, pretending to consider. *Yeah, I'm gonna join the math club. Why not? I'm already a social pariah.* "That's an idea." Nadia glanced at the clock above the door. "Can we talk about it another time? I should probably get going." On the bright side, he'd grilled her long enough that she wouldn't run into anyone on the way to her locker.

"Of course." He looked back to her worksheet. "I'll see you in class tomorrow."

"See you then." Nadia stepped into the empty hallway: wide and exposed, with hideous fluorescent lights. Metal boxes lined the walls like rows of vertical coffins. To spare herself the misery of running into her ex-boyfriend between classes, she loaded her backpack every morning and carried all of her textbooks until the end of the day. Her locker was right beside his, and three down from her ex-best friend's.

They'd become exes on the same day.

She rounded the corner and saw a flash of dirty blond against the grey metal. Her chest tightened. Matthew looked up before she could turn back. Nadia continued at a casual pace.

"Hey, Judas," she said. "Where's Delilah?"

"Those are two different stories." He leaned against her locker, blocking access. "We need to talk."

"No, we don't." She stopped in front of him. "We are no longer dating, so I don't have to pretend to be interested in your opinion. Move."

Matthew pursed his lips. "Don't be like that. I'm sorry about Hannah's party." He didn't look sorry at all. "I didn't tell her to throw you out."

"Nice to know your minions have your back, huh?"

"Paige says you won't take her calls."

"Why would I?" Nadia dropped her bag. It hit the floor with a solid thud. She kicked it against the metal wall and imagined it was Matthew's head.

"So you're just gonna ignore us for the rest of your life? Not even you can pull that off."

"I'm pretty sure I can."

"We didn't mean for this to happen."

Her eyes rolled away from Matthew's gaze.

"Paige really misses you."

Like I care? She studied the Exit sign over the stairs.

"This is so stupid."

Nadia glared at him. "I trusted you."

"It was an accident."

"An accident?" she scoffed. "How does that work?"

"Quit being stubborn."

"No, I'm really curious. You saw each other at the mall and some invisible force magnetically pulled you together?"

"People don't want to choose between you and Paige, but they will."

"Or maybe you were at the movies? And suddenly your clothes just *fell off*. I've heard of that phenomenon. Happens all the time."

"She's lived here her whole life. You've been here two years. Who do you think they're gonna pick?"

"You might want to see a doctor. That could get embarrassing."

"You know as well as I do, if you and Paige make up you'll be back in with everyone else."

Nadia narrowed her eyes. "What's with the sudden interest in my social standing?"

"It's not just about you. Paige is devastated."

"Fortunately, she has you to console her. Lucky girl. Now get off my locker."

"I'm not moving until you agree to talk to her. She's outside."

Nadia took a deep breath and leaned toward Matthew. She stopped an inch from his face, and spoke slowly, enunciating each word. "If you do not move, I will forcibly move you."

Matthew hesitated a second before leaning to the right.

"Good call." Nadia opened the lock.

"Look, it's been two weeks. I understand if you can't forgive me, but you guys were like sisters. And she's been miserable *for days*." He dropped his head back and stared at the ceiling.

"How inconvenient for you. Let's recap: first you hook up with my best friend. Then you tell everyone about it—well, everyone but me. Next, your jackass cousin kicks me out of her house in the middle of a party." She felt the heat rising up her neck, over her cheeks, through her scalp. Thinking about the party made her sick to her stomach.

Nadia shouldn't have gone to Hannah's house. She'd wanted to show her face, like she didn't care about Matthew and Paige. In retrospect, she was sure everyone knew she wasn't invited. No one would go with her. They all had "pre-party plans." They didn't want to align themselves with the loser, show up with an uninvited guest. Two years of her life, and she was still an outsider. She took another breath.

"I really didn't know she would do that," Matthew said.

"Whatever."

"Paige and I wanted to tell you sooner. But we didn't want to hurt you."

"Obviously."

"Knock it off."

"*You* knock it off. You're with Paige and that's fine. I don't care." It wasn't fine. Nadia loved Matthew and Paige knew it. The whole school knew it. It was one thing to lose her boyfriend to some random girl, but to her best friend? She couldn't be more humiliated. "But leave me alone. I'm not interested in a friendship with either of you."

Nadia slammed her locker and walked toward the front door, praying he wouldn't follow.

"You're just mad because you hate to lose."

"Not much of a loss," she called over her shoulder. But it was.

A horrific loss. Not just Matthew; her friendship with Paige had been the center of Nadia's life. And now she felt a constant void.

Nadia pushed through the double doors into the humid afternoon. She used to look forward to the short walk home. Paige had joined her almost every day. They'd do homework together and Paige would stay until dinnertime. *I miss her so much.*

Nadia clamped her lips together and lowered her head. *Don't you dare cry.* The sidewalk blurred as she wiped at her tears.

3 DREW ANDERSON
WEDNESDAY, SEPTEMBER 7

Drew Anderson had just finished her second agonizing day of classes at Desert Mountain Academy. Now she was headed into town to treat herself to a pedicure. Her new roommate, Libby Bishop, had declined Drew's invitation to the salon. Instead, she had insisted on meeting the other members of their study group at the library to quiz each other about some random war that took place a thousand years ago.

She could already tell this would be a tough year. Academically she'd be fine, but her roommate was kind of—oh, what was the word—*fastidious*. Libby followed Drew around their bedroom, cleaning up after her with disinfecting wipes. She tried to do it when Drew wasn't looking, but Drew had already caught her. Twice.

Who alphabetizes their medicine chest? Drew shook her head.

But her obsessive-compulsive roommate wasn't even the most interesting thing so far. A rendezvous she'd witnessed last night won the grand prize. It was so unusual, in fact, that Drew took the time to write about it in her diary at two o'clock in the morning. Of course, she never named names. She would not lose another friend that way.

She turned off Scottsdale Road into a shopping plaza that

advertised Fiona's Nail Salon and Desert Moon Books. She'd get her toes done, then grab a cinnamon latte at the coffee shop that would inevitably be tucked into the back of the bookstore.

Inside, she checked in with Fiona and selected a polish. Drew carried a magazine in her purse just in case, but the store gossip was much more interesting than "How to Tone Your Tummy by Spring." A half hour later, toes freshly painted, she slipped into flip-flops and padded next door for her latte dessert.

She spent too much time flipping through celebrity glossies; it was dark by the time she left the bookstore. Drew crossed the dimly lit parking lot quickly, now wishing she'd found a closer spot. As she approached the car, she saw someone leaning on the passenger-side door. Her breath quickened. She slowed her pace as she peered through the darkness, trying to see the man's face.

"Good evening, Drew," he said, and she immediately recognized his voice.

"You scared me." She laughed, relieved. "What are you doing here?"

"I have to talk to you. Can we go somewhere private?"

"Sure." Drew was always up for some juicy gossip, and what else could this be? She unlocked the doors and climbed into the car. She drove toward school, north on Scottsdale Road.

With the lights of town behind them, her passenger requested she pull over into one of the many trailhead parking lots along the road. She consented, and left the car idling after she'd put it in park.

"What's up?" Drew asked.

"You saw me last night."

She hesitated for a second and then nodded.

"What did you see?"

She tried to look confused. "Nothing."

"Did you tell anyone?"

"No."

"Not even your roommate?" He stared at her intently.

She shook her head. "You're not the only one who snuck out. I broke the rules too. I'm fairly certain Libby wouldn't approve."

"What were you doing, lurking around?"

"I wasn't lurking. I was *stealing*, but I wasn't lurking. I helped myself to a little mint chocolate chip, that's all."

"At one o'clock in the morning?"

She shrugged. "I don't know what to tell you. I couldn't sleep. I like ice cream. And you? What were you doing?"

Her accuser sighed and lowered his car window. The hot night air filled the cabin.

"Who was that guy you were with?" she asked, trying to draw out his story. After a moment, "Okay, it's none of my business." *Maybe it was a romantic encounter.* Drew actually knew the other guy; she'd recognized him. *That would be highly inappropriate.*

"Are you sure you kept quiet?"

"I already answered that. Are we done here?" Drew stepped on the brake and grabbed the gearshift.

"What is that?" The passenger pointed out the driver's side window, squinting through the darkness.

Drew turned toward her window. "Where?"

And the last thing she heard—besides the gunshot—was, "Oh, my mistake."

4 NADIA
FRIDAY, SEPTEMBER 9

The only acceptable thing in Nadia's life was that today was Friday, which meant an entire weekend without having to look at Matthew's face. Sweet, luxurious freedom.

Her friends still averted their eyes when they passed in the hall. She couldn't find a lab partner in chemistry, so her teacher had assigned one. He was a sigher. "Can you pass me that beaker?" *Sigh.* "Did you fill out the lab report?" *Sigh.* "Look out—your solution is on fire." *Sigh.* It was exhausting.

A week ago she'd smartened up and downloaded a playlist to her phone, so at least she could listen to music on the way home. Then she could pretend not to notice Matthew and Paige as they drove by. But when her father found out, she'd been forced to endure a twenty-minute lecture on the importance of "situational awareness."

"Nadia, your personal safety is at risk. A young woman walking down the street, unaware of her surroundings—it's irresponsible. When you leave this house, you need to pay attention. Who do you see? What are they doing? Do you hear footsteps behind you? Open your eyes and your ears."

Her father's occupation repeatedly compelled him to thwart Nadia's attempts to act like a normal teenager. He was a professor of criminology; he understood the dark side of human nature.

She rounded the corner to her house and, as if she'd conjured him with her thoughts, saw her father's Camry in the drive. *Is he checking up on me?* Nadia yanked out the earbuds and shoved them into her bag. *That's not really his style.* But he never left work early and wasn't due home for hours.

Maybe we're moving again. She climbed the front steps. *That would rock.*

Inside, Nadia dropped her bag on the bench in the foyer and kicked off her sneakers. She slammed the front door, announcing her arrival.

"Nadia?" her mom called. "We're in here."

"Dad, what are you doing home?" Nadia yelled as she crossed the living room. She pushed through the kitchen door and grinned at her father. "Did you get fired?"

He stood with his back to the sink. The sun filtered through the window, creating a halo around his coppery brown hair. Beneath his closely cropped beard he suppressed a smile. He'd removed his jacket and rolled up the sleeves of his oxford. He seemed relaxed, which meant he'd been home for a while.

Nadia had her father's blue-green eyes and her mother's dark, wavy hair, though Nadia's had more curl toward the ends. Her complexion, a fusion of her parents' Irish and Lebanese, was a light olive that she thought looked sallow most of the time; too dark to be fair and too light to be dark.

"Good for you," Nadia continued. "You finally told your boss to take this job and—"

"Sweetheart," her mother said, nodding toward the kitchen table.

Nadia turned around and noticed a fourth person in the room. Her face burned as she said, "Oh, we have company." She glanced at her dad. "A little heads-up would've been nice. I was joking, by the way. My father would never tell off his boss. You're not his boss, are you? I'm kidding—I know him. Great guy." *Stop talking.*

"You must be Nadia." The man smiled and extended his hand. He stood a foot taller than her, with wide shoulders and a narrow waist. He had silver hair and wore a dark suit, well-tailored, with a knife-like crease in the pants. "My name is Marcus Sloan. I work as a recruiting agent for Desert Mountain Academy outside Phoenix, Arizona. Your father was just showing me your trophy collection." He gestured to the case along the wall. "Very impressive."

"Sorry. He does that."

"I can see why. The Mid-Atlantic Championship? Nicely done. I don't meet many students with a competitive interest in cryptography."

"Competitive? Nadia?" Her dad laughed. "Not our girl."

Nadia narrowed her eyes at her father's sarcasm. "So I'm a little driven." She turned to their guest. "Cryptograms are just a small piece of the competition. Once the clues are decoded, it's more of a scavenger hunt. Anyone could do it."

"Yes, I'm familiar with the Smithsonian's annual Cipher Search Competition. You're the youngest winner in history. I've been looking forward to meeting you," Mr. Sloan said. "Which brings me to why I'm here. An opening has become available and I'd like to offer you a position as a first-year student."

"First year?" Nadia shook her head. "I'm a junior."

"We run an intensive two-year program for juniors and seniors. The curriculum focuses on ingenuity and problem-solving, so we provide a project-based, hands-on learning environment. As I've explained to your parents, tuition, room and board is paid for in full by the United States Government."

"But I didn't even apply."

"Why don't we sit down, and I'll explain." Mr. Sloan pushed his coffee to the side and folded his hands on the table. "Our school was founded to serve the country's most academically elite. Our primary goal is to remain competitive with up-and-coming nations, like China, who now place a great deal of emphasis on education. It's a government-sponsored private school, so we don't accept applications. We recruit students based on their overall grade point average, among other things."

Nadia looked down. "I don't have the highest GPA in my class." Matthew did, which annoyed her. She came in second place. Again.

"Do you remember the standardized tests administered at the end of your sophomore year?"

"Sure. We take them every May." She loved standardized tests.

"We have a series of eighty benchmark questions scattered throughout the exam. Those questions weigh more heavily on our decision to recruit than GPA. The average student answers ten, maybe fifteen of those questions accurately. The students we recruit get about sixty of them."

"How many did I get?"

Mr. Sloan paused and glanced at her father. He cleared his throat and answered, "All of them."

Nadia smiled. Matthew would be furious if he heard that. He made everything a competition. "So what were the questions?"

"A variety of problems involving spatial ability, abstract thinking, pattern recognition, moral judgment." His cool eyes flitted between Nadia and her dad. She had the feeling his response was deliberately evasive. "Based on your answers, we believe you fit a certain profile that we value at Desert Mountain. I'm sure you'll need to discuss this with your parents. I've shown them our website. I encourage you to peruse the site as well."

"The campus is certainly beautiful," Mr. Riley said.

"Thank you. We're very proud of it."

"School started weeks ago. Why are you inviting me now?" Nadia asked.

"Sadly, one of our students passed away. She was in a car accident."

"Oh, her poor parents," Nadia's mom said.

"Yes, it's a terrible tragedy. We are all still feeling the loss. But unfortunately, with such a small student body, we need to keep each position filled."

"How many students are enrolled?" Nadia asked.

"The Academy has fifty juniors and thirty seniors. We have a few students transfer out every year. Not everyone is suited to the program. Because of the heat, the Academy starts a little later in the year than East Coast schools, so you've only missed four days of classes. Your roommate will catch you up in no time. I fly back tomorrow, and I'll need your decision by then. If you decide to join us, we'll arrange your travel. Due to the challenging nature of our curriculum, you would have to transfer immediately."

He turned to her parents. "Mr. and Mrs. Riley, thank you for seeing me. Your daughter would be a fine addition to our school. I'm staying at the Bridgeport Hotel in Arlington. Please call me with any questions." He placed his business card on the table as he stood. "You should know that our graduates have first pick of all the Ivy League schools."

"Thank you for coming, Mr. Sloan. We'll be in touch." Nadia's dad escorted their guest to the door.

And there it was. A lifeline. Her way out.

No more avoiding her locker, no more heart palpitations every time the phone rang—*is it Matthew? Paige?*—no worries about junior prom. Everyone was already talking about Homecoming. If Matthew had broken up with her for any other reason she still could've gone to the dance. She would've gone with Paige, shown up in a killer dress and spent the evening deliberately ignoring him.

When her dad returned to the kitchen Nadia asked, "Did he just show up?"

"He called yesterday. We were expecting him," he said.

"And you didn't tell me?"

"We didn't see the need until we'd discussed it."

"But I can go, right?"

"I think it's a terrible idea," her mom said. "You're sixteen years old! And you haven't even looked at the school."

"Zaida, honey, we need to talk about this. I've done some research. This is a phenomenal school. It's a once-in-a-lifetime opportunity," Nadia's father said.

"It's very sudden." Her mom crossed her arms over her chest. "Nadia, do you even want to go? And miss your junior year?"

"Well, let's see, I simultaneously lost my boyfriend and my best friend. I was recently humiliated in front of the entire junior

17

class. I spend my lunch period in the biology lab with the *mice* so I don't have to eat alone in the cafeteria. What am I clinging to, Mother?"

"There's no need for sarcasm."

Shut up or you'll blow it. Nadia took a breath. "You're right—I apologize. But it sounds like a perfect fit. Hands-on study? That's right up my alley." She'd never imagined boarding school. Her family was solidly middle class: two cars, a yearly vacation. They certainly couldn't afford private school. "And if it doesn't work out, I can always transfer back, right?" *Whatever it takes, I'll make it work.*

"You hate moving! You throw a fit every time you have to change schools!"

"That should give you some indication of how desperate I am."

"Well, I'm sorry. You can't go."

"Mom," Nadia pleaded.

"It's out of the question." She strode from the room.

Tears burned Nadia's eyes. "Dad, *please*," she whispered.

"I'll talk to her. She worries about you, that's all. She's your mother. It's her job." He lowered his voice. "I think she'll come around." He hugged her and left the room.

Nadia stood alone in the kitchen and felt a flicker of something she hadn't felt in weeks.

Hope.

5 LIBBY BISHOP
SUNDAY, SEPTEMBER 11

Libby Bishop stood at her bathroom counter and rearranged the flowers in the glass vase for the third time that hour. She had placed clear marbles in the bottom for texture, chosen lilies for their strong fragrance and added enough greenery to make the white flowers pop. When she was satisfied with the new arrangement, she cleaned the pollen off the marble counter with a sanitizing wipe, reapplied her lipstick and turned to the bedroom.

She wanted everything to be perfect for her new roommate. Her momma had told her many times you never get a second chance to make a first impression, and with her daddy's high profile, she'd had plenty of practice. That's why she always introduced herself as Libby and not by her full name, Liberty. That's also why she loathed her Southern drawl. She knew what people thought when they heard it: at best, they'd think her uneducated and prissy; at worst, racist. She didn't miss that part of Georgia one bit.

Her room, now half-vacant, was exceedingly tidy. Drew's belongings had been cleared away immediately. The whole thing was awful to think about, and Libby couldn't bear to dwell on the details. Plus, it wasn't as though she'd lost a close friend. Drew was distant; Libby never felt that special connection. Despite living together all summer they'd scarcely gotten to know each other. But it was unsettling all the same. Especially since Libby had been invited along that night. If she wasn't such a conscientious student, she might've been in the car too.

Well, maybe *conscientious* wasn't the right word. Libby simply did not consider spontaneity a virtue. She much preferred a plan.

To cheer her up, her momma had encouraged her to redecorate her room, make a fresh start. And her momma was an expert at new beginnings.

Libby had chosen deep earth tones for the duvet and arranged the coordinating boudoir pillows just so. She'd dressed the windows from floor to ceiling in chocolate brown silk with the slightest sheen, and filled the space between the twin beds with a soft white wool shag. She considered making Nadia's bed up with the extra set of linens she'd purchased, but she didn't want to seem pushy.

Libby settled into her desk chair. She peeked inside the top drawer, making sure the false bottom she'd installed was properly secured. The only plus to living alone was the guarantee of privacy. *Let's hope my new roommate isn't as nosy as the last one.* Satisfied her secrets were safe, Libby closed the drawer, smoothed her skirt and flipped open her political science textbook. She had no intentions of reading right now but she didn't want to seem as though she was sitting around waiting for Nadia Riley to arrive, which she was. It made her uncomfortable, being at loose ends like this. No schedule, no plan. She looked at the clock on her nightstand. Just after noon. *It'll be hours before she gets here.*

Libby went back to the bathroom to recheck the flowers. *And I'm so glad I did. Look at this one! It's like a raccoon's been gnawing on the petals.* She lifted the wastepaper basket to the vase and carefully removed the offending stem. She wiped the counter again and returned to her desk.

I probably should'a washed my hands while I was up.

Libby slid her fingers under her thighs and frowned. *You don't have to. Those wipes are clean. They've got bleach in 'em. Doesn't get any cleaner than bleach. Just don't think about it.*

To distract herself, she read the titles on her bookshelf out loud. *"The Making of a Navy Seal, Unarmed Combat, Diplomacy in a Terrorist World*—oh, for heaven's sake," she said, as she rushed to the bathroom to wash her hands.

6 NADIA
SUNDAY, SEPTEMBER 11

Two days after Marcus Sloan's visit, Nadia flew into Phoenix. She hadn't told anyone about the Academy. Her mom would call the front office tomorrow, let them know about the transfer. Word would get out that she'd been recruited to a boarding school in Arizona. Matthew would be sick with envy. Paige would wonder if he was jealous because they chose Nadia over him, or if he was sulking because he missed her.

She tried to ignore the flash of sadness. This was probably the most exciting thing that'd ever happened to her. She wanted to share it with someone.

Knock it off. Don't let them ruin this.

Nadia followed the other passengers to baggage claim. A man stood to the side, holding a sign printed with her name. He eyed the women, moving from one to the next, until his gaze settled on Nadia.

"That's me." She smiled and pointed to the sign.

He didn't return her smile. "May I see your ID?"

"Oh, sure." Nadia dug through her carry-on and offered her passport.

The driver studied her picture. "What is your mother's maiden name?"

"Azar."

"And your recruiter?"

"Mr. Sloan?"

"The name of the hotel where he stayed?"

"Um, the Bridgeport? In Arlington, I think."

Apparently satisfied, he returned her ID and smiled. "Welcome to Phoenix."

Nadia laughed. "Do you get many impostors?"

"Let's get your bags."

A blast of searing heat assaulted her as they left the terminal. They drove north, leaving the beige city behind, into the rocky foothills of a low mountain range. Dusty stretches of desert replaced shopping malls; gated communities faded into thick stands of sage-green cacti.

Nadia's stomach hurt. *It's like any other new school. I'll be fine. I always am.* She sighed and rested her head on the seat-back. *But what if I'm not? What if no one likes me?*

Keep whining, Nadia, and no one will.

After an hour, the driver turned onto a winding dirt road, barely wide enough for the car. Ahead, a massive sand-colored wall stretched across their path, extending in both directions. A security booth policed the iron gate that blocked the road.

An armed guard stepped forward. He scanned the driver's eyes with a laser gun and nodded them through.

Nadia's stomach tightened. "What was that?"

"A retinal scan."

"They don't know you by sight?"

"The dean of students likes to keep track." The gate closed behind them.

Inside the wall, it was another world—a literal oasis in the desert. Against the backdrop of vermilion mountains, eight buildings formed a semicircle around a lush carpet of grass. The lawn sloped gently toward her; the driveway ran along the bottom of the hill at the base of the half-circle. Flower beds packed with purple and white pansies lined the concrete path curving along campus.

"Dean Wolfe is expecting you." The driver pulled to the building on the far right. An etched stone marker read *Hopi Hall*. He nodded toward a slender woman waiting on the steps. "That's his assistant, Ms. McGill. She'll take you from here."

Ms. McGill smiled. Freckles covered her crisp features. "We're glad you could come." She handed Nadia a bottled water. "Drink this. It's a hundred and eight today."

"Thank you so much." Nadia chugged the icy water. The afternoon sun filtered through the palm trees over her head and danced across the jute-colored wall. The flickering light made her head swim. "I think I was a little dehydrated."

Inside, Ms. McGill's heels clicked along the travertine. She led Nadia to a sitting room at the end of the hall. "I'll get your uniforms. You're about five-three?" Nadia nodded. "Have a seat. Dean Wolfe will be with you shortly."

"Thank you." Nadia stepped into the cool, dark room. A bank of windows covered the far wall. To her left the mountains erupted like crumpled paper; to the right, the distant city nestled in the saddle of the valley. Glass-covered bookshelves lined the walls, like soldiers standing at attention. A brass nameplate bolted to the heavy door in front of her read Thadius Wolfe.

Nadia sank back into an oversized chair, then changed her mind and sat forward, embarrassed her feet didn't quite reach the floor when she reclined. She sat awkwardly erect on the edge of her seat, ankles crossed. She waited.

And waited.

Finally, the door opened. "Miss Riley? I'm Dean Wolfe." His smooth voice resonated through the room.

"It's nice to meet you." Nadia stood to shake his hand.

Thadius Wolfe, attractive in a distinguished sort of way, had deep-set eyes and dark hair streaked with grey. His huge frame filled the doorway. He looked powerful, and not just physically. "Please, come in."

Indigo drapes largely concealed the window behind his desk; a matching oriental rug covered the floor. A small lamp with a sunset-orange glass globe cast a tiny pond of light onto a file labeled Riley, Nadia.

She sat in one of the two wingback chairs, hands in her lap. The soft leather whispered as Dean Wolfe reclined into the other navy chair.

"Mr. Sloan explained that you're replacing another student, so you understand classes have started for the semester." The Dean plucked a speck of lint from his pant leg and dropped it on the rug.

"Yes. I was sorry to hear about the accident."

"It's a horrible thing, losing such a young person." He paused for a moment, then cleared his throat. "You'll need to relinquish your cell phone at this time."

Nadia raised her eyebrows as he continued. "Communications between students and the outer community are restricted. If you need to telephone your parents, your dormitory assistant will make arrangements."

She nodded. "I guess my bags are in my room?"

"Security is checking them. They will be delivered when they're done."

"Glad I left my contraband at home," Nadia joked.

He didn't smile. "You are required to wear a uniform on campus at all times with the exception of Saturdays and Sundays. All classes are mandatory. You train in jujutsu three days a week. In addition, first-year students are required to complete basic strength training five days a week. There are *no* casual Fridays."

"Dean Wolfe, Director Vincent is on line one." Ms. McGill's voice sounded over the telephone's intercom.

"Excuse me."

Nadia stood. "Should I wait outside?"

"No, no. Sit." He picked up the phone. "This is Thadius Wolfe. No, sir, not at the moment. Yes, we shipped everything to her parents. As a matter of fact," he glanced at Nadia, "she's here with me now. Yes sir. I'll speak to you then." He hung up. "Where were we?"

"No casual Fridays."

"Right. Laundry is delivered weekly to your room. Do you have any questions?"

She almost asked about room service, but he hadn't seemed to enjoy her first joke. She shook her head.

"You've been assigned to a standard team: four juniors, a senior advisor. Your success at Desert Mountain is largely determined by your ability to function as a group. I cannot overstate the importance of team unity. You eat together, you work together, you train together. Do you understand?"

Nadia smiled. "Not a problem. I love working with others," she lied.

"Ms. McGill will introduce you to your roommate, Libby Bishop."

"Sounds great."

Dean Wolfe presented Nadia with her class schedule. "We have one more item of business, then you're free to go."

"Okay." She glanced at the paper. *Psychology, Political Science, Diplomacy . . . Arabic? Seriously?*

"It's time to meet the psychiatrist."

7 JACK FELKIN
SUNDAY, SEPTEMBER 11

Jack Felkin sat on the second-story patio outside the Navajo Building and looked across campus. The misters attached to the overhead beams did little to cool the air. He wiped the sweat from his neck and glanced at his roommate's notebook.

That figures. Noah was drawing a caricature of the kid at the next table. "Don't you have anything better to do?" Jack asked.

Noah grinned. "What's better than this?"

"It's a real comfort knowing guys like you will be in charge of our Nation's security."

"You know what your problem is? You take yourself too seriously."

"Great. And now you sound like my mother." She claimed he buried himself in his studies to avoid real life. Sure, he'd always been a committed student, perhaps to a fault. But there were so many books to read, languages he should learn.

"Don't worry about me," Noah assured Jack. "I'll get my work done. Hey, I've been meaning to ask you, is Libby seeing anyone?"

Jack shook his head. He and Noah were seniors, and both had been chosen as team leaders. He didn't understand Noah's willingness to waste study time in pointless pursuits: sketching, speculating about girls. More annoying than his slacker attitude was the fact that Noah's inattention to academics didn't seem to affect his GPA. He and Jack were still neck and neck. "Stay away from her. I don't want you poisoning the well."

"Don't be like that."

"I'm not kidding," Jack said.

"I think we'd be really good together."

Jack did his best to block out Noah's voice. Something had happened Friday afternoon, right on the heels of Drew's death, and it had nagged at him all weekend.

"The poor girl just lost her roommate," Noah said.

Jack and a group of classmates had been leaving Improvised Munitions. In the hallway around the corner, two of his professors had stood talking. He'd caught bits of the conversation: something about a double agent on campus. They obviously hadn't known the students were there.

"I should console her," Noah continued.

"Seriously," Jack said. "Don't mess with my team." *What if it's true?* The idea of a threat to the school troubled him—Desert Mountain meant everything to Jack.

"Afraid she'll figure out I'm better than you?"

Jack smiled. "I'm concerned about team cohesion, not that she'll suddenly lose all sense of reality."

Jack's grandfather had been a war hero, and he'd instilled in Jack an intense loyalty to the United States. As an extension, he felt intrinsically indebted to the Academy and, more specifically, the dean of students.

As if on cue, Dean Wolfe turned up the sidewalk from Hopi Hall. Jack straightened in his seat. He peered over the balcony, watching. Someone followed—a girl he didn't know. *We don't get a lot of visitors.*

"Why don't you ever go out?" Noah asked. "Girls call for you all the time."

"I'm busy," Jack said. Dean Wolfe escorted his guest toward the library. She rushed to keep up, leaning into the hill as she followed. A lock of hair slipped from her bun and fell along her face.

"What are you looking at?" Noah twisted around in his chair. "Who's she?"

"How should I know?"

Wolfe stopped in front of the library. He pointed toward the patio—toward Jack—and the girl looked up. Her full lips parted slightly as the loose curl blew across her cheek.

"Wow," said Noah. "Not bad, huh?"

Jack's breath quickened. He leaned back in his seat so his face was out of sight.

No. Not bad at all.

8 NADIA
SUNDAY, SEPTEMBER 11

Nadia followed Dean Wolfe up the sidewalk to the library. He pointed to the stone fortress at the top of the hill. "The Navajo Building houses the dining hall and the student lounge." On the upper patio, students gathered at tables, books and papers spread around them. A rush of anxiety washed over her. She was glad for the uniforms. Maybe she could fake fitting in. He gestured toward a shaded path lined with olive trees. "And the psychiatrist's office is through here."

Nadia hesitated.

"It's standard procedure."

"Okay. I, uh—why?"

"He's the school counselor."

"I see." *So why didn't you say, it's time to meet the counselor?*

Across the lawn Nadia's recruiter, Marcus Sloan, stepped from the side door of a Japanese-style building and glanced around. When he saw Nadia and the Dean, he stopped.

Wolfe narrowed his eyes as they settled on Sloan. "He's got some nerve," he muttered.

"I'm sorry?"

"Wait here," he said. "Marcus!" Dean Wolfe marched toward him. Nadia barely caught his next words. "She's here; are you happy?"

Is he talking about me? She tried to watch the interaction without looking directly at them. She could no longer hear the words, but it was clear they were arguing. Dean Wolfe pointed at Mr. Sloan in quick, decisive movements. Sloan stood with his arms crossed, a small smile on his lips. Nadia waited in the crushing heat, nervous about their argument, nervous about meeting the shrink.

When the Dean returned, she asked, "Is everything okay?"

"Everything's fine." His tone was sharper now. "Dr. Cameron is expecting you. Through here." He showed her to a small waiting room. "He'll be out in a minute. If you have questions, stop by my office." He left before she could answer.

Nadia had never visited a psychiatrist. *He's a guidance counselor. It's no big deal.* She paced back and forth across the terra-cotta tile.

Dr. Cameron's door opened and he invited her in. His stark office, devoid of personal effects, was nothing like she'd anticipated. The naked concrete floor and bare walls gave the feel of an interrogation room. She sat in the only chair available, a folding chair with a metal frame and built-in seat cushion. Nice as far as folding chairs go, but she'd expected a couch. Dr. Cameron pulled his seat from behind the desk.

"Nadia, I want you to know I'm here for you. If you ever need to talk, please don't hesitate to come by."

"Thank you."

"I like to get to know each of our students personally. I hope that, in time, you'll come to consider me your confidant."

"Okay." Nadia rubbed her arms. The AC vent directly above shot a constant stream of cold air across her back.

"As part of your orientation, I have a few questions to ask. Have you ever been approached by anyone claiming to represent the US government?"

She raised her eyebrows. "What?"

"Please answer the question."

"No, I haven't."

"Do you work for an agency not associated with the United States?"

Nadia laughed. "Is this a joke?"

Dr. Cameron smiled. "It is not."

She stopped smiling. His pleasant expression didn't waver. "Okay. No. I don't have a job. I mean, I worked at Mr. Softee's Frozen Yogurt Shack one summer, but I got paid cash, like under the table, so . . ." Her voice trailed off. *Should I have admitted that?* "I mean, I don't think I made enough money that I would've been taxed, even if I had received a proper check—it's not like I was deliberately engaged in tax-evasion. I'm not even sure that counts." *Stop talking.*

She shifted her weight. Crossed her legs, uncrossed them. Crossed the other way. She considered moving her chair from the arctic zone, but if she moved toward him he would think her too forward—aggressive. If she moved back, he'd think she was subconsciously trying to escape. She'd watched enough television to know that with a psychiatrist, a cigar is never a cigar.

"Are you nervous?" Dr. Cameron asked.

"A little."

"Most people are their first time in. Try to relax; I'm not here to judge you. Consider this a getting-to-know-you visit. Please fill this out for me." Dr. Cameron handed her a booklet and a clipboard. "Be as honest as you can. If you're unsure about something, take a guess."

Nadia opened the book and read the first few questions. *Do you hear voices? Are people out to get you? Have you ever been abducted by aliens?* She filled in the circles and turned the page. *Please finish these sentences: I love my father, but ___; God is ___; I wish my country were ___.* Nadia glanced at Dr. Cameron before scratching out her answers.

Twenty fill-in-the-blanks later, Dr. Cameron said, "Okay, I'm going to administer a polygraph."

"A lie detector? Why?" Freezing now, she rubbed her thighs to warm her hands. She'd be shivering even if his thermostat wasn't set at forty. Nerves made her cold.

"Don't worry; my questions are general. Nothing too personal or embarrassing." His voice was friendly, encouraging.

For the next hour, he pelted her with questions: *Have you ever used illicit drugs? Do you believe that an inefficient national leader should be removed from office, using whatever force necessary? Have you ever been photographed in a compromising situation?* For the first twenty minutes, Nadia considered each response: what her answers might reveal, what private information Dr. Cameron could ascertain. Eventually, mentally exhausted, she gave up, answering from her gut: *no, yes, I don't know.*

Finally, he powered down the machine and asked, "That wasn't so bad, was it?"

"That's your idea of 'nothing too personal'?"

Dr. Cameron smiled. "Now, there are a few things we need to discuss. First of all, if you ever have comments or concerns about your fellow students, I ask that you bring them to my attention immediately. Secondly, what I'm about to tell you isn't meant to frighten or threaten. I'm merely informing you of the rules. All right?"

Nadia nodded, rubbing her arm where the blood pressure cuff had been.

"We have carefully prepared a program of study designed to fast-track the best and brightest our nation has to offer. As such, at Desert Mountain we take security very seriously. Our specialized curriculum is geared toward a career in intelligence. Do you understand what that means?"

"I'm not sure."

"We are the preliminary training school for a very specific branch of the Central Intelligence Agency. If you graduate, you will be invited to join."

"I'm sorry . . . I'll be invited to join the CIA?"

"A branch of the CIA. Our program stresses both mental and physical development because we train recruits for one purpose: to serve in the CIA's Black-Ops Division. The division is off-books; it's not subject to Congressional oversight. This gives us the freedom to perform vital, high-risk missions with complete anonymity—it is absolutely the most critical arm of our nation's intelligence force. However, everyone who works Black-Ops—field agents, communications specialists, tech staff, medics—must be in top physical form. Any one of these assets may, at a moment's notice, be forced to evacuate their location, assist with a high-target extraction or fight for their lives and the lives of their fellow officers."

Nadia nodded along. "You're telling me I've been recruited as a spy?"

"Don't get ahead of yourself: you've been recruited as a trainee. As I was saying, your workouts may feel excessive, but the instruction we provide serves a purpose. Your physical reactions will become so ingrained in your muscle memory that you will react to a threat before your conscious mind realizes you're in danger."

Nadia smiled involuntarily. "No kidding?" *The CIA!*

Dr. Cameron smiled back. "No kidding. Whether or not you remain in this field is entirely your decision, but in the meantime, we do have specific protocol. You are not to discuss the curriculum with anyone outside of our community. Not your parents, not your friends, not the waiter at your favorite restaurant. If you do, the Patriot Act enables the government to take you into custody. You will be held as a suspected terrorist indefinitely and without formal charges."

"No problem," she said. *This is so cool. I'm gonna be a spy!*

"I'm sorry to put this on you all at once. We prefer to familiarize the juniors with our program slowly, but as a transfer student you don't have that luxury."

"I understand." Nadia tried to suppress her smile. *Grinning like a lunatic at the psychiatrist might not be the best way to start my career.*

He handed her a sealed plastic bag. "Please use the swab on your inner cheek. I also need a tiny sample of your hair. A half-inch from the end will do nicely."

Nadia swiped her gum line and placed the swab in the included vial. Dr. Cameron helped her with the fingerprint kit, then gave her a wet-wipe to clean her hands.

"There is one other thing I need to tell you about." Dr. Cameron hesitated. "The recruiter may have downplayed what you've missed."

Nadia shook her head. "I don't follow."

"Your cohorts arrived in June. While it's true classes have just formally begun, our new recruits trained all summer. In addition to extensive physical instruction, they were required to complete an exhaustive list of prerequisite reading. As a result, they've started with a strong background in the coursework. Mr. Sloan wouldn't have chosen you if he felt this was a problem, so rest assured, you can catch up. But it will be challenging. Do you have any questions?"

Nadia took a deep breath. "I wouldn't know where to begin."

Dr. Cameron smiled. "I'll send my report to the Dean and, unless you hear otherwise, you have nothing to worry about. You can wait outside. Ms. McGill will be along momentarily."

Nadia stepped out of his office. *So I'm a little behind. Who cares?*

Ms. McGill led her across campus to the girls' dorm, an adobe-style building surrounded by soft desert grasses. She introduced Nadia to the woman at the front desk. "Your dormitory assistant, Casey Tarlian."

Casey's red hair surrounded her face in a mass of coils. She wore a peasant blouse and a pair of faded jeans. She came out from behind the desk, teetering on lime-green platform shoes.

"Glad you made it," Casey said. Her translucent skin reminded Nadia of a butterfly. "I'm sure your roommate is anxious to meet you."

I know exactly how she feels.

9 LIBBY
SUNDAY, SEPTEMBER 11

An excruciating five hours later, Libby's new roommate finally appeared. Nadia arrived before her luggage—not that Libby would've gone through her things. She respected other people's privacy and expected the same courtesy. Casey showed Nadia to their room, then returned to her post as Libby stood to make her own introduction.

"It's a pleasure to make your acquaintance, Nadia."

"Nice to meet you."

Libby was a tad disappointed about Nadia's size—she was no bigger than a minute. She'd been hoping for a roommate with whom she could swap clothes. Drew had been heavier than Libby. Not that it mattered, because their tastes were so different. Libby would never have worn baggy pants and shapeless sweatshirts. The appearance one presented to the world could be considered a direct reflection of one's internal state, and Libby took great care putting forward an image of grace, competence and beauty. Even when she didn't feel that way.

Nadia was cute, though, in an athletic, outdoorsy sort of way. Her wide mouth provided a generous smile. She wasn't wearing makeup. She looked pretty enough without it, but she might do with a dash of color. Her lashes were dark and long so she didn't need mascara, but a sweep of eyeliner would do wonders. *And everyone ought to wear a little concealer.*

"Am I completely invading your space?" Nadia asked.

"Not at all! I'm so glad you're finally here. Most of the kids are nice enough, but everyone tends to hang out with their own team, and after Drew died—God rest her soul—it's like I'm a pariah. No one knows what to say to me."

"I was sorry to hear about her," Nadia said. "It must have been devastating."

"Thanks. Honestly, we weren't that close." Libby never was sure how to respond to the sympathy, as she was uncomfortable exaggerating her own importance. "I feel so bad for her parents."

"What happened?"

"The details are a little sketchy. You know how rumors go. One teacher said it was a ten-car pileup, another thought she fell asleep at the wheel. I don't know." She shook her head. *I can't think about it anymore.* "Anyway, I'll introduce you to our teammates at dinner. Alan Cohen," Libby wrinkled her nose. "He's a bit fussy but super smart, and Damon Moore, who's absolutely gorgeous." She cringed as the word left her mouth—*goh-juss.* "He's a doll; everyone loves him."

"I love your accent."

"That's sweet of you to say."

Nadia lingered near the door. "I didn't realize security would search my bags."

"I know, it's embarrassing. Just the thought of someone rifling through my underthings." Libby shuddered. "But it's like that here: your rights and privileges no longer apply." She smiled to soften the statement.

Nadia nodded. "I just left Dr. Cameron's. He mentioned—I had no idea I would be so far behind."

"I'll help you get caught up," Libby reassured her.

"Thanks. Hopefully I won't take up too much of your time."

"Oh, honey, don't give it another thought. I hate living alone."

Nadia shifted her weight from one foot to the next. She glanced at her watch.

"Where are my manners? Please, come on in." Libby stepped back toward the wall. "Make yourself at home."

Nadia moved toward her bare bed. "Your room is spotless."

"You mean *our* room," Libby said. *And how good of you to notice.* She found visual clutter exhausting. She'd lined the books on her shelf according to color and height, placed everything on her desk at a right angle, and corralled the items on her dresser into pretty wooden boxes. The clothes in her closet hung precisely, sorted by type and color. Shoes lined the bottom, toes facing out, also arranged by color. "I tend to be a little obsessive when it comes to cleaning. I'll try to keep it under control. I've already decorated but if it's not to your liking we can change whatever you want."

"No, it looks great."

"I bought an extra duvet set if you'd like to use it. The throw pillows are very comfortable. I pile them up and do my reading in bed," Libby said. Her roommate remained quiet. "But you don't have to," she added quickly. *Honestly, Libby. You're gonna scare this poor girl off. Who cares if the beds don't match? You'll learn to live with it.* "It's no big deal, the bedding. Have I—is something wrong?"

Nadia turned toward Libby and shook her head. "Not at all. The whole campus is stunning—it looks like a resort. I'm just a little overwhelmed." She tucked a loose curl behind her ear.

"The grounds are beautiful, no doubt about it. Hard to believe we're in the desert."

"And the curriculum looks interesting."

Libby nodded. "It certainly holds my attention."

Nadia lowered her voice. "Are we—am I allowed to talk about it? With you, I mean?"

Oh, that's what's distracting her! Libby exhaled with relief. *Poor thing. I bet Dr. Cameron dumped everything on her at once.* "Absolutely. You can ask me anything."

Nadia grinned. "Okay. The Black-Ops Division of the CIA? Seriously? Is that as cool as it sounds?"

Libby returned her roommate's smile and answered, "You have no idea."

10 NADIA
SUNDAY, SEPTEMBER 11

A few minutes later Nadia's bags arrived.

"What did you think of Dr. Cameron?" Libby asked. "He's positively perfect. Except for making me cut my hair." She frowned as she examined the ends of her silky blond hair. "He has no idea how difficult it is to get it straight. I had to take two more inches off just to even it out."

As her stomach rumbled, Nadia realized she hadn't eaten since breakfast. "Am I keeping you from dinner? I can unpack later."

"Oh, heavens no," Libby answered. "Dinner runs for an hour; we won't miss it. And I'm sure we'll both feel more settled if you unpack now. You know, just get it out of the way. It won't take but a minute."

Nadia turned into her closet to hide her smile. *I agree one of us will feel more settled, but it's not me.* She pictured her bedroom back home: clothes strewn across the floor, stacks of magazines precariously balanced on her desk. *Keeping my room clean will be harder than catching up in class.* Compulsiveness notwithstanding, Nadia liked Libby immediately. Her refined Southern accent was nothing like the sharp country twang she heard in Virginia.

Nadia unpacked under Libby's steady gaze. She had the feeling she was being evaluated, despite the light-hearted chatter.

She tried to look inconspicuous as she glanced back at Libby's closet for pointers on how to group her clothes.

I've been recruited as a spy and my main concern is organizing my closet.

Twenty minutes later, the smell of basil and freshly baked bread filled the air as Nadia followed Libby through the buffet. In the dining room, small tables dressed in dark linens hosted hushed conversations. Libby led Nadia to the back corner. As they approached, one of the guys at the table stood up. He smiled at them, a flash of white against dark brown skin. He was at least ten inches taller than Nadia. Broad and muscular, with a shaved head, he reminded her of a fireman, or maybe a soldier.

"That's Damon," Libby whispered. "I told you he was hot."

"No kidding," Nadia whispered back.

At the table Libby said, "Nadia Riley, meet Damon Moore and Alan Cohen."

Damon shook her hand. "Nadia, it's so great to meet you. Don't worry about starting late." He held on to her longer than necessary, flirting a little. His voice lowered slightly as he said, "I'm available for whatever personal assistance you may need. We take care of our own. Right, Alan?"

Nadia bit her lip to keep from grinning.

"It seems we have no choice," Alan said. He looked up from his pasta and brushed a thick lock of hair away from his eyes. He stared at Nadia's face, then glanced down to her shoes and back up again. "We are only as strong as our weakest link."

"I guess that makes me the weak link," Nadia said, trying to make a joke.

Alan returned to his dinner and, without a flicker of emotion, responded, "Indeed it does."

11 ALAN COHEN
SUNDAY, SEPTEMBER 11

Alan Cohen did not like change. He did not want a new teammate, he did not care to reconfigure the entire group dynamic, and he did not like Nadia Riley.

"She's cute, right?" Damon asked as they cut across the lawn toward the library after dinner.

"I guess," Alan said. Admittedly, Nadia had appealing eyes and a pleasing symmetry to her features, but looks were not everything. "Still, I do not like her."

"Why not? You just met her ten minutes ago."

"She does not seem particularly bright."

"And how did you assess that so quickly?"

"She talked Libby out of our evening study session. It is bad enough we have to teach her everything she has missed, but now Libby will be a day behind as well. Do you know how long it will take to show Nadia what we have learned in jujutsu? Or catch her up on a summer's worth of work? It will dominate our entire month. Perhaps longer. Mark my words."

"Why you gotta be like that?" Damon shook his head. "You're so negative. I don't even want to be around you when you're like this. I'm skipping study group, too." He turned away.

"Then technically, it is no longer study group. It is me alone at the library."

"That's right," Damon said over his shoulder. "You alone."

Alan shook his head. *Damon only cares about what she looks like. What if she turns out to be an idiot? She will drag down the entire team.* He pushed through the library doors. Cold air surrounded him, instantly drying the sticky spot between his scapulae. *Libby is no genius, but at least she can hold her own.* He found a table against the wall and opened his diplomacy text to chapter two. He sat quietly, focusing his eyes on the upper left quadrant of the page.

Alan was accustomed to a rigorous academic program, having previously attended an elite private school in Manhattan. Education had always been the top priority in his home, which meant the workload here was not unduly challenging. But even he could scarcely afford to skip an evening's study. And he did not need additional time with Nadia to know that he would continue to surpass his teammates intellectually. In fact, he likely eclipsed the entire junior class.

Alan moved his attention to the lower left quadrant. *A flowchart,* he scoffed. *Child's play.* On to the upper right section of the textbook.

No one assimilated languages faster than Alan. When he was a very young child, his family had lived with his grandparents in Jerusalem for a few years, so he was already fluent in Arabic. His father had taught him Hebrew. The Chinese and Spanish he was learning rolled easily off his tongue. He also spoke French (his mother's maiden name was *Badeau*) and enough German to get by. A few more weeks in the dojo with Hashimoto Sensei and he would probably know a good bit of Japanese as well.

Alan studied the final quadrant and turned the page. The information entered his consciousness like a photograph, and then somehow managed to file itself away in an organized system of folders. He would be able to retrieve the knowledge at a later date by searching his mind for the proper file. To say he had a photographic memory was inaccurate. A stack of photographs did not aggregate data. His mind, however, did.

This was not to say he excelled at all tasks. Martial arts, for example, continued to pose a challenge. Kick here, block there: his brain rejected kinesthetic learning. He needed time to process physical activities. Also, he was a bit skinny. Even having just met Nadia, he knew he would remain the least athletic of his foursome.

Alan looked up from his book. The tables around him were cluttered with foursomes. He was the only one studying alone. A girl at the next table glanced up, and Alan smiled. She looked away. He returned to his text.

He did not understand the fluid, constantly changing dynamic between men and women. Nor did he have the slightest idea of the qualities girls found appealing. He considered himself attractive. Not like Damon, but his eyes were a handsome light hazel, flecked with brown, and his mother said they matched his hair perfectly. He had neat, nicely arched eyebrows and clear skin. For the last several thousand years, those were the qualities that attracted a mate. It made evolutionary sense: before man knew medicine, hair and skin were the best indicators of good health. But so far, they had not helped him.

Secretly, he felt jealous of his roommate. Damon was intelligent—not as smart as Alan, but everything came easily for him. He obviously related well to girls, a skill Alan had yet to master. Everyone liked Damon. He had an easy way of being in the world. He made others feel comfortable and important. Besides his excessive flirting—which Alan believed he engaged in solely to mask his intellectual shortcomings—Alan had no real complaints. Unlike his complaints with Nadia.

Oh well. We were a person shy of our four-man team. At least she is not hideous.

Of course, if anyone learned the truth about him, none of it would matter anyway.

12 NADIA
MONDAY, SEPTEMBER 12

At five forty-five the next morning, Nadia's new roommate gently shook her awake.

"I'm so sorry," Libby whispered. "Do you want to skip? It's your first day so you probably won't get in too much trouble. I'll tell Sensei I let you sleep."

"No, it's good, I'm up," Nadia answered, half-asleep. "He's the martial arts guy, right?"

Libby nodded. "Maikeru Hashimoto Sensei. And he is *old*-school."

"Let me brush my teeth."

Libby showed Nadia how to put on her *Gi* and tie the belt. Nadia pulled her hair into a ponytail and smiled in the mirror. *I look like a ninja.*

"C'mon, honey. We're late." The girls rushed next door. "Being late to the dojo is not good. Open the *shoji*." Libby pointed to the sliding bamboo and rice-paper doors. She slipped off her shoes and added them to the long row neatly lining the wall. Nadia did the same.

The bamboo floor gleamed as they hurried down the hall to the large room at the end of the building. Thick blue mats covered the floor. They found spaces in the back, side by side, and Nadia felt reasonably sure their teacher didn't notice as they snuck in.

Hashimoto Sensei instructed as the students performed jumping jacks, push-ups, sit-ups and snap kicks. He barked his orders—half the time in Japanese—while circling the mat. Nadia's legs, weak from kicking, threatened to give out as Libby reminded her they still had to run several miles around campus.

"Let me introduce you to Sensei," she said.

Libby bowed as she reached their teacher. "Hashimoto Sensei, may I present my new roommate, Nadia Riley."

Sensei studied Nadia with dark eyes. Salt-and-pepper hair, cut short against his head, matched his neatly trimmed goatee. His movements mirrored his stature: compact, precise; nothing frivolous. He bowed and, out of courtesy, she did the same. He spoke tersely, each syllable sharp and crisp. "Nadia-san, welcome." Sensei straightened and faced Libby. "Libby-san, in the future please introduce a new student *before* instruction begins. I do not like interruptions to my lesson or surprises on my mat."

"I apologize, Sensei. I'm afraid we overslept," she replied with another bow. "We'll see you tomorrow morning."

"You have never been late before." Sensei stared at Nadia as he addressed Libby. His expression said, *I can see this is your fault, new girl.*

"No, Sensei," answered Libby.

"Do not be tardy again."

"No, Sensei," she repeated.

"He's a little scary," Nadia said as she followed Libby through the dojo.

"You have no idea."

They joined the pack of students pouring toward the Navajo Building. Behind the dining hall, a tall wooden gate led them to the running trails carved into the desert beyond the concrete wall.

Looks like our perimeter is secure, Nadia thought as she took in the multiple security cameras mounted along the wall and the heavy chain and padlock piled on the ground beside the entrance. "What's with the excessive security? Are we not safe?" She tried to sound casual. She didn't want Libby to know how nervous she was on her first day.

Libby laughed. "No, we're safe here. The wall keeps the coyotes off campus. Come on." She began a slow jog and Nadia trotted beside her.

"And now we're on the other side of the wall." Nadia scanned the low shrubbery for coyotes.

"Don't worry. Coyotes aren't aggressive and they don't hunt in packs. Plus, there are plenty of rabbits around for them to eat. They're more of a nuisance than anything."

"And the cameras? Also for the coyotes?"

Libby wrinkled her forehead. "I never thought about it."

Nadia, already breathless, did not respond.

After their run, the girls trudged back to their room to get ready for class. While Libby showered, Nadia made her bed—something she never did at home, but Libby had made hers first thing. As she yanked the frame away from the wall to smooth her comforter, something dropped to the floor.

She crawled under the bed and retrieved a book.

It was a leather journal with a gold dragonfly embossed on the cover. Nadia glanced toward the bathroom before turning to the first page. The author had been at the beach, sunburned and miserable. She flipped to the last entry, halfway through the book.

September 7

I'm in the bathroom with a flashlight so I don't wake my roommate (who demands a solid 8 hours for "beauty renewal"). On my way back from the dining hall (ice cream, what else? I know, diet starts tomorrow) I saw Oso and Culebra talking near the bushes by the dojo. Culebra gave Oso a black duffel. I tried to be still because I was kind of standing under a light but I think Oso saw me! He totally froze when he looked my way. I pretended not to see him and ran back here as fast as I could. What were they doing? What was in that bag? Sooo weird. Something is not right.

The entry was scribbled, almost illegibly. *This must be Drew's.* Nadia did the math in her head, counting the days backward. The last entry was the day of Drew's death. Two days before Nadia met Marcus Sloan.

The shower stopped. Nadia shoved the diary under a pillow as Libby came into the bedroom.

"What are you doing?" Libby looked past her to the pile of pillows.

Nadia glanced toward her headboard, confirming the book was hidden. "Just making the bed." She stood and smoothed the covers.

"Oh." Libby nodded. "It looks nice."

"I'll take a shower and we can go." *I can't believe I read Drew's diary.* Nadia walked past Libby into the bathroom. *Okay, I can believe it; I can't believe I almost got caught.*

13 DAMON MOORE
MONDAY, SEPTEMBER 12

After the morning workout, Damon Moore took a five-minute shower and booked up the hill to the Navajo Building. As usual, he arrived to an empty dining room. A few years ago he might've wandered in at the last minute like the rest of his classmates, oblivious to his surroundings, one of the herd, but no more. A hard lesson learned.

He didn't mind being early—especially when it involved food. His father used to joke that Damon would sell his soul to Satan for a good steak. And showing up first meant Damon could observe his environment without the distraction of other people.

He selected a generous assortment from the buffet, and then took his regular seat, back against the wall at the corner table. Immediately, he noticed the change in position. Damon lifted the tablecloth: vacuum tracks in the carpet. Housekeeping had rearranged the furniture to clean. He stood, moved the table four inches to the right, sat back down and continued his surveillance. The security camera over the door had malfunctioned; it remained motionless, and normally by this time it would've swept the room twice. Everything else seemed copacetic. Satisfied, he eyed his plate, piled high with scrambled eggs, bacon and waffles smothered in fruit compote.

Training himself to notice every detail hadn't been easy. If he'd bothered to learn these observational skills earlier, his whole life would be different. His father's sudden heart attack, for example. There had probably been signs: sallow skin, labored breathing.

Initially, the heightened attention had worn him out; his senses had been constantly on alert, his eyes scanning, watching everyone, everything, waiting for something terrible to happen. But rather than suffer through chronic anxiety, Damon had systematically retrained his brain. So now when something seemed off, he didn't panic: he looked for explanations.

He devoured his eggs and returned to the buffet for another glass of orange juice. Nadia was making her way down the line. Damon watched her for a second, considering. *Don't even think about it. Teammates are definitely off-limits.* He touched her shoulder, matched her smile. "I'm at the same table as last night. Need a hand?"

"No thanks, I'm good."

Back in his seat, his incessant hunger slightly abated, he relaxed a bit. As far as he could tell, he was the only student at Desert Mountain who'd ever gone to bed hungry. Alan rarely cleaned his plate, and Libby threw out more food than she ate. He stood as Nadia approached.

"Assigned seats?" she asked, carefully setting her overstuffed plate on the table.

"Not officially, but this one's mine. I like to peruse the room as I eat. Makes me feel like royalty."

"Consider it sacred." She took the chair across from his, her back to the room. The worst seat at the table, and one he would accept only at gunpoint. "That buffet is amazing. I'm used to Lucky Charms and a banana."

Damon laughed. "I know. I've easily gained fifteen pounds since June." Bottomless bowls of pasta, made-to-order omelets, seconds on sandwiches. If Sensei's workouts weren't so intense, he probably would've packed on an extra thirty by now.

"Well, it must be muscle weight, because I don't see an ounce of fat." She took a swig of her cranberry juice. It looked too clear. She must've watered it down. "You're from Baltimore, right?"

"I am. Libby briefed you?"

Nadia smiled. "Just names and locations."

"You feeling okay? Your blood sugar high?"

She paused, her fork midair, and stared at him. "It's not high, but I can't eat sugar in the morning. It makes me feel sick. How'd you know that?"

"Your plate," he lied. "All protein. You were kidding about the Lucky Charms, right?"

Nadia glanced at her breakfast then back at him. "You're really observant."

"Not really. My mom's a reference librarian, so I hear about everything from managing diabetes to the aerodynamic qualities of titanium."

He and his mom hadn't shared many meals together. She worked most nights, picking up extra shifts to pay off the hospital bills. Afternoons and evenings, Damon had kept busy. Quiet time unsettled him, so he joined after-school clubs and took classes through Baltimore's Parks and Recreations Program. He joined the debate team, rowed crew, learned to paint. He took up chess, tried boxing, joined the drama club. He attended free lectures at the local universities. One regrettable semester he tried his hand at the violin. Whatever occupied his mind.

Wednesday afternoons, however, had been sacred. At four sharp, Damon would arrive at his branch of Baltimore County's Public Library, where his father used to take him every week for story hour. Continuing the tradition in his own way, he'd greet the director, say hi to the kids, then browse the shelves. A fast reader with myriad interests, he spent his leisure time discovering new theories, honing new skills, exploring new worlds.

At least, he used to. Until everything changed.

Damon tried the fruit compote. It tasted like strawberry jam. He polished off his bacon as Alan approached, fresh from the shower, hair soaked, looking like he'd just taken a swim. Poor kid never remembered to brush his hair. Probably too busy sharpening his tongue.

"I see we have another voracious eater," Alan said, eyeballing Nadia's plate.

"Hey, I earned this," she answered. "That workout was tough."

"We are not training to be Sumo wrestlers. You may want to slow down."

"Did he just call me fat?" Nadia asked Damon.

"It's entirely possible."

Behind Alan came Jennifer, the flirty blonde from Noah's team, and her roommate, Niyuri. Jennifer was the kind of girl who wanted all the guys to notice her, a trait Damon found particularly unattractive. His eyes glanced off Jennifer's as he met her roommate's smile. *But Niyuri might be just what I'm looking for.*

He studied her carefully as the pair moved toward their table. Five-four, one-ten, with cinnamon skin and long black hair. Her chin came to a soft point, shaping her face into a heart. It made her look happy all the time. He liked that about her.

Damon stood as Libby joined the table, then quietly turned his attention back to Niyuri. She was fluent in both Japanese and Italian. Her comments in class leaned more toward the abstract and philosophical. Some mistook her as flighty, but Damon didn't think so. She just thought a lot. Her fork slipped from her napkin roll and fell to the carpet. She leaned forward to catch it and bumped her head on the table.

"Ow," she said softly, rubbing her forehead.

Damon swiped Alan's napkin roll as he sidestepped his roommate.

"Hey," Alan protested.

He knelt beside Niyuri's chair. "Are you all right?" he asked, handing her Alan's unrolled silverware. He touched the red mark on her forehead.

"Just careless." A pink hue colored her cheeks as his hand brushed against her. "I was hoping no one saw that."

He feigned confusion. "Saw what?"

She grinned. "Thanks."

Yeah, he decided. *She'll do just fine.*

14 NADIA
MONDAY, SEPTEMBER 12

When Professor Sherman dimmed the lights to show her psychology class a movie, Nadia felt immediate relief. She'd been a little worried about catching up, but a movie? A monkey could follow along.

Twenty minutes later, however, her confidence had vanished.

"That was the President's exit interview," Dr. Sherman said as she raised the lights. "What did everyone think?" Hands popped up. "Jennifer?"

"He's obviously lying."

"How can you tell?"

"He's looking up and to the right, rather than down to the left, which indicates he's inventing a truth rather than remembering a past event," Jennifer said.

"Nice try, but that's a myth. Who else? Damon?"

"He exhibited a cluster of deceptive behaviors. He pulled his earlobe, repeated the interviewer's questions and offered irrelevant details. The truth is simple; when folks lie, they talk too much."

In Virginia, Nadia's first class had been Literature and Composition, reading Thoreau. Apparently at her new school she would learn to be a human lie detector.

"Excellent, I'm pleased you read your assignment. And what

was the other big tell in his nonverbal communication? Anyone?" Dr. Sherman raised her shoulders. "The shrugging—pay attention, people. These are skills you will need."

In her next class, Computer Science and Information Systems, they discussed basic hacking techniques. Their homework assignment was to circumvent the security system of a fictional network and download the database.

"Isn't that illegal?" Nadia asked Libby.

"Sure, but it's not a *real* network. Good skill to have though, don't you think?"

In math, they learned tricks to help memorize long series of numbers. "When do you think he'll teach us how to open a Swiss bank account?" Nadia joked.

"We covered that on day two. I'll give you my notes."

Chemistry turned out to be a lot more fun at spy school than public school. The class mixed common drugstore ingredients to create a stable explosive that required a high velocity strike to detonate. Their professor demonstrated the smoky explosion with a rubber bullet on the front lawn.

Political science, taught by the dullest man in the world, dragged on for a decade. Professor Hayden towered above his class as he paced the aisles. He discussed *ad nauseam* recruiting methods used by al-Qaida, Boko Haram and ISIS. "Our nation, founded on religious freedom, will never be safe from terrorist activity."

A brutal hour later, the students convened in the dining hall for lunch. Nadia and Libby reached the table before the boys. *I can't believe it's only one o'clock. I feel like I've been here a month.*

As they settled in, Libby placed her hand on Nadia's arm. "I can't tell you how excited I am to have you as my roommate. I have a really good feeling about this year."

"Me too." Nadia smiled.

"It's tough when roommates don't click."

"Oh yeah?"

"Yeah. I've been in boarding schools my whole life, so I've had my share of strange girls. The sleepwalker who ended up everywhere. The hippie who shaved her head the first of every month, which I wouldn't have minded, but she saved her hair in a shoebox under the bed. I try not to judge, but that was odd." Libby shuddered. "One girl stole from me. I caught her in the act and she still denied it. Can you imagine?"

A pang of guilt struck Nadia. *Did she see me reading Drew's diary? Should I tell her? If I confess, maybe she'll think I have a shred of integrity. But if she doesn't know, I should probably keep it to myself.*

"I mean, did she honestly think I'd believe she had the exact same pair of earrings my daddy gave me for my thirteenth birthday?"

No, she definitely knows. Why else would she randomly offer that she had a good feeling about us? She's testing me.

"They were *custom* made!"

Nadia winced. *For Pete's sake; it's like living with the telltale heart.*

"You okay?"

Nadia cleared her throat. "I have something to tell you."

"What is it?"

"I feel awful about it."

"What?" Libby's eyes were wide.

Nadia paused. "I found Drew's diary."

Libby drew in her breath. "Did you read it?"

"A little."

"You read a dead girl's diary?" Alan yelled. Nadia hadn't seen him standing behind her.

The dining room fell silent. All eyes turned toward Alan. His mouth hung open as he stood gaping at Nadia. Her face was on fire. Beads of sweat collected on her upper lip. She stared furiously at him. The dead silence turned to whispers as groups of students huddled together, pointing at her as they gossiped.

Damon stepped between Nadia and the rest of the room, blocking her with his body. He turned to a neighboring table. "Can we help you with something?" he asked, loud enough for the room to hear. He waited until people looked away to take his seat. Then, quietly to Nadia, "You read her diary?"

Nadia nodded. She looked at the table, then back up at Damon. "But in my defense, I didn't know what it was. I mean, I knew it was a diary, but it could have been there for years, right? There were no names." She turned quickly to Libby. "Obviously, I knew it wasn't yours. It was wedged under my bed. I would never read *your* diary."

"She did not write about us?" Alan asked. "I am mildly insulted."

"I'm not sure; I couldn't tell. She used code names or something." Nadia snuck a glance at her roommate.

"Why would she do that?" asked Libby.

"Perhaps to safeguard against disrespectful roommates who might, hmm, what might they do?" Alan shot Nadia a contemptuous look. "Oh, right. Read her diary."

"You be nice," Libby said to Alan. "I'm sure Nadia had no idea it was Drew's diary."

"What kind of code names?" Damon asked.

"Made up names. Like *Oso*, whoever that is."

Alan rolled his eyes. "*Oso* is Spanish for *bear*, Einstein."

Nadia narrowed her eyes at Alan. "Name-calling? Really?" She turned to Libby. "I swear I didn't know what it was. And I only read the last entry. I'm so sorry. I promise you, I *am* trustworthy. Most of the time."

Damon laughed. "Don't sweat it, girl. There's nothing wrong with a little moral flexibility. That's probably why you were recruited. So what did it say?"

"Absolutely not," Nadia said to Damon. "It's bad enough I read it. I'm not going to gossip about it."

"Did you give it to Jack?" Alan asked.

Nadia shook her head. "I don't know him."

"He's our team leader." Libby searched the room. "I swear he was here a second ago, but now I don't see him."

"I'll give it to Ms. McGill and she can send it to Drew's parents."

"You should really give it to Jack," Alan said.

"Do you remember the date of the last entry?" Damon asked.

"September Seven."

"No way!" Alan said. "This is the day she, you know—"

"Drove her car into the side of a mountain?" Damon finished. "Did she have like a premonition or something?"

Nadia didn't answer. She pursed her lips and looked down at the table. Truthfully, she was dying to share what she'd read. *But even I have limits to how low I'll go.* And Libby's expression made it clear she didn't approve.

"Was it at least interesting?" Damon pressed.

Nadia leaned forward and whispered, "Big time."

"You have to tell us," Alan said.

"It's out of the question."

"Then why did you even bring it up?" Alan glared at her.

"I thought I was having a private conversation with my roommate," Nadia said.

"Good for you, Nadia." Libby faced the boys. "You two ought'a be ashamed of yourselves. It's none of anyone's business."

Early Monday evening, just after sunset, the student snuck down to the parking lot beyond Hopi Hall. He would rather leave campus entirely but this was where he kept his cell phone, hidden in the bushes along the wall. And this location, on the far side of school, was as private as any.

He pulled his hood over his head and dialed an off-campus number.

"Hello?" answered a tired voice.

"We have a huge problem," the student said.

"This better be good. What is it?"

"The dead girl left a diary."

Long pause. "What did you say?"

"She kept a diary," the student answered. He glanced over his shoulder.

"Did you read it?"

"No. But someone else did."

"Who?"

"Nadia Riley."

"The new girl?" the older man asked.

"Yeah."

"How do you know?"

"I overheard her at lunch."

"Did Drew write about our meeting?"

"Maybe. I know she saw us. She might have heard everything we said. She promised me she kept quiet, but it never occurred to me to ask about a diary."

"This is a disaster. Can you get the diary?"

"I followed Nadia all afternoon. She gave it to the Dean's assistant. For whatever reason, Ms. McGill took the book directly to the kitchen incinerator. She never even opened it."

"What did you expect her to do? Keeping a diary is against school policy. All sensitive documents are destroyed. You have to take care of this Nadia situation immediately. She could ruin everything we've been working toward—years of training down the tubes," the older man said.

"I know. And another thing—Drew wrote in code."

"What code?"

"I told you: Nadia is the only one who read it. But if she figures it out, my position will be revealed."

"From what I hear about her, it's very likely she'll figure it out. And if Nadia realizes what's going on, revealing your position will be the *least* of your problems. Do you have any idea what will happen if you're found guilty of treason?"

The student's heart beat faster. "Maybe I should call Agent Roberts."

"You have no business calling him. You have a question, you come to me. Do you understand the basic principle of a chain-of-command?"

"I just thought—"

"We don't pay you to think. We pay you to act." The older man paused. "Do you know why I never address you by name?"

"Yes, of course. In case someone is listening."

"That's only partly correct. As a double, you are required to compartmentalize everything that happens to you. Separate this life from your other life. If the real you wants A, this you requests B. You must think differently, act differently, speak differently. Split your personality. Do you understand?"

"As a matter of fact, no. I was chosen for this role because of my intellect and personality, not in spite of it."

"Don't flatter yourself. You were chosen because it was convenient. Because we did something for you, and, as a result, you owe us."

"First of all, I owe Agent Roberts, not you. Secondly, the only reason I am indebted is because Roberts wanted me, so he figured out how to get me. And lastly, I know my role. Does it seem like this is my first day? My training began long before I arrived at school." *And I was taught by better men than you.* "Instead of a lecture, how about you just give me my orders?" The student glanced over his shoulder.

"Fine. Get rid of Nadia Riley before she connects the dots."

"How do you want me to do it?"

"I don't care, but make it look like an accident."

16 NADIA
MONDAY, SEPTEMBER 12

Late Monday evening after dinner, Nadia and her roommate stepped out of the Navajo Building into the blazing night. "Any chance we're done for the day?" she asked.

"'Fraid not. We're off to the library. Alan and Damon'll meet us there."

"This has been the longest day of my life," Nadia said. Afternoon classes had consisted of Arabic, Mandarin Chinese and Spanish. Thanks to her uncles, she knew a few phrases in Arabic, though nothing she could repeat without getting detention. But she found herself physically unable to make some of the sounds.

"I know. I can barely speak English, let alone Arabic and Chinese."

"And this heat! I can't breathe. Doesn't it bother you?"

"You get used to it. At least, that's what they keep telling us."

"Do you guys always study together after dinner?"

Libby nodded. "After dinner, between classes, during breakfast, on weekends. It's a habit we fell into this summer. We had so much material to process. Add that to the physical training; it's the only way we could keep up. I couldn't do it alone. None of us could. Well, except maybe Alan, who never passes up a chance to mention how much smarter he is than the rest of us."

"Not a team player?"

Libby laughed. "You could say that."

Nadia frowned. "I'm really behind, aren't I?"

"A little," Libby admitted. "But I promise you, if you want to be here, we will not let you fail. I wasn't kidding when I said I do not like living alone." They reached the library. "And can you imagine being the only girl on the team?"

"I don't know. Damon's undivided attention might not be such a bad thing," Nadia said, smiling at Libby.

Libby grinned. "He has this way of talking to you like you're the only person in the world. So I can enjoy his undivided attention *and* have a roommate."

Nadia pushed through the revolving doors. Cool air and the smell of freshly printed books surrounded her. Dark glass walls framed with brushed steel beams rose from the carpet. A row of black cabinets ran perpendicular to the front door. The sign above the enclosed area read Authorized Persons Only.

"What's in there?" Nadia pointed.

"Restricted case files," Libby said. "Some of the information is classified, so it's not available for student review."

"Case files of what?"

"I really couldn't say. Keep moving." Libby ushered Nadia out of the entryway.

Polished wooden bookshelves filled the room. A student climbed a ladder and glided silently along the brass bar, reviewing the row of books. The girls walked down a few open steps to reach the lower level and found Alan and Damon in the back corner of the room. The boys were speaking Arabic.

"English, please," said Libby, smiling sweetly at Alan. "He's already fluent," she said to Nadia, "but he won't tell Dr. Shaheen because he likes feeling superior to us. You believe that?"

"Lucky you. My mom's Lebanese, but I never learned," Nadia said.

"Good for her," Alan answered.

"Are you Arabic?"

"My last name is Cohen." When Nadia didn't answer he

continued, contempt soaking his words. "I am *Jewish*. You have heard of Israel, right?"

"Yeah, I'm familiar with Israel. Isn't Israeli Mossad the only intelligence group better than the CIA?" She'd learned a little about both agencies while studying the origins of ancient ciphers.

"What? Why would you even say that?" Alan demanded. "You do not know anything about either one, do you?"

"Have you guys started the math assignment yet?" Libby asked.

"What's your problem?" Damon asked Alan.

"I just wonder where her loyalties lie," he answered.

Nadia turned to Damon. "He's kidding, right?"

"Easy, tiger. Complimenting Mossad doesn't necessarily make her a traitor," Damon said.

"Because we really should get started," Libby said.

"Historically, our people do not get along. The Arabs and the Jews," Alan said.

Damon nodded. "Well that explains the open hostility."

"It is her." He pointed to Nadia. "Your kinsmen are a bloodthirsty group."

Is he serious? Nadia did her best to ignore his jab. "So how do you know Arabic?"

His cheeks flushed. "It is none of your business. Why are you interrogating me?"

"Not interrogating. Making conversation," she said.

"Well, how about you do not."

"I had a little trouble with the second section," Libby said.

"It's a simple question," Damon said. "Just tell her."

"I have no inclination to share my life story with her," Alan answered.

"All right, now! That's enough," Libby said, her voice too loud for the library. She glanced around. Softly, she continued, "I'm sorry, but we've really got a lot of ground to cover."

Nadia's teammates went over their lessons in surprising detail. Back home she'd never taken school this seriously—she didn't know anyone who did, not even Matthew. *Is it possible I'm in over my head?* Everyone else had been recruited months ago. She was only invited because someone had died. That made her the last choice—the least capable student here. She wished she'd asked Dean Wolfe about her academic standing when they met. *'Course, then he'd know I constantly doubt myself. He probably would've cut me from the program right then. And I will not go back home.*

"Are you even listening?" Alan asked.

Oh, fantastic. They've been talking the whole time and I have no idea what anyone said. "Of course I'm listening." She couldn't ask them to start over. She'd look like a complete idiot. *I'll ask Libby if I can copy her notes.*

Nadia sighed and looked around the room. Her classmates sat in huddled groups, hunched over foot-high stacks of index cards, open texts, piles of notebooks. *Yeah. I don't belong here.*

And that's when she saw him. Her breath caught in her throat.

He stood at a bookshelf skimming the titles. His forehead furrowed in concentration, full lips moving slightly as he read. His skin was a beautiful dark olive; it almost glowed. He ran a hand over his cropped black hair. Then, as though he could feel Nadia's stare, he looked up—directly into her eyes.

Her cheeks flushed and she quickly looked away. She took a deep breath and glanced back. He walked toward her; his lean body taking long, smooth strides. His eyes did not leave hers.

He reached the table and offered his hand. She took it to shake hello. With his other hand he gently pulled on her arm, forcing her to stand. He smiled, his eyes still locked on hers. Her mouth opened, but she couldn't find words. For what seemed like minutes (but was probably only a second or two) they stood staring at each other. She couldn't look away.

Finally, Libby broke the silence. "Nadia," she said, "meet Jack."

17 JACK
MONDAY, SEPTEMBER 12

Earlier that day, during his Advanced Documents class, Jack had received a summons from Dean Wolfe. He was halfway out the door before the bell finished ringing, a flutter of excitement in his stomach. He rushed to Hopi Hall.

Maybe it's a commendation for my analysis of Slavic satellite surveillance. His instructor had insisted Jack read the paper aloud in class.

He adjusted his shirt collar and checked his reflection in the glass bookshelf. Jack ran a hand over his black hair—more out of habit than necessity—before knocking. "You wanted to see me, sir?"

"Close the door," said the Dean. "Please, have a seat. How is your semester progressing?"

"Excellent, thank you."

"And your summer?"

"No complaints."

"You worked as a camp counselor, right? With inner-city kids?"

He's been keeping track of me. That's a good sign. "Yes sir. My summer was very rewarding, but I'm always glad to be back at school."

"You strike me as a loyal, dedicated student. A patriot. Would you say my assessment is correct?"

"Absolutely." Jack straightened a bit. "I'd do anything for the Academy."

"I'm pleased to hear it." Dean Wolfe thumbed through an open file on his desk. "It seems your peers think highly of you, and your instructors offered glowing end-of-year-reports. Last spring you reported a student for cheating on an exam; he was expelled. You two were close."

"He was my best friend." It almost killed Jack, turning him in. But lying and cheating—not to mention disobeying orders— were absolutely unacceptable. No excuses.

"And one of your biggest rivals."

Jack hesitated. *Does he think that's why I spoke up?* "Yes sir. I suppose that's true."

"Relax, son. It wasn't an accusation. In fact, your choice of friends indicates you aren't intimidated by other people's accomplishments. You stick with the winners. That's part of what makes you a successful leader."

The compliment sent a warm feeling through his chest. "Thank you, sir."

Wolfe paused for a long moment, tapping his pen against the desk. "Jack, I'm afraid I have troubling news. We've suffered a serious security breach. It appears Drew Anderson's death was not an accident. Furthermore, I believe one of our students may be a double agent. Immediately following the incident with Drew, Marcus Sloan came to me recommending a new student, a transfer. Her name is Nadia Riley." Dean Wolfe's chair rasped as he rocked back.

Nadia Riley. She must be the one I saw him with yesterday. "Drew was murdered? I don't understand. You suspect the new recruit? Or the recruiter?"

"At this point, I don't know what to think. Albert Vincent, our CIA director, has received intelligence that we have at least one double in our student body. Until we discover who has penetrated our network, no one can be trusted. Since nothing implicates Drew Anderson as the traitor, her murder leads me to one of two conclusions. Either she discovered the identity of the mole, or—"

"Or the mole wasn't initially invited and she needed to clear herself a spot on campus."

"Exactly. To explore the first hypothesis, tell me what you know about Drew's roommate."

"Liberty Grace Bishop, only daughter of Senator Wentworth Bishop. She's from Savannah, Georgia; parents married; older brother. She's attended a series of prestigious private schools. Good grades, excellent standardized test scores. Her personality inventory reveals a slight tendency toward obsessive-compulsive behavior, but it also indicates that she respects authority and is extremely loyal. Her family is from the Deep South; I suspect she's a patriot, born and bred."

"Excellent assessment. Tell me about Damon."

"Damon's a natural. He's attentive, perceptive, intelligent, well-spoken. His manners are impeccable. His mother is a librarian. His father died of a heart attack." Jack cleared his throat. "He has no siblings. His psychological profile describes his sense of justice as very black-and-white. He despises weakness. I don't see him waffling between right and wrong."

"Alan Cohen?"

"Alan is the team's greatest intellectual asset. He's an only child. His father is a doctor, his mother sits on the board of several charities." Jack paused. He didn't want to bad mouth his subordinate.

Dean Wolfe seemed to sense Jack's reluctance. "Go on."

"Alan does not share Libby and Damon's gift for putting others at ease. I can't imagine he'd be selected for undercover work. As you know, a covert agent must be nuanced, captivating. At the very least, unassuming." Alan was the antithesis of disarming. "How can I put this? His awkwardness makes others uncomfortable."

Wolfe nodded approvingly. "Good work, Jack. It sounds like you really know your team. Let me tell you a bit about the new girl. Our recruiter suggested her last spring and I refused to admit her. I didn't want her attending our school."

"She's not qualified?"

"On the contrary. Miss Riley earned a perfect score on the questions the CIA embeds into the standardized tests. Marcus Sloan thinks she's a genius."

"And you?"

"No one scores perfectly on that exam. It's possible to have too much of a good thing. She fits the CIA's profile too well, as though she's been prepped. And even if she wasn't, bringing someone like her onto campus is like starting a nuclear countdown. Overqualified applicants turn into rogue agents. I've seen it before at the CIA. It's only a matter of time until something snaps. And when that happens, regardless of her allegiance, her handler will cease to be in control. The security of Desert Mountain Academy is my highest priority."

"Why take the risk? Can't you just expel her?"

"Not without reason. Especially since her mother is Middle Eastern. We can't be accused of racial profiling. Now, I could rearrange the teams and assign her to someone else, but I firmly believe you are the best man for the job."

Jack looked down as his cheeks warmed. "Thank you, sir. That means a lot to me."

Dean Wolfe nodded. "You've earned my trust. I want you to keep an eye on her; report any unusual activity to me. But don't assume anything. We must be certain before we move—we get one chance. When we find the double, we need to arrest and interrogate, not expel. And if we make a mistake, the real double will disappear."

"I understand. Given that off-campus communications are carefully monitored, I assume a double agent would need an on-campus handler. Any leads? Maybe a faculty member?"

"I've been considering that question myself."

"Does anyone travel extensively over the summer?"

"The foreign language professors all take refresher immersion courses. Our recruiter travels constantly. He takes three to five days off every month, during which time he is not required to report in. He has more freedom than any of us. And, of course, Hashimoto Sensei says he spends his summers in Japan, but I never see his receipts so I really don't know. He doesn't seek reimbursement for travel expenses because his trips are not school-related. But I have no other reason to suspect him." Wolfe continued, "Obviously, this information is well above your pay grade, so to speak. I'm placing my trust in you. Do not disappoint."

"No, sir. Thank you."

"Excellent. That's all for now." Dean Wolfe waved his hand in dismissal and resumed the paperwork on his desk.

Jack hesitated. "Sir, may I ask a question?"

"What is it?" The Dean did not look up.

"How did Drew Anderson die?"

Wolfe stopped his work and rubbed his forehead. His fingernails were buffed to an understated shine. After a moment he looked at Jack. "She was shot in the back of the head, execution style. I don't need to tell you: this information does not leave this room. We teach strategies of war, Jack. Techniques of clandestine service, skill sets specific to Black-Ops. If this information were leaked, a foreign agency would know exactly how we train our up-and-coming agents, which would inform their counter-intelligence training." Dean Wolfe leaned forward and lowered his voice. "More detrimental, however, is the devastation that would be inflicted on our government if an enemy organization managed to plant a mole at this level—the beginning of training. Such an individual would have the potential for an extended and damaging career posing as an agent of the United States of America."

After dinner Jack headed to the library. First-year students always gathered for evening study sessions. He'd catch up with the new girl there.

Jack forced himself to stop smiling. He was elated Dean Wolfe had confided in him. To be trusted with something like this was unprecedented. This assignment had implications far beyond the academy, to his career and future with the CIA.

He spotted Damon and Alan at their usual table. Damon, the natural, with his back to the wall. Alan, the less-natural, scowling at the girls at the next table for whispering too loudly. Knowing Libby would be along soon, Jack positioned himself between shelves.

Desert Mountain demanded excellence in all things. Competition was fierce among his classmates, but it was nothing Jack couldn't handle. He'd been competing with his brothers his whole life. Now, probably to please their father, they were both in medical school, while Jack studied here at the Academy, content with the secret knowledge he was serving his country.

He straightened the books directly in front of him, then checked his watch. *Where are they? This is cutting into my study time.*

A minute later Libby and Nadia walked through the door. Nadia moved confidently, shoulders back, chin high. Her hips swished a little as she walked. She laughed at something Libby said, a quiet laugh with a slightly crooked smile. Jack realized he was smiling with her. He moved closer, to a bookshelf near their table, pretending to be deep in thought.

After a few moments he glanced in their direction; Nadia stared at him. *Am I being too obvious?*

If she is a double, she's been trained to read body language, he reminded himself. *Maybe she saw right through me. I guess there's only one thing to do.* He adjusted his messenger bag and marched to her table.

18 NADIA
TUESDAY, SEPTEMBER 13

Tuesday morning after exercises, Nadia and her team ate breakfast as the sun rose higher. The light glinted off the city below, burning through the hazy cloud that settled on the valley.

"Do you want to hear something annoying?" Alan asked.

"Why wouldn't we?" Libby answered.

"I called my parents last night and the phone kept clicking. And I noticed a distinct pause between everything I said and everything they said."

"The phones are tapped," Damon said.

"What?" Nadia asked.

"Phones are tapped. That's the delay. Everything you say is pre-screened. If the operator doesn't like it, your folks don't hear it."

"Good to know," Nadia said.

"How do *you* know?" Alan asked. It sounded more like an accusation than a question. Nadia noticed Alan tended to stay on the defensive.

"What else could it be? It's a basic security measure."

"What's on today's agenda?" Nadia asked.

"Diplomacy with Dr. Moran, followed by Phys Ed with Sensei. We get a light load on Tuesdays and Thursdays. If I had to guess, I'd say we're doing archery in gym class." Damon nodded toward the lawn, to the line of targets arranged at the bottom of the hill.

"How do you know so much about everything?" Alan demanded.

"First of all, I'm looking right at the targets. Secondly, they went over all this in orientation. You were sitting right next to me."

"Don't feel bad," Libby told Alan. "I don't remember that, either."

"Certainly you are not comparing your intellect and recall to—"

"Hey, guys." Jack interrupted Alan as he stepped onto the patio. He pulled a chair next to Nadia's. His clean smell surrounded her. "I need to speak to Nadia for a minute."

"Off we go, then," Alan muttered, as the team gathered their dishes.

"I'll see you back at the room," Libby said, collecting Nadia's plate.

"Thanks." Nadia adjusted her ponytail. *I just finished working out, I'm all sweaty and exhausted, and he sits right next to me.* Add that to yesterday's fabulous first impression—she'd been so flustered when they met she made a complete fool of herself, answering all his questions with one word: *fine, fine, good, fine.* He took her to the language lab in the library, a glass room lined with laptops and headphones. She completely ignored his instructions as he pulled up the Arabic program, and instead spent her time watching his beautiful hands fly over the keyboard.

"How was your workout?" Jack asked.

"Good," Nadia said. *You're doing it again. Speak in complete sentences, loser.*

Jack continued, apparently oblivious to her embarrassment, "So, I meant to ask: how'd it go at the shrink's office?"

Shocking, nerve-wracking, unsettling. "Fine, I guess. I don't know what he was doing, so I'm not entirely sure."

"Basic fact-finding. Are you a US citizen, do your parents work for the government or any foreign agencies, are you patriotic, do you respect authority, you know," he winked at her, "the basics."

Who winks? But he looked adorable when he did it, his eye crinkling at the corner. Nadia tried not to smile. "Right. The basics. What's with that test?"

"The booklet? You'll take that a few times every semester. They mix it up a little—reword the questions, test us when we're tired after a long drill, ask them orally. On and on."

"Why?"

"The more often they administer the test, the less likely it is we can deceive them. If they question us when we're fatigued, we don't have the energy to fabricate a lie, or even remember what we said last time. It's best to be honest. Inconsistencies are a huge red flag."

"Some of those questions were bizarre. I get, 'do you hear voices,' but what about, 'is your stool black and tarry?' What is that?" The words were out of her mouth before she could stop them. *Oh my God. Please tell me I did not just ask the beautiful boy about fecal matter.*

"Good question. Black stools can indicate either stomach ulcers, which may mean an anxiety disorder, or an overindulgence of alcohol. Both diagnoses are problematic to our line of work. Asking a direct question like 'are you an alcoholic' would be too easy."

"I haven't heard back from Dr. Cameron. Does that mean I passed? I'm in?"

"You're not out."

"Getting a straight answer around here is impossible."

"We're all basically kept on a need-to-know basis." He placed his hand over hers and her stomach jumped. "Remember, this is a covert training facility. Your parents don't even know the truth."

She tried to focus on his words instead of the fact that he was holding her hand. "Yeah, I don't understand why our parents can't know."

"For one thing, by not advertising our curriculum, we lessen the risk of enemy organizations infiltrating the school."

"What about the kids who leave? Do you really think they don't say anything to their friends back home?"

Jack glanced at the empty tables around them. "Only team leaders are supposed to know this, but before a student is dismissed he's required to spend a week in a deprogramming session."

"Hmm. And now we're conspirators." She studied his eyes. "That's interesting."

"What?" Jack looked confused.

"You told me something I wasn't supposed to know. You've created a bond between us; now we share a secret. What I don't know is why you told me."

He laughed lightly, probably more out of politeness than humor. "That's very good. Have you already trained somewhere?"

"Not even close." Nadia smiled. "My father is a criminology professor. He specializes in political assassinations and hostage situations. It's a technique used by kidnappers to bond with potential abductees."

He stared at her for a moment. "I'm not a criminal."

"Of course not," she said quickly. *Nadia, shut up.*

"And I have no plans to ransom you. If I took you, I think I'd keep you." He smiled again, teasing her. "In any case, after a week of deprogramming, no one talks."

"Sounds a little threatening." The heat of the morning pressed down on her. She wiped her forehead with the back of her arm. Was this what she wanted? A life of secrets; lying to her parents? On the other hand, how unbelievably exciting. A future filled with mystery and intrigue, and she was flattered they chose her. Nadia bit her lower lip as she realized Jack was still holding her hand. She hoped it wasn't sweaty. "So if it's so hush-hush, why *are* you telling me?"

His smile widened as he brought his index finger to his lips. "I could get in a lot of trouble for sharing." He leaned in, his mouth brushing against her ear as he whispered, "So please, keep it between us."

His closeness sent a shiver down her back. *Ignore it, Nadia. Did you learn nothing from Matthew?* "My lips are sealed."

Jack stood and pushed in his chair. "Listen, why don't you meet me at the gate after dinner and we'll run a few laps around campus." He said it matter-of-factly, like who would say no to such an offer?

Seriously? More running? Is he insane? "Sounds fun. I'll see you then."

19 DAMON
TUESDAY, SEPTEMBER 13

Tuesday afternoon at the library, Damon made an impulsive decision. If Alan didn't stop banging the table, Damon would be forced to snap his neck. He didn't want to do it; he kind of liked Alan. But he needed to finish his homework.

Damon refocused on his translation a half-second before Alan shifted his weight, once again slamming into the table. Damon violently scratched out the Chinese character he'd been writing, cracking his pencil in half. This was a *library*. The most sacred of spaces.

He dropped the pencil shards and examined his palm for splinters. The light fixture above his head hummed. A bad ballast. Maintenance would swap out the fluorescent tube and, in a day or so, they'd come back to fix the light properly. "Fantastic," he mumbled, pulling a sliver of wood from his thumb.

Alan glanced over. "Oh, you broke your pencil." His knee pumped up and down.

The AC unit kicked on, adding a dull drone. "So I did."

"You should try to be more careful." Alan chewed on a cuticle as his eyes returned to the staircase. He obviously had news. And until he spilled, no one was getting anything done.

"Hey, man. What's up?" Damon asked.

Alan broke into a wide grin. "I will wait until the girls arrive."

75

Damon rubbed his head. Four brutally long minutes later, Libby and Nadia came down the steps.

They were barely at the table when Alan started in. "Did you guys hear what happened?"

"Can you be a little more specific?" Libby asked.

"You know Drew's car accident?" The look of satisfaction left his face. "The reason this one is here?" He jerked his head at Nadia.

"Come on, man." Damon understood his roommate's hostility toward Nadia. Alan had just established his place on the team when Drew up and died. Now he was forced to prove himself all over again. Damon felt bad for him, being so insecure, but he didn't like bullies. "Lay off her."

"Thank you, Damon," Nadia said. "And what are we studying this afternoon?"

"I am in the middle of a story!"

Nadia turned to Alan. "I think you've overestimated our interest in what you have to say. I can't speak for everyone, but personally, I don't give a rat's—"

"As I was saying before I was so rudely interrupted by the girl who probably thinks *habeas corpus* is a city in Texas—"

"I know what *habeas corpus* means."

Alan scowled at Nadia. "Oh yeah? Well for your information, I happen to—I have—I might—"

"What are you saying?" she asked.

Damon tried to suppress his smile. He liked how Nadia stood up for herself. More than he hated bullies, he hated pushovers.

"Honestly, that's enough," Libby said. "I'm gonna have to take someone out behind the woodshed."

Libby, on the other hand, went out of her way to avoid conflict. Even when the conflict wasn't hers. Not that she was weak, but she obviously felt uncomfortable with discord. He usually did the opposite, charging head-first into the fire. Often spraying lighter fluid on the flames just for fun.

Libby continued, "Nadia, even though I'm sick to death of people talking about that poor girl, why don't we hear him out?"

She sighed. "It's just easier that way. Now what's this about the car accident?"

"Thank you." Alan glared at Nadia. "No accident."

"What are you talking about?" Damon asked.

Alan's agitation visibly faded as he doled out his gossip. "I overheard some teachers. Drew was shot. She was murdered."

"Come on," said Damon. "None of our teachers would talk about a murdered student in front of a first year."

Alan looked smug. "They were speaking Arabic."

"No way," said Nadia. "How would the school keep something like that secret?"

"The senior professors are all retired CIA operatives. Do you really believe them incapable of covering up the death of one insignificant girl?" Alan answered.

"I beg your pardon, but Drew was not insignificant," Libby said.

Alan scoffed. "Please. Her parents are nobodies."

Nadia took a deep breath and opened her mouth, undoubtedly to read him the riot act, and as much as Damon would've enjoyed hearing the exchange, Alan surely had more information. "That can't be right," Damon said. "They found her car. She drove into the side of a mountain. It was completely torched."

"It could have been staged," Alan argued.

"Why would anyone want to kill Drew?" asked Libby.

"They did not say. But I heard the word *khawan*."

"So? What does that mean?" Damon asked. Alan was milking this for all it was worth.

"It means *traitor*," he whispered. "You know, like a double agent. Who knows what the CIA would do to a treasonous student."

Libby looked troubled. "At least a life sentence. Maybe the death penalty."

"I am thinking either she was a mole and the CIA had her killed, or it is someone else and Drew found out, and *they* killed her." Alan's excitement was obvious.

"A girl is dead," Damon reminded him. "Show some respect."

Alan raised his eyebrows and shrugged. "I did not kill her."

"Well then, by all means." Damon extended his arm. "Please continue," he said, his sarcasm wasted on his roommate.

Alan nodded like he was accepting an apology. "Thank you."

"That's completely unbelievable," said Nadia.

"You think I am lying?"

"Here we go," Damon mumbled.

"No, Alan. If I thought you were lying I would come out and say it. I meant the story was unbelievable."

"Maybe it is you," Alan said to her. "Maybe you are the double. You needed a place on campus and failed to receive an invitation based on merit, so you killed Drew to open a slot."

"Yeah, I'm a double agent. This whole struggling-to-catch-up thing is just a big act. Not bad, huh? But you caught me. I killed Drew. And you know what?" Nadia leaned across the table into Alan's space. Her voice dropped an octave. "You better watch your back, because you're next."

Damon laughed as Alan slammed his book shut and stomped away from the table. He shook his head. "Fifty bucks says he made that up, just to have a good story to tell."

"I don't know," said Libby. "He's occasionally insensitive, but I don't think he'd out-and-out lie."

"Occasionally?" repeated Nadia. "That's cute."

Damon shrugged. "Yeah, I guess you're right." Alan *was* a horrific liar. Like when Damon grilled him about girls. Alan said he'd hooked up plenty of times, but Damon could tell he was lying. Alan had shifted his weight, looked away, repeated the questions. As if that weren't enough, a minute later he turned a splotchy crimson, scratching at his neck like a cat with fleas—it looked like an allergic reaction.

The strange thing was, it had happened another time too, when Damon asked Alan about his family. Alan said he'd lived in Jerusalem with his grandparents as a little kid because his father had been working for Doctors Without Borders. Two minutes later he was covered in hives. He claimed he'd eaten peanuts at lunch or something. But he never had any trouble with peanut *butter*. It didn't add up.

"In any case," Damon continued, "what's done is done. Drew's death was tragic, but there's nothing we can do to change it. The truth comes out when it needs to. It always does."

20 NADIA
TUESDAY, SEPTEMBER 13

On their way from the library to dinner, Nadia asked Libby, as casually as possible, "So, does Jack have a girlfriend?"

"Not a chance, and it's not from lack of offers. He practically has his own fan club. Sadly, his single-minded pursuit of academic excellence leaves little time for a social life."

I must've misread his signals. Her stomach sank. *Of course I did, why would he be interested in me?* Nadia knew she was cute, but he was on another level. *Anyway, what difference does it make? That's the last thing I need.*

She turned her attention back to Libby. "Do you like him?"

"*Like* him, like him? No, he's not my type."

"Greek god doesn't do it for you?"

Libby laughed. "Actually, no. I prefer the Scandinavian look: blue-eyed blondes. You should see his roommate, Noah. I'd tell you to go for Damon, but he's got his eye on Niyuri—you know her from class. She's one of Noah's, which makes it interesting because they're our rival team this semester. She's cute as a bug. And sweet, too."

"So he's smart, then?"

"Damon? Absolutely."

"No. Jack."

"Oh yeah. Smart as a whip. We lucked out getting him as our team leader," she said.

"So all our competitions are against Noah's team? Doesn't that create an awkward living situation for him and Jack?"

"I believe they do it that way on purpose," Libby said. "One more challenge to overcome."

"Jack asked me to meet him at the gate after dinner."

"Is that right?" Libby asked, her smile teasing.

"We're just going for a run." Nadia wondered if Libby could tell she was nervous. "It's no big deal." She pulled the dining room door open.

Alan and Damon, already at the table, were discussing the upcoming Fall Formal. "I'm taking Niyuri," Damon announced.

"You're already making plans? It's over two months away," said Libby. "You're such a girl!"

"Whatever," said Damon. "You gotta lock that down."

"Lock what down?" Alan frowned. "What do you mean?"

Damon stared at him for a moment. "I asked her before someone else had a chance."

"Oh. Well, I am disinclined to attend. I hate dancing," Alan said. "As you can imagine, it is not exactly my *milieu*."

"It's mandatory," Damon said.

"Mandatory?" Alan asked.

"Yeah," answered Damon. "As in, you don't have a choice."

"I know what mandatory means," Alan snapped. "But why?"

"It's part of the curriculum. Here's the deal: imagine you have a job at the Spanish embassy," Damon began.

"Why Spanish? Why not Israeli?" asked Alan.

"What's the difference?" He paused long enough to glare at Alan. "So you're working at the embassy and there's an event, a formal occasion. You're on assignment, you need to meet and greet. How can you blend if you don't know how to mingle? If you're standing along the wall the whole night?"

Nadia nodded. "I see your point, but I'm with Alan on this one. Can't we just go over it at the dojo or something?"

"Fitting in takes years of practice. People have to like you but not remember you. Meanwhile, you need to train your eye to notice every detail of your surroundings. Right? Close your eyes. Okay, now what color are my eyes?"

Nadia smiled. "Like dark chocolate."

"Alan's?"

She shrugged. "I want to say . . . light brown?"

"Hazel," Alan interjected.

"How many emergency exits in this room? No—keep your eyes closed."

"I don't know, three?"

"Which way is north?"

Nadia opened her eyes. "Are you kidding me? I don't even know where the bathroom is. I'd be dead by now, wouldn't I?" She tended to be hideously unobservant about her surroundings, despite her father's constant efforts to the contrary. She focused on people instead. Body language, innuendo. "I am so in over my head."

"As we have noticed," Alan said.

"Nah, these are skills you can learn, but they take practice and discipline."

"You close your eyes," Nadia instructed Damon. "How many exits?"

He made a face. "*Please.* Don't insult me. Four exits: two on the south wall, the main exit on the north wall, and one to the west. The alarm will sound if you open that door. Two cameras and four motion sensors are mounted along the ceiling. Your eyes are green unless you're wearing navy, then they look blue. Right now you have on a pair of pearl earrings you borrowed from Libby. I know they're hers because she wore them last Thursday. You've touched your ears three times during this conversation, which tells me you think the pearls are real and you're afraid you'll lose them. Don't sweat it; they're not real."

"He's right," Libby whispered. "They're fakes."

His eyes opened. "Have I satisfied you?"

"Nobody likes a show-off," Nadia answered, as Libby tried not to laugh.

Nadia was so nervous about meeting Jack, she hardly touched her dinner.

He was waiting at the gate. "Let's go slow so we can talk. I want to ask you about something."

Nadia's stomach fluttered. "Okay." *Is he going to ask me to the dance?*

They started down the path. The evening air was hot against her skin.

"Do you think you'll be able to catch up in your classes? Because if you feel overwhelmed I can find you a tutor. It's important to start out strong."

His slow pace was like her medium. "Yeah, I'm okay. I don't need any help."

"You missed a lot this summer."

"I'm fine, really."

"Great. No worries, then. I just wanted to touch base with you."

"That's what you wanted to ask me?" Nadia said the words quickly so he wouldn't know she was already winded.

"Yeah. I'm your team leader, so if you need help with anything, I'm your man."

Nadia couldn't figure out why he'd invited her here to ask a question he could've asked anywhere. *Unless he thought I might be embarrassed for needing extra help. In which case, he's gorgeous and thoughtful.*

"I got it," she said finally. "But thanks for the offer."

Libby wasn't in the room when Nadia returned from her run. She peeled off her sweat-soaked clothes and turned on the shower. *Two days and I'm already exhausted. I need to get in shape.*

She stood under the water for a long time. The cool stream washed the prickly heat from her scalp, the stickiness from her skin. After twenty minutes, finally refreshed, she stepped onto the tile and wrapped herself in a thick towel. In the bedroom, as she selected a pair of pajamas, a flash of color caught her eye. Something moved across the floor—not a mouse, something large and bright. It ran under her desk.

Nadia dropped the pajamas and jumped onto her bed. A black-and-orange lizard the size of her thigh huddled beneath her chair. His beaded scales shimmered in the soft bedroom light.

What the hell is that? Her legs shook. A thick, forked tongue slithered out of the animal's mouth. "Is anyone there?" she yelled at the closed door.

The lizard scurried toward her, sharp claws clicking across the floor. A low wail escaped her lips; a strange sound, one she'd never heard. He veered right and disappeared under Libby's bedskirt.

What do I do? Wait for Libby? What if it bites her as she comes in the room? I can't take that chance.

Libby's bed stood between Nadia and the door.

Holding her towel tight, Nadia jumped onto her roommate's bed. She leaned forward and turned the knob.

Nadia leapt into the hall and slammed the door. Two steps toward the lobby, she realized her towel was caught. It ripped off her body and lay in a damp heap on the floor. She stood naked in the hallway.

"Oh my God! What are you *doing*?" a girl called from the lobby. "Put some clothes on!"

Nadia's face burned. Six, maybe seven girls had gathered at the end of the hall to watch the scene. She yanked on the towel. It didn't budge. She grabbed with both hands and pulled as hard as she could. The damp towel slipped from her fingers and she fell onto her butt. Scrambling to her feet, she opened the door enough to free the fabric and slammed it shut again. She sprinted to the lobby.

From behind her desk, Casey asked, "Nadia, are you all right?"

Nadia shook her head. "There's a giant lizard in my room."

By now, everyone on her hall had grouped to the lobby.

"A lizard?" Jennifer asked. "Are you joking? You're afraid of a lizard?"

"No, you don't understand. This thing is like a baby dragon."

Casey telephoned maintenance. A few minutes later a man in a steel-blue jumpsuit arrived.

"Everyone decent?" he asked. He rocked on his heels. "What's the problem?"

"Giant reptile in my room." Nadia sat on the lobby sofa, gratefully wrapped in Casey's bathrobe.

"I'll have a look," he said.

Nadia waited impatiently, scowling at the group of girls chatting by the front door. A few minutes later the man returned, empty handed.

"Where's the lizard?" Casey asked.

"I'll have to call animal control. It's a Gila monster. I'm not going near that thing." He removed his baseball hat, wiped his brow with the sleeve of his shirt and shook his head.

"What's a Gila monster?" Nadia asked.

"You've heard of rattlers and scorpions, right?" he asked.

"Yeah."

"Well, they're nothing compared to this."

"What do you mean?"

"A Gila monster is ten times deadlier than all of them. It grabs onto its victim and doesn't let go. Nothing you can do to unclamp those jaws. Docs in the ER say people come in with the lizard still hanging off their arm."

"How did it get in my room?" Nadia's voice was high and shrill.

"I don't know. These lobby doors close automatically, for the very purpose of keeping out the desert creatures. But that's not even the strangest part." He paused.

Nadia raised her eyebrows. After a second she lifted her hands, exasperated, and asked, "Well? What is?"

"Gila monsters are extremely rare. I've lived here thirty-five years and never seen one outside the zoo. Don't know anyone who has. They live underground, they're completely nocturnal and they almost never surface." He chuckled. "You're one lucky lady."

"How do you figure?"

"Cause you didn't get bit. That would've been lights out for you, sweetheart."

21 JACK
WEDNESDAY, SEPTEMBER 14

Wednesday evening, shortly after dinner, Jack headed to the air-conditioned comfort of the library. He found a quiet armchair along the wall and studied his fledglings from across the room.

So far, Jack's assessment of Nadia was remarkably inconclusive. She wasn't mediocre at anything, which is what he'd expected from a trained agent making a decided effort to appear *untrained*. She was either great at a task or awful, never in the middle.

Yesterday afternoon, for example, a few hours after inviting Nadia to meet him for a run, Jack had stood on the patio outside the dining hall as the juniors reported to the main lawn for Phys Ed. Sensei demonstrated the use of a bow and arrow, then allowed the students to practice. Jack admired Nadia's posture: firm stance, erect spine, strong arms.

"Look," Sensei called to his class. "Notice her form. Nadia-san, fire."

Nadia drew back the bow. Her body straight, her hands steady, she released the string. The arrow flew clean and fast. It pierced the target, second ring from center.

No way was that her first time. She was way too comfortable with the weapon for a newbie. Perfect form.

But then last night when they'd gone for a run, she could

barely keep up. She was either out of shape, or she'd deliberately panted to seem weak. He'd funneled her ahead of him on the trail to observe her cadence: smooth, efficient. A born athlete. Jack couldn't quite figure it out.

Nadia looked up from her books, her movement drawing Jack back to the moment. She glanced toward the library entrance, checked the ceiling. *What is she looking for? Surveillance cameras? Points of entry?* Besides yesterday's red flag, when she'd accurately identified his motives for confiding in her (in about a nanosecond), she seemed like a typical recruit. Her eyes stopped on Jack. He smiled and strolled across the floor to her table. "How's it going? You guys helping our girl catch up?" He placed his hand on Nadia's shoulder. She smiled back.

"We are not miracle workers," Alan said.

"Sarcasm," Nadia said. "How refreshing."

"Furthermore," Alan said to her, "Desert Mountain is not a nudist colony. We heard about last night. I do not know what protocol was in *Virginia*, but here we remain clothed, at all times."

"Whoa, what are you talking about?" Jack asked.

Nadia's face reddened. She said to Alan, "I don't think that's a problem you'll be facing anytime soon."

"Come on, now. We're a team," Libby said. "Let's not say anything we might regret."

"And what's your aversion to contractions?" Nadia continued. "Because it doesn't make you sound well spoken; you just sound pretentious."

Alan's face flushed. "I use contractions all the time."

Jack grinned and sat down on the edge of their table. "Wait, nudist colony? What's this now?"

"You're kind of on my things," Alan said, pulling at some papers under Jack's thigh. "I am discriminated against because I am eloquent." He scratched at his throat.

Jack leaned to the side, freeing Alan's papers. "Go back to last night."

"We had a Gila monster in our room. Nadia's lucky she wasn't injured. Y'all shouldn't be joking about this."

"No kidding. Were you there, too?" Jack asked Libby.

Libby averted her eyes. "I was not present." She patted Nadia's hand. "I should'a been."

Nadia shook her head. "I was really worried you'd walk in and get bitten. I'm glad you didn't come home."

"When was this?" Jack asked.

"Right after our run."

"Man, you got lucky, huh?" Besides the occasional scorpion in the shower, he'd never heard of an animal breach in the dorms.

Nadia raised an eyebrow. "So I've been told."

"I just thank God you're okay," Libby said. "I would've been devastated if anything had happened to you."

"I would have been fine," said Alan.

"Never mind him." Damon shot Alan a look.

"I promise you, despite nearly irrefutable evidence to the contrary, there is no curse associated with being my roommate," Libby said.

"Hey." Jack nodded to Damon. "Can you come give me a hand with something? I have a dresser I need to move, and if I wait for Noah, it'll never get done."

"Right now?" Damon asked. "For real?"

"It won't take long." Jack stood and turned away, knowing full well Damon would follow.

Outside, the city lights sparkled in the distance. They began the walk across the lawn.

"What's this about?" Damon asked. "I know you don't need help redecorating."

Jack smiled, pleased with Damon's quick assessment of the situation. "True enough. I'm curious what you think of the new recruit. I'd hate to lose another team member."

"Especially one who looks like her, right?"

Jack laughed. "It never crossed my mind."

"I like her. She's funny. And not intimidated by Alan. You know he made Drew cry?"

Jack shook his head. "I didn't know that."

"Yeah. He's nice enough to Libby; it's hard not to be, you know? But, man, if someone rubs him the wrong way, forget it. It's like he gets these personal vendettas. Deliberately sabotaging his own team."

"Hmm. I'll keep an eye on that. You think Nadia will be able to catch up?"

"Yeah, no problem. Even if Alan refuses to help, she's still got me and Libby."

"So she and Libby are getting along?"

"Seem to be."

"What's Alan's problem with her?"

Damon shrugged. "I couldn't say."

Come on, Damon. You don't miss anything. "Take a guess." Damon remained silent. "I'm not asking because I'm a fan of high school gossip. It's my job; I need to know what's going on."

Damon hesitated. "He's pissed he's gotta help her catch up. He'd rather be a man down than fall a little behind."

"Is he a pain to live with?"

"A little, but he's all right." Damon rubbed his face. "Except he talks in his sleep. Bad enough I gotta listen to him all day, you know what I mean?"

The boys reached their dorm. Jack pulled the door open. "How's everything going with you?" he asked quietly.

"I'm great, man. No complaints." Damon smiled.

Jack watched him carefully. "Good. Hey, thanks for your help."

"No problem."

Thursday morning, Jack cornered Alan after breakfast. "How's it going?"

"How is what going?"

"You know, life in general."

Alan raised an eyebrow as he gave Jack a sideways stare. "Have you met my teammates?"

"What's the problem?"

"Where should I start? Damon? Though recruited to a top-notch school, his interests appear purely social, and let me tell you: he cannot spare the study sessions."

"Not everyone has had your advantages."

"Well, Libby has, and she is not much better."

"What's wrong with Libby?"

"Have you heard her speak? *Ah do declayah. Can y'all fetch me some sweet tea?* I do not know if this is a result of inbreeding, which frequently occurs in her part of the country—"

"Hey," Jack said sharply. "She's your teammate. I don't want to hear you talking about her like that."

Alan looked genuinely surprised. "Then do not ask my opinion. Anyway, why do you care what I say?"

Jack shook his head. Alan wouldn't understand the necessity of team cohesion. That they must trust their unit without question. "One day your life may depend on her."

"God be with me if this is true."

Jack sighed. Talking to Nadia's teammates was not proving as helpful as he'd hoped. "What about Nadia? Things okay with her? Do you have any concerns?"

"Are you joking right now? She is the worst of them—a complete idiot." Alan scraped his remaining pancake into the trashcan.

"How so?"

"She is unintelligent, combative and unpleasant. I need you to move her to a different team—better yet, send her home. I can deal with Libby and Damon, but Nadia? We were informed during orientation that we will frequently be graded as a unit. She is a detriment to us all." He pressed his finger into Jack's chest. "Including you."

Jack firmly moved Alan's hand aside. Alan paused, probably

realizing he'd just poked Jack in the chest. He looked away as he set down his dishes.

"Believe it or not," Jack said, "I don't get to pick and choose my team." *Else you would not be on it.*

"Well, something has to be done. I refuse to work like this." Alan looked squarely at Jack. "You get rid of her, or I will do it for you." He turned on his heel and walked away.

22 NADIA
FRIDAY, SEPTEMBER 16

Friday morning, Nadia found an envelope wedged under her bedroom door. She read the message aloud:

> This weekend is your first survival course. Two opposing teams will be dropped at an undisclosed location in the desert. Your objective: Locate the coordinates given to your team leader, collect a package from the indicated area and return the item to campus. You will carry one water bottle, a field knife and a tranquilizer gun (see Hashimoto Sensei to secure your weapons).

"Did they mention this at orientation?" Nadia asked.

Libby shook her head. "This is the first I've heard of it. Come on, we'll ask Sensei when we get to the dojo. He *loves* answering questions."

After the students gathered on the mat, Sensei entered the room. "Several of you received a summons this morning. The survival course, an Academy tradition and critical element of training, is a simulated mission: You must retrieve a package and return to campus as a group. You are issued a knife and tranquilizer gun. The knife is for fire-building. It is not a weapon. For those of you not incompetent, the trip will take two days and one night."

Nadia smiled. *Finally, something I'll do well.* She glanced at the worried faces around her. *What's the big deal? It's a camping trip.*

"This exercise requires physical stamina and mental discipline. You will move from sunrise to sunset. You will be hungry and tired. And keep in mind, your group travels only as fast as its slowest member. Do you understand?"

Several students raised their hands.

"Lower your hands! I have said everything you need to know. If you have been called to the survival course, see me after exercises and I will distribute weapons. One team at a time."

Instead of their usual morning run, Nadia's team followed Sensei down the hall while Noah's juniors waited in the lobby. He stopped at one of the closed doors and pressed his thumb onto the keypad. A green light flashed and he shielded the keypad with his body before entering a password. The lock clicked open and he led them inside.

"I did not know we had a shooting range," Alan said.

"We do not. I do." Sensei led them past ten firing stations, each with a paper target at the end of a long aisle. The targets were printed with a human silhouette; the stations partitioned off with glass.

When they reached the door at the far end of the room, Sensei again placed his thumb onto the keypad and entered a code. "Wait," he ordered.

The students peeked inside. Stainless steel pegboard lined the walls. Guns, ammunition, knives and swords covered every square inch. Nadia had never seen a gun up close, much less hundreds lined up together.

Damon whistled softly. "It's like a high-tech, lethal candy store. I could have some fun in here."

Sensei emerged from the room and distributed handguns. "Choose a lane. We will now have target practice. You do not need ear protection; these guns are equipped with silencers. Use both hands to steady your aim. Face forward, eyes open and fire."

Nadia held the gun awkwardly in her hand. She wasn't sure what to do with her arms. *Lock my elbows? Relax?* She flinched as she squeezed the trigger with the tip of her index finger. Nothing happened. She wrapped her entire finger around the trigger, held her breath and pulled harder. The gun fired and she stepped back to catch her balance. The kickback was stronger than she'd expected.

"Do not hold your breath. Press the trigger after you exhale," Sensei instructed.

Nadia fired again. He corrected her stance, adjusting her form so her left hand supported the right as her arms were extended.

"These firearms, designed especially for your training at Desert Mountain, are lethal weapons. They have been modified to hold magazines of either tranquilizer darts or bullets. It is impossible to tell by glancing at this gun whether or not your ammunition is lethal. We train with these weapons specifically to sharpen awareness of your combat situation: never take for granted your opponent will behave as expected. Never assume your enemy is dead. You must relinquish all weapons to me immediately upon your return."

The team took several practice shots before Sensei showed them how to bring the target forward. Damon's paper man had a grouping of holes around the heart. Libby's had a nice cluster in the head. Sensei raised his eyebrows in approval.

"My brother takes me hunting," she said.

"And you, Damon-san?" Sensei asked.

"Skeet shooting."

"Next," Sensei ordered.

Alan's had miscellaneous holes: two in the shoulder, four in the neck, a few in the heavy white border around the silhouette.

"Where'd you learn to shoot?" Libby asked.

His face flushed and he scratched his collarbone. "Just lucky." He pulled at his shirt, fanning his chest.

"What's the matter, honey? You feeling all right?"

"I am fine."

Sensei pulled Nadia's target forward. Her paper was pristine. "Nadia-san, it seems your proficiency with a bow and arrow was an aberration." Sensei shook his head and addressed her team. "I suggest if you need to subdue your opponents, someone else take the shot."

Nadia sighed. *Look at that, I'm the worst on my team. What an unexpected turn of events.*

Saturday morning the group met Jack at the front gate. They climbed into one van as Noah's team entered another. They drove an hour before the van pulled over.

"We get out here," Jack ordered. "Noah's team will be dropped on the other side of the target, equal distance from the destination. The good news is since it's your first time, we get a map." Jack held up a topographic map.

"And the bad news?" Alan asked, his voice tight.

"Everything else. Now come on." Jack led them into the desert. "And no talking. We each have one bottle of water and we don't know whether or not the stream will be dry. See the dotted blue line?" He pointed to the map. "That means it's an occasional stream. Depending on how much it's rained here we may or may not get to refill our bottles. Talking dries out your mouth."

They continued in silence along the narrow path. A collection of cactus parts accumulated on Nadia's pants. A few of the sharper spines poked through the fabric and scratched her legs. She brushed at them as she walked. Two of her fingers swelled slightly from the pricks, but Nadia refused to stop and pick them out. She wouldn't be the one to hold up the team.

Hours later, when the sun disappeared behind the mountains, they stopped for the night. Nadia couldn't even guess how many miles they'd traveled. Her fatigue was nothing compared to the raw hunger scraping at her gut.

Jack demonstrated how to make a bow drill—which basically consisted of a couple of sticks and a shoelace—to start a fire. By the time he'd finished the temperature had dropped significantly. They huddled around the small flame. As the fire dwindled, she regretted sitting for so long. Her muscles had stiffened; her legs and feet throbbed.

"Gather plant debris for bedding," Jack said, "but watch for rattlesnakes and scorpions."

Are you kidding me?

"We'll spoon. It's the best way to keep warm," Jack said.

Libby inspected small piles of fallen leaves before pushing them together. She picked through her meager bedding, chucking rocks and large twigs off to the side. Alan got on his knees and shoveled dirt into a pile like a bulldozer. Nadia rolled her eyes and half-heartedly gathered some leaves before collapsing on the ground. A few hours later, she regretted her carelessness. The cold desert floor sucked the heat from her body and she woke often, shivering despite being wedged between Jack and Libby.

This is miserable. What am I doing? I can't even handle one stupid camping trip! She couldn't bear the thought of quitting—it had only been a week. *I just need a little more time to acclimate.*

As she finally drifted off, Jack roused the group. "The sun's almost up. Let's move."

They hiked along the foothills of a low mountain. Nadia's body ached; muscles she'd never felt tightened and seized. She kept her eyes on the dusty ground and trudged behind Libby, planting her front foot in the exact spot Libby's back foot vacated. *One more step,* she repeated. *Just one more step.*

They walked for hours. By mid-afternoon the heat had become unbearable. Nadia's t-shirt, soaked with sweat, clung to her skin. Her canteen had been empty since late morning. Her feet burned, her lips were chapped and she felt sick to her stomach. She wanted to go home.

I can't go home. Tears stung her eyes. *I don't belong there either.*

"We're here," Jack whispered. "Everyone, quiet. Noah's team

might be close." He unholstered his gun. Alan and Damon drew their weapons. Libby shrugged and readied hers as well. Nadia was the last to draw.

Jack moved like a mountain lion stalking prey. The team followed, keeping low to the ground. "I see the package," he whispered.

In a small clearing, a white envelope sat on a wooden crate, weighted down with a rock. Jack stepped forward to retrieve the item.

When he rejoined the group Alan whispered, "What is it?"

"I don't know," answered Jack.

"Open it," he urged.

"Absolutely not. Our mission is to return to school with this package. What's inside is none of our concern." They retreated, retracing their steps.

An hour later, they stopped at a small stream. Before rehydrating, Libby vigorously scrubbed her hands in the water, then dampened her handkerchief and wiped her face. Nadia filled her bottle and sat down hard on the ground. Her gun dug into her ribs so she reached for it, to move it around. She leaned back and pulled the weapon from its holster.

A sudden, sharp pain pierced her foot.

"Oh my God!" Nadia cried. "I think a scorpion bit me!"

Immediately dizzy, she swayed to the side and hit her head against a scrawny tree. The animal's poison was attacking her central nervous system. Next her muscles would lock, then full paralysis would set in. Without the anti-venom, she'd be dead by nightfall.

Jack rushed to her side. "What happened?"

She clutched his hand. "Jack, please. Tell my parents . . ." Her lips and tongue tingled. The words felt thick, like hunks of bread. The earth lurched toward her.

"Nadia!" He caught her in his arms. "You shot yourself in the foot!"

Her vision warped. She tried to answer, but the sedative in

the dart worked fast. Her eyes closed as the drug coursed through her veins.

Nadia came to with a splitting headache. She struggled to focus. She was moving—how was she moving? Someone carried her. A shoulder dug into her abdomen.

"Look who is awake," Alan said. "Sleeping beauty."

"She didn't do it on purpose," Libby snapped.

Nadia was slung over Jack's shoulder, his strong arm secure around her legs. *This is the most humiliating moment of my life.* With every step her head pounded. "Can I have some water?" she whispered, her tongue thick and dry.

"We're almost home," Jack said, not slowing his gait. "Can you hang on until then?"

"I feel really sick."

"Please don't puke on me," Jack said.

She didn't answer; she'd fallen back asleep.

23 ALAN
SUNDAY, SEPTEMBER 18

Given that Alan was ordered to bring up the rear on the way home from the survival course, he spent a large part of Sunday afternoon watching Nadia swing like a pendulum across Jack's back. She regained consciousness long enough to complain about being thirsty, but not long enough to hear his request that she return home at the first available opportunity. A request which, for whatever reason, seemed to annoy Libby much more than did Nadia's screwing up in the first place.

Alan parted ways with his teammates the moment they crossed through the back gate. Before he dined, before he showered, before he returned his gear to the dojo, Alan marched across the lawn to the tree-lined path leading to Dr. Cameron's office.

"Alan," Dr. Cameron greeted him. "What can I do for you?"

"May I?" Without waiting for an answer, Alan charged inside and pulled the door closed. "I have serious concerns about one of my teammates."

Dr. Cameron turned his papers face-down. "Who?"

"It is Nadia Riley."

"Has she done something?"

"Oh please. What has she *not* done?" Dr. Cameron looked at him quizzically, and Alan quickly reviewed what he had just said. "I mean, what hasn't she done? We just finished our survival course. Jack Felkin had to carry her back to school because she shot herself with a tranquilizer dart."

"What?"

"I am not kidding. She has failed all three quizzes administered this week. Her grades are disgraceful, but I do not—I don't think she cares! She is a distraction during study sessions. Constant interruptions, and she is not even trying to catch up. How did she get into this school? I left an exceptionally well-regarded institution to attend Desert Mountain, and I refuse to allow my academic record to be marred due to an incompetent teammate."

"I can see you're very upset about this."

"Of course I am upset! Would you not be? It is bad enough I have to train with other people, but forcing me to carry her weight is unacceptable."

"I thought you said Jack carried her."

"Yes—he did. I did not mean literally carrying—"

"Alan. I'm teasing."

Alan paused. "I do not think it is the best time for a joke."

"Listen, would you like to sit?" Dr. Cameron gestured to the folding chair.

Alan shook his head.

"Okay," he continued. "I hear your concerns, and they are absolutely valid; however, an important part of your training involves learning to work with others."

"I do not *like* working with others."

"I understand. But you cannot enter into the field of intelligence if you are unable—or unwilling—to be part of a team."

"I am willing to concede that teamwork is required; however, equipping me with incompetent teammates is unreasonable and unfair."

"I can assure you, we do not admit incompetent recruits. Perhaps Nadia has qualities and talents you haven't yet discovered?"

"No. She does not. She is not good at anything."

"Okay. You have two choices. You can wait it out and hope

she's not invited to return next semester, or you can work with her, in a dedicated effort to improve your team."

"I do not want to be part of this team."

"We've established your feelings about that."

"Can you not move me to a different team?"

"There are no vacancies."

"Well, maybe I will just go home." Alan made the threat before he thought it through. Even if he could convince Saba to let him transfer, he did not really want to. Desert Mountain Academy was so exclusive, one could not even apply. His old school was impressive, absolutely, but with enough money anyone could get in. *Well, maybe not Nadia.*

"How about this: give it one semester. If Nadia manages to pass her classes and return, I will look into vacancies on another team. Academically, we always lose a few students before winter break."

Alan chewed on his cuticle as he considered this. He shrugged. "We can always hope." *Knowing my luck, this will be the first semester in history that no one fails.*

That evening, Alan signed out a car and drove into town. Though exhausted from the survival course, he needed time away from the troglodytes. Plus, he had a phone call to make. A call that could not *under any circumstances* be traced back to him.

He drove to the bus station west of town. Inside, along the wall of dirty windows, he found a bank of telephones. Alan chose the farthest from the door and, back to the wall, used a tissue to pick up the receiver. Not because he was worried about fingerprints, but because the station smelled like vomit. He dialed his international calling card number, followed by fourteen digits. The line rang in Tel Aviv.

"Shalom." The voice sounded a million miles away.

"Shalom, Saba," Alan answered.

"My son," his saba said in Hebrew. "Where are you?"

The ninth circle of hell. "At a bus station."

"Alan. You took a vehicle from school? They have GPS trackers."

"I have bigger problems than campus security."

"If anyone questions you, say you stopped to use the facilities, all right?"

"This is a mistake. I cannot do what you asked. I—I am not the right person."

"Yes, you can. I will tell you exactly what to do."

Alan sighed. A homeless man shuffled across the station, pushing a grocery cart loaded with trash bags. A woman bounced a fat, drooling baby on her lap. He felt nauseous.

"Are you listening?"

"Yes, Saba."

"You must blend. Get close to people. Be part of the team."

"But—"

"Aryeh, I have been doing this my whole life. No one likes to suspect their friends. Eat too much, watch football. Act like an American. Remember your training."

"But these people are—"

"Enough." His grandfather answered sharply. "You did not have to go. You insisted you could handle it. You said to me: *This is what I want.* So, now you must make the best of the situation." His voice softened. "Relax. Take a girl out for dinner."

Alan rolled his eyes. "I really only know two girls. One is a senator's daughter—"

"Not her."

Great. "The other is a complete moron."

Saba chuckled. "This is not a bad thing. She is pretty, I bet."

"She is all right."

"Use contractions, Aryeh. Americans are lazy. They use contractions all the time."

"She's all right." He never remembered the contractions. He was good about the adverbs, but not the contractions.

"Aryeh, you must tell me something. Has your loyalty shifted?"

Alan hesitated a fraction of a second. "Of course not, Saba. And please stop calling me that. My name is Alan."

"Because I have told you before: The United States is not loyal to her children. If anything happens in the field, the CIA will disavow you as an agent. It is not like this in Mossad. Here, we are *all* family. We never leave anyone behind."

"Yes, Saba."

"Family before country, Alan. Always."

Unless the country is Israel. "Yes, Saba. Of course."

24 NADIA
SUNDAY, SEPTEMBER 18

Sunday night, after waking from her drug-induced sleep, Nadia took a walk around campus. She kept to the shadows, not wanting to be seen. She'd figured someone might choke on the first trip, but she never dreamed it would be her.

Every time I think I've reached the height of my embarrassment, I'm proven wrong. She might've enjoyed the irony if the stakes weren't so high.

Marcus Sloan had told her not everyone made it to the next level. The senior class had twenty students fewer than the junior class, which meant two out of every five kids either got tossed or quit. Failure was not an option.

It's time to get serious.

First step, she needed a tutor, and as much as Nadia hated the idea, she knew whom to ask for help.

At breakfast on Monday, Nadia dragged her chair around the table next to Alan's. She smiled. "How are you this morning?"

"What do you want?" he asked, not bothering to hide his contempt.

"I think we got off on the wrong foot," she said. "Occasionally, I can be a little . . ."

"Aggressive?" he asked. "Antagonistic? Incompetent?"

"Direct," she said. "I've clearly offended you, and I apologize."

He eyed her suspiciously. After a moment he answered, "Very well."

"And I have a favor to ask."

Libby and Damon, who were carefully watching the exchange, shared a glance.

Nadia continued, "I'm having a little trouble with my schoolwork. Between catching up on summer reading and learning the new material, I'm a bit overwhelmed. I was wondering if you'd be willing to tutor me?"

Alan took a long time to finish chewing. "Perhaps you should go home."

Be nice. It's this or facing Matthew. "I understand I'm not your favorite person, but you'd be helping our whole team. After all, my performance reflects on you, as well."

"Your work ethic is abysmal."

"It's been a long and difficult week. That's why I'm coming to you." She tried not to sound irritated.

"I'm surprised you are astute enough to acknowledge your shortcomings. I would not have credited you as one with accurate introspection."

Keep your mouth shut. "Yeah, well. I'm an enigma. Can you help me or not?"

His eyes narrowed as he studied her. Almost to himself, he said, "We would be required to spend a great deal of time together."

"I am aware." She could practically see his wheels turning as he calculated the hours he'd be forced to spend with her.

After a heavy sigh and a sneer, which Nadia chose to interpret as his attempt at a smile, he answered, "Fine. We will convene after dinner."

25 AGENT 77365
MONDAY, SEPTEMBER 19

An hour before dinner on Monday evening, the student pulled on a pair of shorts and a long sleeve shirt before heading toward the running trails. When he reached the east side of the outer wall, he slipped off the path and into the brush. He stayed low as he stole through the desert.

A few miles out, he retrieved his phone. He assembled the pieces: handset, battery, memory chip. "I got your message," he said to his contact. "What do you want?"

"The Gila monster was a good idea, but a rattlesnake would have been more efficient."

"For your information, anti-venom is readily available. And a rattlesnake comes with a built-in alarm system."

"So why not a scorpion?"

"Again, anti-venom. It's the equivalent of a spider bite. Only dangerous without modern medicine." *Where did this moron train?* "Is this why you needed me to call? So you could lecture me?"

"Believe it or not, I have better things to do than coach you through adolescence. Someone knows about you. And the administration's on a manhunt."

"Thanks for the news flash. I have one for you: everyone knows about Drew's execution. If you and your *colleagues* could refrain from gossiping in front of the students, I would be very grateful."

"I realized our error shortly after the conversation. I thought we were alone."

"You realized your error?" the student repeated. "How many other people overheard?"

"I don't know. I'm sorry. Was it a severe setback?"

"No. I covered it well. Does the administration know about me *specifically*?"

"Not yet. And you'll never believe who they suspect."

"Who?"

"Nadia Riley."

"Because her family is from the Middle East?"

"Don't be ridiculous. Wolfe has good reason to suspect her. Not only did she arrive on campus late—giving the appearance that someone hand-picked her—but she received a perfect score on the CIA's questions in the standardized tests."

"How is that relevant?"

"Do you know how difficult it is to get a perfect score? It's been done maybe twice. *You* didn't do it."

Then maybe you should have recruited her.

The man continued, "The logical conclusion is someone coached her."

"Did they?"

"Not at all. Her mind is just suited to our line of work."

"Great." He glanced at his watch.

"This actually works out well for us. Why don't you do your patriotic duty and help them out?"

The student looked around. "You still want her neutralized?"

"I have a new plan. I need you to get as close to her as you possibly can."

"But what if she figures out Drew's code?"

"It doesn't matter. Your new mission is to convince everyone she's the double. When we're finished with her, no one will believe a word she says. Do you have plans to see her?"

"As a matter of fact, I expect to see her very soon."

"Good," his contact answered. "Because she's our new fall guy."

26 NADIA
TUESDAY, SEPTEMBER 20

Nadia had noticed on the survival course that while she'd barely managed to take one more step, her teammates hadn't seemed the least bit fatigued. If Jack hadn't had to carry her back, she might not have made it. She'd always considered herself reasonably athletic. Discovering she had no endurance bothered her. With a tutor now squared away, she gathered her courage and made an appointment at the dojo.

"Sensei, I'm having a hard time. I'm struggling in class, I'm exhausted, I feel—"

"What do you want?"

"I bombed the survival course. I was weak. I held back my team. Please help me."

"Not to mention rendering yourself unconscious with a tranquilizer gun," he added.

"Yes, thank you for reminding me."

"If you recall, I suggested you not discharge your weapon," he continued.

"Oh, it was quite by accident, I assure you."

"There are no accidents!" His raised voice startled her. "Only a lack of discipline! And I have seen nothing from you to indicate you are worthy of my individual instruction."

Nadia's cheeks burned. A hot rush of tears threatened to fall.

"Hashimoto Sensei." Nadia bowed deeply at the waist. She continued in a shaky whisper, hoping she'd memorized the correct word, "*Kudasai.*"

She remained in the bow for what felt like five minutes. Her lower back began to ache. Unfamiliar with Japanese etiquette, she now feared she'd overcommitted. But she couldn't possibly stand after this long without being dismissed. She watched his feet for movement, almost hoping he'd turn and walk away just to relieve her from this uncomfortable position.

"Get up and stop this nonsense," Sensei instructed. She straightened. "Who taught you *kudasai*?"

"I looked it up. It means *please*, right?"

He stared at her for a long time. "I will help you. If you do exactly as I say."

"Yes—thank you! Absolutely."

"I will give you one month; no more. If you fail to reach your peers by then, your position here will likely be reevaluated. We will meet here every morning, one hour before sunrise."

"No problem. What time does the sun come up?" she asked.

He sighed and cast his eyes toward her feet. "Do not make me regret my decision."

She shook her head. "I'll figure it out. Will I still be required to train with my classmates?" Nadia didn't do the math, but that sounded like a lot of time in the dojo.

"Required or permitted?" he answered.

"Thank you," she said, a false smile pulling on her lips.

Seven days a week, Nadia met Sensei in his dojo. He had a long bamboo stick that cracked like a whip when he hit something. Usually, that something was her.

The first day she walked in and *crack!* across her thigh. The split end of the stick stung like a giant rubber band snapping against her body. "What was that for?" she asked, rubbing her leg.

"Bow when you enter a room of learning."

"Couldn't you just tell me that?"

"Now you will never forget. Do not ask questions. I will tell you when you need to know something. Follow me to the mat. Stand with your legs three feet apart. Good. Now bend deeply at the knees, toes forward, back straight. This is Horse Stance. Make a fist and bend your elbows, your left hand across your abdomen. This is low guard. Place your right fist facing out across your forehead. This is high block. One hundred blocks with each arm, go!"

"One, two, three—"

Crack! "Count in Japanese!"

"But I don't speak Japanese!"

"Then you will be in this position for a long time."

Nadia spent that afternoon in the language lab. By the next morning she could count to a hundred in Japanese. Once she learned one through ten, it was easy.

Sensei taught her defensive moves first—escapes and blocks. He hit her hundreds of times before the instinct to deflect a blow became muscle memory. Then they moved on to strikes. She learned to kick and punch, use pressure points and joint locks. He taught her choke holds by knocking her unconscious. She came to with a dull headache.

"Really?" she asked him, rubbing the back of her neck.

"I warned you several times to tap out, but you refused. You are too stubborn. When blood stops flowing to your brain, you have seven seconds until you lose consciousness. If not quickly revived, death shortly follows."

Every day they ended in his meditation room, where she learned Zazen breathing. "This will teach you discipline," he instructed, adjusting her posture on the tiny meditation bench. "Once you learn to breathe, you will not tire as easily. Inhale through your nose as you count to four. Exhale slowly through your mouth as though blowing through a straw while you count to eight. Eventually, one breath will last sixty seconds."

Each day brought more pain. When she stood her legs throbbed, when she sat, knives stabbed into her back. Lying down brought little relief, and her neck ached from hundreds of head raises. She limped around campus, her movements stiff and awkward.

Worse than the physical pain, her crush on Jack continued. Granted, between the extra workouts and Alan demanding they spend every spare moment studying together, she didn't have that much time to think about Jack. She certainly didn't want to like him. But every time she spotted him her heart raced. Occasionally he'd stop and say hello, ask about training. She was still too embarrassed to thank him for carrying her out of the desert. As a result, she made a point to keep their conversations brief.

A few weeks into her extra training, after a particularly long night studying with Alan (during which he mentioned that her naïve grasp of computer linguistics was holding up the entire class), Nadia arrived at the dojo twelve minutes late.

Exhausted, she rushed onto the mats, bowing to Sensei. "I'm so sorry I'm late."

"I do not train tardy students. Leave my dojo."

"But I—"

"Now!"

Nadia's eyes filled with tears. *I tried. I really did.* Her lower lip began to shake.

She shouldn't have come—she'd never be good enough for the CIA. She would go home, resume her hideous life. Maybe the public shame of losing Matthew to her best friend would've subsided. Maybe no one would remember how she'd been kicked out of Hannah's party.

I remember. Nadia burst into tears.

"Are you crying?" Sensei demanded.

She nodded, wiping her nose on her sleeve.

"Stop that!" He took a step back.

Nadia tried to stop. "I don't even know why I'm here. I'm wasting everyone's time."

"It is one day. You will not be late again."

"I was the last choice!" She struggled to stifle her tears.

"What?"

"I was only invited because someone died. But the recruiter said I answered all the test questions correctly. Why was I the last choice?"

"I do not answer questions."

She looked at the ground. Her face felt hot and she started crying again.

Sensei sighed. After a moment he relented. "Many factors contribute to recruitment."

She sniffed. "Like what?"

"In addition to standardized tests and grade point averages, there are personal issues to consider."

"Like?"

"We are wasting time."

Nadia was silent.

"You are behaving like a child," Sensei said. "Why must you know?"

"I'm completely incompetent. My invitation was a huge mistake. I don't belong here. I know it and you know it—probably better than anyone."

He took a deep breath and slowly exhaled. "The Academy prefers two working parents. Less time is spent monitoring the child. Children of divorce are desirable. They are eager to please and more willing to take risks. We like students with siblings, or at the very least, to have come from boarding school. It is less strain on the family when a child goes away. If I remember correctly, and I always do, you do not meet any of those criteria, which would explain your delayed invitation."

"Really?"

"Yes, of course. Does this satisfy your curiosity?"

Nadia nodded. "Thank you," she said softly, wiping her eyes.

"My morning is already ruined. We might as well have a lesson. Go and wash your face."

Later that afternoon, before the puffiness had disappeared from her eyes, Nadia found herself face-to-face with Jack. She was entering the language lab at the library when he called out in a loud whisper.

She turned toward him. His long strides quickly closed the space between them.

"Hey," she said, studying the carpet.

"Hey, yourself. How's it going?"

"Good, thanks." She nodded, smiling. Feeling like an idiot.

He lifted her chin. His brow furrowed. "Are you okay? Your eyes look a little red."

Even his eyebrows are perfect. "Yeah, I'm fine. I think it's allergies."

"Really?" He seemed skeptical. "Most people get them in the spring."

"Listen, I've been meaning to say something: I know it's long overdue, but thank you for carrying me out of the desert. I'm really sorry about the whole shooting-myself-in-the-foot thing. And I'm embarrassed it's taken me this long to say it. As you might imagine, I was not eager to rehash."

He laughed. "It's okay. I'm sorry for *you.* I imagine your friends will be merciless about that for some time." They stood in front of the language lab, his hand on the doorknob, her clutching an armful of books. The silence stretched a little too long. "I guess I should let you go in."

"I guess I'd better."

He didn't move. "So speaking of things long overdue, let's go out this weekend. How's dinner and a movie?"

Did he just ask me out? Nadia skillfully suppressed her grin. "This weekend?" She pretended to consider. "I think I'm available." *Seriously, Nadia? Are you an idiot? Don't you ever learn?*

"Great. Saturday night, eighteen-hundred? I'll meet you in front of Hopi Hall." Jack smiled and pulled open the door.

Shut up, it's one date. What's the worst that could happen?

27 JACK
THURSDAY, SEPTEMBER 29

The last Thursday morning in September, Jack rushed to the Dean's office to give his first official report. So far, no definitive evidence indicated that Nadia was anyone other than whom she claimed to be.

Jack knocked on the Dean's open door. He hadn't stopped smiling since Nadia agreed to a date, which concerned him a little.

"What have you learned?" Dean Wolfe asked, waving toward his wingback chairs.

"She trains excessively at the dojo. Every morning like clockwork, an hour before sunrise—and that's in addition to the regular junior-class regimen." Jack couldn't help but admire her dedication. She worked harder than anyone he knew. He tried to keep the respect out of his voice; *report the facts, not the feelings.* "If she is the double, I'm betting Sensei is her handler. They spend an exorbitant amount of time together. And if so, he's very good."

"What do you mean?"

"She's actually working out. She now runs at the head of the pack. If he's going over casework, he's making her exercise at the same time."

"What else?" Dean Wolfe asked.

"Well, she's very bright. She requested Alan Cohen as a tutor, so she's up-to-speed in all her classes. Also, if she is guilty, she's certainly a gifted actress. I mean, she shot herself in the foot with a tranquilizer gun on the first survival course. She's either brilliant or innocent. I've kept some distance; I don't want to scare her off. Sometimes I think she knows I'm checking up on her."

"How so?"

"I catch her staring at me a lot."

"Hmm. Anything else?"

"Early on I shared some information meant only for team leaders. I know it's against policy, but I thought it would be a good way to win her trust. Nothing critical, of course."

"Smart."

He paused. "I got the sense she knew why I was sharing."

"Really? What gave you that impression?"

Because she came out and said it. "Just a feeling. What does her father do?"

"He's a professor. Criminology, I believe."

Jack nodded. *So she was telling the truth.* "I'm taking her out this weekend. Dinner and a movie." He forced a neutral expression. *Why does that make me so happy? Am I excited about impressing Dean Wolfe? Doing undercover work? Or is this about getting closer to Nadia?*

Wolfe raised his eyebrows and nodded. "Excellent; the closer, the better. I'll make a car and expense account available. Have you given any thought to the Fall Formal?"

"I intend to invite her. It's at a hotel downtown, so I figure if she's meeting someone from another agency, the dance provides a perfect opportunity. If I escort her I can keep a closer eye. But I can't ask her yet. No one likes a sure thing."

"No, I agree. It's cat-and-mouse, eh?"

"Yes sir." Jack felt himself smiling. *It is about Nadia.* He hesitated before he asked, "Have any other suspects emerged? I would be happy to broaden my investigation."

"Just stay focused on your assignment."

"No, of course. I just thought maybe . . ." *I hope it's not her.*

"I'm very satisfied, son. You're doing exactly what I asked. Thank you."

"It's my pleasure, sir." *Stay focused,* he reminded himself, as he felt a flicker of excitement in his stomach.

28 NADIA
SATURDAY, OCTOBER 1

"This is a mistake," Nadia said for the third time in two days. "Do you think I should cancel? I think I'm gonna cancel."

Libby sat on her bed reading a magazine. "Like I said the last seventeen times you asked, no, I don't. What are you so worried about? Jack's a good guy. I'd trust him with my life."

"I know. But I've been burned before."

"Who hasn't? Is this about the guy from home?" she asked. Nadia nodded. "All right, tell me what happened."

"I can't talk about it."

"Come on," Libby coaxed.

"It's too humiliating."

Libby slowly flipped the pages of her magazine. "More humiliating than shooting yourself in the foot and having to be carried back to school thrown over the shoulder of the hottest guy on campus?" She smiled sweetly at Nadia. "That humiliating?"

"Hey, thanks for the reminder." Nadia groaned as she leaned against the wall. "Fine. I'll tell you." She took a deep breath, then sighed. "I'd been dating Matthew for almost a year. I was totally crazy about him, which I can't understand now, because he's very self-centered and way too competitive—and that's coming from me." Libby rolled her hand in a circle, as in *let's move on*. "Anyway, about a week before school started he hooked up with my best friend. I didn't know, but apparently everyone else did."

Libby winced. "I'm guessing no one told you."

Nadia shook her head. "Of course not. But it gets worse. Matthew's cousin Hannah always has a back-to-school party for the entire grade. It's a huge deal—caterer, bartender, DJ—the whole thing. And it's kind of understood everyone's invited. So I showed up about an hour into the party. It was packed—I had to park like two blocks away. I went through the house and out back by the pool to get a drink. People were hanging around inside, outside, you know."

Libby nodded.

"I'm at the bar ordering a sprite and cranberry when Hannah walks up to me. She literally screams, 'I can't believe you are so rude that you'd show up at my party uninvited.' The entire patio falls silent. *Everyone* is staring. Including Matthew and Paige. Just *staring* at me." Nadia's heart pounded as she told the story. "I was so embarrassed I couldn't move. My legs went numb. I tried to set my drink back on the bar but I missed and the glass shattered on his deck. Then she started yelling about that. I had to walk through all those people to get out. It was the single worst moment of my life."

"That's awful. Your face is red just talking about it." Libby stood and put her arms around Nadia. "But Jack's not like that. He'd never hurt a flea."

Nadia tried to smile; she shrugged like it didn't matter. "It's my own fault. I shouldn't have trusted Matthew." *But I expected better from Paige.* She turned toward her closet and pretended to flip through the hangers as tears stung her eyes.

She and Paige had been inseparable since the first day of freshman year. Paige's leg had been in a cast. Nadia, standing behind her in the lunch line, volunteered to carry Paige's tray. "I don't make the offer lightly," she'd said. "It's a lot of pressure carrying this little tray across the cafeteria. I'm always afraid I'll trip and my food will go flying."

"I know exactly what you mean," Paige said, "and I'm forever in your debt."

For two years, they were closer than sisters. They spent every day together. But at the party, Paige had stood to the side, mute, as Hannah threw Nadia out of her house.

It's one date. Just don't fall for him. She sighed again. "I don't have anything to wear."

"Here, let me." Libby opened her own closet and selected a slim black sweater. "Try this with your jeans and boots. You can borrow a strand of pearls."

"It's so soft. Cashmere?"

Libby nodded. "You know what? You can keep it. Alan said it made me look like a corpse."

"He's a real charmer."

"Don't ever ask him how you look unless you really want to know."

Nadia held up the sweater and checked her reflection. "I still feel like he's looking for any excuse to ridicule me."

"I believe it's unintentional."

"Of course you do. You only see the good in people."

Libby smiled. "While that may be true, social grace is not his forte. And he's incapable of telling a lie. He'd make a terrible field agent and he knows it. He'll stay behind the scenes: analysis, or maybe a computer specialist. He'd make a great translator. But can you imagine if the enemy captured him? They wouldn't have to use torture. They'd say, 'Please tell us who you work for, and don't lie.' He'd sing like a mockingbird."

Nadia watched Libby rearrange the clothes in her closet to ensure each hanger was separated by the same amount of space. "And if *you're* captured, the enemy can drop a pile of clothes in the middle of the floor."

Libby laughed. "Please, I'll tell you anything! Just let me fold those sweaters!"

At six o'clock Nadia found Jack waiting in front of the administration building. He drove to the Mesquite Grill on Scottsdale Road.

A half-hour later, in the darkened restaurant, Nadia found it difficult to concentrate on the menu. She scanned the words over and over, but she couldn't focus. Jack's fitted European-style oxford and dark-washed jeans accentuated his strong, lean form. His legs touched hers under the tablecloth and she swore she could feel the heat from his body surrounding her.

Relax. He's just a guy.

"So how is it for you, being away from home for the first time?" Jack asked.

"It's okay. My parents are pretty cool. I sort of feel guilty being here. I'm sure it's been hard on them."

"Are they overprotective?" Jack asked.

"My mom is, about some things."

"Like what?"

Nadia smiled, thinking about her mom. "Stupid things. What if the house catches fire, what if you're at a party and your friends are drinking and you don't have a ride home, what if a meteor falls from the sky, what if, what if . . . She likes me to be prepared. She even made up this code phrase for us, just in case."

"What do you mean?" Jack smiled with her.

"Like if I'm at a friend's house and I don't want to be there, for whatever reason, I call her and say, 'I forgot to tell you, but the plumber called,' and she knows to make up an excuse to come get me." She blushed as she spoke. *Why am I telling him this? I sound like a little girl.* It was like her mouth had its own mind—Nadia wanted to sit quietly but she couldn't seem to shut up.

"I love it! We should have a code phrase."

"For what?"

"For our long and lucrative career together at the CIA. And by 'lucrative' I mean extremely dangerous work for little pay and no public recognition. Any ideas?"

She laughed. "Right, lucrative. How about: 'the piano needs to be tuned'?"

"No good. If we have to say this to each other over the phone it can't be so out-of-context." Jack chewed on a fry.

"Okay. 'It's getting chilly, so grab a sweater.' Always appropriate."

"Perfect," Jack agreed. "Picture it: twenty years from now, I'm captured by an elite terrorist cell stationed in Taipei. They threaten me, they know I'm working with someone. 'Call her in,' they order. So I make the call, 'Sniper? It's Blade.' "

"I'm Sniper?"

"Sure. After you shot yourself in the foot how could you not be Sniper?"

"I guess I had that coming."

" 'Sniper, it's Blade. Meet me at the extraction point, but bring a sweater. It's cold outside.' And you'll know that means run, save yourself! I love it." He laughed as his eyes locked onto hers. "Tell me more. Do you have a boyfriend? I like to know if I should watch my back."

"No boyfriend." Nadia smiled to herself.

"You don't have the slightest accent. Did you grow up in Virginia?"

"No, we moved around a lot."

"Where all have you lived?"

"Do you want the whole list?" she asked reluctantly.

"Sure, we've got time."

"Okay. I was born in Michigan, then we moved to Belize, then Maine, then Guam . . . California, Texas, upstate New York, Pennsylvania, Maryland and finally, Virginia." She knew the next question; it was always the same.

"Was your dad in the military?"

"Witness protection program."

Jack's eyes widened. "For real?"

"No, I'm kidding. He never got tenure."

He smiled. "Very funny. Was it hard moving around like that?"

"A little. I was a shy kid. I remember having to stand up in front of the entire class and introduce myself every time we moved. It was excruciating." Nadia covered her face with her hands. She'd spent her entire childhood being the new kid. Every couple years they'd pack up, move halfway around the world, and start over. That's when her obsession with codes and puzzles began. She'd been too reserved to introduce herself around the neighborhood, so her mom bought books of games to keep her occupied. Nadia would sit for days, scratching out code after code while her mom unpacked another new house, her dad familiarized himself with another new job.

"So tell me something about you no one else knows," Jack said.

"I don't have any secrets."

"Everyone has secrets. How about something most people don't know?"

Nadia thought for a minute. "I can read your palm."

"No way."

"True story. Let me see." Nadia pulled his hand across the table. She ran her fingers softly over his calloused palm, his smooth wrist. His skin was warm. "Oh, this is very good."

"What do you see?"

"I see a long and happy life. Your career will be extremely rewarding. You will marry only once and have two children."

Jack withdrew his hand. "That's so generic."

"I'm not finished." Nadia yanked his hand back and pretended to study the lines in his skin. "Okay, your father chose your name. Your mother disagreed; she wanted something more uncommon."

"Hmm. Not bad."

"What was it?"

"What was what?"

"The name your mother chose for you."

"Hermes. God of speed and war."

"I hate to break it to you, but Hermes was a messenger. And the God of thieves, not war."

"Is that right?"

"I'm afraid so."

"Well, my mother never was much of a scholar." He nodded to his palm. "What else do you see?"

"This is interesting. It says here," Nadia lightly traced the cup of his hand, "your parents are divorced. You have an older brother. Your mother is a gifted cook." She glanced at his face. "You're closer to your mom than your dad. In fact, you and your father are often at odds."

Jack's hand tightened. His face remained expressionless.

"You think of Dean Wolfe as a father figure. In turn, Dean Wolfe respects you a great deal."

Jack pulled away. "Impressive." He shifted in his chair and signaled for their server. "Can we get the check?"

Oops.

"Need anything else?" the waitress asked.

He tossed two twenties on the table. "We're good."

"Jack?" Nadia said.

"We gotta go."

"I hope I didn't say anything—"

"Not at all," he interrupted. "I just realized the time." He placed his hand on the small of her back and led her toward the door. "The movie is right up the block."

29 JACK
SATURDAY, OCTOBER 1

"Did you like the movie?" Jack asked, as he drove Nadia back to school. Keeping her engaged in mindless small talk required his full concentration. The feeling of disappointment that had settled deep in his gut refused to soften.

"I did."

He glanced at her; Nadia watched the darkened scenery through the passenger window. She'd been quiet since the restaurant. *She's not as clever as she thinks. The question is: does she know she messed up?*

Nadia turned to him. "Tell me about your family."

Like you don't already know. "Well, you were a little light on the body count: I have *two* older brothers and a younger sister," Jack said. "I'm from San Diego, my parents *are* divorced, my dad's a vascular surgeon and my mother owns a Greek restaurant. And you were right—she's an incredible chef. That's about it."

"Succinct," Nadia said. "What do you do for fun?"

"I'm doing it now."

She laughed. "Anything else?"

"I miss driving along the coast. I like running too. It clears my head. And I spent last summer working at a camp for underprivileged kids."

"Admirable."

"Not really; I got way more out of it than they did. The kids are amazing." For a brief second, Jack's smile was genuine. "They're all so happy to be there, you know? It was like rediscovering the world—I see life through fresh eyes when I'm with them."

"Do you like your family?"

"Most of them. Holidays are the best, when my brothers are home from college and we can all hang out. I miss my siblings."

"That's awesome. I wish I had a sister or brother."

"Yeah, but in this business it can be a liability," he answered.

"What do you mean?"

"Oh, you know." He shot her a quick look. "It's easier to risk your life for your country if you aren't worried about loved ones grieving when you die. But I love the work. Everything about it." *Especially catching traitors.*

"You don't mind lying to your family about what you're learning?"

It's better than lying to my country. "The way I see it, I'm protecting my family. The less they know, the safer they'll be."

"Do you see both your parents a lot?"

"You ask a lot of questions."

"Sorry." She smiled. "I dominated the conversation at dinner; I don't know anything about you."

"I live with my mom. My dad works like crazy. They had an ugly breakup. I still see him, but, as you guessed, we're not close." They pulled onto the dirt road leading to school. At the gate, Jack signed in with the guard. "Thanks, Jeff," he said, as they were waved through.

"Why don't they scan the students?" Nadia asked, pointing to her eyes.

"I dunno. They only do employees." Jack pulled into the lot behind Hopi Hall. "I'll walk you home."

Jack took her hand and didn't let go as they walked along the path to the girls' dorm. He hated himself for it, but he liked her touch.

She turned to him. "Thanks again." Nadia glanced at his face, then down at the ground.

She wants me to kiss her. And so I won't. He lifted her chin and looked into her eyes. The color in her cheeks deepened and his breath quickened. *Oh my God. I want to kiss her too.*

He leaned toward her as her eyes closed. His mouth lingered near hers, then he lifted his chin and touched his lips to her forehead. Her body moved into his. She took a deep breath. Jack closed his eyes—it took every ounce of strength not to press her against the wall. He wanted to feel his hands inside her thick hair, their bodies close together, his lips on hers.

Jack forced himself to step back. "I'll see you tomorrow," he said abruptly, and walked away.

Five hours later, at 0330, sleep continued to elude him. He rolled onto his back, eyes trained on the ceiling.

He could've fallen for her easily. No girl had ever read him like that—so quickly, so dead on.

She shouldn't have told me what she knows.

He'd worked it out during the movie: Nadia Riley was absolutely the double agent. Before she'd arrived on campus, she'd studied a dossier of her teammates. She missed enough of the details that if he hadn't already known about her, he wouldn't have been suspicious.

But how did she know about my relationship with Dean Wolfe? That wasn't in any dossier. He'd never spoken to anyone about the Dean. Not even Dr. Cameron.

Jack sighed. *At least Wolfe will be happy. And I'm here to serve my country, not find a date to the prom.*

His expanding disappointment aside, the investigation did intrigue him. *How long has she been training? Who does she work for? What could she teach me?* Jack understood why she'd been chosen. There was something about her—he couldn't quite put his finger on it. She was disarming. Like in the car, when he was talking about his summer. He'd forgotten for a second that she was the enemy.

His stomach twisted as he pictured her, leaning against him outside her dorm, her lips so close to his. Her scent—soft and summery, like coconuts. How she'd looked at him. He knew when a girl liked him.

Seriously, Jack? That's spycraft 101. She was trained to attract you.

Intellectually, he understood his feelings were stupid and childish—she was putting on a show. But emotionally . . .

What kind of agent will I be if I fall for every girl who comes along?

But it wasn't every girl, it was this girl. And this was the *only* girl.

What does that say about me? That the only girl I fall for is an enemy spy? Dr. Cameron would have a field day with that one.

You know, maybe she's just intuitive. Maybe she has a gift for reading people. I don't have any proof that she's the double. It could be anyone. Maybe she scored so highly on the entrance exam because she's a genius. It would be awesome if she were innocent—she's just my type. Determined, hard-working, goal-oriented, perfectionist.

Jack sighed and forced himself back to reality. *Knock it off. It has to be her. No one is that intuitive. And who studies cryptograms for fun? Not to mention, she was evasive about her family and where she grew up. And that code game with her mother?*

But if it was more than a game, why'd she tell me about it?

Jack checked the clock. 0359. His eyes returned to the ceiling. *She shot herself with a tranq gun. No way would a pro do that, not even for a cover story—it's excessive.*

He sighed again. *Really? How long are you gonna go back and forth with this? Your first priority is to Dean Wolfe and your country.*

Of course, on the off chance that Nadia was innocent, Jack would love to be the one to clear her name. *I need to know the truth. This assignment requires aggressive action.* He closed his eyes as a new plan took shape.

30 NADIA
FRIDAY, OCTOBER 7

Since their date last Saturday, Nadia had the feeling Jack was deliberately avoiding her. She wasn't the best conversationalist, but she'd thought he'd had a good time. *Until I read his palm.* Of course, she hadn't actually read his palm. She'd just paid attention.

She knew his mother was a good cook by the way he'd ordered his salad—Kalamata olives instead of Spanish, grilled shallots instead of raw onions, and olive oil and balsamic in lieu of Thousand Island. And he looked way too exotic to be named Jack. She'd guessed his father named him because his last name was Felkin, as opposed to, say, Kronopolis, which meant his mother—who might have given up her maiden name—was the one who'd bestowed him his beautiful dark olive skin.

And the thing with Dean Wolfe? Jack was obviously an overachiever, which probably meant his father was excessively critical (which also meant he would prefer his mother's company). Matthew's father was the same way; that's why he'd felt a constant need to compete with her. And she'd guessed Jack's parents were divorced and he had at least one sibling based on what Sensei told her about how the Academy selects recruits. The older brother was a shot in the dark.

Next time she'd keep her deductions to herself. Not that there would be a next time.

She replayed their conversations in her head, poring over each detail. *I sounded like a fifth grader telling him about the code with my mother. And joking about Witness Protection. How is that funny? That's not funny.*

Maybe he was just being friendly. Taking her out because she was new. But why kiss her forehead when he walked her home? Is that something a team leader would do? *Yeah, I guess it's kind of big-brotherly. That would explain why I didn't get a real kiss.*

It doesn't matter, she finally decided. *I don't want to go down that road anyway.*

In mid-October, after a solid month of physical training, Nadia bowed deeply to Sensei. Although the constant pain had subsided, she was grateful the four weeks were over. "Thank you for everything." As a result of her hard work, Nadia noticed visible veins in her arms from hundreds of push-ups. Her stamina—along with her confidence—had increased threefold. And she looked *fabulous*. "I am now on par with my classmates." She was actually much further ahead than her friends, but she didn't want to sound arrogant. Sensei appreciated humility.

Sensei gave her an appraising look. "Contrary to my expectations, you have proven yourself an earnest student. But I am still unsatisfied with your handgun skills."

A week into private lessons, Sensei had insisted she begin target practice—with the silencer removed. "If you do not familiarize yourself with the concussion, you will freeze the first time you hear a shot." After a lecture on gun safety (which Nadia politely suggested may have been more useful *before* she was given a firearm, and to which he responded *crack!*), he handed her the weapon.

"Nadia-san, remember your archery. Face your target. Open both eyes. Ready the gun and press the trigger."

She'd held her breath and squeezed. With her stronger biceps, the recoil was much less noticeable and she easily controlled the kickback. The bullet pierced the edge of the target on her first try. "Look, I hit the paper!"

"This time aim for the man," Sensei had answered without amusement.

Now he went on, "You may continue your private training three days a week."

Nadia stayed low in her bow so he wouldn't see her cringe. "Hashimoto Sensei, your offer is beyond generous," she said, straightening. "But why would you continue to spend time on me? Why do you care if I fail or succeed?"

Anger flashed through his dark eyes. Before she could blink, he dropped to a crouch and swung his leg toward her, catching her ankles and sweeping her feet into the air. She fell flat on her back. He pressed his pole to her throat. "I do not answer personal questions! I will expect you in my dojo three mornings a week."

She nodded hastily.

"Get up. How dare you imply I have wasted my time."

"My apologies." She scrambled to her feet and quickly bowed again, wincing. "*Arigato*. But must you use the stick?"

Crack! "It is only pain. When you are in pain one of two things will happen: The pain will be so great that you will die, or the pain will eventually go away. Either way," he smiled and bowed his head, "no more pain."

Nadia no longer hid behind her textbook in political science, and she'd started to pick up the nuances of Arabic and Chinese. Alan turned out to be a very proficient tutor. He focused on her study skills; she'd never learned *how* to learn. Alan, raised in private schools, had perfected note-taking years ago. He knew the value of an outline, flashcards and most importantly, rewriting class notes.

In Diplomacy the class studied dead drops, or leaving a package in a designated area to be retrieved later by another agent. They practiced brush-passes: a computer disc, a USB drive, an empty envelope. They'd go two at a time, while the other pair offered a critique. At first it was obvious, any bystander could see the object change hands. During one attempt, Nadia's hand got stuck in Damon's jacket as they passed. He didn't notice until he'd pulled her to the ground, tearing open his pocket.

After a while they became skilled enough to complete unde- tected brush-passes right in front of the other pair. Occasionally when Libby and Nadia returned to their room for the night, they'd find a message from the guys slipped into a pocket or dropped in their bags.

Nadia's favorite section came next: cryptography. Studying under the same instructors who'd taught actual agents allowed her to further hone her decoding skills.

"How did you solve this one?" Alan asked of a particularly difficult problem.

"Look at this symbol. In this word it's used side-by-side, so it's most likely *s, t, e,* or *o.* It appears again at the beginning of this three letter word, which is probably *the.* So the symbol is *t.* Get it? You should be good at this. It's all about language. If you can remember letter frequency, you'll have no problem." She raced through these assignments eliciting a rare, albeit backhanded, compliment from Alan.

"I am surprised you are so good at codes, given your lack of propensity for foreign languages."

Nadia wasn't offended; she'd realized weeks ago that Alan was more clueless than malicious. "You know, you don't have to say every little thing that pops into your head."

"I am physically incapable of telling a lie. My face gets red and splotchy and I grin like the Cheshire cat," he answered. "Once in a while I break out in hives. I cannot imagine how I was selected for intelligence work."

"So you never lie?"

"Out loud? Never. I could not begin to guess what the other person wants to hear, so why bother making up a lie?"

"What does 'out loud' mean?" Nadia laughed.

Alan fanned his face with his notebook. "Everyone lies to themselves a little, right? I just meant—I mean—I try to avoid compromising conversations."

"Compromising? Like what?"

His face reddened. "Nothing."

"Come on. What aren't you telling me?" Nadia poked his ribs.

"Stop it." He pushed her hand away. His nostrils flared a little as he spoke.

"All right. Sorry." She hadn't seen him angry in a long time. Annoyed, yes. Aggravated—plenty. But not angry. "So can you tell when someone's lying to you?"

"I take people at their word. It does not occur to me they might be lying."

Nadia shook her head.

"What?"

"I'm naturally suspicious. And when I ignore my intuition, I get burned."

"Damon is the same way," Alan said. "Makes for a lousy roommate."

"But a pretty good spy."

31 LIBBY
SUNDAY, NOVEMBER 6

"Come on, honey. Rise and shine." Libby pulled opened the curtains and sunlight poured across her roommate's bed. She never understood why people would want to sleep in. Her momma used to call her *Little Bit of Sunshine*. 'Course, that was ages ago. "Time for breakfast."

Nadia would probably sleep all day if Libby let her. She'd been moping around for weeks, ever since her date with Jack. Not so much that anyone else would notice, but living in such close quarters provided Libby maximum exposure to Nadia's moods. True, Jack had been keeping his distance. Libby told her not to read too much into it; she'd heard the seniors were working on an intense project all last month. Plus, Jack knew how hard Nadia had been trying to catch up. Likely, he was just being thoughtful; giving her space to focus on work. But Nadia would hear none of it; she was sure she'd blown her chances.

"Get up," Libby said. "It's a beautiful day."

Nadia groaned as she dragged herself to the bathroom. "Fine, I'm up. But we are no longer friends."

Without thinking, Libby began straightening the items on Nadia's dresser. She continued to her desk, strewn with papers. *It's a miracle she can find anything.* When she heard the shower running, Libby went to her closet and pulled out a container of sanitizing wipes. In a flash she'd scoured the doorknobs and the top of Nadia's desk.

Libby noticed her compulsion to clean increased exponentially with stress. With Thanksgiving right around the corner, she'd had to sit on her hands a couple times to control her urges. She didn't think Nadia minded so much, but dipping a napkin into her water glass to scrub the chocolate milk mustache off of Alan's face probably wouldn't go over too well.

Libby smoothed Nadia's bedding. She'd recently received her marching orders for the holiday and she was just sick about them. Every time her mind flicked onto the topic her stomach lurched.

She frantically wiped Nadia's nightstand and the switch on her bed lamp. Before she reached the headboard, Nadia emerged from the bathroom. Libby frowned and dropped the wipes into the small wastepaper basket between their beds.

Nadia tilted her head. "Are you okay? You look upset."

Libby threw a smile on her face. "Do I? No, I'm fine." She sat on the edge of her bed. "I was just missing my momma. Isn't that silly?"

"No, it's really sweet." Nadia began sifting through her closet.

Libby *was* worried about her mother. This past year her daddy had spent most of his time in Washington. By himself. Caroline Bishop was a people-person and, like her daughter, she did not care to be alone. Libby's previous schools had never been more than a two-hour plane ride from home, and always in the same time zone. Libby had felt so guilty about moving across the country she'd almost declined her invitation to the Academy, but her father had insisted.

"Ready to go?" Nadia asked.

"Let me check my face." Libby dashed into the bathroom and reapplied her lipstick.

The girls met Casey in the hallway. "I was just coming to your room. Nadia, you have a call."

At the front desk, Libby waited as Nadia picked up the phone, said hello and instantly scowled, which created a sharp crease between her eyebrows.

She shouldn't make that face. It's just not pretty. Libby drummed her fingers on the edge of the desk. She caught herself and stopped almost immediately, but Nadia must've noticed her impatience because she waved Libby over and held up the phone so they could both hear.

"Can you repeat that?" Nadia asked.

A man's synthesized voice spoke through the line, "The rook sings at first light. Prepare for the meet." The line went dead.

"What on earth was that?" Libby asked.

Nadia shook her head as she replaced the receiver. "I don't know. Probably one of the idiot boys."

"Are they still teasing you about the survival course?" Casey asked.

"I'll be hearing about that until I graduate."

"Oh, you poor thing," said Casey.

Wish I had time for these ridiculous games. "All set?" Libby asked. Nadia and Casey turned toward her, eyebrows raised. "I'm sorry, did I interrupt?"

"No, I'm ready," Nadia said. She pulled open the lobby door. "Are you sure everything's okay? You seem a little . . . stressed lately."

Pull it together. Libby smiled brightly. "No, everything's fantastic." Her daddy's advice echoed in her ears: *If you don't like what people are saying about you, change the conversation.* "Though I do mean to find out which one of those boys is still picking on you."

Libby followed Nadia through the dining hall, and they joined Alan and Damon at their usual table. "Whichever one of you telephoned my roommate," Libby said, "she didn't get the message. So how about you lay off?"

"What are you talking about?" Alan asked.

"So it was you?" Libby asked Damon.

He turned to Nadia. "Baby girl, if *I* call you, there'll be no question."

Libby smiled at Damon's flirtatious tone. "All right, no one wants to confess. Bunch of chickens. But on a brighter note: less than three weeks until Thanksgiving. Everyone going home?"

"Of course." Alan looked at her like she'd sprouted a second head. "It's Thanksgiving."

Damon shook his head. "I'm not."

"Neither am I," Nadia said. "Plane tickets are so expensive and winter break is right around the corner."

"Oh, that's too bad," said Libby.

Nadia shrugged. "Last week Sensei offered additional lessons over break, so at least I'll have something to do. Damon, you have plans?"

"Not yet, but things are definitely looking up. I'll have you all to my—"

"I can't wait to go home," Libby said. "I love Thanksgiving! My brother will be home from college, my momma will make all my favorite things to eat—her pecan pie is to *die* for. We'll do some Christmas shopping; we may even decorate the tree. We cut our own, you know. It'll be so much fun!" She clapped her hands before noticing her friends had stopped eating. Six eyes were glued to her face. *Uh-oh.*

"Why are you talking so fast?" Alan asked.

Libby felt her face flush. "Am I? Sorry. My mouth moves a million miles a minute when I'm excited." *Or nervous.* Her gaze fell on Jack and Noah as they entered the room.

Damon narrowed his eyes as he studied Libby's face. He followed her line of vision, then looked back at her. "Are you kidding me?"

"I don't know what you're talking about." Libby dropped her eyes.

"*Noah?*"

"What are you guys talking about?" Alan asked.

Well that was fortuitous timing. Libby shrugged. "What's wrong with Noah?"

"Oh, hell no." Damon said. "He's the leader of our rival team. You don't need to be consorting with the enemy."

"You're taking Niyuri to the Fall Formal—she's *on* his team!" Libby said.

"That's different."

"How?"

"It just is," Damon said. "Noah's not good enough for you. You're not going to the dance with him, if that's what you're thinking."

"Is that why you are acting so weird?" Alan asked.

Libby ignored Alan's question as she addressed Damon. "What are you, my daddy?"

"Seriously, Damon," Nadia said. "You jealous?"

"No, I'm not jealous. I'm just saying. She can do a whole lot better."

Nadia laughed. "What, like you?"

Damon gave Nadia a sly smile. "Blondes aren't my type." He winked.

"Well, Libby, if Noah does not ask you to the dance I would be willing to take you," Alan said quickly, his eyes darting between Nadia and Damon. "It is only two weeks away. At this point, I suspect you are frantic to secure an escort."

"Really? A pity date?" Libby asked. Alan's clumsy attempt to break the connection between Nadia and Damon managed to further agitate her, though she wasn't sure why. "Think I'll hold out for the real thing."

"Suit yourself." Alan shrugged. "Nadia, I suppose we could go together."

Nadia paused for a moment. "Alan, can I give you some advice?"

"If you must."

"How can I put this?" Nadia took a deep breath. "When you ask someone on a date . . . Girls like to feel special. Like they've been *chosen*. Don't just go around the table asking one after the other."

"Honestly, Alan." Libby's tone was sharper than she'd intended. *Just as well they think I'm bent out of shape about some stupid dance.* She glanced up at Damon. *He doesn't miss a trick; I need to be more careful.*

"So, no, then?" Alan asked.

"It's a very generous offer," Nadia said. "But I must decline."

Who cares about the damn dance? Libby pushed her omelet around the plate. *I have more pressing concerns than my social life.*

32 NADIA
SUNDAY, NOVEMBER 6

On Sunday night Nadia went for a run on the hiking trails beyond the wall. She was rounding a blind corner when she literally bumped into Jack. She fell backward and skidded off the rocky path. Sharp pebbles pierced her hand as dozens of spikes stabbed into her back.

"Nadia! Are you okay?" Jack rushed over. "You landed on a barrel cactus!"

"That would explain the searing pain," she snapped. "Can you please get the spines out of my shoulder?"

"These hurt. It's like getting a bunch of fish hooks stuck in your back. Don't move," he instructed.

Nadia clenched her jaw to keep from screaming. She picked at the rocks embedded in her palm. The raw skin throbbed.

Jack gently brushed her ponytail out of the way. "It's quite a coincidence running into you. I was just talking about you at dinner."

"Oh yeah? What about?" She tried to sound casual, which wasn't easy, given the extreme pain. "Had someone not heard the story of how I humiliated myself on the survival course?"

"Don't be silly. Everyone's heard that story."

"Very funny."

"No, one of my friends was thinking of asking you to the fall dance."

Nadia rolled her eyes knowing Jack couldn't see her face. "Is that so?"

"Yeah, but I told him I thought you already had a date."

"Well, I don't."

"Yeah, I know. I asked Libby yesterday."

"You asked Libby to the dance?" She turned her head slightly in Jack's direction.

"Hold still. No, I asked Libby if you had a date."

"Then why did you tell your friend I was going with someone?" Nadia twisted all the way around to look at him.

"Stop moving! Because I was hoping you might want to go with me."

"Oh." She turned back around to hide her grin. "Okay."

You're making a huge mistake. He's been avoiding you for a month. He doesn't like you that way.

"Excellent," Jack said, as he dug another spine out of her shoulder.

Shut up, Nadia. No one cares what you think.

33 LIBBY
MONDAY, NOVEMBER 7

Bright and early Monday morning, Libby got called to Dr. Cameron's office. After a good night's sleep and an intense morning workout, her mood had brightened, but even if it hadn't, she didn't mind the doctor's interviews. Not only was he handsome, but she found his disposition most agreeable. She smiled as they exchanged pleasantries.

"And how is your family, Libby?" he asked.

Her stomach jumped. *What now?* "Why do you ask? Is something wrong? Have you heard something?"

He shook his head and looked concerned. "Should I have?"

"'Course not," she said quickly. "I just meant because sometimes my daddy's in the news. You know, because of his work." *Shut your mouth, Liberty Grace.* "Everyone's just fine, and it is so good of you to ask." Libby knew better than to discuss family business.

"How is your roommate getting along?"

"She's doing great."

Dr. Cameron smiled. "Good." He looked at his hands resting in his lap. "I understand she spends a lot of time at the dojo."

Libby nodded. "She takes private lessons. After what happened on the survival course—well, I'm sure you heard. She felt a little behind, but she's on track now." As the heat kicked on, a

142

flutter of movement caught Libby's attention. Her eyes flitted to the corner behind the door. A dust bunny scurried along the baseboard like a cockroach running from the maid's broom.

"Have you noticed anything that concerns you?"

Oh my goodness, it's the size of a tennis ball. Don't they clean in here? Libby glanced at her folding chair. *I bet this chair never gets wiped down.* The thought of sitting on other people's filth made her queasy. She scooted to the edge of her seat and looked back at the dust.

"Libby?"

"Hmm?" *Look away.*

"Have you noticed anything that concerns you?" he repeated.

Look away! Libby tore her eyes away from the dirt and looked at the doctor. "Concerns? About Nadia? No." Libby shook her head. *Did I touch the back of the chair when I sat down?* She chewed her lip, trying to remember. *I'm sure I wouldn't have been so careless.* Dr. Cameron remained mum. The silence stretched on. "What do you mean? About Nadia? Like what?"

He shrugged and raised his eyebrows.

Pay attention. You sound like a crazy person. "Everything seems fine . . ." Libby's voice faded. Dr. Cameron's gaze was unwavering. Libby shifted in her chair. "You know, she studies and works out. That's about all any of us have time for. She's almost always with me."

"Except at the dojo, right?"

"Well, yeah. And when she's studying with Alan. Sometimes they study alone." Against her will, her eyes moved like a magnet to the corner of the room.

Dr. Cameron reached for a file on his desk. He opened the manila folder and shuffled a few papers. *Don't look at the floor. Focus on his words or you'll be expelled. They don't want crazy spies. At least, not this kind of crazy.*

"Do she and Alan get along?" he asked.

Libby forced a light laugh. "She gets along with Alan as well as anyone, I suppose." *Don't look at the floor!*

Dr. Cameron smiled.

"It's just, he's not always easy to get to know. But he's a great guy. I mean, you know. He's nice. A little awkward sometimes." Libby stopped talking. She squinted and rubbed her forehead. She managed to maintain eye contact. "I'm sorry, what was the question?"

"Is he particularly adversarial toward Nadia?"

"No more than anyone else. He and Damon both tease her a lot. Like that ridiculous phone call the other day." Libby rolled her eyes.

"What phone call?"

"Oh, one of them called our hall. Whoever it was disguised his voice and said, *the pawn sings at dawn*, or some stupid thing like that. Alan's more mean-spirited, but Damon's the one who would think of something clever to say, so I'm not sure which one of them is messing with her. Maybe they're working as a team. It's nice Alan's making a friend, I just wish it wasn't at Nadia's expense."

"Why are you so sure it was them?"

Libby shrugged. "Who else would it be?"

Dr. Cameron wrote something on his yellow pad. "You can go ahead to class."

Libby hesitated. "I'm sure it was all in good fun. They don't mean anything by it."

"I'll let Dr. Sherman know you're on the way."

Libby stood. "You know, push comes to shove, those two would do anything for her. We all would."

"Don't forget, Libby. This conversation stays between us."

She nodded as she left his office. She wasn't sure why, but she felt like she'd just betrayed her friends.

34 NADIA
TUESDAY, NOVEMBER 8

Nadia found another note slipped under her door on Tuesday morning. She read aloud:

> This weekend is your team's second survival course. This is a noncompetitive, solitary mission for each junior member. Your objective: Spend twenty-four hours alone in the desert. You will be driven approximately twenty miles from campus. After spending the night, you will hike back to school. Your equipment includes one water bottle, a knife and a one-way tracking device (this allows us to locate you if you fail to return in a timely manner).

"Twenty-four hours alone in the desert? I don't like the sound of that at all," Libby said, biting her lip. "Come on, before we're late for exercises."

Damon and Alan were already at the dojo. They confirmed receiving a second order.

"Good thing we do not require tranquilizer guns, huh, Nadia?" Alan said. "No one would be there to carry you out."

Damon jumped in, "You think you'll be able to sleep without a sedative? If not, I could sneak something over to your campsite."

"You guys are hilarious," Nadia snapped.

The rest of the week blurred into a stream of forgotten lectures and sleepless nights. Instead of paying attention in class, Nadia worried about the weekend, which then forced her to stay up late studying what she'd missed. She found little relief during morning meditation.

"I can't do it. What if something happens and no one is there to help me?" she asked Sensei after they'd trained on Friday.

"You are a different person than you were one month ago. It is not a competition, so you will not carry a gun. Your overnight is short, so you will not build a fire."

"I don't get to make a fire?" she asked, growing more concerned. At least fire would keep the animals away.

"We cannot have novice students building fires all over the Southwest. The climate here is too dry. If a single spark is left to smolder, the desert will be consumed by flames."

"So why do I need a knife? In case I'm attacked by a wild animal?"

"Do not be absurd. It is for emergencies. If you were lost and the temperature dropped, *then* you would be permitted to build a fire."

"But I—"

"Enough! Nadia-san, you must understand: fear is a chemical reaction in the body, a warning administered by your brain to pay attention. Nothing more. How you channel your fear determines the course of your life. Always. Fear runs only as deep as the mind allows."

Later that afternoon the team waited beneath the enormous iron gates at the front of the school. The van arrived and they climbed in; Damon in the far back, Alan in the middle, Nadia and Libby on the front bench seats.

The drive from school was quiet. Alan chewed his cuticles until one bled, then stuck his finger in his mouth. Nadia turned away. *At least I'm not the only one who's nervous.*

She ran her palms along the plush seat and slid her hands under her legs. The familiar anxious chill settled over her, starting with her hands and feet. *Stop worrying. If it wasn't safe, they wouldn't send us out alone.*

She leaned forward to speak to the driver. "Has anyone ever been hurt during their solo?"

"Not too bad," he answered, watching her through the rearview mirror. "I think we had a scorpion bite once, but I guess the kid was grabbing for wood without looking first. It's those bark scorpions you gotta watch for, the little guys." His eyes returned to the road and he swerved back into his lane.

"Nadia, shut up," Alan whispered, his voice tight. "He cannot drive and talk."

Nadia closed her eyes and concentrated on her breath. *In for four, out for eight.*

The driver pulled onto the shoulder. "First stop," he called.

"I'll go," said Damon, climbing out of the van. "See you guys. Good luck. And for the love of all that is holy, whatever you do, don't—" He slammed the door.

They drove another fifteen minutes. Nadia volunteered at the next stop. She figured she'd rather be sandwiched between two classmates than stuck out on the end. *We've been driving fifteen minutes at what, forty-five miles an hour?* That put Damon about . . . eleven and a half miles away. She wondered how far a scream would travel.

Nadia watched the van drive off, and then took a moment to orient herself. *We headed east from the school, then due south. The driver turned right onto this road, so I need to go—north. Keep the afternoon sun on my left.*

The land was flat, but uneven, which forced her to watch the ground. She wove between knee-high plants, avoiding the shadows where snakes might hide. Nadia spotted a trail of dark green brush in the distance and made a beeline toward it, knowing it would be near a stream. If she could follow the water until nightfall she wouldn't have to worry about dehydration. Worst case scenario, she'd fill her bottle once tonight and again in the morning. She could definitely make it back to school on that.

When the evening sky burned dark orange and pink, Nadia searched for a safe place to sleep. She remembered how quickly the black night had swallowed the desert on the first survival course. There were no streetlights, no flashlights, nothing to spear the darkness.

Nadia found a sturdy tree to use as shelter. She pushed fallen leaves together with her feet, huge sweeping motions that made her inner thighs tight. The smell of loose dirt filled the air. She stomped around a bit to chase off any neighbors and, when the dust settled, placed her knife and water bottle at the base of the tree.

She stretched out on the ground and looked through the branches. A sparkling river of stars crossed the sky. Coyotes called in the distance. She thought about the last time, and Jack's arm around her body. His dark hair, the way his skin smelled after being in the sun. She pulled a layer of leaves onto her torso and closed her eyes.

35 JACK
FRIDAY, NOVEMBER 11

The constant effort to stay one step ahead of Nadia proved taxing. Late Friday evening, Jack drove toward town, relieved his errand was near completion. The sky was dark and clear; the road deserted. His team should be selecting their campsites right about now. He wondered if Nadia was as nervous as she'd appeared, or if she'd carefully scripted her vulnerability, knowing Jack's inclination to protect.

He'd been so conflicted since their date. He'd spoken to Libby—grilled her, really. Copious details about Nadia's schedule, her topics of conversation, word choices, background. Jack looked for anything to confirm his misgivings, any scrap of new information to take to Dean Wolfe. But he'd come up empty.

He began to feel like he was searching for evidence that didn't exist.

Jack pulled into the parking lot of the darkened office building and drove around back. *I guess I'll know soon enough.*

He parked away from the streetlights and stayed in the shadows as he approached on foot. He knocked softly on the back door. As it opened, a wedge of light spilled onto the asphalt.

"Come on in," Samuel said. "You got the package?"

Jack nodded and handed Samuel a small box.

Samuel whistled as he looked inside. "Nice. Real?"

"Of course. What kind of guy do you think I am?"

Samuel laughed. "First class, all the way. She stepping out on you?"

Jack shrugged. "You tell me."

"You know my motto: trust but verify. Close-range burst transmission?"

"Sounds good."

"Gimme a minute." Samuel disappeared down the hall.

Jack moved a stack of broken radio parts off the only chair in the room and sat down. The plastic shelves along the wall sagged under the weight of metal boxes and spools of wire. A graveyard of discarded speakers cluttered the floor.

A nagging voice in his head asked, *Are you sure you want to do this? To Nadia? Without the Dean's approval? You're crossing a line.*

He tapped his foot to drown out the voice. *This is the fastest way to prove her innocence.*

"Stop tapping your foot," Samuel said as he entered the room. "I stayed open late for you."

Jack quieted his body. "Sorry. Song stuck in my head."

"You going out? There's a new club downtown, supposed to be pretty hot."

Jack passed Samuel an envelope as he took back his box. "No, I think I'm gonna go for a run in the desert."

Samuel counted the hundreds. "You're a wild man." He looked up and smiled. "It's all here."

"Trust but verify." Jack smiled back.

"All right, Jason," Samuel said. "Good luck, man. Let me know how it works out."

"You bet," Jack said as he stepped into the night. The door slammed shut behind him.

36 NADIA
SATURDAY, NOVEMBER 12

Nadia woke to warm, yellow fingers of light spreading across the desert. The air held the crisp promise of a new day. Quail began to call. An unstoppable grin spread across her face as she stretched awake.

I did it!

She stood to scatter the leaves evenly around her tree. Jack had taught them about the school's *Leave No Trace* philosophy: when she left the environment, it was to look as though she'd never been there. Nadia suspected this rule was probably more about being a good spy than a responsible steward of the earth, but when Jack had explained it on their last trip she hadn't had the energy to ask.

Beside the stream, she crouched and uncapped her water bottle. As the cool water flowed over her fingers, she scanned the ground for rattlesnakes. She lifted the bottle to her lips and something caught her eye.

Nadia leaned in for a closer look. There, in the loose dirt beside the stream, was a footprint. And it was not her own.

Her heart pounded as fear flooded her veins. She shot up and searched the low desert brush along the horizon. She held her breath and listened for snapping twigs or the crunch of gravel.

Noises surrounded her; lizards rustling across fallen leaves sounded like buffalo.

Knock it off. Fear is a chemical reaction. Nothing more. It doesn't mean I'm in danger.

She reexamined the print. A man's shoe. Brush marks led away from the footprint, as though someone had tried to erase his tracks with a branch. *Am I being followed?* The marks clearly led away from the stream, but as the sandy soil turned to rock and scrub, she lost the trail.

Nadia tried to relax, to slow her quickened heartbeat, to force rational thought. *It could be weeks old. Who knows when it last rained?* This didn't soften the knot forming in her stomach.

Maybe Jack came by to check on us. Would that be part of his job?

Nadia stayed alert as she chugged a bottle of water. She reached behind her back to secure her knife and realized her weapon was missing.

No! She dropped her bottle and ran back toward the tree. On her hands and knees she filtered through the dispersed debris. *Sensei's going to kill me.* Nadia searched the far side of the tree, the path to the stream, around the water. Her knife had vanished.

Did someone steal my knife? She shook her head. *I must have misplaced it.* Nadia looked again, meticulously scouring every inch of ground she'd touched since removing the knife from her waistband the previous night.

I know I didn't lose it. I put it right next to my water bottle.

The sun burned away the pleasant cool of morning. After a lengthy search, Nadia gave up. *I need to get moving. Even at a fast clip, it'll still be five, maybe six hours before I'm home.* She hurried, feeling exposed in the open desert.

She took only one break, pausing for a few minutes to rest in the shade of a palo verde tree. Rubbing her thighs, she leaned against the light green bark and closed her eyes. A branch snapped and her eyes shot open. She felt someone watching her. Nadia scrambled to her feet.

It's in my head. I'm tired. Ignore it.

She began walking again, much faster than before.

Her legs were numb from constant movement, and hunger gnawed at her stomach. The faster she hiked, the more apprehensive she grew.

Stop looking over your shoulder, she ordered. *Nothing is there. It's impossible to sneak through the desert. You'd know if someone were tailing you.* But no matter what she told herself, Nadia couldn't shake the distinct feeling that had settled over her.

She felt like prey.

37 DAMON
SATURDAY, NOVEMBER 12

Minutes after returning to campus from his solo, Damon stood in the waiting area outside Dr. Cameron's office, debating how much trouble he'd get in if he failed to show. Demanding an interview the second he finished the survival course? Bad enough Damon hadn't slept last night; now he had this to deal with. He took a deep breath and knocked on the door.

"Good to see you," Dr. Cameron said. "Have a seat. How is everything?"

"I can't complain. How about you?" Damon made his way into the interrogation room. He'd been forced to see plenty of therapists and none of them had an office as barren as this. Stripped down of all comforts.

"Classes okay? You just got back from your solo, right? Did you enjoy your time alone?"

Expressionless, Damon studied Dr. Cameron's face. "I guess."

"Do the survival courses challenge you?"

He glanced at his watch. "I actually have a paper due Monday. If you don't mind, I'm a little pressed for time."

Dr. Cameron smiled. "You don't like coming in here, do you?"

Damon paused for a beat. "It's nothing personal."

"Is there anything you'd like to talk about?"

"No, Dr. Cameron. You called me."

"How's your roommate these days?"

Damon shrugged. "He's fine, I guess."

"And your other teammates?"

"Everyone's great."

"How is Nadia doing? Has she had any trouble catching up?"

Damon shook his head. "Not at all. In fact, she's good at everything."

"How so?"

He shrugged again. *What part of that is unclear?* He stared at Dr. Cameron. Dr. Cameron stared back, a whisper of a smile on his lips. "I don't know. She's smart, she's quick. I don't know what else to tell you."

"What do you want to tell me?"

"Nothing."

"Who would you say is the weak link on your team?"

Alan. "We don't have one."

"What about Alan?"

"Alan's sharp."

"Libby, then?"

"I don't mean to be disrespectful, but I really do have a lot of work. My team is rock solid, no one does anything that concerns me, everything's cool."

"Why would you mention being concerned, Damon? I didn't ask if anyone did anything that concerned you."

Dammit. "I don't know. A hunch, I guess."

"That's an interesting hunch."

"Not really. Isn't your job to investigate security issues on campus? I mean, look at this room. No windows, harsh lighting, one exit. A folding chair? No pictures of your family or soothing landscapes. The walls are grey cinderblock. This office is not for therapy. You ask me about Alan, Nadia, Libby. It's no huge leap to assume you're digging for information."

Dr. Cameron smiled. After a moment, he said, "That's only part of my job. I'm also here for *you*. For all the students. When you need to talk, or unburden yourselves."

"Yeah, okay. But I'm just saying."

Dr. Cameron leaned back in his chair. "Damon, I'd like to talk about your brother."

And there it is. Damon sighed. He leaned forward, elbows on his knees, head in his hands. "Sorry, but I don't talk about him."

"Do you feel responsible?"

He didn't answer. When his dad died, he'd tried to step up, to fill that role for his brother. He'd watched his mother struggle as she clawed through her grief, fought desperately to keep their house. That morning he'd wanted to hang out with his friends. Just once, without his little brother clinging to him. "I need you to help me out," his mother had said. That's all he did, was help her out. He took his brother everywhere. So they went to the playground. Chips of cold April rain pelted Damon's neck as he sat with his back to the park, pissed off, messing with his phone. Not paying attention.

"Damon?"

After his brother died his mother forced him into therapy. What a waste of time. "How do you feel?" the psychologist had asked. *How do you think I feel?*

"Do you think you could've done something differently?" Dr. Cameron asked.

Of course I could have. If I'd gotten up when he asked me to. If I hadn't been so distracted and self-involved. If I'd paid attention, my whole life would be different. "I don't talk about my brother. With anyone. Ever."

"Damon, I won't insult your intelligence by explaining survivor's guilt, or by reassuring you that it wasn't your fault, but it is important to talk about things that bother us. If we don't, they can take on a life of their own."

Damon shook his head. He'd stood at the cemetery and, for the second time, watched a box descend into the earth. This time, half the size as the last. They'd added trinkets: his brother's blanket, his favorite book. At the last minute, Damon snatched the tiny yellow bear from the casket. His mom didn't notice. She didn't notice anything. It took months before she could go back to work.

Dr. Cameron remained silent. Damon waited. *I've played this game before. First one to talk loses.* Another minute passed.

"Okay. We don't have to talk about him today."

I win. Damon lifted his head. The Doctor's expression was wrong. Off somehow. No furrowed brow, no sympathy. Damon knew the tell-me-about-your-dead-brother face, and this wasn't it.

"What do you think about Nadia spending so much extra time at the dojo?"

Oh, that's his angle. Bond over my dead brother and I'll rat out my friends. Nice try, Doc, but this ain't my first rodeo.

"Damon?"

'Course, the faster I give him something, the faster I'm out of here. And as long as we aren't talking about my brother, what do I care? "I don't know. She needed extra work. That was obvious after the first survival course. She's got a lot of heart, though, taking the initiative, getting the help. I still don't understand how she shot herself." Damon snorted. "It's almost as though . . ." He deliberately trailed off.

" 'As though' what?"

He shook his head. "Nothing—it's crazy."

"You're not suggesting she did it on purpose?"

"No, of course not. See what I mean? Crazy. Nobody would do that."

Dr. Cameron pursed his lips. He crossed his legs. His eyes didn't leave Damon's face.

Damon continued, "I mean, why would she? It's not like it got her out of the solo. I'm sure that went fine, right?" Dr. Cameron didn't speak. "Oh, is she not back yet?" Damon looked at his watch, eyebrows raised. "Wow. What is she up to?"

"Have you spent much time with Sensei?"

"Only in class." Pause. "He's careful with his time."

"What do you think of him?"

"I like him. He's very traditional. Very reserved."

"He seems to have warmed to Nadia."

Damon smiled. "Yeah, well. Nadia's clever. She's exceptionally good at cracking code, which is strange because she's only so-so with foreign languages."

Dr. Cameron jotted something onto his legal pad.

"And Alan is insane with the languages. He can pick them up like that." Damon snapped his fingers. "But not so much with code." Dr. Cameron did not write that down. *Interesting.*

"What do you think about Nadia having previously studied cryptography?"

He shrugged and met Dr. Cameron's gaze. "Quite a coincidence." Damon sat perfectly still in his chair. *Don't fidget. Don't swallow. Don't even blink. You'll be out in a second.*

"You think it was by design? That she somehow knew about the Academy?"

"I have no idea. I can only think of one reason to learn a skill like that." He kept his eyes steady on the doctor. "But maybe I just lack imagination."

Dr. Cameron paused for a moment, studying Damon. Then, finally, "Is there anything else?"

Damon looked toward the ceiling and squinted. "I don't think so."

"Okay." Dr. Cameron handed Damon a booklet of shrink tests. "If you could take a few minutes and fill these out."

Fantastic. Just what I wanted to do. Damon smiled. "I'd be happy to."

38 NADIA
SATURDAY, NOVEMBER 12

Nadia's pace had become nearly unsustainable when she spotted the concrete wall of Desert Mountain Academy in the distance. Overcome with relief, she slowed enough to catch her breath and regain composure. The pride she'd woken up with quickly returned, and with campus in sight, she felt like an idiot for succumbing to fear. She'd spent twenty-four hours alone in the desert! Four months ago she wouldn't have believed it possible.

Of course, now she had another demon to face. Nadia made an effort to stop smiling. *But I'm so proud of myself!*

She went to the dojo to tell Sensei about her knife. She found him in the meditation room, and waited silently while he finished. When he looked up, Nadia bowed.

"Ah, Nadia-san, thank you for waiting." He bowed on the ground before rising, then again to her when he stood. "How well did you perform?"

"Very well. I seem to travel much faster when I'm not drugged. Thank you for your help."

"You did the work. The physical challenge was not as great as you expected," he said.

"No, you were right. It was all in my head."

"You have your knife for me?"

Nadia looked at her feet. "I seem to have misplaced it."

"What?"

She forced herself to make eye contact. His lips formed a stern line. "I'm so sorry. I don't understand how it happened. I put my knife and water bottle together when I went to sleep, and this morning my knife was gone. I didn't notice until I saw the footprint by the stream, and by then—"

"What footprint?" Sensei's brow creased.

"I don't know, but it wasn't mine. Did Jack come by to check on us?"

A look of concern flashed through his eyes. "Nadia-san, tell me exactly what happened."

"I saw a footprint and kind of panicked. But then I remembered what you said about fear not being real, so I tried to calm myself down." She watched Sensei's face. "Anyway, that's when I realized I didn't have my knife. I searched for over an hour but never found it. And I think someone tried to erase their tracks—you know, with brush?" Maybe it was contempt on his face, and not concern. She couldn't decide. As usual, his carefully guarded expression revealed very little. "Do you think someone might have followed me? Or that my knife was taken?"

He straightened his spine and crossed his hands behind his back. "I suspect you lost it. Perhaps you kicked it during the night."

Nadia's self-satisfaction evaporated as she registered his look of disappointment. She almost wished someone *had* been stalking her. That they'd stolen the knife. "Sensei, please forgive me." She bowed her head. "I don't know how this happened."

"Dr. Cameron has requested you. See him before returning to your room." Sensei bowed curtly and left her in the hall.

Nadia sighed as she left the dojo. *So much for a hot shower and early lunch.*

A few minutes later, across the lawn, she knocked on the psychiatrist's door. "You wanted to see me?"

"How was your solo?"

Nadia settled onto the folding chair. "Better than I expected."

"No problems?" He pulled his chair around the desk to sit in front of her.

She hesitated. "I lost my knife."

Dr. Cameron cringed. "How did Sensei take the news?"

"Not well."

"Sometimes they aren't secured properly to the waistband. I've recommended belted knives. If the sheath is threaded through your belt, it's impossible to lose. But the draw isn't as smooth, and the potential for injury outweighs the benefit."

I know I didn't drop it. Should I tell him I think someone else was there?

Dr. Cameron handed her a steel clipboard with a packet of papers. "I need you to fill these out."

No. I'll either seem paranoid or it'll look like I'm avoiding responsibility. Nadia flipped through the packet. All the psych tests, reformatted, just as Jack warned. "No problem," she said, offering Dr. Cameron a tight smile.

An hour later on the way back to her dorm, Nadia ran into Jack.

"How did it go?" he asked.

She ran her hands over her hair. Last night she'd braided it in two long plaits that hung over her shoulders. It was a childish style, and now she regretted not taking more care. Libby probably returned looking like she'd just left a photo shoot. Nadia was covered in dirt—she hadn't even brushed her teeth. "It was amazing!" She broke into a broad smile.

Jack laughed. "That's awesome! You look really happy."

"I am. I know it must seem stupid, but I was terrified."

"No, not at all. It's scary your first time out—especially if you're not a camper. Good for you. I'm so glad it went well." He reached over and touched her shoulder.

She tried, unsuccessfully, to stop grinning. "Thanks."

"Let's grab a bite after you get cleaned up. I'll meet you on the patio." He nodded toward the Navajo Building.

"Sounds good. Give me an hour?"

"I'll save you a seat."

"Hey, let me ask you something. Were we out there alone? I mean, do you check on us or anything?"

He shook his head. "Check on you? How do you mean?"

Nadia opened her mouth. *You'll sound completely insane.* "Nothing. Never mind."

39 JACK
SATURDAY, NOVEMBER 12

I'm in serious trouble.

He'd realized it the moment Nadia returned from the desert. Her clothes were covered in dust, her face smudged with dirt. She wore her hair in two messy braids.

She looked adorable.

Jack hated the idea that Nadia might be a traitor. His devotion to country absolutely took priority over his feelings for any one individual. But she was amazing—beautiful, intelligent, strong. The kind of girl he'd pick as a partner. He desperately wanted it to not be her.

It can't be. She's too transparent. Nadia was elated after her solo. An accomplished agent—hell, even a second-year student— wouldn't think that was a big deal. His gut insisted it wasn't her.

He'd considered alternate suspects. No one stood out among the junior class. Alan briefly flashed across Jack's radar because of his multilingual upbringing, but Alan could no more be a covert agent than Jack could be a penguin.

Jack had hung out with Nadia all afternoon. After a late lunch they'd gone to the library. She studied diplomacy while he studied her. Sometimes she moved her lips a little as she read. Her facial expressions reflected her thoughts—a smile, a look of confusion.

She was never neutral. *If she were trained as a spy, she'd be blank. A constant poker face, no matter what went on inside.*

After dinner they'd watched a movie in the student lounge. She'd fallen asleep on his shoulder. His arm had gone completely numb, but he hadn't wanted to wake her.

Now, in the darkened documents lab at 2300 hours on a Saturday night, Jack tried to focus on his assignment. Two sets of false identities were due Monday morning and he'd barely begun. He hunched over the lab table, peering through a lighted magnifying glass at the stamped seal on a Bermudian passport. He'd fallen behind in his work and it was all Nadia's fault.

He looked up from the eyepiece, staring mindlessly at the wall, and smiled as he pictured her curled up against him, sound asleep.

To tell the truth, she'd been under his skin since their first date. *No way is she the double. And my investigation will clear her. That would be perfect: single-handedly exonerate Nadia, expose the real double and impress Dean Wolfe.* Jack felt ninety-nine percent sure that Nadia was innocent.

Unless it's an act. Could it be?

He groaned out loud. *This is unacceptable. Remember why you're here. Would you rather impress the girl—who may or may not be an enemy of the United States, or the Dean of Students? Who can without a doubt alter the course of your entire life?*

Jack's head ached from the smell of fresh ink and rubber stamps. He pinched the muscle between his thumb and index finger—a tension-relieving technique Sensei had taught his class—and forced his attention back to the purple customs seal splayed out under the magnifying glass. He needed to replicate the symbol, the variances in the ink. The right side of the image blurred from over-pressing, sharpened in the middle, and vanished toward the left, fading off the page like invisible ink. The key, Jack decided, was not to apply even pressure. A busy officer wouldn't bother to rock the stamp back and forth onto each passport.

I wonder if Nadia's ever been to Bermuda, he thought, looking back up at the wall.

40 NADIA
SATURDAY, NOVEMBER 19

The morning of the Fall Formal, Nadia was full of nervous energy and unable to focus on homework. She paced the small bedroom until Libby threatened to move out, then sat on her bed and pretended to read a magazine. She was about to go for a run when Casey knocked on the door. "Jack's here to see you."

Nadia met him in the lobby.

"Noah and I rented a limo. We'll meet you outside Hopi Hall at eighteen-hundred?" He flashed his brilliant smile and her stomach fluttered. "We'll all ride together."

"Sounds great."

"I also wanted to give you these." Jack handed her a small black box.

Nestled inside she found a pair of earrings: large, square-cut amethysts set in gold. The sun pouring through the skylight glinted off the stones and cast dancing prisms across the room. Except for a gold ring with a shaving of emerald she got for Christmas last year, Nadia had no real jewelry.

"They're beautiful," she said. *But what does he expect in return?* "I can't accept these." She held the open box toward him.

"I know, I know. It's way too early in our relationship for jewelry, but I want you to have them. I promise, no strings attached."

"Thank you." Nadia's cheeks warmed as she averted her eyes. *Relationship? I like the sound of that.*

"I'm glad you like them." He kissed her cheek and turned toward the door. "I'll see you soon."

Nadia dressed for the dance like she dressed for any event—quickly. Libby took one look and said, "Absolutely not."

"What's the matter?" Nadia asked, turning toward the mirror. She wore a black satin dress, strappy heels and Jack's earrings. She'd pulled her hair into a high bun.

"Sit down," Libby ordered, pointing to Nadia's desk chair. "Face me."

Nadia did as she was told. Libby stood quietly, studying Nadia's face, her hair. Nadia glanced down at her dress, then back up at her roommate, feeling childish in comparison. Libby's gown had been custom made; the perfect shade of red for her creamy skin, the most flattering cut for her even proportions and long legs. The material shimmered slightly as she moved, catching the light.

Libby yanked out Nadia's hairband. "Head between your knees and shake. All right, now flip your hair back." She retrieved a makeup palette from the bathroom and applied eyeshadow and liner, then a sweep of mascara. She handed Nadia her lipgloss as she removed one of Jack's earrings.

"No, I have to wear those!" Nadia said.

"They don't go with this dress and you're not wearing them. Gloss your lips."

"They were a gift from my date, and I am wearing them."

"It's out of the question. You'll wear these," Libby said, handing Nadia a pair of gold drop earrings. "Jack will understand."

"But—"

Libby held up her index finger. "I am going to the dance with Alan. *Alan.* I am in no mood to be trifled with."

Nadia scowled at Libby as she exchanged her earrings.

"You'll thank me later," Libby said sweetly.

Twenty minutes later, Nadia trailed behind Libby as the girls walked toward Hopi Hall. Libby's heels were two inches higher than Nadia's, but her pace was as smooth as ever.

Jack waited by the limo door. "You're not wearing your earrings?" He slipped Nadia's corsage on her wrist.

"I wanted to, but Libby won the argument." She touched her ears. "I hope I didn't hurt your feelings. You don't want to get between a Southern belle and her idea of fashion."

He laughed. "No worries. You look amazing."

"And so do you." Jack was more striking than usual in his black tuxedo. The other guys looked good too—it's hard to look bad in a tux—but Jack looked like . . . well, *James Bond*.

They arrived at the Scottsdale Ritz-Carlton, where the sweet, heavy smell of mimosa trees hung thick in the air. Occasionally, far off in the distance, silent flashes of lightning seared through the sky, casting a dramatic backdrop for the sharp mountains.

Music filtered through the lobby and beckoned them to the back terrace. Thousands of tiny white lights glistened around the swimming pool. Jack took Nadia's hand and immediately led her to the dance floor.

"No one's dancing yet," she said.

"I don't care. I want to be close to you." He pulled her in, his arms strong around her body. Her hands slid over his shoulders. Her legs felt weak as he murmured, "You look beautiful." He pulled back and looked into her eyes.

I could stare at him for hours.

He moved his hand to the hollow at the back of her neck. His mouth hovered over hers. Softly, like a whisper, his lips brushed against her. Nadia sensed him hesitate for just a moment, then he kissed her again, harder this time, with a sudden force that seemed out of control. They breathed each other in; no one else existed. The kiss ended and Jack pulled her close again, their bodies pressed together as they moved as one. Nadia leaned against his chest, trying to catch her breath. *Uh-oh.*

The song finished and Nadia reluctantly followed Jack to their table.

Damon took her hand as she arrived. "Niyuri deserted me. An emergency involving a folded contact lens. Come dance with me."

Jack grabbed Damon's sleeve. "Let's get some drinks instead."

Damon dropped Nadia's hand and smiled tightly at Jack. "Sure."

Noah pushed past Nadia to reach Libby. "You look fantastic," he said.

"Don't mind me," Nadia mumbled.

Libby's face lit up. "Why, thank you Noah. My date didn't say."

Alan glanced at Libby. "Oh, yeah. You do look nice. And you know I would tell you if you did not."

"You mind if we dance?" Noah asked Alan.

Alan shrugged. "I do not care. We only came together because she did not have a date." He didn't seem to notice Libby's glare. A moment later, he cleared his throat and said, "Nadia, perhaps we should dance?"

"Oh." She glanced toward the bar; Jack still waited in the queue. "Okay."

He led her to a quiet spot and put one hand on her shoulder, one on her waist. He kept his distance, a foot of light shining between them. They swayed awkwardly to the music. Alan avoided her eyes.

I feel like I'm in junior high. "What's up, Alan?" she asked, as the silence stretched into awkwardness.

He glanced at her. "You look particularly attractive this evening."

"Thanks. You too." Another minute passed. *I guess an uncomfortable silence beats the usual barrage of insults.*

Nadia scanned the crowd for Jack. She found him just as Jennifer, the beautiful blond from Noah's team, pulled him to the dance floor. *Great. Of all the girls for him to dance with.*

Alan stopped swaying. "Do you mind if we do not finish the song?" Before she answered, he disappeared into the crowd, leaving her alone.

Why am I not surprised? Nadia shook her head and returned

to their table. As she searched the floor for Jack and Jennifer, a waiter in a crisp white shirt and gold vest approached.

"Nadia Riley?"

He wore too much gel in his jet-black hair. His slippery eyes jumped around the table. He looked like the kind of guy she'd avoid at a party. "Yes," she said.

He placed a stack of cocktail napkins beside her. "Inside the top napkin is a disc. When I walk away, put it in your purse. When you get to campus, drop it in the trashcan outside the girls' dormitory. Tell no one."

"What?" Nadia leaned toward him.

"Standard protocol. Think of it as a pop quiz," he said, rearranging the tray of drinks Jack had brought.

My first dead drop! With a slight smile, she slipped the napkin into her purse.

I mean, seriously. Is this is the coolest school ever?

41 ALAN
SATURDAY, NOVEMBER 19

At 2350, Alan stood in the shadow of the dojo, watching Jack and Nadia say goodnight. They kissed briefly and Jack started to leave. Nadia dumped the trash from her purse. Jack turned back toward her, probably to collect another kiss, but before he could, Nadia went inside. Alan narrowed his eyes as Jack reached into the trashcan. *I really do have unfortunate timing.*

For weeks Alan had followed Saba's orders, made up excuses to spend time with Nadia. But lately, she spent more and more time with Jack. He could not compete with Jack. Not even *Damon* could compete with Jack. And Saba was not pleased. His latest reprimand had been delivered that afternoon.

Twelve hours earlier, Alan had driven to Tempe. He parked in front of a bookstore across from the metro station, where he found a semi-secluded pay phone.

"*Shalom*, my son. Tell me your progress."

"I am not certain. I think I have become part of my team," Alan answered in Hebrew. "But it is difficult to say."

"What about the girl you mentioned?"

"It is not going as well as I would like."

"Alan. I don't understand the problem."

"She is dating our team leader. He is a senior. I am not—"

"Do you know what women like?"

Alan rolled his eyes. "Not even a little."

Saba chuckled. "Do something daring. Break the rules. A dramatic gesture to make her feel special."

"Saba, I am not very good at breaking—"

"Enough. You were given choices, no? Tell me what they were."

"I do not think—"

"What were they?"

Stop interrupting me! Alan sighed. "Train here, train in Tel Aviv, train nowhere."

"And what did you choose?"

"Saba, I understand my choice."

"No one forced this on you. I could have, but I did not. What was the only condition of your choice?"

Alan remained silent. *Why would I answer? He will not let me finish my thought.*

"If you had come here, I would tuck you under my wing. We could choose assignments tailored to your interests. You wanted to fly on your own. Now, you become a man." His voice hardened. "You will stay the course. You will get close to this girl. You will become an agent of the CIA. And you will report everything back to Mossad." The line went dead.

Alan's hand shook as he replaced the receiver. His Saba had never hung up on him. He prayed it was a bad connection and not anger that ended the call.

Now, standing in the dark, Alan knew he must proceed with his mission. He pressed himself against the dojo wall as Jack jogged down the path.

Alan peeked into the girls' lobby. Casey was not at her desk. He rushed down the hall to Nadia's room, knocked softly and thrust his hands into his pockets. The folded note was pressed securely against his thigh. He only needed a minute alone in her room.

Nadia gasped when she saw him. She pulled him inside by his lapel. "Have you lost your mind? We'll both be expelled."

She was not exaggerating. The school allowed no unsupervised coed visits in the dorms. "I understand my visit is unorthodox."

"What's wrong? Where's Libby?"

"Noah said he would walk her home. I think they are still down by the limo."

"Then what are you doing here? You can't wait for her."

"I came to see you," Alan said. "I owe you an apology."

"What are you talking about?"

"The way I left you on the dance floor. I behaved badly. I—needed some air all of a sudden." His cheeks warmed.

"Seriously? Of all the things you've said and done, that's what you're sorry for?"

His heart pounded. Its weight and size seemed to increase as it beat against his ribcage. *What am I doing here?* "I know I have been kind of a jerk—you do not have to nod, I just said *I know*."

"Well it's true. You can be fairly hostile," Nadia said.

Alan opened his mouth and then closed it again. He looked down, sure he would see the lapel of his jacket thumping up and down with the rhythm of his heart beat. *This is a mistake.* His face burned hotter. He pulled at his bow tie. "I am sorry about the dance."

"Have I done something? Is it because I needed extra help?"

He took a deep breath. "I find myself in an unusual situation. Though I cannot explain why, I seem to have developed feelings for you beyond friendship. I—I have a small crush on you."

Nadia opened her mouth.

He raised his arms in front of his body like he was stopping traffic. "You do not have to say anything. I know you and Jack have a thing. He is obviously quite fond of you. I mean, I just saw him out front collecting your trash from the garbage can as a memento."

"What?" Nadia narrowed her eyes.

"It is a crush." Alan scratched at his neck. *Keep talking.* "The thing is, I have never really had a girlfriend, or even strong feelings for a girl, and I am not sure what is appropriate—"

"What did you say about the trash?"

"What?"

"The *trash*, Alan," Nadia enunciated, drawing Alan's eyes to her mouth.

"Oh yeah. It was strange to me, too." Alan shrugged and forced himself to look away from her lips. "Are you okay? You look pale. Maybe you should splash some water on your face. I can wait here." He sat on the edge of the closest bed and glanced at his watch.

"I—I don't feel very well."

"I am happy to wait while you get a drink."

"Please, I need you to go."

"Right." He stood, eyes on the floor. "I am sorry. I should not have come. I made things worse." *And my mission failed.*

Nadia sighed. "No, Alan. Thanks for the apology. Don't worry about it—it's fine."

Alan offered a slight smile. "I will see you later."

42 NADIA
SATURDAY, NOVEMBER 19

Although Libby had been asleep for hours, positively blissful after dancing with Noah most of the evening, Nadia didn't even try to close her eyes. She listened to her roommate's rhythmic breathing as she stared at the ceiling.

Why would Jack intercept my dead drop? Is he the double Alan heard about? Was I used as a messenger—a go-between for him and his handler? She scanned the dark corners of the room, as though answers were tucked away in the shadows. *Maybe Jack didn't take it. Maybe Alan made the whole thing up. Maybe Alan is the traitor. He's deflecting suspicion.* Nadia frowned. *But he's the one who told us about the double. Why would he do that? Unless it's to throw us off track. Because why would a double agent report his own presence? It's genius.*

She shook her head. *No, he wouldn't try to frame Jack. He'd pick an easier target. Someone who doesn't know what they're doing. So if Alan's telling the truth, why did Jack take the package?*

Then, all at once, it came to her.

Her assignment was to make the dead drop. Jack's must've been to retrieve the dead drop. For all she knew, Libby and Damon had done the same thing. Nadia couldn't ask them about it; she'd been specifically instructed not to tell anyone, and secrecy was part of the training. She definitely couldn't ask Jack—he was her team leader. He'd be forced to give her a bad report for breaking confidentiality. She didn't want to put him in that position. And suspecting Alan? As a double agent? She smiled to herself.

That's probably why Jack was acting so weird when he dropped me off. They'd shared an amazing moment on the dance floor, but after dancing with Jennifer, he'd seemed distracted, distant the rest of the night. *He was thinking about his assignment. It wasn't about Jennifer at all.* She exhaled deeply and closed her eyes.

Seriously, Nadia, chill. Not all guys lie and cheat.

The next morning, Nadia joined her team on the flagstone deck outside the dining hall.

"You're late," Libby said. "Is anything wrong?"

"By like, two minutes. I'm fine," Nadia reassured her. "That's a little OCD even for you. Are you worried about something?" The pile of work she pulled from her backpack reminded her she hadn't slept much.

"No, ma'am. I'm right as rain. Absolutely fine. Like sunshine on daisies," Libby said quickly. "Just excited about Thanksgiving, I guess."

Nadia studied Libby's face, her plastic smile. "Glad to hear it." *Maybe she didn't sleep well, either.*

"Why are you talking so fast?" Alan asked.

"Hey," Jack said, as he stepped onto the patio.

Nadia's pulse quickened when he smiled. "Look." She pulled on her earlobe. "Your earrings." The memory of his kiss flooded her thoughts and her face warmed.

"They bring out the green in your eyes. I knew they would." Jack sounded pleased.

"I hope you weren't upset with me last night," Libby said to Jack. "The earrings really are beautiful, but they weren't right with her hairstyle. You understand."

"I don't, actually. But no, I wasn't upset," Jack answered.

"I'm glad to hear it. In retrospect, I might've been a bit pushy." Libby smiled, then asked him, "What are your plans for Thanksgiving?"

"I'm driving home. San Diego."

Nadia tried to hide her disappointment. She didn't expect him to skip Thanksgiving with his family for some girl he just met, but she'd really hoped he'd be staying at school.

Jack continued, "I have to give Jennifer a ride. She lives less than an hour from me." His eyes did not leave Nadia as he spoke.

"Oh," Nadia said. Her heart sank as she pictured them on the dance floor. *Maybe she is the reason his mood changed last night.* "That's nice of you."

"I'd invite you along, but we're going to my grandmother's and she doesn't do well with new people."

"Don't worry about Nadia. I'll be here." Damon smiled. "I won't let her out of my sight." He slid his hand over hers.

A flash of anger crossed Jack's face; just as quickly, he returned to neutral. Nadia knew it was petty, but she liked it.

Nadia extracted her hand from Damon's as she answered, "I would never impose on your family. Anyway, I've already made plans for the weekend. Sensei's going over some advanced weaponry with me. I couldn't cancel this late even if I wanted to; it would be rude." She forced a smile and tried to ignore the annoying voice in her head.

It kept whispering: *Jack and Jennifer; Matthew and Paige.*

43 JACK
SUNDAY, NOVEMBER 20

Ten minutes after their encounter on the patio, thoroughly disgusted with both himself and his traitor girlfriend, Jack dumped his uneaten lunch into the trash and rushed back to his dorm. He'd had one simple task: keep an eye on Nadia Riley. Bad enough he'd let her successfully complete a brush-pass at the dance last night, but then, like an idiot, he'd tried to rationalize it. He'd actually considered the possibility that the waiter made a mistake—that he mistook her for someone else. *After* he watched Nadia put the napkin in her purse! There was no reasonable explanation for the exchange, but a huge piece of him couldn't believe what he'd seen.

Maybe I don't want to admit I was wrong about her.

Jack slammed his bedroom door. His head throbbed. He wanted to punch something—put his fist through a wall. An immature, overly emotional response, all because he got played. She'd lied to him, betrayed everything he believed in. Acted like she wanted him.

He strode to his desk and grabbed a book from the shelf. Their kiss last night—it felt so real. The heat of her mouth as his lips hovered over hers. His hand buried in her thick hair. Her body against his, her hands on his neck, her scent, the softness of her skin. Finally, contact: deep and desperate. It wasn't until she pulled away that he realized they were surrounded by people. He was furious with himself for losing control. But he was so drawn to her. He wanted more.

This isn't about me being wrong. This is about me falling for her. The pain he now experienced knowing she was the traitor forced him to admit that his feelings ran much deeper than a simple crush. And he'd just revealed his emotional state to his entire team.

And what the hell is Damon's problem? Is he hitting on her?

He tried to refocus on his anger. He'd rather be outraged than heartbroken. And as much as he wanted to explain away her dead drop, he couldn't. He knew the critical nature of the mission because he'd done something totally inappropriate: he'd looked at the disc himself.

In all his time at the Academy he'd never so much as glanced at the information he was sent to collect. The survival courses were staged—simulated missions—but still, not a peek. Until last night. He'd opened the disc on his laptop—it wasn't even encrypted. The file contained detailed schematics of a one-man fighter jet.

An hour had passed before it occurred to him to stake out her dorm. Someone else would be looking for the package. At 0115 he'd snuck from his room, concealed himself in the tall grass and waited, muscles tensed, ready to attack. The sprinklers turned on just before daybreak, soaking him. Now he was stiff, tired and disgusted with himself for acting like such an amateur. He'd had one chance to discover the identity of the receiving agent, and he blew it.

He shook his head. *I can't believe I admired her dedication. She wasn't working hard to catch up—just reviewing skills she already knew.*

But things were looking up. Nadia was finally wearing the earrings, and Jack couldn't wait to check the sound quality of Samuel's bug.

He'd hidden the receiver in a book Noah would never touch, carved out the center with a razor blade and buried the device inside. Jack shoved *The Anthology of Early American Literature* into his bag and jogged to the language lab, where no one would give headphones a second thought.

Back against the wall, he pulled up the Spanish program, just to be safe, and settled into his chair. With the book on the desk in front of him, he plugged the headphones into the receiver.

Nadia's conversation rang loud and clear.

Alan spoke first. "We will meet you at the library."

A moment later, Libby whispered into the microphone. "What're you gonna do about him?"

"He asked me to pretend it never happened," Nadia answered.

"How awkward."

"I know. I wish he'd never said anything."

"I'm sure it'll blow over."

"I hope so. Did you see Jack dancing with Jennifer last night?" Nadia whispered.

"No, but I bet she was like white on rice."

"I hate that they're driving together."

"I don't blame you there."

Jack pulled the headphones from his ears. What a waste of time. Obviously, Nadia wasn't going to share anything significant with Libby, and he didn't want to hear her lies about how much she liked him. As far as Nadia was concerned, he was just part of her cover.

The next morning, a half hour before Dean Wolfe arrived on campus, Jack went to Hopi Hall. He paced the sitting room, glancing at his watch every few minutes. When the dean arrived, Jack followed him into his office, uninvited, and closed the door.

"Do you have new information?" Wolfe opened his briefcase and stacked several files onto his desk.

"Your instincts were right. Nadia's the double. I intercepted a dead drop."

Dean Wolfe stopped shuffling his papers and looked up. "What?"

"Here." Jack handed him the disc.

"Did you look at it?"

"No," Jack lied, maintaining eye contact.

"Do you know who was meant to retrieve the disc?"

Jack shook his head. He wasn't about to tell Dean Wolfe how he'd botched that. "I'm confident Hashimoto Sensei is her handling agent. She's staying here for Thanksgiving and they've scheduled training time."

"Can you stay for the holiday?" Dean Wolfe asked.

"Not without telling my parents what we do here."

"I understand. Good work with this disc, Jack. I'm impressed."

Jack lowered his eyes as he accepted the compliment. *At least something good comes of this.*

"I need to share something with you. Sit down." Dean Wolfe pulled a digital recorder from his briefcase.

Uh-oh. He looks concerned. Jack's heartbeat quickened. *Is it possible he picked up the transmission from the earrings?* Jack settled into a wingback chair. *Calm down. Samuel wouldn't be so careless.*

The Dean pressed a button, and a deep, synthesized voice said, "The rook sings at first light."

Jack opened his mouth and Wolfe held up his hand. Nadia answered, "Can you repeat that?"

The message repeated, and then, "Prepare for the meet."

Wolfe stopped the tape. "She received this call a few weeks ago. Apparently, he was referring to the dance."

And I'm just now hearing it? For weeks I've been trying to prove her innocence. Jack took a deep breath and exhaled his anger before he spoke. "Sir, with all respect, the more information you share with me, the faster we can get this done."

"I share what I am authorized to share."

"Can you arrest her? Between that phone call and this disc—"

"We weren't able to trace the number. She could claim the message was a joke. And, obviously, I haven't reviewed the disc. For all I know, it's a recipe for chocolate-chip cookies."

"I understand," Jack said. *She's a traitor!* But he couldn't reveal anything more without incriminating himself. "What's our next move?"

"You're on the right track. Stay close; keep me informed."

Jack hesitated, trying to decide whether or not to tell Wolfe about the earrings. He should've cleared it with him first, but he'd been so excited about doing actual undercover work that he hadn't bothered with the proper channels.

No, that was a lie. He hadn't asked for permission because he didn't want the Dean to turn him down. Jack wanted to present irrefutable evidence one way or the other. He wanted to be a hero. To please Dean Wolfe, to clear Nadia's name.

"Is there something else?" Wolfe asked.

"No, sir," Jack answered.

"Then close the door on your way out."

44 NADIA
WEDNESDAY, NOVEMBER 23

Classes ended early on Wednesday and the students traveling home trickled off campus, a handful at a time, until only a few remained. Both vans drove back and forth to the airport all afternoon, and most of the cars got checked out for the weekend. Nadia sat on the patio high above campus, watching the scene.

Nothing felt right. The air wasn't sharp, the leaves didn't turn. Thanksgiving in Virginia meant thick sweaters and crackling fires. She and her dad would walk through the neighborhood and pick their favorite tree. Hers would be the maple on the corner, bright orange and crimson. He'd choose an oak—deep rust and chocolate brown. Right now her mom was probably baking: apple and pumpkin pies, a cranberry-pear crisp. Tonight they'd pop popcorn and watch a movie.

After an hour or so, Damon joined her. "You okay?" He gave her ponytail a gentle tug.

"A little homesick."

Damon stared for a moment. "That's not all."

"Yes, it is."

"Come on. You're worried about Jack and Jennifer."

"No, I'm not," Nadia lied.

"Please," Damon said. "You can't con a con. Do you trust him?"

"Sure," she answered. But she wasn't sure, and Damon probably knew it. "I have no reason not to." Nadia searched Damon's face to see if he knew something about Jack that she didn't. He revealed nothing. *Come to think of it, I never know what he's thinking.*

"Jack has no idea how lucky he is."

"Yeah? Is that why you were antagonizing him the other day?"

Damon laughed. "I'm just playing with him. He's got a jealous streak; makes him an easy target. Listen, if he so much as brushes against her, I'll snap his neck."

Now Nadia laughed. "I appreciate that. How's everything going with Niyuri?"

Damon nodded. "She's a sweetheart. I don't know why she's wasting time on a guy like me."

"None of us do. You're passable at best."

He smiled and turned toward her, staring so intently they might've been the last two people on earth. "You busy all weekend?"

How does he do that? "I think so. Why, what's up?"

"I thought you and I might hike into the desert for an overnight. Now, I won't allow firearms. I can't have you drugging me. Or yourself. But no chaperones, either." He winked at her. "And you know what they say: what happens in the desert stays in the desert."

"I'm pretty sure that's Vegas. Nice try, though."

"Hey, fish gotta swim."

"Sounds like fun, but I can't. Unless Sensei cancels on me, which he's never done."

"You two are awfully tight." His tone was innocent; for once, no innuendo.

Nadia smiled. "Yeah, he's been so generous with his time. And his self-discipline is fascinating. He showed me how to slow my heart rate when I'm stressed—I can teach you if you want."

"That'd be cool."

"He answers my questions before I ask, which is good, because I'm not allowed to ask questions." She laughed. "He's almost like a spiritual advisor. This may come as a surprise to you, but after the first survival course, I didn't think I was gonna make it. If not for Sensei, I probably would've been kicked out by now."

"Nah, you're good," Damon said. "It's nice you have him, though."

"How about you? You have anyone?"

He shook his head. "I've always been kind of a loner. I guess my brother and I were close."

"I didn't know you had a brother."

"I don't." Damon paused. "Anymore."

"What?"

He turned his eyes to the empty lawn. "He died."

Nadia's hand flew to her mouth. "Oh my God."

"Since then, I don't know . . ." His voice drifted off. "I have a hard time. You know, making connections."

She wanted to say something—she didn't want Damon to think he couldn't talk to her. *But what do I say? I understand?* Of course she didn't understand. For lack of anything better, she asked, "What was his name?"

"Gabriel."

A heavy pause followed the word. "Do you want to talk about it?"

He didn't answer. He stared across the field, looked up at the sky. Avoided her eyes. Finally, he said, "I don't talk about it."

"I'm sorry. I didn't mean to pry." They sat in silence. A soft breeze carried the sweet smell of the desert onto the patio. Nadia brushed a few hairs from her face.

He cleared his throat. "It was a hit-and-run."

"Oh, Damon." She turned in her seat to face him.

He was quiet for a long, long time. "We were at the playground near our house. He was eight years old." Damon's jaw tightened. A few moments later, he continued, "The car just took off." He picked at a flake of loose paint on his chair.

Nadia focused on keeping her body still. Any movement might bring him back to the present, remind him that he didn't want to talk. She had a thousand questions: *What happened? Did the police find them? Are they in jail?*

"I heard him—I heard a scream. The brakes screeching. Then the . . . a thud." He met her eyes, then quickly looked back at his chair. "I called 911. They sent an ambulance." He continued picking at the paint, sending tiny flurries of black enamel onto the patio. "He was still alive when we reached the hospital. He was in surgery for hours. But in the end, his little body just couldn't hang on."

She wanted to scoot her chair closer to his, to lessen the space between them.

"My mom never got to say goodbye." He shook his head. "I never got to say goodbye."

"Oh, Damon," she whispered. Her eyes stung.

He scraped the paint from under his thumbnail and winced. He opened his mouth, closed it again. A minute later he continued, "But the worst part, worse than waiting at the hospital, not knowing if he'd live or die—the absolute worst part is that it was completely my fault."

"No," Nadia said. "I know that's not true."

"I haven't told you everything." Damon cleared his throat. "I took him to the park. I was supposed to be watching him. I wasn't paying attention. I was screwing around on my phone. I had my back to him, Nadia."

"Damon, I—"

"There was no one else there. It was cold and pissing rain and he kept asking me to push him on the swing. I turned around to tell him to quit bugging me." His voice tightened. "That's when I noticed the car. Before it happened. It registered in the back of my mind that something was off. This SUV swerved over the line, skimmed the curb. I figured the driver was messing with his phone, or the radio . . . I don't know. He wasn't going that fast. There were two other men in the car—I assumed somebody would be watching the road. If I'd paid any attention at all to what was going on around me, Gabriel would still be alive."

Nadia took his hand. *That's why he notices everything.* She tried to keep her voice steady. "You have to know it wasn't your fault." The comment sounded hollow. Meaningless, and not at all comforting.

"Of course it was. I should've called the police before it happened, reported the car. Told Gabriel to stay away from the road."

"I'm so sorry." She wiped at her eyes.

"If I had just paid attention." He turned toward the open lawn. His eyes narrowed as he shook his head. "I promise you this: that is the last detail I will ever ignore."

His words hung in the air like a heavy cloud. The gentle breeze that swept through campus didn't move them. The seconds grew into minutes as she and Damon sat in silence. The minutes piled on top of each other like rocks, each individual one adding to the weight of the whole. Her sadness spread deeper inside, and for that she felt guilty. *What right do I have to be sad about one stupid holiday when Damon will never see his brother again?*

After a long time, Damon sighed. He cleared his throat. "I think I'm gonna go for a run before dinner. Maybe we can catch a movie in the lounge tonight?"

"Sure. Whatever you want."

But that was the last Nadia saw of him for the next four days.

45 LIBBY
WEDNESDAY, NOVEMBER 23

Wednesday afternoon, Libby gathered her bags—packed with her favorite cool-weather sweaters—and caught the last shuttle to the airport with five of her schoolmates. She clutched her boarding pass in her hand and complained to anyone who would listen that she was not pleased about taking the red eye. I mean, come *on*. A flight at two-o'clock in the morning? It was *inhumane*. Normally, she didn't like to complain. The world had enough negativity without her adding to the heap. But extenuating circumstances called for extenuating measures.

The last of her shuttle companions boarded his plane at nine-fifty that night. Libby breathed a heavy sigh of relief, dropped her boarding pass in the waste basket and took the mile-long escalator downstairs to the rental car desk. Twenty-seven minutes later, she pulled onto I-10 East toward Tucson.

Traffic thinned near the south end of Phoenix and Libby stopped to grab a bite. While she waited for her order, she went to the ladies' room to braid her hair. She fixed it tight against her skull and pinned it in place.

Back in the car, Libby carefully arranged a wavy, medium-length, auburn-colored wig against her scalp. She pushed a pair of non-prescription eyeglasses onto her face. The dark plastic frames matched her new hair. "And I *still* look good."

Libby dialed her cell phone. "It's me," she said, too tired to hide her Georgia drawl.

"How are you, sugah?" His familiar voice reassured her.

She sighed. "I don't want to do this."

"I know you don't."

"Is there any other way?"

"We all have our orders. This one happens to be yours. We all got obligations we don't like."

"I know, Daddy. I just really don't feel good about this."

"If there was anything I could do to get you out of it, you know I would."

"I know you would." Libby took a long breath, trying to keep the tears out of her voice. She wasn't trying to make him feel bad, it was just—well, he was her *daddy*. When she was in trouble, he was her first call. But even he couldn't fix this mess. "You'll send the address and relevant file to my phone?"

"Already on the way. Be careful, baby. Lot a crazies out there."

"I will, Daddy. Love you."

"I love you, too."

Libby shut off her phone. She clamped her hand over her mouth and choked back a sob.

Less than two hours later Libby pulled into the Tucson Regency Resort and Spa. She handed the rental key to the valet and strolled toward the front desk. Flashing her sweetest smile, she batted her eyes at the desk clerk. "Good evening, Charles. I'm Amanda Downing." She took out her wallet—the one with Amanda Downing's license and credit cards. "I believe you have a reservation for me?" Libby toyed with a curl on her wig.

He clicked away at the keyboard. "Ms. Downing, of course. The Presidential Suite is ready for you. As requested, we have provided a laptop and full-color printer." He used two fingers to summon a bellboy. "Garret will show you to your room. Is there anything else I can do for you at this time?" He swiped her card and verified the picture on her driver's license.

"I can't imagine."

Libby followed Garret to the elevators. They rode all the way to the top floor. Figured her daddy got her the Presidential Suite. *It's the least he can do, making me be here like this.* Her heart pounded harder just thinking about it. Garret led her inside.

"We've set up your office in the bedroom to your left; the master suite is on the right. Our menu of spa services is here," he pointed to the coffee table, "and in-room dining is, of course, available around the clock. Shall I place your bag in the bedroom?"

"No, you can leave it out here. Is there a password for the wireless?"

"The gentleman who made your reservations sent a personal wifi."

"Perfect." Libby fished into her wallet and grabbed a twenty. An extravagant tip, but it was her father's money and right now she didn't care too much about looking out for him. Hell, she'd just thrown a four-hundred-dollar airline ticket into the wastebasket. "Thank you."

Garret showed himself out and Libby eased off her jacket. *First things first.* She booted the computer and searched through her handbag. The Photocrop program she'd purchased on the way down installed quickly. She removed the flashlight—actually a USB drive—from her keyring and pulled up a dozen pictures on the screen.

A dull ache grew at the back of her skull. She rubbed her neck as she examined the photos. They were taken last year, right about this time. Her momma and brother, each holding up a glass of wine, toasting the camera. One of Libby decorating the Christmas tree.

"Oh shoot," she said out loud. "It's that dang sweater." The black cashmere she'd given Nadia. Libby pulled that photo into the trash and looked for another. She and her brother in front of the Christmas tree, wearing matching footed pajamas—a gag gift from her momma. She and her momma leaning over the roasted turkey with forks and knives in hand.

The only picture she could find of her daddy was from the summer. Standing on their yacht, deeply suntanned, looking handsome as ever. *This might be problematic.* Her father did not presently have a tan, what with being in Washington all season, and it was entirely possible one of her friends would see him on television over the holiday.

I bet I can lighten him right up.

Libby cut her daddy out of the photo like a surgeon removes a tumor. She brightened the light, lessened the contrast, decreased the saturation and carefully inserted him into the picture with her and her momma.

Libby searched the background of the photos for telltale markers. Just for good measure, she found a calendar and stuck it on the kitchen wall. She changed the year to make it current and printed the proof of her perfect holiday.

"And a happy Thanksgiving to me."

46 NADIA
THURSDAY, NOVEMBER 24

Nadia spent Thanksgiving morning at the dojo and the afternoon in the language lab. In the early evening she went for a run, sprinting along the hiking trails beyond the wall. During her cool-down lap she practiced slowing her breath to slow her heart rate.

She had just finished showering when Casey knocked on her door. "You have a phone call, sweetie," she called.

Nadia pulled on her robe and jogged to the front desk. "Hello!" she sang, expecting to hear her mother's voice.

"Nadia, it's Jack."

"Oh hey, Jack. Sorry, I thought you were my mom." She winced, embarrassed by her over-enthusiastic greeting.

"Are you homesick?"

"A little. How's it going?" She balanced the cordless phone between her shoulder and chin and tightened her robe.

"Good. I wanted to say hi, let you know I was thinking about you."

Nadia was glad he couldn't see her grin. "That was thoughtful." She hesitated, trying to think of a casual way to ask about Jennifer without sounding like a psycho girlfriend. *Did you get Jennifer dropped off okay? Did she keep her hands to herself? Are you hooking up with her?* She kept her mouth shut.

"Are you wearing your earrings?"

"No, I just got out of the shower. I'm not even dressed yet, but I'll wear them to dinner."

"Sweet. Think of me when you do. I'm going to my dad's tomorrow, so I doubt I'll have a chance to call again, but I wanted to wish you a happy Thanksgiving. I miss you," Jack said.

"Me too," she answered, suddenly shy. She hung up the phone and noticed Casey shivering outside. Nadia waved her in.

"I thought you'd like some privacy," Casey said.

"Do you think I could use the phone later? To call home?"

"Of course. Whenever you want. If I'm not here, today's code is 9-7-6-9. But make sure you call by midnight or that code won't work."

The staff prepared a traditional Thanksgiving meal, which made Nadia more homesick. Damon never showed for dinner. She'd hoped he would cancel his trip.

She liked being around him. He always seemed so interested in what she had to say. And the way he'd confided in her: she was honored for his trust.

Why am I thinking about Damon? Nadia fiddled with one of her earrings. She pictured Jack in his tuxedo, holding her close as they danced. The way his kiss sent a warm rush through her entire body. She felt herself smiling.

She hurried through dinner and returned to her dorm, walking quickly down the path to escape the cold night.

Casey wasn't in the lobby, so Nadia slipped behind her desk and into the chair, dialing as instructed.

"Happy Thanksgiving!" her mom said.

"Happy Thanksgiving, Mom!" Nadia called back. "I miss you!"

"Nadia, we miss you, too! Did you—"

Feedback screeched through the phone. She moved the receiver away from her ear. "Mom, what did you say?"

"I asked about your holiday," she repeated.

"It was great, how about you?"

"Sweetie, I can barely hear you."

Nadia moved the receiver back to her ear and the screeching resumed. "Something's wrong with the phone," she said loudly. "Can you hear me?"

"You're breaking up. Do you want to call me back?" her mom asked.

The desk blurred as Nadia's eyes filled with tears. "No, it's okay." She steadied her voice so her mom wouldn't worry. "A bunch of us are gonna watch a movie in the lounge. Everyone's waiting on me. I love you. Tell Dad."

"Okay, sweetheart. Love you, too!"

Nadia hung up and hurried down the hall, desperate to get to her room before she started crying. She fumbled with the lock and rushed inside, slamming her door. She fell onto her bed, sobbing quietly. She pictured her parents, turning out the lights, getting ready for bed; Jack at home with his brothers and sister; Libby curled up on the couch with her mom. Even Alan, surrounded by family, watching the snow fall on Central Park. Everyone she knew was with someone they loved.

Her thoughts turned briefly to Damon, and with them another surge of guilt for feeling sorry for herself.

For some reason she didn't fully understand, she wished he was there with her.

47 AGENT 77365
FRIDAY, NOVEMBER 25

"You are the most incompetent agent I have ever worked with," the young man said into his cell phone.

"May I remind you, I'm still your superior," the older man answered sharply.

"Wrong. You are my professor on campus; that is your cover. I do *not* answer to you, despite your *chain-of-command* delusions. It's been months, and Nadia Riley is still at school. What is taking so long?"

"You're right to be concerned. It's only a matter of time until Riley figures out she's being set up. And that you're the one doing it. You should've gotten rid of her when you had the chance."

"When exactly do you think that was? First you tell me to send her home, then you tell me to frame her. And what are you doing? Besides creating all these problems in the first place?"

"You've no one but yourself to blame. You haven't done a very good job planting evidence. Set her up, we'll give her to the CIA and all our problems disappear," the professor said.

"Are you kidding? I arranged an incriminating phone call, the dead drop at the dance. What more do you want? A dead body in her closet? Why does this all fall on me?"

"Get a hold of yourself. You have the most access. I can't do it—I have a classroom full of students watching me. But you need to give us something big."

She needs to disappear. I need her gone from school and out of my life. I still have her knife. I could plant her bloody knife somewhere. But whose blood would I use? He sighed. The last thing he needed was another complication. And framing her for treason was not the same as framing her for murder.

An hour later, at 0225 on Friday morning, he finished forging a Canadian plane ticket. At 0315 he wrote out a message using a complicated cipher code. By 0400, he was back in bed, sleeping like a baby.

48 NADIA
FRIDAY, NOVEMBER 25

At seven o'clock on Friday morning, Nadia met Hashimoto Sensei at the dojo.

"I let you sleep in because it is a holiday weekend," he said.

"How thoughtful of you," she replied, with only a hint of sarcasm in her voice. "What are we doing today?"

"This morning we will study jujutsu. Your ground fighting skills are unacceptable. Are you ready to begin?"

"*Hai.*"

"Take off your earrings. I do not allow jewelry in the dojo. It is too easy to be injured or to injure another."

"Sorry, I forgot. I slept in them last night and I don't usually do that."

"To say you are sorry implies an accident, and what is an accident?" he asked.

"A lack of discipline," she recited, placing her earrings on the window sill.

A minute later, she stood at attention on the mat, awaiting instruction.

"Nadia-san." Sensei slowly circled the mat as he spoke. "Do you know the difference between ninja and samurai?"

Nadia shook her head, eyes forward.

"Both are deadly. Ninja is silence, stealth and cunning." Sensei stopped an arm's length away on her left. "But there is more: Ninja cannot be trusted. He sells himself to the highest bidder."

A flash of movement in her peripheral vision as his bamboo pole flew toward her face. Nadia ducked the blow and deflected his stick, forcing Sensei's shoulder away from her. She struck at his throat with the blade of her hand. His hand caught hers an instant before she made contact.

Sensei smiled and bowed. "*Yoku dekimashita*. Well done."

She grinned and returned his bow. As Sensei moved to the front of the room, Nadia stood back at attention.

"Samurai, also, is clever. Strong, disciplined, proud. But he is loyal. He serves one master, like his father before him. He believes in honor above all. While ninja fights in shadows; samurai harnesses light. Nadia-san, *you* are like samurai. You consistently demonstrate self-restraint, self-discipline and a desire to improve yourself through a rigorous study of martial arts. You have impressed me. Otherwise, I would not waste my time."

Her cheeks flushed, embarrassed—but pleased—by his praise. She knew this was Hashimoto Sensei's deepest compliment.

If Sensei saw how she was feeling, he ignored it. "I trust you are happy in your studies?"

"*Hai*, very much."

"Excellent. I believe this semester is a new beginning for you. This is why I am willing to share my experience. This afternoon I will show you the covert-operations room, but first, you must understand something. No one is permitted in that room except me. In the history of the Academy, I have shown the covert-ops room to only one other student. Bring your passport this afternoon."

"I need my passport to get into the covert-ops room?" Nadia smiled. "Where exactly is it?"

"One hundred snap-kicks. *Hajime!*"

After a quick lunch Nadia returned to the dojo. She followed Sensei down the south wing, where he stopped in front of a metal door.

He turned to enter his password, but he didn't shield the keypad with his body. Under most circumstances Nadia would have turned away out of courtesy, but she was watching the keypad because, unlike the weapons room, it had no thumbprint reader, and she wondered why. *I guess the weapons room needs more security?* Sensei entered his password: *abunai*. The door clanged softly as the lock released. "Come in."

Nadia stepped into the tiny room, about the size of her and Libby's bathroom. Richly grained wood panels, each the size of a kitchen cabinet door, lined the walls. The empty room contained two recessed bookshelves, both stacked with books.

"This is the covert-operations room," Sensei said with moderate ceremony.

Nadia had the feeling she should *ooh* and *ah*, but she really didn't see anything special. Literally, an empty wood-paneled room with a couple bookshelves.

"We will begin here." Sensei turned to the wall on their left. He ran his hand over the panel. "This salvaged wood came from a Buddhist monastery that was abandoned during the First World War. Each plank was hand-carved and smoothed by young monks." He pressed the panel and a hidden cabinet opened with a quiet *click*.

Nadia smiled. *Room not so lame anymore.*

"This row of cabinets contains surveillance equipment." He held up an unabridged *Merriam-Webster's Dictionary*. "Look closely."

She leaned in for a better view. "What about it?"

"Run your hand down the spine."

Her fingers slid down the binding. The canvas was smooth—until a slight indentation over the 'o' in *Dictionary*. "What is it?"

He opened the book, exposing a hollow cavity filled with wires and a small black box. "This is a camera, audio and visual." He held up a box of lightbulbs. "These are strictly audio."

"In the lightbulb? No kidding."

"A wiretap can be hidden anywhere: inside a pencil, sewn into the button on a sofa, concealed in a ring." He returned the items to their shelves. "The next cabinet contains *counter*-surveillance equipment. These tools are used to sweep for wiretaps, to make sure the integrity of your environment has not been compromised." Sensei picked up a thick wand-shaped device and turned it on. He quickly scanned Nadia's torso. "You are clean," he joked. He rarely joked.

"A bug could be anywhere, right?" Nadia asked. "I know the school has security cameras outside all the buildings, but you don't think our bedrooms are wired, do you?"

"No. It would be a serious violation of civil rights, especially since you are minors." Sensei gestured to the second wall, opposite the door. "This cabinet houses equipment for dead drops. Have you learned about dead drops in class?"

"Yes, in fact—" She wasn't sure she should tell him about her dead drop. The waiter had said not to tell *anyone*.

" 'In fact' what?"

I better not. "We learned about them weeks ago."

He held up a small tin. "A magnetic box can be attached to a park bench or under a car." He showed her a can of shaving cream with a false bottom, a pair of hollowed chopsticks, even a glass eye with a pocket to conceal a message. "You have your passport?"

Nadia reached behind her back to pull the passport from the waistband of her *Gi*.

I bet he'd be able to confirm that Jack was supposed to retrieve my dead drop.

Sensei selected a thin, foot-long stick from the cabinet. He flipped a switch and a blue glow filled the room.

Why is that still bothering me?

Sensei held the light over the pages. "A customs official uses this wand to identify counterfeit passports. The light detects security threads in the paper, which are sensitive to ultra-violet radiation."

"Excellent," Nadia said. *It just seems strange Jack allowed himself to be seen by Alan. Why didn't he come back later—after everyone was asleep? Sensei won't mind if I ask. He won't give me a bad report.* "May I ask you a question?"

"You just did. Nadia-san, I believe you know my policy on questions. I will tell you if there is something you need to know." He turned away.

On the other hand, it isn't fair to put him in that position. Making him choose between me and the rules. Nadia chewed on her lip. *No, asking him wouldn't be right.*

"This bookshelf contains training manuals from all major branches of clandestine service, past and present: CIA, KGB, MI6 and so on."

Nadia set her passport on the bookshelf. She was thumbing through the *Flaps and Seals* section of the CIA training manual, which indicated the best methods for opening an envelope undetected, when Sensei continued.

"In this cabinet we have fingerprinting equipment and lock-picking kits."

Nadia let the book flop shut and slipped it back on its shelf.

He held up a jar that looked like clear rubber cement. "This is liquid latex." He used the brush inside to spread a thin layer on the back of her hand. It dried immediately.

"Shake my hand." He returned the jar to the shelf. "Hold still," he said, and slowly peeled the second skin from the back of her hand. He held it up to the light. "Now you have my thumbprint."

"Very cool!" Nadia said, reaching for the latex print.

He put it on the shelf, closing the cabinet.

Sensei turned to the remaining wall. "This area contains special, close-range weapons."

"More weapons? You're kidding—you have an entire room full of guns, knives, swords and baseball bats."

"I do not have baseball bats, and I never joke about weapons." He pressed the door, revealing a large box filled with two-inch-high ugly, metal guns. Nadia might not have been a very good shot, but she'd learned to appreciate the beauty of a finely crafted firearm.

Sensei continued, "These are modeled after CIA deer guns. They are single-use—one shot—designed to allow an agent to kill his enemy in order to retrieve his enemy's gun. They were created during the Vietnam War. To be accurate they require a close range. The short barrel produces an extreme concussion. Ideally, a weapon like this would be used out-of-doors to minimize hearing loss."

"We won't use these, will we?"

"Not in school; except to train, of course. If you become a field agent you will use similar equipment. Some students will work inside the Agency's Black-Ops Division as computer analysts or linguistics specialists. Others will take cover jobs, perhaps in a foreign embassy. Only the best of you will have the opportunity to serve as field agents. Nadia-san, I believe you will be that good."

Her face warmed at his continued praise.

"Remember, though, close-range weapons require a *specific* kind of agent."

"I don't understand."

"Self-defense is one thing, but assassination is entirely another. When completing elimination orders, it is easier to shoot someone with a sniper's rifle from hundreds of yards away than to look into their eyes as they die. It becomes very personal."

Could I really kill another human being because someone ordered me to? Nadia readily accepted the career path offered at Desert Mountain Academy—so far she loved it. But her thoughts lingered only on the positive: world travel, exotic missions. . . . She deliberately avoided contemplating the negatives: deep cover, no contact with her family, capture, murder. Those ideas overwhelmed her. She chose to believe she'd be so well trained by the time she had a mission that her actions would be second nature.

Sensei continued, "This weapon is discreet and convenient: a poisoned pen. Click out the needle and stab." He offered her the pen. She reached for it, but he didn't release his grip. Nadia looked into his eyes as they stood holding the pen. "Hit the jugular for a kill shot." The tiny hairs on the back of her neck stood up and she shivered. She felt his eyes on her as she examined the pen.

"This final shelf contains code books: advanced cipher translations, one-time pads and the like. And that concludes our tour."

They returned to the lobby. "We took longer than I anticipated. You may relax before your evening meal."

"Thank you." Nadia bowed.

"*Arigato.*" He returned her bow. Just as she was sliding the shoji closed he called out, "Nadia-san!"

She opened the screens. "Yes?"

He held out his hand. "Do not forget your earrings."

49 DAMON
FRIDAY, NOVEMBER 25

Damon had been alone in his room for thirty-eight straight hours, ever since his conversation with Nadia. He'd successfully buried his guilt for months, then one hour with her and his conscience arrived for an extended visit.

For six years Damon had helped raise his little brother. But when Gabriel's life depended on him, Damon had dropped the ball. Afterward, his mom had sat on the edge of Gabriel's unmade bed. Not hearing, not seeing, growing paler and more emaciated by the day. She'd refused to look at Damon, and he'd known why. Her eyes had burned with accusation: *This is your fault. This never should've happened.*

And deep down, he knew. Gabriel's death was his fault.

Damon groaned out loud. It was now well into Friday morning, and he desperately needed air. When he was sure Nadia was at the dojo, he grabbed his rucksack and a change of clothes and headed out the back gate to start his "camping trip."

He hiked north, knowing any vehicles moving in and out of school would be from the south. The brisk walk helped; exercise always cleared his head, and the sun warmed his tensed shoulders. He'd screwed up, talking to Nadia like that. Exposed too much of himself, telling her things he'd never told anyone. But when he thought about her—those green eyes, the messy ponytail, her open smile . . . Something about her caught him off-guard. A vulnerability she didn't share with anyone else.

In any case, whatever this connection between them, it had to stop. It left Damon feeling uneasy. Physically distancing himself from her seemed his only viable option. He paused to dig a water bottle out of his pack.

I don't understand why she's wasting her time on Jack. She could do so much better. Jack's insecurities were a dead giveaway of his inherent weakness. His reaction at the Fall Formal when Damon had asked Nadia to dance spoke volumes. And Damon had no tolerance for a weak leader.

He reached the highway and stuck out his thumb. He thought about ways to break them up. With Jack's lack of confidence, Damon could easily plant the idea that Nadia had someone on the side. Or maybe hide a love note from Jack to another girl. As far as Damon was concerned, he'd be doing her a favor.

There wasn't much in the way of traffic. About an hour passed before an eighteen-wheeler pulled over, the air-brakes screeching and hissing. Damon broke into a sweat at the sound. He pressed his water bottle to the back of his neck.

"Hitchhiking's not safe, son," the trucker said as Damon climbed into the cab.

"Oh, it's cool." Damon flashed a smile. "I'm a trained assassin."

The man chuckled. "Where you headed?"

"Phoenix," Damon said. "The Holiday Inn."

Having made his decision, Damon returned to campus early Sunday evening. He waited at the back gate, watching his classmates filter in. Nadia sat alone on the patio outside the dining room. He had to work to stay hidden; she kept looking in his direction, almost as though she sensed him there. When Jack crossed the lawn toward their dorm, Damon started back to his room.

They reached the lobby together. "Hey, man," Damon said, pulling open the door. "You have a good break?"

"Yeah, it was fine. Did you and Nadia hang out?"

"I had a great holiday. Thanks for asking."

"Sorry. How was your weekend?"

"Outstanding."

"Oh yeah? Did you keep an eye on my girl?" Jack asked.

He cleared his throat and averted his gaze. "You know, I really didn't see her." Jack looked toward the door as more students entered the lobby. Damon rolled his eyes. *Your girl. Give me a break.*

Jack turned back to Damon. "There were like, eight students on campus. How could you not see her?"

"I know, it's weird, right?" Damon laughed. "I hardly believe it myself. I was here the whole time."

"Not even at dinner?"

"Nope." Damon turned toward his hallway. "Must've just missed her."

Damon hated to skip his evening meal, but he couldn't risk running into Jack and Nadia at the same time. Not right now, when everyone would be talking about their weekend. In any case, he had work to do.

Fifteen minutes after the dining hall opened, Damon headed to the girls' dorm. He had a limited window. He needed to be in and out before Casey finished eating. He strode to the front desk. If anyone asked, he was leaving a note for Niyuri.

His breath was easy, his heart rate slow. Compared to what he'd been through back in Baltimore, this was an afternoon at Camden Yards.

A proactive move, really. A preemptive strike.

A glance down both wings satisfied Damon he was alone, so he made his way to Nadia's door. With steady hands he prepped his kit. It didn't take but a second or two to pick the lock and slip inside.

50 NADIA
SUNDAY, NOVEMBER 27

Nadia's classmates returned en masse on Sunday afternoon. She waited on the patio, one eye on the front gate watching for Jack and Jennifer, the other on the back gate looking for Damon.

After about two hours sitting in the same hard chair, trying to casually scan the perimeter every few seconds, Nadia got disgusted with herself. *You'll see them when you see them, loser.*

She met up with Alan in her dorm, of all places. She was walking in while he was leaving the lobby.

"What are you doing here?" she asked, apprehensive of the answer.

Alan's face blushed. "I—uh—Libby."

Nadia nodded. *Liar.* "Did you find her?"

"She is not here yet. See you."

Nadia stepped out of the way to avoid being trampled during his hasty departure.

Libby arrived an hour later with a suitcase full of new clothes. She'd gotten highlights and a matching mani-pedi, but Nadia noticed dark circles under her eyes. Jet-lag wasn't kind to Libby.

"You don't mind if I tack these on the wall, do you?" Libby asked, as she hung her Thanksgiving Day pictures by the door.

"Of course not." Nadia's reply was unenthusiastic. *Wish I'd gone home.* "Did you have a good trip?"

"Oh, honey. It was amazing." Libby talked as she put away her clothes. "Momma and I spent all day Friday at a spa. I had the best facial—and the massage! Honestly, it was just . . . amazing. Then she treated me to a prickly pear moisturizing body treatment—"

"You went all the way to Georgia for a spa treatment using desert plants?"

Libby turned to face Nadia, a smile plastered on her face. "I *know*. Isn't that *funny*? Course, in Savannah prickly pear is an imported exotic. Anyway, that's enough about me. How was your holiday?"

"It was fine." Nadia looked away. She briefly considered sharing Damon's story, but it didn't feel right. If he wanted to tell Libby, he would. She crossed the room to Libby's side, pretending to admire the pictures. "Looks like you had a blast."

"Yes, ma'am, I did."

Nadia studied the photos on the wall. "Hmm."

"What is it?"

"Nothing." She glanced back at Libby. *That's strange.* Her eyes returned to the pictures.

Libby's hair looks three inches longer today than it was on Thanksgiving.

51 JACK
SUNDAY, NOVEMBER 27

Jack was psyched to be back at school. Thanksgiving hadn't been the warm celebration he'd anticipated. His brothers hadn't come home and his sister spent her weekend skiing with friends. Jack's mother insisted he visit his father. Dr. Felkin was on call, and in the two hours they were together he received seven phone calls. Between life-saving conversations, he managed to give Jack a lecture on the virtues of pursuing a medical career.

"Medicine's not everything, Dad," Jack answered.

"What could be a more noble calling?"

Oh, I don't know. Hunting terrorists? Finding and disarming nuclear weapons? Most of the time, Jack didn't mind keeping his studies surreptitious. It gave him a secret power over his father. But occasionally, when Dr. Felkin launched into his if-you're-not-a-doctor-you're-nothing speech, it took all of Jack's willpower to remain silent.

So stepping back onto campus, even with all his worry over Nadia, was a welcome relief.

Before he left for the weekend, Jack had attached the receiver for the wireless transmitter in Nadia's earring to a voice-activated tape recorder. He dropped his bags, grabbed the American lit book and raced to the language lab, excited to hear what he'd missed.

The recording opened with feedback. Then pieces of a conversation between Nadia and her mom. He rewound the tape, straining to decipher their words. When Nadia complained about connection, he realized what had happened. His heart skipped a beat. The frequency waves of the wireless transmitter had interfered with the telephone. The bug caused the noise.

Had Nadia realized it too? *Does she know I wired the earrings? Does that have something to do with why Damon didn't see her this weekend?* He leaned onto the table, eyes wide, while he listened to the rest of the tape. She was talking to Sensei—he said something about "earrings." Then the recording stopped. *Four days, and I have three minutes of incoherent conversation.*

Jack glanced at his watch—almost dinnertime. The second he saw Nadia he'd be able to tell if she found the mike. Her reaction would give her away. He packed up his equipment and left for the dining hall.

Libby, Alan and Nadia were already seated, eating their chicken parmesan.

"Did you miss me?" Jack asked, approaching Nadia from behind.

She jumped as he touched her shoulder. "You scared me. When did you get back?"

Jack couldn't get a read. If Nadia had found the bug, she was definitely playing it cool. She wasn't wearing his earrings. He couldn't ask about them; he'd brought it up too many times already. "Not long ago. How was your break? Spend a lot of time with Damon?"

"Not much. I was mostly at the dojo and Damon went camping. It's nice to see you."

She's lying to me. I wish Damon were here so I could confront her. "Yeah, good to see you too. I'm gonna go unpack, but I'll catch up with you later. Maybe we'll go for a run tomorrow night." Jack playfully kissed the top of Nadia's head.

That was useless. What was she doing over break? There's no way she stayed on campus and Damon never saw her. It doesn't make any sense. Jack absentmindedly chewed his lower lip as he walked down the path. *Maybe they're both lying. Maybe they hooked up and forgot to get their stories straight.* He swallowed, not liking the thought of Nadia with Damon. He passed a group of girls entering their dorm.

I'm sick of her games. Why should she call the shots? I need hard evidence, so I can end this once and for all.

The next morning Jack woke at 0500. He went for a run, showered and ate breakfast. By 0800 he'd chewed the whites off his fingernails. At 0915, confident all other students were in class, he snuck into the girls' dorm.

He hurried past Casey's empty desk. She wasn't needed during the day. It was after classes, in the afternoons and evenings, that the school required a chaperone.

Jack moved silently down the carpeted hallway to Nadia's room. He tried the doorknob—locked. He slipped a small tool out of his pocket and proceeded to pick the lock. It took longer than he expected. Beads of sweat collected on his forehead. A deep breath only slightly calmed his nerves. After two minutes of intense concentration, the door clicked open. With one last glance toward the lobby, he crept inside.

He started with the medicine chests in the bathroom: deodorant, hair gel, sunscreen. The room smelled like coconuts and vanilla. It reminded him of summer. Like Nadia. *Focus.*

Back in the bedroom, he spotted a wooden jewelry box on one of the dressers. Black velvet lined the compartment, and the earrings he'd given Nadia sat in the center. Her other earrings were pushed into a pile toward the back, with a silver bracelet, a shell choker, a ring made of blue glass. He replaced the lid. Above her desk, he inspected the bookshelves.

He walked to Libby's side and looked through the containers arranged on her dresser. Hair ties, makeup, jewelry. He was closing the last box when he noticed a bit of paper jutting out from underneath. A worn note read MISS YOU, SUNSHINE! LOVE, MOMMA.

He crossed back over to Nadia's side and picked up her jewelry box. Taped to the bottom he found an unsealed envelope. He opened the flap and removed a ticket stub from Air Canada Airlines, issued to Nadia Riley, from Phoenix Sky Harbor to Vancouver, Canada. The date of departure was Thanksgiving, returning on Saturday night. *Finally, some actual evidence.* He pulled the ticket from the envelope and stuck it in his pocket.

Why would she keep a ticket stub? She screwed up and forgot to throw it out—that's why she hid it. He shook his head. *Rookie mistake.*

Jack stood quietly in the middle of the room, considering his next move.

What was she doing in Canada? Meeting another agent? Sensei must have gone with her—his voice was on the recording. It occurred to him Canada would be freezing this time of year.

Nadia's closet door was ajar; he searched the rack for her jacket. It took him a minute—it was all the way in the back. The coat wasn't heavy: red fleece, with a reflective stripe along the hood. His search of the pockets revealed a note printed in cipher text, scribbled on a crisply folded piece of yellow notebook paper. Jack wiped his palm on his khakis, and then jotted the code on his hand using a felt-tip pen from Nadia's desk. He stuck the paper back in her coat. *Did she write it or receive it?*

He checked the clock on her nightstand. *I need to get moving.* He let himself out and locked the door.

Jack glanced at his sweaty palm as he hurried down the hall. He kept his hand open and flat, cautiously preserving the message. *I'll go to the library, crack the code and then report to Dean Wolfe.* He nodded as he imagined the Dean's response. Jack forced himself to focus on the positive. Nadia might've outplayed him on the operative field, but she would not win an emotional battle.

He rushed across the lawn and through the revolving doors of the library. His eyes surveyed the room as he approached the reference desk. This time of day, the building was deserted. The librarian sat typing at her station. The clicking of the plastic keys interrupted the dull drone of the heating unit.

She smiled as he approached. "Jack, why aren't you in class?" Her fingers continued tapping across the keyboard.

"Good morning, Dr. Wilson. You look very nice today." He leaned against her desk. "I'm working on a special project. I need to use the cipher computer."

Her smile widened. "Your flattery is transparent, but I'll help you anyway."

The cipher computer, locked in a small room behind the language lab, wasn't available for general use—otherwise, students would never learn to crack a code. But Jack was in a hurry and didn't have time for games. He followed Dr. Wilson down a narrow corridor of closed doors. She jiggled the key in the lock and opened the room. "Close it up when you're done."

Jack waited for her to leave before entering the numeric code. The screen flickered as one letter popped up after another. T-A-W-S-I-T-U-O-C . . . He waited. S-Y-O-B-G-N . . . Finally, the last three letters in the sequence appeared. Jack grabbed a piece of scrap paper from the stack beside the monitor and jotted down the results.

TAWSIT UOCSY OBGNIHC.

He stared at the letters. Sit *is the only word I see. Maybe it's every other letter.*

TWI UCY BNH, *no, no.* AST OS OGIC . . . *nothing. Maybe it's backwards.*

CHINGBO YSCOU TISWAT. *SWAT* jumped out immediately. *A SWAT team?* Then *BOY. Boys, cout, swat . . . Ah,* boy scout. *Boy scout is. Ching boy scout is wat.* Suddenly he saw it—the sentence wasn't in order. It wrapped around.

Boy scout is watching.

Jack's heart raced. He struggled to catch his breath.

Someone warned her. She knows I'm watching.

A new surge of panic gripped him as he realized what he'd done.

And I just stole a ticket stub from her room.

52 NADIA
MONDAY, NOVEMBER 28

Monday morning was brutal. After the four-day weekend, each professor tried to cram three days' worth of material into one hour. Nadia furiously scribbled her class notes. After first period her hand already felt as though it would snap.

She and Libby stopped by their room before lunch. Libby talked nonstop about her holiday and how wonderful it had been to see her family. Her mother made the *best* meal and she and her brother played touch football with all the neighborhood kids and blah, blah, blah, perfect American Thanksgiving.

"Gimme one second," Libby said as she stepped into the bathroom, prattling on through the closed door. Nadia rolled her eyes, thoroughly annoyed with her roommate's sunny disposition. *Knock it off. It's not her fault your family can't afford two plane tickets.*

Nadia glanced toward the photographs hanging by the door, but her eyes stopped on Libby's dresser. The boxes were askew; the backside of each wasn't perfectly lined up with the wall.

"What happened?" Nadia asked, as Libby came out of the bathroom.

"Well, if you must know, I peed."

Nadia laughed. "Not that, *that*!" She pointed to the dresser.

"Did you borrow something?" Libby asked.

"No way. I know better than to mess with your system."

"Are you sure? Because I don't mind if you did."

"I promise it wasn't me."

Libby turned toward Nadia, her face pale. "Someone's been in our room."

"Why would someone come into our room?"

"I don't know, but I guarantee I didn't leave it like this, and you didn't touch it, right?" Nadia shook her head. "Check your things." Libby rushed to her desk and pulled open the top drawer. Just as quickly, she pushed it shut. She examined the boxes lining the dresser, then her dresser drawers.

Nadia opened her jewelry box. She didn't have anything worth stealing, except maybe the earrings from Jack. "Thank goodness." She slipped them on. "I would've been devastated if these had been stolen."

"Nothing seems to be missing," Libby said. "What do you think happened?"

Nadia thought for a moment about the surveillance equipment she'd seen over the weekend. *But why would anyone want to listen to our conversations?*

She'd promised Sensei she wouldn't discuss their lesson, and in any case, she didn't want Libby to panic. "I don't know. I'm sure it's nothing," she said finally. "Let's go to lunch."

They found the guys at their usual table. "Someone was in our room," Libby said breathlessly, the instant she sat down.

"For real?" asked Damon.

"You wouldn't know anything about that, would you, Alan?" Nadia asked, spreading her napkin in her lap.

"Why would I?"

"It wouldn't be the first time you were in our room."

"That's my boy!" Damon laughed. "You were in their room? How did you pull it off and *what* were you doing?"

Alan glared at Nadia. Obviously he hadn't told Damon about his awkward confession.

Knowing Alan's inability to lie, Nadia did it for him. "Dropping off Libby's wrap after the dance."

"Hold up. You risked getting expelled over a sweater? What were you thinking?" Damon shook his head. "We need to talk, 'cause I tell you what: if I show up at Nadia's door in the middle of the night, it's not gonna be about a sweater."

Damon took a bite and Alan scowled.

Nadia winced and mouthed, "Sorry."

"So how do you know someone was in your room?" Damon asked.

"My dresser was out of order," Libby answered. "As you can imagine, I'm fairly particular about my things. And I don't mind telling you, I feel violated."

"What's the big deal?" Alan asked. "It was probably some girl on your hall."

"Doing what?" Libby asked.

Alan shrugged. "How should I know?"

Nadia took a few quick bites of her salad, then pushed away from the table. "I need to stop by the dojo. I'll see you guys in class."

Nadia found Sensei in the meditation room. She waited in silence until he'd finished.

"You are not in uniform," Sensei said, before turning to face her.

"Can I talk to you about something?" she asked, her face suddenly hot.

"Of course."

Nadia hesitated. "I think someone was in our room this morning, uninvited." She felt foolish saying it out loud.

"Why would you think that?"

"Um," she hesitated. "Libby's dresser—"

He nodded. "Enough said." He studied her face for a moment, his dark eyes unwavering. "What do you need from me?"

"Well, it doesn't look like anything was taken, so I'm thinking maybe something was left behind," she said tentatively.

"Ah. You wish to sweep your room," he replied, not quite a question, not quite a fact.

"I was wondering if you'd lend me a piece of equipment for counter-surveillance. I could bring it right back," Nadia continued, gaining confidence. He hadn't laughed at her—that was a good sign.

He paused another moment before answering. "Come with me."

They walked down the south wing to the covert-ops room. Nadia looked away as he entered his code, even though she'd already seen it, and made a mental note to look up the definition. She was curious what *abunai* meant, mostly because she was curious about Sensei.

Inside, he opened the second cabinet. "This is easy to use. Anything within a six foot radius will elicit a signal. The closer you are to the listening device, the faster it beeps." He flipped the switch and the machine beeped. He shut it off and opened the first cabinet, full of surveillance equipment.

"I must have left something on the other day." He frowned. Nadia imagined he was not accustomed to mistakes. He flipped the switch and pointed the device at the shelves. The beeping continued.

Sensei set the gadget aside and checked the equipment he'd shown her over the weekend. "I do not see it. I do not understand." He searched the cabinet once more, then turned to Nadia. Leaning against the wall, he stared at her for a long moment. His eyebrows knitted together. Then, slowly, they relaxed. His mouth opened and he nodded. Sensei put one finger to his lips and motioned her into the hall.

He followed her out and closed the metal door behind them. He tried the device again. The beeping resumed. He swept her feet, up her legs and torso, down her arms, then her head. The machine made a continuous noise, like the sound of a flat-line on a heart monitor. Sensei turned it off and noiselessly removed her earrings. He made a gesture, indicating she should wait, and jogged up the hall with her jewelry. Seconds later he returned and checked her again. Silence.

"Have you always had those earrings?"

She shook her head. "They were a gift from Jack Felkin."

He nodded. "Nadia-san, is there a chance your boyfriend might be spying on you?" he asked gently.

"No way. I mean, he's not even really my boyfriend. We've only gone out a couple of times." *Why would he even suggest that?* "And the earrings were in my room this morning. Anyone could have bugged them, right?" Quietly she asked, "You know him, what do you think?"

"I would be surprised. Jack is a promising student, a hard worker. But a clever hawk hides his talons. Perhaps he planted a listening device as your suitor, not as a spy."

"Why would he? I mean, I'm sure he's much more secure in this relationship than I am. Anyway, why would he need to break into my room to bug them? He could've done it when he gave them to me, and someone was *definitely* in our room."

A thought flickered, a quick warning. She couldn't quite put her finger on it. *Jack does ask about the earrings a lot. But that's because they mean something to him, right?*

She continued, her conviction weakened. "Jack wouldn't violate my trust. I don't think. He certainly wouldn't risk getting expelled just to find out if I like him." If he was caught in her room, he'd be out, no questions asked. And his loyalty to the Academy was unquestionable. He could be the poster boy for Desert Mountain.

"It does seem unlikely he would jeopardize his position at the Academy." He handed her the device. "Take this with you. If this is a professional job there will be more. Bring it back when you are confident your environment is secure. You are comfortable sweeping the room?"

She nodded.

"No one must know you have this. I showed you the covert-ops room under special circumstances. I trust you will respect the confidential nature of our lesson."

"Yes, of course."

"Nadia-san, there is something else I must tell you." His gaze remained steady. "The director of the CIA received reliable intelligence that a trainee had been recruited as a double agent before he—or she—arrived on campus. Director Vincent also suspects the student is not working alone. He requested I keep watch for unusual activity. I am quite certain we have *at least* one double, and I am not the only person looking for him."

"Wait a minute. Are you saying someone thinks it's me?" she asked. "Someone bugged my room because they think *I'm* the double?"

"This I do not know," he answered quietly.

"But that's crazy. Why would I be a suspect?"

"I am afraid I cannot answer that question, either."

Nadia paused. Alan's intel about the double was accurate. *What if . . .* "Sensei, do you know anything about Drew? Is it true she was murdered?"

"It seems possible. I will give you a stun gun to keep in your room."

"Why do I need a stun gun?" Her voice was erratic. "Do you think I'm in danger?"

"For peace of mind," he said. "If I thought you were in danger I would give you a tranquilizer gun. Though it would be of little help to *you*."

His joke barely registered as she asked, "You don't think it's me, do you?"

"If I believed you were guilty, I would not give you a weapon. I trust you as you trust me. You have never given me reason to doubt your allegiance, and in fact have proven your dedication to me and your studies time and again. I am confident in your loyalties." Sensei paused for a moment. "Nadia-san, you must always be ready to defend yourself. This is why I insisted we continue individual instruction. So when the time comes, you can protect yourself and those around you. When I was half your age, I lost my father. Had I known what you know now, he would likely still be alive."

Shock registered on her face before she could stop it. "Hashimoto Sensei, I—"

"Wait in the lobby; I will return your earrings." His curt nod indicated the conversation was over.

In the front room, Nadia slumped onto a floor cushion and leaned against the wall. Somewhere in the dojo a radio blared, then silence.

She pulled at a curl in her ponytail and tried to calm herself. *So what if someone thinks I'm the double? What's the worst that could happen?* Her heart pounded against her chest. She'd be questioned, but of course she'd be clean. *They'd need evidence. Right?* Sensei believed in her; that had to count for something. He'd never shared anything personal before. Was that a sign of respect? A warning?

She remembered what Dr. Cameron said about the Patriot Act. They could legally detain her for as long as they wanted. She hugged her knees and lowered her head. *What would happen to my parents? What would the Academy tell them?*

Sensei appeared with the stun gun. "I have removed the device. Here are your earrings."

53 JACK
TUESDAY, NOVEMBER 29

Tuesday morning, Jack waited on the sidewalk in front of the library. He paced for a while, swore, tried the front door for the third time. The morning brightened and he slipped on his sunglasses. Finally, Dr. Wilson arrived.

"Morning, Jack. You know I don't open for another half hour?"

"I was hoping I could sneak in a little early." Jack took her briefcase, freeing her hand to unlock the door.

"The cipher computer again?" she asked as they entered the building.

"No, ma'am, the language lab."

"Sure, go on in. You know where the lights are, right?"

"Yes, thanks," Jack answered.

He fired up the computer in case she came to check on him, then removed the American lit book from his bag. He turned on the recorder.

Nadia was talking to her friends; he fast-forwarded the tape. The next conversation was between her and Hashimoto Sensei. *Finally.*

She was telling him someone had been in her room—but nothing was missing. *Good, that means she hasn't noticed the boarding pass.* It also meant Jack could return the ticket before she realized he'd taken it.

Sensei offered her a piece of counter-surveillance equipment. Then shuffling, a beeping sound, and silence. Jack pressed the headphones against his ears, trying to decipher the noises. Without warning, deafening music blasted through the speakers. He yanked the headphones off and turned down the volume. Ears still ringing, he listened again. Nothing but static.

He couldn't figure out why Sensei would crank music in the dojo. Then it dawned on him. A warm rush spread through his body. *He needed the noise to mask the sound while he destroyed my equipment.* Jack tried to take a breath. He couldn't fill his lungs. The lack of oxygen left him lightheaded and dizzy.

They found the bug. Nadia and Sensei found the bug.

Jack trudged down the sidewalk to the Dean's office to update him regarding the holiday break. Now that Nadia knew she'd been bugged and he still had no concrete evidence, he really regretted not asking permission for aggressive surveillance.

Jack stopped in front of Hopi Hall. He rubbed the tip of his loafer against the stairs until scratches appeared on the toe, then looked at the palm leaves bending above his head.

Stop stalling.

He forced himself inside. Down the hall, Wolfe's door was closed. Jack knocked softly and leaned his ear against the dark wood. "In a minute," the Dean called.

The glass-covered bookshelves surrounded him like soldiers. His eyes glazed over. He felt sick imagining what Dean Wolfe would say.

After several endless minutes, the door opened. "Have a seat."

"Was the disc I intercepted helpful?" Jack asked, hoping for a positive start to the conversation.

Dean Wolfe either didn't hear or chose to ignore the question. He walked around the edge of the room, smoothing the fringe of his Persian rug with his foot. He didn't look at Jack as he spoke. "Do you have any new information?"

"Yes sir, I do. I have reason to believe Nadia took a trip out of the country over the holiday."

"Where did she go?" He did not sound particularly interested.

"Vancouver."

"Vancouver, Canada? Not exactly the Mecca of the underworld." Dean Wolfe chuckled.

"No, sir. But she specifically told me she didn't leave campus last weekend."

The Dean abandoned his task and sat next to Jack. "Lying to your boyfriend about your plans over the holiday isn't really the kind of evidence I'm looking for." Dean Wolfe smiled a kind, fatherly smile. "Do you have any other information?"

Jack's face burned with embarrassment. *He thinks I'm reporting that my girlfriend lied to me. Can't he see this is important?*

Jack considered for a moment what the consequences might be for his unsanctioned behavior. He'd planted a piece of surveillance equipment, broken into her room and stolen a ticket stub she'd deliberately tried to hide. He couldn't tell Wolfe about the cipher text without revealing how he'd found it, nor could he tell him about Nadia discovering she was being watched—*or* that her first stop was her handling agent, Hashimoto Sensei.

I need more evidence. Then he'll see her Canadian trip wasn't a vacation. He'll reward my initiative, rather than reprimand me for making such a colossal mistake—what was I thinking, taking the ticket? I'll put it back. He'll never have to know I was there more than once.

"Listen, son." Dean Wolfe seemed to be carefully considering his words. "Perhaps it's time to pass this assignment along to someone else."

"What? No!" Jack quickly composed himself. "Sir, I don't think that's necessary."

"I'm not blaming you. Maybe you're not her type? Perhaps we should bring Noah into the fold."

"Dean Wolfe—"

"It's nothing personal."

"Sir, with a little more time, I'm *sure* I can get you what you need."

The Dean sighed and leaned back in his chair. He stared at Jack for a long moment. "All right. You have until Friday."

"Thank you, sir." Jack stood to shake the Dean's hand. "I won't let you down."

Jack caught up with the first years as they filtered through the back gate after their morning run. He leaned against the wall and waited for Nadia. He did his best to look relaxed, but his stomach lurched every time someone rounded the corner. His mouth felt like he'd been licking the hiking trails. He was furious with himself for disappointing Dean Wolfe, not to mention falling for a traitor.

Nadia and Libby walked through the gate together, hands on their hips, panting. "Hey, Jack," Libby said.

"Hi, Libby." His voice sounded strange in his ears. "Hi, Nadia."

"Hey," Nadia said. "What are you doing here?"

"I was at the library and thought I'd come by to say hello. I haven't seen much of you since we got back. Do you want to get together this evening? Maybe—well, you probably don't want to think about a run right now, but we could study together or something." Jack was talking too fast. Winded from speaking, he tried to catch his breath.

"Are you okay?" Nadia asked. She touched her cool hand to his forehead.

"Yeah, I'm a little light-headed. I haven't eaten yet."

"I'd love to get together. Maybe we can practice archery on the lawn?" She made a gesture, like pulling an arrow across a bowstring.

Nadia's words weren't giving anything away. Jack nodded and forced a smile. "Sounds like fun."

She pointed her imaginary weapon at him, closed one eye and released. The arrow pierced his chest. "I gotcha."

We'll see about that.

*　*　*

An hour before dinner, Jack met up with her on the front lawn and waited while she assembled the targets. He shifted his weight from one foot to the other.

Dean Wolfe's faith in him had faltered and the enemy spy might know he was tailing her, but neither was an excuse for letting anxiety take the stronghold. Much of his career in clandestine services would involve deceit, impending danger, the unknown. He couldn't even handle the stress of working from campus—a relatively safe and controlled environment. *I'll never be able to function undercover. I'm a wreck.* Nadia didn't seem the least bit uncomfortable. She concealed her feelings like a pro. He hated that she was constantly one step ahead. Outwitting him at every turn. *She's so much better than me.*

She turned to him and smiled. "I put them close together so we can talk while we shoot."

"Talk about what?"

"Nothing in particular. I just meant talk, like hang out."

He followed Nadia across the lawn. They took a few shots, each landing close to center. Jack stood to Nadia's left, and as they fired he watched her back. Her posture was impeccable. *Why does it have to be her?*

"You're not bad," Nadia said, turning to look at him.

"I was thinking the same thing about you."

They continued for a few more minutes, Nadia apparently concentrating on the task at hand and Jack focused only on Nadia. When he could no longer take the silence, he asked, "Are you okay?"

"Yeah." She dropped her arms and looked at the ground. "Something happened the other day to me and Libby. I guess I'm a little distracted. But I don't want to talk about it right now."

"Are you sure? You can talk to me about anything."

Nadia smiled. "I know. But I need to think about something else for a while."

"You'll let me know if you change your mind?"

Nadia nodded and resumed fire.

54 NADIA
WEDNESDAY, NOVEMBER 30

On Wednesday morning an angry column of clouds rolled over the mountains. By mid-afternoon Phoenix had disappeared under a slate-colored blanket. Nadia and her classmates hurried across campus, heads down, jackets clutched tight. By dinnertime the line between earth and sky was indiscernible.

"Hurry up," Nadia called to Libby through the bathroom door.

"I'm going as fast as I can," Libby answered pleasantly.

Nadia slouched at her desk, scowling, arms crossed. She spent half her life waiting around because Libby refused to leave the room without looking perfect. Nadia groaned out loud. She was so miserable she couldn't stand herself. *Stop taking it out on Libby.* She shoved her hands in her jacket pockets; on the left side, she discovered a note. One of the guys must have slipped it in when they were practicing brush-passes, but she didn't remember wearing her jacket before tonight. She unfolded the paper to reveal a coded message.

She sat up and pulled out a fresh piece of notebook paper. Nadia examined the cipher, jotted down a few possibilities for a key code, then scratched them out. She wrote a couple notes, another possible solution, and then it came to her. She translated the numbers and sat back, staring at the message. *Ah, it's backwards.* She flipped the letters around.

Nadia penciled a line between *t* and *i*, and *s* and *w*. Carefully, she tore the paper between *g* and *b* and rearranged the slips. She rewrote the message on a fresh page: *boy scout is watching*.

"Definitely Alan," she muttered aloud.

"I'm ready," Libby said as she emerged from the bathroom. She'd freshened her makeup and brushed her blond hair over her shoulders.

"You look really nice," Nadia said, feeling less hateful. *Who knew cracking a code could cheer me up?*

"Well that's good, because no one cares what's on the inside, right?"

Nadia smiled. "Hey, did you get hair extensions over Thanksgiving?"

"'Course not. Attach someone else's DNA to my body? The very idea. Why do you ask?"

Nadia pointed to the photographs on the wall. "Your hair looks much shorter in the pictures."

Libby spun around to look at the wall. "Oh *that*. Right. I had a thingie in my hair—you know. It goes around back and kind of puffs up the rear." Libby turned back toward Nadia and pushed on the back of her hair. "See? Makes my hair look shorter in the front. You know the thing, right?" Nadia shook her head. "No? Hmm. Must be a Southern thing. Whatcha got there?" Libby nodded at Nadia's hand.

"Oh. It was in my pocket." Nadia held the note out for Libby.

"Boy scout is watching? What does that mean?"

"I have no idea. I don't always get Alan's jokes."

"I know what you mean. You ready? I could eat a horse."

A few minutes later, the girls met Alan and Damon at their usual table. Before sitting, Nadia tossed the note onto Alan's plate. "I found this in my jacket. I don't get it."

"Do you mind? I am trying to eat." He plucked the paper off his dinner.

"What's it supposed to mean?" Nadia asked.

Alan read the note. "I have no idea; it is not mine."

"Are you sure?"

"Am I sure? Of course I'm sure. I think I would remember writing a cryptic message and hiding it in your coat. Anyway, code is not my thing."

Her chest tightened. "Damon?"

"Sorry, baby girl. I can't help you," he answered. "I am a lot of things, but a boy scout isn't one of them."

"So no one knows anything about this?" Her voice wavered.

"What's the big deal?" Damon asked.

"Nothing," she mumbled. If her friends didn't deliver the message, who did? Maybe it was a warning. Someone trying to tell her she was suspected as the double agent. But the note, buried in her jacket pocket, might've stayed hidden for months. If someone wanted her to find it, they should've put it in a more conspicuous location.

A terrifying thought jumped to her head. Her mouth watered as a wave of nausea flooded her stomach.

"Are you all right?" Libby asked. "You don't look so good."

"I feel sick," Nadia whispered. She dropped her head between her knees. Her breath came quick and shallow. Her heart pounded against her temples as blood rushed to her face.

Maybe it wasn't a warning.

Maybe it was a setup.

The next morning, after a restless, sleepless night, Nadia forced herself out of bed. Tension twisted her muscles into steel cables. The anxiety in her chest pressed against her ribs, squeezed at her heart. She couldn't shake the feeling she was being set up. Thoughts of the note, her missing knife, the phone call, the wiretap—maybe even the Gila monster—snaked in and out of her consciousness.

Am I in danger? Is that why Sensei insisted I continue training? No, if his concerns were more than fleeting thoughts, he'd take proactive measures to protect her. Of course he wanted her well trained—she was joining the CIA's Black-Ops Division.

During her morning run, exhausted from lack of sleep, Nadia mentally evaluated her friends. Libby had infinite access to Nadia's things. But Nadia had access to Libby as well. *If she was up to something, I'd know. Wouldn't I?* Libby's behavior had been a little unusual lately; more obsessive cleaning, talking too fast. Nothing alarming, but enough that Nadia had noticed.

During the dead drop exercises in October, Damon had demonstrated his proficiency at sleight-of-hand. In fact, he was good at everything spy-related: the way he could read people at superhuman speed, his quick mind, his surveillance skills. *But can I blame him? He believes ignoring one tiny detail got his brother killed.* To Damon, the power of observation meant life or death. *Plus, he really shared himself with me.* No, she and Damon had a definite connection. If he was going to frame someone, it wouldn't be her.

Alan was hiding something. Something big. She could feel it. Every time the two of them got past superficial layers of conversation, he clammed up. *But he couldn't engineer such a complex scheme.* His poker face was nonexistent.

Nadia considered confiding in Jack. She trusted him—for the most part. But he was her team leader. He would be required to report anything she said to Dean Wolfe. What if this was all part of an elaborate training exercise? If she couldn't handle the pressure she'd be cut from the program immediately.

At least it was Thursday, which meant a light class load and only a few weeks until winter break. Thinking about the holidays on the way back to her dorm reminded her: she'd left her passport in the covert-ops room over the weekend. She trekked back to the dojo and, after enduring a lengthy lecture on caring for her valuable belongings, collected her ID and returned to her room to get changed.

After breakfast, Nadia and Libby walked to Diplomacy. Nadia sank into her chair and opened her bag. "Oh no. I don't believe it!" She slammed back in her seat. "I left my stupid paper on my desk."

"You know, honey, I don't mean to pour salt in the wound, but it just takes a second to file your things away."

Nadia glanced at the clock. "Do you think I have time to get it?"

"Hurry up. I'll tell Dr. Moran why you're late."

Nadia sprinted across the lawn, through the lobby of her dorm and down the hall, key in hand. She unlocked the door and charged to her desk to grab the paper. As she turned back toward the hall, movement caught her eye. A shadow behind the door. Nadia drew a sharp breath.

Without thinking, she lunged toward her nightstand and grabbed the stun gun. Her voice shook as she said, "I have a weapon. Come out slowly. Hands over your head."

Stillness settled on the room. Nadia crept toward the hall. When she got close enough, using all her strength, she side-kicked the door.

A gasp as the door slammed into a body.

"All right!" he called. "Put down your weapon."

She knew the voice.

Jack slunk out from behind the door.

Her heart beat furiously. "You scared me to death! What are you doing here?" She lowered the gun as relief eased through her body.

"I came by to drop off a note."

"Why didn't you leave it at the front desk?" She felt like an idiot, assaulting her boyfriend like a cage fighter. *Overreact much?*

"I wanted to put it on your pillow. To surprise you." He was breathing fast. She must've startled him, too.

She shook her head. "You risked getting expelled to leave me a note?"

"Nadia, I . . . I'm in love with you. I had to tell you—I couldn't wait any longer."

The urgency in his voice flattered her. She opened her mouth, then closed it. Smiled at him. Finally, "I don't know what to say."

Like a chameleon, his face changed. "That's why I'm here." His forehead relaxed, his eyes softened and he returned her smile. He moved toward her, reaching for her hands. "To tell you I love you."

Earlier Thursday morning, just after sunrise, the student left school through the back gate. Slipping off the trail that time of day was no easy task, but his options were limited. He hiked about a mile from campus and pulled out his cell.

His contact answered, "Yes."

"Where do we stand since Thanksgiving? What happened with the ticket?"

"It wasn't enough. This has dragged on far longer than necessary. It's time for the elimination," the older man said.

"Wait. I think that would be a mistake."

"You don't get paid to think. You get paid to act."

"Yeah, you mentioned that a time or two. But if we kill her, the CIA will be forced to investigate. We will draw *more* attention, not less."

"Listen, if she disappears, all suspicions about a traitor go with her. We'll plant evidence in her room; the CIA gets their double and everyone's happy. We'll make it look like her own people betrayed her."

The student glanced over his shoulder. "If we are planting evidence, we should keep her alive. Let the CIA question her. She knows nothing about us."

"It's a lot easier to frame a corpse. Anyway, the hit's been ordered. This comes from higher up."

"Why her? Maybe it can be someone else."

The man snorted. "Like who?"

"Maybe a guy? I never have access to the girls."

"We aren't interested in switching horses midstream."

"Well," the student stammered. "I need help. I can't do it on my own."

"Why can't you do it? Did you get too attached?"

"No," he said. *Yes,* he thought. *I cannot kill her. I refuse.*

"Do you remember what we did for you?"

"You know what?" the student asked. "You caused this mess—begging me to meet you in the middle of the night because you were unable to complete a simple dead drop, killing Drew after she saw us, then *talking* about it. I have no choice but to call Phoenix."

"Do not go over my head on this or you will regret it," the older man warned.

"Who do you think this is? Do you take me for an idiot? I have an insurance policy of my own, you know."

"I'm not sure I understand what you're saying."

"Let me speak slowly so you can follow along: I have every telephone conversation—including this one—on tape. I have documents, orders, fingerprints, photographs. I am the Library of freaking Congress. Do what you need to do, but know this: You take me down, I will drag all of you down with me. So save your threats for someone else." He ended the call and sat in the dirt.

The situation had spun out of control. Someone had to go down for this. Sure, he cared for Nadia—more than he should, but not so much he was willing to spend the rest of his life in jail convicted of treason. And if the CIA got called in, anything could happen. *But killing her makes no sense.*

The student took a deep breath and dialed headquarters.

"Hawkins' Insurance, how may I direct your call?" the receptionist asked.

"Agent Identification Number 77365," he answered.

"Please hold."

A moment later, the gruff voice of his handler's boss, Agent Roberts, said, "What do you need?"

"My contact is panicking. Adding to the body count is a serious mistake. It will draw more attention and prolong the investigation."

"What do you suggest?"

"Evidence in Riley's room. A dead drop obviously meant for her. Pretty much any other course of action. Another hit is excessive and unnecessary."

"Did you talk to your contact about this?"

"I tried, but he refused to listen."

There was a long pause. "I understand your reluctance. You're fairly new. If you can't get the job done, it's okay—*this* time. We can send someone to walk you through it."

"It's not about that." It was partly about that. But the thought of anyone killing Nadia sickened him. "This is a *mistake*."

Roberts' voice hardened as he said, "This is not your call."

Careful. "Yes sir. I understand."

Another long pause. "I will consider your opinion."

"Yes sir. Thank you."

"In the meantime, lay low. There's enough heat on your end as is. We'll have a decision within the week." Agent Roberts hung up.

The student nodded to himself. *Roberts is a reasonable man. He will retract the hit order, and we can continue as before with a frame job.*

Of course he knew this day would come sooner or later. But it never occurred to him he would care so much for the target.

He stood and brushed the dust from his pants. *I wish it could be someone else.*

The CIA knew about a double agent on campus because some girl needed ice cream in the middle of the night. *Shooting her was a mistake. He could have knocked her out, blown up the car; made it look like an accident.* But his contact claimed that would not do—

some hero-wannabe passing by might pull her from the flames. As ordered, the student had rolled down his car window. He watched silently as the shooter squatted beside the car.

I had no choice. All I did was lower a window. He popped the battery off the back of the phone and hurled it into the desert, then pulled out the memory card.

He was in too deep to give up now.

56 NADIA
THURSDAY, DECEMBER 1

Ten different emotions competed for Nadia's attention. Relief, joy, confusion, disbelief—all fighting against the wave of adrenaline that had just flooded her body. She wanted to tell Jack how she felt about him. How happy she was, how much he meant to her. That she was totally falling for him. She opened her mouth to speak, but something stopped her.

Something didn't feel right. She couldn't identify her trepidation, but something was definitely off. He moved toward her, his hands seeking hers. And then she realized what she'd seen: a micro-expression that flashed so quickly across his face she almost missed it. His transformation was too sudden. From scared of his overwhelming emotions, to . . . self-satisfaction. That's what was wrong—he looked smug. Nadia narrowed her eyes. "Let me read the note."

"I—I haven't written it yet," he stammered.

She took a step back. "Why are you here? In my room?" *Unless . . .* Slowly, the pieces fell together. The bugged earrings, the intercepted dead drop.

Jack was framing her. He'd come to plant evidence.

"It was you," she whispered. "You're the one who broke in. You stalked me on my solo and stole my knife—I knew I didn't lose it! The wiretap, the coded message—it was all you." Her legs weakened. She wanted to sit down, to put the fight on hold until feeling returned to her lower body.

But Jack moved forward. "You betrayed your country. For what? Money? Power? I found the cipher in your jacket. *Boy scout is watching.* I know it was about me. Am I being followed? Is that how you knew I was here?"

"You're the double," Nadia said. "You tried to frame me."

"Give it a rest! I know it's you. Wolfe knows it's you. And we know who your handler is, so don't even think about taking me out—there's no way you'd get away with it. I found your plane ticket." Jack clutched a small slip of paper. "Who'd you meet in Canada?"

He's not here to kill me or I'd be dead by now. The thought gave her enough courage to step forward. "Give me that." Nadia wrenched the ticket from his hand. "You forged this."

"Are you kidding me? It's over. We've got you," Jack said. His eyes flashed with anger.

"Oh yeah? Then explain this!" She pulled her passport from her dresser and threw it at his head. He flinched as it bounced off his temple. "Do you see a Canadian seal anywhere? You forged a plane ticket, but you couldn't fake a customs seal because my passport was locked up at the dojo!"

Jack opened her passport and rapidly flipped through the pages. He searched it again, this time carefully scanning each page. Closing the booklet, he held it in both hands. He stared at the cover. Then, in a low voice, he said, "You could have used a fake passport."

"But I put the ticket in my real name? That doesn't even make sense. Oh, I'm such an idiot—I can't believe I trusted you." Nadia gasped as she remembered the dead girl. "Oh my God! You killed Drew!"

"Of course I didn't kill Drew. I'm not the double, Nadia." Jack tossed the passport onto her desk and rubbed his forehead. "And I'm starting to think maybe you're not, either."

"Prove it," Nadia challenged.

Jack hesitated. "Fine." He paused again. "Dean Wolfe assigned me to you."

"What does that mean?"

"He ordered me to watch you. He had reason to believe a double agent infiltrated the student body, and you were a suspect. You were *the* suspect."

She closed her eyes. *Oh my God. That's why he's been dating me.* The realization felt like a kick to the stomach. *And I almost told him how I feel about him.*

She squared her shoulders, refusing to give him the satisfaction of seeing her humiliation. "I'm sure he'll be happy to confirm your story. We'll go to his office right now." Nadia pointed to the door.

They crossed campus together, arm-in-arm, the stun-gun pressed into Jack's rib cage. One click of a button and he'd be convulsing on the ground. When they reached Hopi Hall, Nadia hid the weapon against her back to protect Sensei.

Dean Wolfe waved them in. "Why aren't you two in class?"

Nadia's face still burned with anger and embarrassment. "Jack broke into my room. He said he was acting under your orders."

"I didn't say he ordered me to break into your room. I said he instructed me to keep an eye on you," Jack said.

"Semantics," Nadia snapped.

"You were in her room?" Dean Wolfe asked with a look of disbelief on his face. "Why, Jack? Why were you in her room?"

Jack mumbled an answer as he stared at his lap.

"What was that?"

"Sir, I was looking for evidence."

"Dean Wolfe." Nadia struggled to control her voice. "Did you authorize Jack to place surveillance equipment on me?"

The Dean sighed heavily. "I did not." He looked at Jack, one eyebrow raised.

"I put a listening device in her earrings," Jack said, answering the unasked question.

Dean Wolfe leaned his head into his open palm and closed his eyes.

"Why do you think I'm a double agent?" Nadia asked.

He sat back and crossed his arms, studying her for a long moment. "Your test scores were impeccable. You did too well, as though you knew the questions before the test was administered."

Nadia shook her head. "But I—"

He held up his hand. "No one is above suspicion at this time. You were specifically chosen from a wide applicant pool and some-one pushed hard for your admittance. If you had come in with the rest of the students, instead of as a transfer, it might not have seemed so suspicious, but the combination of factors raised a red flag," Dean Wolfe gently explained. "We needed a starting point."

"But it's not me," she said, annoyed that her voice sounded like a little girl's. "Someone is trying to make it look like me." She turned to Jack. "Did you plant evidence in my room to score points with the Dean?"

"How could you even ask me that? I would never do that. I didn't *want* it to be you."

"Dean Wolfe, Jack found a plane ticket to Canada in my room, but I didn't go to Canada. He checked my passport—tell him," she ordered.

"That's what it looks like," Jack said.

"Nadia, although Jack was admittedly overzealous in his assignment, I do not believe he is trying to frame you. Having said that, it seems someone else might be. For your protection, I will have additional cameras installed in your dorm."

"In my room?" Nadia winced.

"Of course not. In the lobby and hallway. If anyone tries to break in, we'll know."

"Can we call the CIA?" she asked. "Tell them we have this evi-dence? Get some agents on campus? Maybe they can run forensic tests or something."

"I will send the ticket stub and any other evidence to the lab.

But if we bring agents onto campus, we show our hand and lose the only shot we have of catching these guys. I know this is a tremendous request, but if we don't catch the double, the CIA will be forced to scrap the entire training program. Our higher-ups will reason if one double agent can get in, many can. Nadia, are you able to serve your country?"

Oh Nadia, no big deal, but the future of our nation's security rests in your hands.

"Yes, of course," she answered miserably.

"Wait a minute." Jack turned to her. "If it's not you, why'd you get a dead drop at the dance?"

Nadia's cheeks burned hotter as she thought about the dance. His kiss. How real it had seemed. *I'm so stupid—as far as he's concerned, our entire relationship was an assignment.* "Because I'm being framed! The waiter told me to drop the disc in the trash can. He said it was a quiz or something."

Jack narrowed his eyes. Nadia could see him processing, replaying the events in his head.

"You sure were eager to find evidence against me," she whispered.

"What would you have done? I mean, that phone call? With the rook?"

"Given you the benefit—"

"Okay, listen, you two," the Dean broke in. "We still have a double agent on campus. Evidently, Nadia, it is not you. However, we have no leads. If the double is watching you he may know that Jack is . . . monitoring you as well. Therefore, you are not, under any circumstances whatsoever, to discuss this conversation with anyone. You are to carry on exactly as before. This never happened. Do I make myself clear?"

"Yes sir," Jack said.

Nadia looked away before she answered, "Yes sir."

"Nadia, I don't believe you are in physical danger. To successfully infiltrate our intelligence program, the double needs to remain anonymous."

"What about Drew?" she asked quietly.

"At this point in our investigation, it seems Drew's death was unrelated. I assure you, your safety is very important to me. If I felt you were in harm's way I would place you in protective custody," he said. "All right, you're dismissed. I expect you both to return to classes at once."

Jack held the door for her as they left the Dean's office. In the sitting room he said, "Listen, Nadia, I'm sorry about everything. I knew in my heart it wasn't you." He put his hand on his chest for emphasis. "I just knew it. Now we can put this behind us. Start fresh. I really do care about you."

Nadia struggled to remain calm. She held her fists behind her back, resisting the urge to strike. She looked at his nose, his throat, his solar plexus, counting the ways she could kill him. She took a deep breath, stepped forward and jabbed her finger into his chest. Through clenched teeth she whispered, "Do not *ever* speak to me again."

57 JACK
THURSDAY, DECEMBER 1

Jack's chest burned as his feet pounded against the packed earth. His wet shirt clung to his back. He sprinted through the darkness. The trail curved around the back wall. He ignored the gate and started another lap.

So much for credibility with the dean. I botched my entire career before graduating. My first real assignment and I completely blew it.

I didn't even get the girl.

He thought if he ran hard enough, long enough, he'd be able to forget this morning, go to his room and collapse. It was the only way he'd sleep tonight.

Jack remembered Wolfe's remark after he delivered the intercepted disc. "Jack, I'm impressed." He groaned out loud. *I humiliated myself in front of him—and Nadia.*

He stopped running when he reached the gate. As he walked to his room he wondered if he could ever win back Nadia's trust. *I really liked her—before I suspected her of treason.*

Earlier, when they'd left the Dean's office, she'd said, "You fabricated our entire relationship. I was your *mission*. I meant nothing to you."

"That's not true. I was devastated when I thought you were guilty. When I saw the dead drop at the dance, I tried to explain it away, to give you the benefit of the doubt, but how could I?"

"You gave me those earrings before the dance, hours before the dead drop, so don't pretend that's when you first became suspicious. Nobody bugs someone unless they think it'll pay off. You thought I was guilty before we even met!" When she was angry her eyes turned the color of summer moss.

"I was ordered to watch you. I thought the wiretap would clear your name!"

She'd been standing close enough for him to smell the faint coconut of her shampoo. Her face reddened as she whispered, "You heard me talking to Libby about you." In that moment he'd felt her slip away, like an iceberg breaking off into the ocean. He'd wanted to stop it, but he didn't know how.

Jack wiped the sweat from his forehead and went through the lobby of the boys' dorm. Down the hall, tacked to his door, he found a pink message slip. Noah had scribbled, "Dean Wolfe wants to see you in his office right away."

Jack's stomach dropped. He glanced at his watch as he ran back down the hall—after 2100 hours. *He must be furious to stay this late. I'm getting expelled.*

Jack climbed the steps of Hopi Hall like a man walking to the electric chair. He plodded toward Wolfe's office, knocked on the open door.

"Jack, thanks for coming in."

"I'm sorry you've been waiting. I went for a run and just got your message."

"It's fine. Sit down." He pointed to the wingback chairs.

Here it comes.

"Listen, about this afternoon." Dean Wolfe leaned back. He tapped his pen on the desk.

He's going to tell me to pack my things. My life is over.

"I owe you an apology. I should've been more specific about what was acceptable and what was not."

Jack's mouth hung open as he stared at Dean Wolfe. "What?"

"I regret I wasn't clear."

"Dean Wolfe, I'm the one who's sorry." Jack sat forward on the edge of his chair. "I know I should've gotten permission ahead of time. In my haste to protect the Academy, I didn't bother with the proper channels."

"Well, you saw an opportunity and you acted. Unfortunately, it was the wrong decision. But you showed determination and initiative, and that's important."

"Thank you, sir."

"You understand bugging a fellow student—or breaking into someone's room—is a violation of both school policy and that person's civil rights, correct?"

"Yes sir." Jack nodded. *Well, I do now.*

"Nevertheless, I feel somewhat accountable for your actions. My request lacked explicit instruction, and I probably put too much pressure on you earlier this week when I suggested making a change. I trust nothing like this will ever happen again?"

"No, absolutely not. Thank you. I'm very sorry." Jack scooted back in his seat and relaxed into the leather.

"There is one more thing." Wolfe paused. "Close the door."

Jack jumped from his chair and shut the door. He sat back down.

"Nadia caught you in her room. She discovered she was under investigation. If she is the double, she had no choice but to march you over here and confront us. Claiming innocence doesn't exonerate her, and I'm not convinced she's clean. After ordering you two to continue as before, it doesn't make sense to reassign the case. I need you to stay on assignment."

"Absolutely. I'll do my best," Jack answered automatically. Though thrilled with Dean Wolfe's continued trust, the idea that Nadia might still be guilty caused a sinking feeling in his stomach. He hesitated before asking, "Do you have any other leads?"

"Nadia remains our primary suspect. We've had concerns about Marcus Sloan before. His itinerary doesn't always—" He shook his head and stopped. "I specifically told him I was not interested in Nadia Riley. He ignored my apprehension. It's as though he has some personal stake in her attending the Academy."

Jack remained quiet.

"I think that's all for this evening."

Jack stood and extended his arm. "Thank you."

"I'll see you soon."

Jack let himself out and closed the door. He leaned against the wood and exhaled. His eyes stung. *A second chance. I didn't ruin my life.*

In the morning, I'll redouble my efforts. I've got to find something for Dean Wolfe.

Back in his room, Jack took a twenty-minute shower. He stepped out into the steam-filled bathroom, wiped the mirror with his towel and studied his reflection. He couldn't stop thinking about Nadia, about what the Dean had said—something didn't fit.

She couldn't get to Canada without a passport, and I checked her passport myself. If she didn't take that trip, someone planted evidence to make it look like she did. And why would she keep a ticket stub? She could've flushed it down the toilet. Unless she didn't know it was there.

He squeezed the middle of his toothpaste tube and stuck the brush in his mouth.

The cryptic phone call before the dance talked about a meet. He wondered, though. Nadia didn't seem to acknowledge she understood the message. *But would she? She'd play dumb, right? In case it was being recorded.* But the whole thing—it was sloppy work. Why would she allow her coworkers to contact her on a public telephone?

The dead drop—that incriminated her, for sure. Jack had read the disc himself. *But if it's a frame job, of course it would contain actual information, right? And the disc wasn't even encrypted.*

He spat in the sink and rinsed his mouth. *Maybe I should trust my gut—I thought she was innocent from the start. Well, until I didn't. Then I threw her under the bus.*

I'm going to make a horrible agent.

58 NADIA
FRIDAY, DECEMBER 2

"Nadia-san, the world of espionage is a fragile house of smoke and sand. It slips between your fingers, disappears into air. From now on, illusion and deceit are your companions; intelligence and stealth your weapons," Sensei said as they concluded Friday's lesson. "In the future, you would be wise to remember: when the tiger smiles, it is not because he wants to be your friend."

Nadia covered her face with her hands. "Is that your version of I-told-you-so?" Against Wolfe's orders, she'd relayed the whole story to Sensei. How Jack had strung her along so he could spy on her, how she confronted him, how they'd gone to the Dean. She was so embarrassed she couldn't even make eye contact. This was worse than Matthew and Paige. Worse than that ridiculous party. And she brought it on herself, trusting Jack, being so gullible. *People only take advantage if you let them.*

She'd always believed herself to be a relatively decent judge of character. Sure, she'd made some bad calls—trusting Paige, for example. But she'd hated Matthew when they first met. She found him arrogant and superficial. If she'd stuck with her initial impression she wouldn't have gone out with him, her friendship with Paige would still be intact and she wouldn't be here at Desert Mountain, absolutely humiliated, yet again. After everything with Jack, how could she ever trust her instincts? "I'm such an idiot."

"Look at me!" Sensei ordered. "You are lucky to learn this lesson early in your studies, on such a trivial matter." He gestured dismissively. "He is only a boy. I, too, learned this lesson early, but with the gravest of consequences." A shadow crossed his face; for a moment, Nadia read perfectly what ran through his mind.

"Hashimoto Sensei, what happened to your father?"

His spine stiffened as his expression hardened. "I do not answer personal questions," he said quietly.

"Forgive me," she said, and lowered her head.

A moment later, he spoke. "My decision to leave Asia, to train agents for the CIA, was a difficult one, born of tragedy and betrayal." Nadia raised her head. Sensei turned away as he continued. "We lived in Lhasa, Tibet. My father was a member of the Tibetan resistance fighters, secretly trained by the CIA." Sensei sighed deeply. "He gave his life to secure the escape of Tibet's spiritual leader." He turned his eyes toward Nadia. Looked through her. "Together we crossed the Himalayas. A terrible storm raged. Eventually, we reached the Indian border. But we were miles from our original extraction point, where we had planned to meet his partner. My father secured safe passage for our party, but he stayed behind. His ethical code forbade him to seek refuge without his friend. He insisted, for my safety, that I travel on. I never saw him again."

"Oh no."

"I later learned his partner betrayed us; his loyalties were purchased by the Chinese. If my father had been better trained, if I had been better equipped to sense danger, to intuit a traitor, my father might still be alive."

For a few moments she remained silent, deeply touched that he'd confided this personal information. "Hashimoto Sensei, surely you don't believe you are responsible for your father's death? You were a child."

"Nadia-san, if you and I were involved in a conflict, fighting on the same side, and you survived the battle but I did not, would you not feel responsible?"

"But I have been trained. By you, Sensei. Though obviously, not enough. I didn't see what was right in front of my face."

His voice softened. "Do not be so critical. Even monkeys fall from trees."

Nadia nodded. "I know; I have more important things to worry about than my social life. I asked Dean Wolfe to bring in the CIA but he refused. He says we can't let the double know we're on to him."

"I am afraid he is right. But you are a clever young woman, Nadia-san. I have faith in you."

"The worst part is, I have to pretend none of this ever happened. I have to be civil to Jack when I see him." *How could I have let myself fall for him?*

"He is irrelevant. Have you asked yourself the obvious question? If Jack is not setting you up, who is?"

She'd replayed the events a hundred times. Each time, a new suspect arose. And with each new suspect, a dozen reasons why it couldn't possibly be them. She shook her head. "I have no idea."

Sensei's dark eyes were grim as he studied her. "Finding the truth is like chasing echoes through a canyon."

Nadia joined Libby, Alan and Damon in the dining hall for dinner. She poked a fork at her bowl of beef stew, ignoring her friends as they chatted about the weekend's study session. *It could be any of them.*

"You look terrible," Alan said to her. "Are you unwell?"

She glared at him. *He's always undermining me.* "I'm fine."

"You are looking a little green around the gills." Libby pressed her inner wrist against Nadia's forehead. "Maybe you should go lie down?"

Why? Trying to get rid of me?

"You want me to walk you to your dorm?" Damon offered.

"No, I'm fine," she said. *He's been stuck to me like glue all day.* Twice she'd asked him to back up. *Is it Damon? Or is he making a play because I'm mad at Jack?* She hadn't said anything, but he was a mind-reader about stuff like that. "Not that I don't appreciate the attention, but can you scoot your chair over? I'm practically sitting on your lap."

"If you want to sit on my lap that can absolutely be arranged," Damon said, but he moved a few inches to her left.

"Hey, Nadia." Jack's voice startled her. He was always sneaking up from behind. It was incredibly annoying. Probably so he had the height advantage.

Me sitting while he towers above.

"Jack, you want to join us?" Damon reached around Nadia to drag an empty chair to the table.

"There's not really any room," Alan said, spreading his elbows out on the cloth.

"Don't bother, Damon. I'm not staying," Jack answered, glaring at Alan. "Nadia, can I talk to you for a minute?"

"What's up?" she asked, not glancing from her dinner.

"In private?" Jack yanked out her chair and led her to a quiet corner of the room.

When they were out of earshot of the other diners, Nadia whispered, "What do you want?"

"Let's go out to dinner tomorrow night." Jack offered a tiny smile.

Her mouth fell open. "You can't be serious."

"We've been ordered to continue our relationship," Jack said quietly.

"You mean our *farce* of a relationship," she hissed.

"There's no such thing as a perfect romance."

"Do you think that's funny?"

"A little," he said. "Come on, we can at least be friends, right?"

"You want a friend, get a dog."

"Look, we need to go on a date. I thought we could go downtown and grab a bite. I'll help you figure out who's trying to set you up." Jack's voice was serious now. He leaned against the wall and grabbed her hands. He held his head low, tried to meet her eyes. If Nadia didn't know better she would've thought he sounded concerned.

But she did know better. *I hate him. Why does he have to be so hot?* "Get your hands off me," she said softly. "I would rather pull out my own fingernails than go on a date with you."

He flashed an insincere smile as he whispered, "People are watching." Then, much louder, he continued. "Great, Saturday night. Eighteen-hundred?"

"This isn't the military, jackass. You can say six o'clock."

"It's *Jack*. Just Jack. And I can't wait, either." He kissed her cheek and walked away.

Nadia was seething—furious with Dean Wolfe for making her continue this romantic charade, furious with Jack for pretending to care. Giving her earrings, taking her on a date. The kiss at the dance—she'd been so blind.

Nadia left her half-eaten dinner on the table and went to her room. Slipped under her door she found a survival course summons for the following weekend. *Great.* She slammed the door closed and flicked the light switch. The light flashed and popped, then went dark as the bulb burned out.

Of course it did.

She stomped down the hall to Casey's desk for a replacement.

Back in her room, she climbed on Libby's bed to reach the light fixture. The glow from the hallway wasn't bright enough to change the bulb, but Nadia remembered Libby had a flashlight clipped to her keyring.

She found the keys in Libby's top desk drawer. They weren't hard to locate: the drawer was shallow, and Libby's things were laid out neatly, as usual. Nadia tried the flashlight. *And it doesn't work. Why would it?* She flicked the switch a half-dozen times before unscrewing the battery compartment. Something didn't look right. She turned on the bathroom light.

It was a USB drive, carefully concealed as a flashlight. She'd seen thumb drives disguised as all sorts of things: pens, jewelry, children's toys.

Nadia went back to Libby's desk. Something had caught her attention. *What was it?* Something about the drawer.

Nadia pulled everything out and threw it on top of the desk. She ran her hands along the wood. In the back center was a hole. She slipped her index finger inside and lifted—the false bottom released.

One by one, Nadia removed the contents buried deep inside. A chestnut wig, a crisp stack of cash, a pair of glasses. And a driver's license, issued to Amanda Downing. A brunette Libby smiled at her from the photograph.

Oh no. Her stomach churned as she stared at the evidence. *It's Libby.*

"What are you doing?"

Nadia had no idea how long her roommate had been standing in the doorway. If Libby hadn't spoken, she'd never have known she was there.

59 ALAN
FRIDAY, DECEMBER 2

Saba's insistent directives caused a chronic feeling of desperation deep in Alan's solar plexus. He could think of little else. He had called Tel Aviv over the holiday, and it had not gone well. Saba demanded action.

Why Saba insisted he find a girl, Alan still did not know. But Saba had learned Nadia's name, and she was now the focus of all their calls. When Alan asked, "Why Nadia?" Saba had said, "I have my reasons," and refused to comment further. Possibly, Saba had collected a dossier on Alan's schoolmates and specifically chosen Nadia because she was clever. Maybe he regretted allowing Alan to attend Desert Mountain, and now, concerned for his grandson's safety in the field of intelligence, wished to ally him with an exceptional partner. Perhaps Saba did not believe Alan could take care of himself. Or maybe because Nadia's family was insignificant and, regardless of how the relationship ended, there would be no backlash.

Whatever the reason, Alan was in no position to argue. But he needed Jack out of the way.

Alan followed Libby out of the dining hall. He scowled and asked, "What was so important that Jack had to pull Nadia away from her dinner?"

"How should I know? I was with you."

"I am certain she would rather spend time with him than tend to the trivial matters of life, such as food and oxygen, but I do not appreciate having to clear her dishes."

"I'm not sure you're right about that. Something's off between them."

Alan's heart skipped a beat. "Did she tell you that?"

"She didn't have to. It's plain as the nose on your face."

He shook his head. "I did not see anything."

"What *exactly* were you looking at?" Libby stopped in front of her dorm. She just stood there staring at him, so Alan stopped too. "Well?" she asked.

"Well what?"

Libby rolled her eyes. "Forget it." She pulled open the lobby door.

"Did you want me to get that?" Alan called through the glass. *Why do they not ask for what they want?* He continued along the sidewalk, now irritated with Libby. *I am not a mind-reader.*

Alan could not imagine what Boy Wonder had done to aggravate Nadia. Jack checked up on her a lot. Maybe she thought him too possessive. Girls did not like controlling boyfriends—even Alan knew this much.

Once their break-up became official, he would move in. Ask how she was feeling, if she wanted to talk—according to Saba, one thing would lead to another.

Alan entered his dorm. Down the hall, taped to his door, he found a summons from Dr. Cameron. *On a Friday night?* He ripped the message off the door and headed back outside.

A few minutes later, Alan fidgeted in the metal folding chair. "Why do you not put a couch in here? It might help people relax."

"Are you tense?" Dr. Cameron asked.

"No, I simply meant it would be more inviting. You are trying to get people to open up, right?"

"Would you be more comfortable in a softer chair?"

"I believe I would."

Dr. Cameron smiled. "I'll take that into consideration. Alan, I understand you've been tutoring Nadia. I'm proud of you for working as part of a team."

Alan's heart beat faster at the mention of Nadia's name. "Thank you."

"How's it going?"

"Exceptionally well. I am an excellent tutor."

"So you spend a lot of time together?"

"Yes."

"And do you still have concerns about her?"

"She is not very good with languages," Alan said.

"That's not what I mean."

"What *do* you mean?"

"Has she ever done or said anything that troubled you?"

"Yes, as a matter of fact." Alan pursed his lips.

"Well? What?"

"Apparently, she is dating Jack Felkin."

"And?"

"I do not think this is a very wise decision." *Speak properly*, he reminded himself. *Lazy American.*

"Why is that?" Dr. Cameron asked.

Alan shrugged. "I don't know why girls are only interested in seniors. It's not an intelligent long-term plan; they are only on campus for one year." *And it is interfering with my assignment.*

But their relationship was more than an inconvenience.

Much to Alan's irritation, he found himself constantly thinking about Nadia. His feelings had changed from intense dislike to mild interest and ultimately settled on curious infatuation. Closer examination revealed her clever, witty and—he would admit it—very attractive.

The whole situation confused him. He had intended to use her as part of his cover. His orders were to get closer, so he insisted they continue studying together. In truth, she no longer needed his help. Her logical mind made swift deductions regarding human behavior that would never occur to him. And she was extraordinarily intuitive; she knew the instant Alan hedged the truth—even before he broke out in hives.

Dr. Cameron pinched the bridge of his nose and rested his head in his hand. He sighed. "How is Damon?"

"Fine, except a messy roommate. And he claims I talk in my sleep—but I don't believe this is true. He's kind of a flirt, which is annoying."

"Libby?"

"No, he flirts with Nadia more than Libby."

"I meant, how is Libby," Dr. Cameron said.

"Oh. I don't know." He shrugged. "Fine, I guess."

"What do you know about Nadia's family?"

"Nothing. She lives in Virginia. Her parents are married. They are not wealthy. This is about all I know. Why do you ask?"

"Is there anything you'd like to discuss while you're here?"

He hesitated. Maybe Dr. Cameron was asking these questions because he knew Alan was deliberately trying to get close to Nadia. *Was I followed off campus? Has someone reported me? Oh God, for Dr. Cameron's sake, I hope he does not know anything.* Alan's Saba tended to shoot first and ask questions later. "No."

"Okay. Well, I wanted to let you know a spot has opened on another team. Are you still interested in switching?"

Alan breathed a sigh of relief. This is why he was called in. "Has someone left?"

"A student was expelled."

"Why?"

"Unauthorized use of a cell phone. Security picked up the signal."

He quickly weighed the options—move farther from Nadia to dissipate his feelings but incur Saba's wrath, or stay close and stick to the plan. "You know, Dr. Cameron, I have invested a great deal of personal time into my team. I'm going to stay where I am."

"Good for you. I think that shows real progress. Your final survival course for the semester is next weekend; then exams and a much-deserved break. We'll meet when you return next year."

A survival course! The perfect time to get close to Nadia.

I will cull her from the herd. But how? His grandfather would know what to do. Plant a bomb to distract everyone, then snatch her up seconds before it went off—something flashy. *Maybe she will shoot herself again and this time I will carry her out. Then we will be alone.*

Admittedly, this scheme was not the most sound. The likelihood of Nadia tranquilizing herself twice seemed slim.

Would it be too obvious if I shot her?

"Alan? Is there something else?"

Alan realized he was smiling. He tried to adopt a neutral expression. "No. Thank you very much, Dr. Cameron. You have been extremely helpful."

60 NADIA
FRIDAY, DECEMBER 2

Nadia turned toward the doorway, toward Libby's voice. Her room-mate stood unmoving, silhouetted in the darkness. The soft light from the hall cast an eerie, ethereal glow around Libby's head. Nadia knew Libby had spoken, but she didn't hear the words over her own shallow breath.

"I asked you a question." Libby's voice was higher than usual. She stepped into the room and closed the door.

The bathroom light burning behind Nadia illuminated Libby's face. Now it was Nadia whose features were concealed. "I didn't hear you," she whispered.

Libby tried the light switch.

"It's out," Nadia said.

"I asked what you're doing." Libby's brow furrowed. She didn't look like herself. She looked tired, troubled. The skin under her eyes, usually smooth and bright, was shadowed.

"Is it you?" Nadia asked.

"Is what me?"

"Are you the double?"

"Are you kidding?"

Nadia shook her head. She held up the wig.

"Why are you in my desk?" Libby asked, angry now. She rushed forward and grabbed her things. "How dare you!"

Nadia wasn't frantic, which surprised her. She was . . . relieved. One way or another, it was almost over. "You tried to set me up."

"Set you up with who? I don't know what you're talking about, but I can't *believe* you did this!" Libby shoved the hidden items back into her drawer. She replaced the false bottom and swept everything from the top of the desk inside. Then she started to cry. Her shoulders shook as loud sobs wracked her torso.

"Libby?" Nadia touched her roommate's back.

"Oh honey. I wanted to tell you so bad, but it wasn't my secret to tell." Libby turned to Nadia, her cheeks streaked with mascara.

Nadia grabbed a box of tissues from the bedside table. "Here." She pulled her desk chair over and put her hand on Libby's knee. "You can tell me. I promise I won't judge you."

"You don't understand. I really can't." Libby choked out the words.

"It's okay. Our room isn't bugged. I'm sure of it." It all made sense now. They killed Drew as a warning to keep Libby in line. "They threatened you, didn't they?" *Poor Libby—she must've been terrified.*

"What?" she sniffed. "Did who threaten me?"

"The people you're working for. Because Dean Wolfe can help. We can get you protection. I'm sure you can cut a deal."

Libby took a deep breath. "Nadia, what are you talking about?"

Nadia spoke clearly, as though explaining to a small child. "You're working as a double agent. I'm sure you had a very compelling reason. Is it about your father? Was it blackmail?"

Libby laughed through her tears. First a giggle, then harder, until she was hysterical. She clutched at her stomach.

Nadia moved back a few inches. *She's completely lost it.*

"A double agent? You think I'm a double agent?" Libby's nose was stuffy from crying and she gasped for air. "Nadia, I can barely handle one life—you think I could be living two?" She calmed down her laughter. "Is that why you went through my things?"

"No—I was looking for a flashlight. The bulb went out and I remembered you had a flashlight on your key ring, and then I noticed the fake bottom, and—it doesn't matter." Nadia shook her head. *Does she seriously think she can talk her way out of this?* "Libby, if you're not the double, what are you doing with a fake ID?"

Libby wiped her cheeks with a tissue, then glanced at her makeup smeared across the white sheet. "Oh, I am so embarrassed. I must look a fright."

She's worried about how she looks? Does she understand she's committed treason?

"Let me wash my face. Then I'll tell you."

I caught her—she might think she has nothing left. What if she tries to hurt herself in the bathroom? "Let's talk first. You look fine."

Libby sighed. Her shoulders slumped as she rested her slender hands in her lap. "While I am not pleased you violated my privacy, I must confess: I am so relieved you found out. I have been dying to talk to someone."

Nadia nodded. "Go on."

"I don't even know where to start." Libby looked toward the ceiling. Tears shimmered in her clear blue eyes. A few drops spilled over her lower lids, racing to her chin. "I guess I'll tell you about my Thanksgiving."

61 LIBBY
THURSDAY, NOVEMBER 24

On Thanksgiving morning Libby drove along the foothills of the Santa Catalina Mountains. The top of the highest peak shone white with snow, but in the low desert the day was warm and sunny. She followed the directions given by her father and pulled onto a lavish estate nestled among the hills.

"I'm Amanda Downing," she told the receptionist. "I'm here for a visit."

"Yes, Miss Downing." The receptionist waved toward a man in white. White coat, white pants, white shoes. "He'll show you the way."

Libby followed her guide down the carpeted hall. Sconces lined the wall and cast soft light along the crown molding. Small tables held generous vases full of flowers. Each door was numbered with a silver plate.

Libby's stomach twisted in knots. *It'll be different this time. Look at this place—fit for royalty.*

He stopped in front of 147 and knocked firmly. A minute later he said, "Let's check the atrium."

At the end of the hall the ceiling vaulted skyward, and Libby entered the glass room. Leather sofas and chairs were arranged informally, pulled together for clients and guests. Large, lush plants gave the room a tropical feel. A waiter circulated, holding a tray of bottled waters.

"She's right over there." The man pointed. "You want me to take you?"

"No. Thank you," she said quietly. Libby smoothed her soft wool skirt and adjusted the cornflower blue sweater hanging over her shoulders. She took a deep, shaky breath and began a slow walk to the far end of the room. When she reached her destination she kneeled. She put her hand on the woman's leg and searched her perfect, unlined face.

"Oh for God's sake," the woman said with a heavy Southern drawl. "Get *off* that filthy floor."

Libby smiled and squeezed her hand. "Hi, Momma. It's so good to see you."

A few hours later, Libby and her momma ordered lunch by the pool.

A young woman in a white lab coat approached. "Good afternoon, Mrs. Downing. Are we still on for your four o'clock massage?"

"Like I have something better to do?"

"Excellent." She smiled. "If you're interested, I have an opening for a facial immediately following."

Caroline Bishop turned her full attention to the woman. "I did not care for last week's. I looked like I'd been out in the sun picking cotton all day."

The aesthetician's voice was soothing. "Hmm. Let's try our restorative facial, with organic chamomile, licorice root and white willow powder. It will be perfect for your porcelain skin."

"Oh, that sounds nice, doesn't it, Momma?" Libby asked.

"Fine."

"Remember to arrive a few minutes early so you'll have time to enjoy a glass of cucumber water in the Relaxation Garden."

"A courtyard thick with orchids does not a Relaxation Garden make," Mrs. Bishop said as the woman left the table.

The waiter arrived with their entrées: roasted pork tenderloin with apricot chutney and grilled Alaskan salmon on a bed of black lentils.

"This smells wonderful," Libby said.

"I'm still waitin' on my iced tea," her momma said sharply.

"Oh—I'm so sorry—I completely forgot. I'll bring it right out."

She snorted as he walked away. "He *forgot*. Like he has so many other more important things to do than bring me my damn tea."

"It was an accident, Momma. I'm sure it'll be right out. You want my water? I just opened it."

"I hate this place. It's a *hell*hole."

"Yeah, I can see that." Libby looked across the lush lawn, past the tennis courts, to the line of mesquite trees at the far end of the property.

"I don't belong here. These people—they have *real* problems."

"I'm really proud of you for being here."

Mrs. Bishop leaned forward and grabbed Libby's knee. "You tell your father if he does not get me out of here I will make his life very unpleasant."

"No, Momma. I'm not gonna do that."

"Whose side are you on?" she hissed as she yanked her hand away. Libby winced as her mother's nails raked across her thigh.

The orderly who'd escorted Libby to her mother arrived with a tray of paper cups. "Here you are, Caroline," he said cheerfully. He held one out. Inside were three colorful pills.

Her mother glared at him. "Caroline? What, are we sleepin' together? You may address me as Mrs. Bi—"

"Downing!" Libby interrupted. "She prefers to be called Mrs. *Downing*, if you don't mind." Libby took the cup from his outstretched hand.

He pressed his lips into a thin line. "Yes, ma'am, Mrs. Downing."

"Well. Go on, then!" Her momma waved him away like she was

shooing flies. "Wait—fetch me that umbrella before you go. This desert sun has not been kind to my daughter's fair complexion."

"Oh—I'm fine," Libby said.

"No, darling. You are *not*. Sun damage, like a wealthy husband, is easy to acquire, but most difficult to rid oneself of. Look at Juan over here." She gestured to the orderly.

"Momma!" Libby's face burned hot.

"Mrs. Downing, my name is Caesar, as is clearly printed on my name tag."

Mrs. Bishop continued as though he hadn't spoken. "His face is terribly mottled. And once you lose your looks . . . well, it's all downhill from there."

An awkward silence fell.

"*Why* are you still here?" Mrs. Bishop asked Caesar.

"I am required to stay until you take your medication."

"Well, that is unfortunate, because I take my pills after I eat, and I don't *eat* with the *help*."

Libby covered her face with her hands. *Thank the good Lord I brought plenty of cash. I'll be tipping heavily on my way out.*

"I don't need to watch you eat; just take your pills so I can be on my way."

"I would love to, but maybe you've noticed I find myself without a beverage?"

"Here, Momma. Please, *please*, just take mine."

"*Fine*." Her mother dumped the contents of the paper cup into her mouth, then stuck out her tongue to show the orderly she'd swallowed.

"Thank you, Mrs. Downing. Enjoy your lunch."

After he walked away Libby turned to her mother. She wanted to tell her off, yell at her for being so awful to that poor man, but that was not something Libby was permitted to do. "You know, it's this quarrelsome attitude that got you here in the first place. He's just doing his job."

"Your father is what got me here. He searched for the farthest place from Washington he could find. Far away from him. He's ashamed of me. I can't even use my real name!"

"Momma, that is not true. I begged Daddy to send you here! I wanted you close to me, in case you needed anything. In case he was out of the country or something." This was a flat-out lie. Her daddy had told her it was time to soldier-up. And her mission was caring for her momma. "And he registered you under a different name so that when this is all over, you can go back to being who you were without anyone having to know. Remember, Momma? How much fun we used to have?"

"Do not be naïve, Liberty Grace. It is not *my* good name he's tryin' to protect. He's ashamed to have anyone know his wife's in the nuthouse."

"Not true. And it's not the nuthouse, Momma." Libby sighed and slipped off her sweater. "Lots of people get help for things like this. It's not like when Nana was your age."

"No. He's ashamed of his drunk wife. How's that gonna look if he's tapped as the VP?"

"He's not thinking of accepting that offer anymore."

Her mother looked stricken. "Because of me."

"No, Momma. It's not because of you." *Not everything is about you.* Libby paused as a couple strolled past their table. She leaned in and whispered, "It's because he's thinking about going against his party. Daddy's thinking of running for President."

Her mother sat back in her chair, silent for the first time in Libby's life.

"I don't understand why you couldn't tell me," Nadia said to Libby. "Why you went to so much trouble to lie—disguising yourself, using a fake ID. I mean, you can see how that looks, right?"

"First of all, I'd all but forgotten Alan's story about a traitor. No offense to him, but I don't always take him seriously. He's a bit of a drama queen, bless his heart."

Nadia nodded, conceding Libby's point.

"Secondly, in about two years, I may well be the most recognizable teenager in America. Which, by the way, means all my time here is wasted." Libby's eyes flooded again.

"Not at all! You can do a lot of things with the CIA that don't involve clandestine services. Don't worry about that."

"Nadia. It's Black-Ops. It's all clandestine!"

"Well, maybe you could—"

"But most of all," Libby continued, "appearances mean everything to my family. A public scandal would be absolutely horrifying. My daddy's career'd be over—my momma would *never* recover. I had to wear a disguise." She clutched Nadia's hands. "No one can find out about my momma."

"A lot of people go to rehab. I don't think it has the same stigma it used to."

"You don't know a lot about politics, do you?"

"I don't," Nadia admitted.

"Daddy's opponents will claim marrying a lush demonstrates a lack of good judgment. If he can't sort out his personal affairs, how's he gonna run the country? He can't even keep his own house in order!"

"I guess I didn't think of it that way."

"And my mother, she would be absolutely mortified if anyone found out. You have to *swear to God* you will not tell another living soul about *any* of this—not even Sensei."

Nadia stared into Libby's pleading eyes. "Of course I won't. You have my word."

Libby sighed and looked at the ground. "So. That's it, then. You know the whole, ugly, sordid truth."

"And I love you just as much as I did an hour ago."

Libby threw her arms around Nadia. "I'm so sorry I didn't tell you. Withholding the truth is just as bad as lying, and I promise you, I will never lie to you again."

Nadia returned her roommate's hug. *Speaking of lies of omission . . .* She wanted so much to confide in Libby—about her fake boyfriend, the frame job, her conversation with the Dean. But she couldn't without disobeying a direct order. Not to mention causing a lot of trouble for Sensei.

And, really, Libby had enough on her plate.

Saturday evening Nadia met Jack in front of Hopi Hall. He'd pulled a dark sedan out of the parking lot. He closed her door and climbed into the driver's seat.

"You're wearing your earrings."

"Libby made me."

"They look great."

"I was going to flush them down the toilet, but I think I might hock them instead."

He ignored her. "I need to tell you something."

"Yeah?" she said, avoiding his gaze.

"I'm convinced you're not the double agent."

Nadia rolled her eyes. "I don't care what you think, Jack."

"But Dean Wolfe is not so sure," he continued.

Her head whipped around to face him. "What—why?"

"I don't know. But I thought if you and I worked together we could figure it out." Jack stared at her.

Nadia thought about it for a moment before shaking her head. "You know what? I don't believe a single word that comes out of your mouth. This whole thing," she waved her finger back and forth between them, "is a total lie, and it has been from the start."

"Nadia, believe me or not—I don't care, but the facts are the facts. You're under suspicion, and I still have orders to watch you. Telling you like this—disobeying a *direct order*—it goes against everything I believe in. And if you repeat this conversation to the Dean of Students I'll probably be expelled. My future is literally in your hands."

"Then why *are* you telling me?"

He took a deep breath. "I believe you're innocent. Dean Wolfe seems to have concerns about Marcus Sloan and you're caught in the crossfire. I care about you. And if I don't help you, we might never learn the truth. And if we don't learn the truth, the security of our country is at stake."

She studied his face. *He looks sincere. But his kisses seemed real too.* "I would have to be a complete idiot to trust you again."

"Fine, but I still want to find the actual traitor and I need your help. Who's been in your room besides you and Libby?"

"You."

Jack blushed. "Who else?"

Alan. He's the only one. Could it be? Maybe his I-cannot-tell-a-lie bit is a complete act. But he told the truth about Jack intercepting my dead drop. Wait a minute—maybe he only knew because he was the one sent to collect it.

What if Alan went to get the disc and instead saw Jack taking it? So he came to my room and mentioned it to test my reaction—to see if I'd told Jack about the drop. He lied about having a crush on me as a distraction, to deflect the situation so my guard would be down when he asked about the disc.

Nadia looked out the passenger side window. *It could be Alan. I caught him leaving our dorm Sunday after Thanksgiving. Was he in my room?*

"Nadia? Who else?"

But what about Libby? Do I believe her story? So her mom's in rehab—big deal. Betty Ford was an alcoholic—it's not like Mrs. Bishop would be the first First Lady to hit the bottle. Libby put on a convincing show, but is that all it was?

Nadia glanced at Jack. *It might be him. He's lied about everything. Maybe he's lying about Dean Wolfe. I caught him in my room—maybe he was planting the airline ticket, not finding it.* She sighed.

Is there anyone I can trust?

Nadia spent the next week dreading the survival course. The thought of two full days with Jack Felkin repulsed her. She'd asked Sensei if there was any way to be excused from the trip.

"Hai," he'd said. "If you are dead."

Saturday morning, she and Libby sat on the steps of Hopi Hall waiting for the van. The concrete warmed the back of her legs. Nadia pulled her sleeves over her shoulders and watched the boys cross the lawn.

"Hey, honey. I've been meaning to ask you about something."

"Go ahead."

"The other day when we," Libby's voice dropped to a whisper, "you know, were talking? You said something about setting you up. I don't get what you meant."

So she did catch that. "I just meant like, you were putting one over on me. I'm so sorry—I jumped to a ridiculous conclusion. I know you would never betray me, or our country." Nadia watched for a reaction.

Libby smiled. "If you can forgive me lying to you, I can certainly forgive your moment of doubt." She stood and brushed off.

As Jack spoke to their driver, Damon pulled Nadia aside. "You okay?" he asked.

Nadia nodded. She debated faking a smile, saying, *Of course I'm okay, why wouldn't I be?* But it was Damon. He'd see right through her. "Just an idiot. But thanks for asking."

"You let me know if you need anything. My offer still stands." Damon mimed his stealth kill, twisting an imaginary head, dropping the corpse. "But you gotta help dig the grave, all right?"

"Deal." Her smile was genuine. "I'll keep you posted."

The team loaded into the van: Jack and Damon in the back, Alan in the middle, Nadia and Libby up front. Nadia leaned back in the seat, carefully adjusting her tranquilizer gun in the shoulder harness she'd requested.

"Hey, Nadia," Damon called. "You think we'll need to carry you out this time?"

She rolled her eyes. "Yeah, that never gets old." The van pulled onto the highway.

Alan leaned forward. "Don't worry, Nadia. I am prepared to carry you if I have to."

Nadia turned in her seat. "No one will have to carry me, okay? I can take care of myself." She felt immediate remorse as his smile disappeared. He looked like the last little kid to be picked for a dodgeball game.

"Honestly, boys," Libby piped in. "It's enough already."

"I'm sorry, Alan," Nadia said. "I'm a little tired." He nodded and looked out the window.

"You two worry about your own performance," Jack said. "Now listen up. As you know, each trip becomes increasingly difficult. We're going about twenty-five miles farther out, which means we have to move a lot faster."

"What's the plan?" Damon asked.

"Same deal as before. Our teams will be dropped on either side of the canyon. We'll hike into the gorge, retrieve the package and hike back to school. It will take about half a day to get down there and half a day to get out. We'll sleep in the canyon. Any questions?" Jack asked.

"Can we look at the package this time?" Alan asked.

"How many times do we have to go over this? No," said Jack.

"You're such a boy scout," Damon said.

Nadia's heart jumped at the phrase. She turned toward the back of the van.

"No kidding," Alan said. "You really are."

Damon flashed his beautiful smile. Closed-lipped, Nadia smiled back.

"What's wrong?" Libby asked her quietly.

She shook her head. "Nothing."

After another hour, the van pulled over. "Everybody out," called the driver.

"That way." Jack pointed toward a steep, rocky hill. Beyond a sparse row of ponderosa pines plunged a deep canyon of smooth red rock. "You guys go ahead. Nadia, I need you for a second."

Alan and Libby started through the thin line of evergreens. Damon hesitated, watching Nadia. She nodded to him, and he followed the others toward the hill.

Jack narrowed his eyes, first at Damon, then Nadia. "What was that about?"

"What?" she asked innocently.

His jaw tightened. "You two seem awfully tight. I thought Damon was with Niyuri."

"I don't know what you're talking about."

"Fine." Jack squared his shoulders. "Regardless of your feelings for me, I'm your team leader and I need to know I can count on you to follow my instructions."

She silently studied the landscape.

"Nadia!" Jack said sharply. "I trust we're not going to have a problem?"

She bit the inside of her lip. "No more than usual."

"I'm not kidding."

"Yeah, I got it." She turned away, annoyed with herself for being unprofessional and petty. Regardless of whatever had happened between them, he was her team leader. He'd earned that honor before she ever arrived at Desert Mountain.

They began their descent into the canyon. There weren't many places to get in—or out. The sinuous walls were like weathered beach glass; too smooth for an inexperienced climber to scale without a rope. But every so often a dusty slope, like the one they were on, broke through the endless wall of rock.

The treacherous entry point forced them to move slowly, to check the ground before each step and inspect each handhold before committing. One misstep would mean sliding down the hill, dragging loose rock and cacti with them.

After several hours of picking their way down the mountain, they reached the canyon floor. Smooth stones lined the dry riverbed, a few feet deep in some places. They gave under Nadia's weight, each step like quicksand.

"Hit the head if you have to," Jack ordered, "and let's keep moving. We've got a long way to go."

63 JACK
SATURDAY, DECEMBER 10

Jack sat across from Nadia and watched the shadows of the campfire dance over her skin. Her eyes glistened like stars. Her dark hair framed her face in copper and brown. She looked beautiful in the firelight.

They had just finished day one of the survival course. Although they were ahead of schedule, Jack wasn't willing to slow down. When a group slacked off, the team leader looked incompetent. And regardless of his growing conviction that Nadia was not the double, he was still eager to impress Dean Wolfe—especially if it meant outperforming Noah.

Jack threw another piece of wood on the fire; the sparks swam up into the night sky, disappearing like fireflies. "We should get some sleep," he said.

Nadia made a point of wedging herself between Libby and Damon. Jack clenched his jaw. *How long is she going to keep this up? She would have done the same thing to me if she'd been in my position.*

Jack turned away. Nadia didn't deserve his misdirected anger; he was mad at himself, not her. He'd do anything to make this right, to win her back. But opening his heart right now, exploring his feelings like some lovesick puppy, was an unacceptable distraction. The traitor hiding among his schoolmates demanded his full attention. He needed to put the mission before the team, and the team before himself. If that meant shutting down and compartmentalizing, so be it.

But he didn't have to like it.

Midmorning they reached their destination. A small package waited in the middle of the riverbed, wrapped in brown paper and tied with kitchen string.

Jack put his fist in the air, signaling the team to stop and be quiet. He waved them to a sheltered area behind a jutting wall of stone. He scanned the canyon for movement. "Who wants to get it?"

"I'm on it," Damon said. Jack grabbed the back of his shirt before he stepped into the clearing.

"No, not you. If Noah's team is around, they'll tranq us in a second. It needs to be someone we can carry out. One of you." He pointed to Nadia and Libby. "Or maybe Alan."

Alan narrowed his eyes.

"Sorry." Jack shrugged. He hadn't meant it as an insult.

"Well, Nadia. You got shot last time, so I guess I'm drawing the short stick." Libby didn't move forward as she spoke.

"She did not exactly get shot—" Alan began.

"We *know*," Nadia said. "I'll do it, since I've cleverly researched my tolerance for sedatives. You never know with a tranq dart. The last thing we need is for you to have a bad reaction out here."

"She's right," Jack agreed. "It makes a lot of people sick, and if you start puking you'll dehydrate in a heartbeat. Good thinking, Nadia." He thought a flash of pride crossed Nadia's face as he complimented her, but he couldn't be sure.

"Oh, thank goodness," Libby said. "I'd be black and blue if I hit the dirt. I bruise like a peach."

"You're good," Damon said to Nadia. "I'll cover you."

"We'll all cover you," Jack said. *He needs to back off.* Shut up. even if he may be the agent.

His team drew their weapons and scattered, searching for shelter behind boulders and bends in the walls. Satisfied with their positions, Jack signaled his go-ahead. Nadia raced to the clearing, grabbed the package and sprinted back.

She almost smiled as she handed the item to Jack. "That was easier than I expected."

"Great job," Jack said, and Nadia quickly looked away. He waited as the others reassembled. "We're only supposed to use our weapons at the site of the pick-up, so theoretically, we should be out of the woods. But knowing my roommate, he'll have his team shoot us anywhere, just for fun."

"You're kidding." Libby grinned, like Noah was the cleverest boy in the world.

"I'm not. All right, listen up. We were dropped off on the west side of the canyon, and they're coming in from the east. What I don't know is if we're all traveling south. If we are, then obviously they're behind us. If we aren't, they're up there," Jack pointed up the canyon, "headed straight for us."

"Lay out your plan," said Damon.

"I'll climb up to that low ledge and travel in front of you. That way, I'll see them before they see any of us." He wasn't happy about leaving Nadia and Damon together, but an assault from Noah would cost him the mission. "You guys fine on your own?"

"Please," said Damon. "Don't worry about us; we're professionals."

"Don't leave tracks," Jack instructed.

Alone, he traveled quickly. By midafternoon, satisfied Noah was behind them, he doubled back to find his team.

That's a relief. The last thing we need is an ambush.

64 NADIA

SUNDAY, DECEMBER 11

Yesterday the canyon looked majestic; today Nadia was over it. The uneven path demanded constant attention and the scenery grew monotonous. Every few miles, small caves pocked the layered rock walls. She longed to be home, standing under a steamy shower.

Ahead of her, Libby slowed. The boys continued a few paces, Alan trailing behind Damon, before Libby turned and asked, "What is going on with you? And don't tell me nothing, because I can see something's not right."

Nadia sighed, desperately wanting to confide in Libby. But she couldn't say anything; she had to lie. Before she answered with a benign *I'm fine*, a loud crack echoed through the canyon.

Noah must have found us.

Another shot right behind. Shards of rock sprayed past her head as a chunk of limestone wall exploded. She and Libby scattered for cover.

Alan hadn't quite reached the canyon wall when a third shot cracked down. He screamed as his legs gave out.

Nadia raced across the riverbed to pull Alan to safety. "Help me with him!" she called. Damon rushed toward her. They dragged Alan behind a cluster of rocks. His cries were raw, like a wounded dog's.

Nadia pulled her gun. "Alan, stop crying! It's a tranquilizer dart. It doesn't hurt that much," she shouted over him. *What a baby. You didn't hear me screaming when I got shot.*

"No—look!" Alan's hands moved from his thigh. His fingers were bloody.

There shouldn't be any blood.

"It was not a dart!" he yelled.

Of course it wasn't a dart. Tranq guns are silent. "Damon, on point." She holstered her gun and pressed hard on Alan's thigh. His blood felt warm against her suddenly cold fingers. Her heart pounded.

"Is it bad?" Alan grabbed her shirt. "Answer me!" His fear was palpable.

"I need you to calm down. You're fine." She faked a confident tone. "It's just a scratch." From behind the rocks, she searched the high walls, half draped in shadow. No movement. "Check your weapons. Do we have live rounds?" Nadia didn't believe for a second that Sensei would make such a deadly mistake.

"Tranqs," Libby confirmed.

"Mine too," Damon said.

"Check Alan's."

"Where is Jack? I need Jack!" Alan yelled.

"I'm right here." Jack climbed down from an overhanging ledge. "Those shots weren't from Noah's team. That concussion sounded like a twelve-gauge." He examined Alan's leg. "It's grazed, not deep at all. Wrap it up. We need to move." Nadia did as she was told.

"It really hurts," Alan said through tears, his lip quivering.

"I've got you, okay?" Nadia said quietly. Alan nodded and squeezed her hand.

"I saw a cave about a half-mile up," Jack said. "I'm on point. Libby, Nadia, help Alan. Damon, you're the best shot. Bring up the rear."

"I think we should split up," Damon said. "I'll head south while you guys—"

"Out of the question," Jack interrupted. "Let's go."

They picked their way toward the cave, moving as quickly as possible. Nadia kept her gun out, barely breathing, as they stole through the canyon. They reached the cave and climbed into the shelter of the mountain wall.

"What happened back there?" Jack asked, as Nadia and Libby helped Alan onto the floor.

Alan and Libby hadn't seen anything, and for once Damon had no insight to offer. The shots had come out of nowhere. They'd echoed off the canyon walls—Nadia couldn't even tell Jack the general direction of the gunman.

For the first time, Nadia realized she was in serious danger. Her eyes met Jack's. She knew what he was thinking, because she was thinking the same thing.

Someone messed up. That bullet was meant for me.

RIGHT NOW

65 NADIA

SUNDAY, DECEMBER 11
6:27 PM

Nadia sits near the mouth of the cave, her gun drawn, Jack beside her. Damon and Libby huddle around Alan, try to keep him warm. They can't risk a fire; it would signal their position, and they don't know the location of the gunman.

"That bullet was meant for me, wasn't it?" Nadia whispers.

Jack shakes his head. "I really don't know. What I do know is you guys are my responsibility and I let you down. I'm sorry."

"Nadia," Damon calls from inside the cave. "Trade spots with me. You rest and I'll watch the door."

"I'm good," she calls back, as she stares out at the impending darkness. Quietly, to Jack, she says, "It's not your fault. You couldn't have predicted something like this."

"Thanks for saying that."

She realizes this is the nicest she's been to him in days. She averts her eyes. "So much for the Dean's promise of safety."

"Wait here." Jack steps out of the cave.

Nadia scrambles to her feet and grabs his arm. "Are you insane? You have no idea who's out there. You don't seriously intend to wander around in the dark."

"I don't expect you to understand, but it's my job to ensure the safety of this group. The school won't realize we're missing for at least another three, maybe four hours. I'm not gonna sit here and hope for the best." Jack pulls his arm away.

"I'll come with you."

"Absolutely not." His expression tells her the discussion is over.

He slips from the cave and disappears into the moonless night. That's when she notices he's forgotten his gun.

"Jack!" Nadia whispers as loud as she dares. She picks up his weapon. It occurs to her: Jack appeared *after* Alan was shot.

Maybe it was Jack.

She releases the magazine. Tranquilizer darts. She exhales, relieved. The tiniest breeze brushes against her face. Before her, silent as smoke, stands Jack.

"Just making sure you were all set," she whispers, barely able to speak. Nadia reengages the mag and racks the slide, then offers Jack his gun.

"Right." He grabs her wrist and pulls her close. She feels his breath hot on her face. "If it *had* been me, don't you think I would've swapped out the bullets by now?" He presses his mouth against her ear and whispers, "I'm not incompetent, Nadia. I wouldn't have missed." He pushes her away and recedes into the night.

He has no right to be offended. He's given me no reason to trust him.

So why do I feel bad?

Nadia waits at the mouth of the cave for hours. She doesn't intend to fall asleep, but at some point, Damon wakes her to cover a shift. Grateful for the rest, she crawls deeper into the cave with Libby and Alan.

She knows she'll be safe with Damon standing guard.

you sure?

66 DAMON
SUNDAY, DECEMBER 11
6:29 PM

Damon knows exactly what happened in the canyon. He's been double-crossed.

Nobody was shooting at Nadia—they tried to hit *him* instead. The bullet they told him would end her life got redirected. And he knows exactly who pulled the trigger, because only one agent could be that incompetent.

Professor Hayden. And the first chance he gets, Damon will end him.

Nadia was nowhere near the guys when they were attacked. They must've been ten feet apart. *Not even that idiot could've missed her by that much.* But he and Alan were within a foot of each other.

A competent sniper would've killed Damon with one shot.

He's underestimated the severity of his handlers' response. Damon needs to get the hell out of this canyon. And he needs to do it alone. But right now, he and Libby are wedged against Alan inside the cave. It's a tight fit—barely enough room for the three of them to lie down, and they're forced to curl up like a pile of kittens. Nadia's at the door, and she won't leave.

Damon has no choice but to wait. He wraps his arms around his roommate, tries to stop Alan's shivering.

He whispers in Alan's ear, "When this is all over, you remember how I took care of you."

"What are you talking about?" Alan asks.

A few days ago, Damon discovered Alan's big secret. After hearing about the hit on Nadia, he'd suggested Alan as the fall guy instead. It wasn't personal, just convenient, what with them living together and all.

But Hayden had laughed at him. "Do you know who his grandfather is?"

"How would I know that?"

"He's *Mossad*."

"Mossad? As in Israeli intelligence?"

"Yeah. We don't touch your roommate."

"That can't be right. If his grandfather is Mossad, how did Alan get into a CIA training school?"

"His grandfather's cover is deep."

"So how do you know about him?"

"Agent Roberts was the CIA liaison to Mossad while he was with the Agency. They met once, about thirty years ago."

"No kidding. Does Alan know?"

"I'm sure he does."

Damon couldn't believe Alan had kept it from him. He also wondered how deep and dangerous Alan's grandfather must be that no one in the CIA had record of him—or his association with their new trainee. It probably meant his grandfather was Kidon, an elite faction of Mossad whose sole responsibility was making people disappear. After learning the truth, Damon had to admit Hayden made a good point. He wasn't about to take out the grandson of an Israeli assassin.

Now, in the darkening cave, Damon pulls Alan closer. "You just remember how I had your back."

"Yeah, whatever," Alan mumbles. "I will be sure to send you a thank-you note."

"No thanks necessary. You and me—we're like brothers."

Time feels endless as Damon lies unmoving on the cold ground. Jack leaves; Nadia's breathing deepens. He forces himself to wait another hour, and then another. Finally, he untangles himself from Libby and Alan.

Nadia's asleep against the wall. Seeing her like this, her face relaxed, eyes closed, reminds him of the solo when he found her camp. He'd liked moving through the desert at night, with the animals out. The land pulsed and breathed, unlike the day, when everything hid from the sun. In a strange way, the desert reminded him of Baltimore. His Baltimore—the city at night. It's a whole different town after dark.

He'd had no trouble finding her site. He knew she'd get out of the van right after him. And she'd left a trail like an elephant: crushed topsoil, broken plants. After he found her, he'd sat under a tree and watched her sleep. She'd looked so peaceful. Never in his life had he felt the way she'd looked. He'd erased his tracks and left long before sunrise, but he'd gotten what he went for. He took her knife, in case he ever needed it. Her prints were all over the handle. Damon could've used it a hundred times to frame her. Dipped the blade in blood, hidden it somewhere on campus. She would've been gone in a heartbeat. He never could bring himself to do it. cute·

He shakes his head. This past week, ever since hearing about the hit, he's been shadowing her, trying to keep her out of harm's way. Turns out, being close to him was the biggest threat to her life.

He tells himself that forming an attachment right now isn't an option. But something about this girl gets to him. He never felt this way about Niyuri. Of course, that wasn't the plan. Niyuri was cover.

He holds his breath and tries to slip through the entrance. Nadia grabs the cuff of his pants.

"Where are you going?" she whispers, squinting at him.

"I gotta take a leak. Head on inside. You keep Alan warm and I'll take a shift at the door," Damon says. He smoothes the hair away from her face. His hand rests on her cheek. He wants to lean down and kiss the top of her head.

"Thanks." She nods and gently squeezes his hand.

"Nadia?"

"Yeah?"

He hesitates. "Nothing. Get some sleep."

Damon waits for her to crawl inside before he begins scaling the rock. He moves slowly and steadily up the canyon, choosing each handhold with care. The low rumble of thunder rolls off the walls as he climbs, reverberating against the rock. The cool air smells like rain.

Leaving like this, alone, in the middle of the night—it's what he trained for. Funny how that worked out. The guys who taught him might have been a little too thorough. He suspects they'll regret teaching him to disappear.

When he reaches the top, he hoists himself over the ledge. He drops to his knees, exhausted. With no time to spare, Damon takes several deep breaths before heading toward the lights of Phoenix.

67 NADIA
MONDAY, DECEMBER 12
6:15 AM

Whispers. Cold air wraps around her skin. The ground, colder still, pushes through her clothes. *Where am I?*

"Saba."

Nadia opens her eyes. She holds her breath, listening for the intruder.

"*Khawan,*" he whispers. It's Alan.

Nadia exhales and pushes herself to a sitting position. She rubs her eyes.

"Saba, they found out." He's talking in his sleep. "About me."

Nadia leans toward Alan's lips. His words are barely audible. "I am a traitor."

Her mouth opens as she stares into Alan's troubled face. *It's been him all along.*

She stands, carefully, and draws her gun. She circles Alan, her back toward the entrance. Libby lies beside him—if Nadia is forced to fire, she'll hit her best friend. *Why did his colleagues shoot at him?* She shakes her head. *Not him—they were shooting at me.*

"Hey!" She kicks his shoulder.

"Ow! What are you doing?" Then he sees the gun. "What is the matter with you? Put that down before you shoot me in the face."

Libby sits up beside Alan and yawns. "Why are you pointing a gun at us?"

"These aren't tranqs. I'm loaded with live rounds," Nadia tells Alan.

"Why are you carrying bullets?" Libby asks.

"Because I knew we had a traitor." Nadia's eyes stay on Alan. "Libby, go outside and get Damon."

"Take the gun off of me," Alan says.

Libby moves slowly. "Nadia, what's going on?"

"Get out, Libby."

"All right, I'm going. You just take it easy, okay? I don't know what this is, but I'm sure we can work it out." She backs toward the entrance. "Why don't we all take a nice, deep—"

"Get out!" Nadia yells. Libby leaves the cave. "What have you done?" she asks Alan.

"What have I done? *You* are the one pointing a gun!"

"You were talking in your sleep. You said you were a traitor. *You confessed.*"

"What? This is complete bull—"

"I heard you!"

"Take it easy." Alan holds his hands in front of his body. "What *exactly* did I say?"

"You said, *I am a traitor!* No ambiguity. Who is Saba?"

"Saba is my grandfather."

"More information." Nadia straightens her arms, sighting the gun between his eyes.

"Honey, I'm coming in, okay?" Libby says.

"Where's Damon?" Nadia asks over her shoulder.

"I don't know. He's not out here. Can I please come in?"

"Fine; stay behind me." Then, to Alan, "Saba. Go."

"It is what I call him. You call yours *giddo*, right?"

"You confessed to being a traitor, Alan. I heard you."

"I just—I have not been completely honest about my family." His eyes plead with her. "But if I tell you, I will be kicked out of school."

"If you *don't* tell me, I'll probably shoot you now."

"Nadia, for the love of God, please stop pointing that gun at him."

"My saba—my grandfather—he is in our line of work. In Israel. I swear to you, I am not a traitor."

Nadia narrows her eyes. "You're telling me that your grandfather is *Mossad,* and no one at Desert Mountain knows about it?"

"No one anywhere knows. He has changed his identity so many times *I* do not even know his real name. Well, this is a slight exaggeration. But no one can possibly connect us. I mean, unless they have worked with him or know him personally or something." His eyes stay on her gun.

"Why did you say you were a traitor?"

"Because of him! He is Mossad; I wish to be CIA. Before my training at Desert Mountain commenced, he gave me his blessing—with the caveat I keep him informed of world events discussed by the CIA as they relate to the Middle East. The United States is not good about sharing with her allies, unless she gets something in return. Though I am not certain why he cares what happens in the CIA. He is constantly telling me how much better Mossad performs. He said I could choose, but I—"

"Alan!"

"Right. At first, I agreed. I love him very much, and I did not see the harm. We all want the same thing—a safe world in which to live. But I no longer feel comfortable with our arrangement. It makes me feel . . ."

"Like a traitor?" Nadia asks.

"Uneasy. I do not wish to quietly report to Mossad. If I cannot liaise openly, I will tell him our deal is finished. I swear."

Nadia lowers her voice. "Do you understand what you've done? You've committed treason."

"No! I have told him nothing! But if anyone finds out, I will be expelled."

"If anyone finds out, you'll be sent to Guantanamo Bay!"

"I have done nothing wrong! And I really like it here—I like you all. I mean, I did not at first; I found you very annoying, but now I know you a little better—"

"Shut up," Nadia orders. "Let me think." *Is he telling the truth? This explains why he always looks nervous when our conversations get personal. What about coming to my room? Seeing the dead drop? Just bad timing?* "Why were you in my dorm after Thanksgiving break?"

"What?"

"You said you wanted to see if Libby was home yet, but you were lying."

Alan wipes roughly at his eyes and says, "I do not want to tell you."

"Tell me anyway."

"You are not a very nice girl."

"Noted. Now answer the question."

Alan digs into his pocket.

"Easy," Nadia says, following his movement with her gun. He throws her a folded note. The edges are worn; it looks like he's been carrying it for a while.

She pushes the note toward Libby with her foot. "Do you mind?"

Libby unfolds the paper and reads aloud, "Perhaps you would be interested in joining me for a meal downtown."

Alan glares at Nadia. "Please disregard my inquiry. It is no longer relevant. I planned to leave it at the front desk after the holiday, but then I saw you coming and I lost my nerve."

"And you just happen to have it with you?"

"I have been carrying it around for weeks, trying to work up the courage to give it to you."

"What are you, like twelve years old? Why would you leave a note when you could've just said it to my face?"

"I did say it to your face. After the dance. That did not work out so well. Anyway, consider my offer retracted. Further investigation has revealed your personality to be a bit grating."

She watches him carefully. *Anyone else and I wouldn't buy this story. But Alan? It does make sense.* "You don't sound like an American."

"I was not born here. I learned Arabic, Hebrew and French, all while learning English. I get confused with my languages—*not* my loyalty. I am every bit as American as you, Nadia."

The color is gone from his cheeks. Sweat collects on his forehead. *If he were lying, his face would be bright red.* Nadia lowers her gun. *He can't lie.*

"Thank God," Libby says quietly.

Wait a minute—he can't lie. How the hell did he get past Cameron? Nadia raises her gun. "How did you pass the polygraph?"

Alan sways a little. "I—I—"

"I thought you couldn't lie," she says.

"I have no baseline!"

"What?"

"No baseline—Dr. Cameron asks questions to establish a baseline—I fail those questions, so all of my answers look the same."

"The baseline question is your *name.* Stop trying my patience and give me *all* the information!"

"My name is not Alan!"

Nadia and Libby exchange a glance. "Continue," Nadia says.

"It is not my given name." His voice is weary. "It is the first question Dr. Cameron asks, and my face reddens, and my heart races, and my blood pressure soars. Because *Alan* is not my name. I was named for my Saba's father. My given name is *Aryeh.*"

"What's that now?" Libby asks.

"Yes, I know. It sounds like I have phlegm in my throat. When I was young, my teachers could not pronounce the name and I would have to correct them. The other children made fun of me. They would hawk loogies on the playground and then say, 'Oh, someone is calling you.' I went home crying every day. My mother felt sad for me. The next fall, I transferred to a new school. She enrolled me as *Alan.* But it is a lie, and it makes me feel guilty. Like

I am turning my back on my heritage. Recall how your mother felt after 9/11."

Nadia had mentioned it once, one night while she and Alan had been studying. For years after the attack, her mom stopped telling people she was Middle Eastern. She'd been afraid for her family's safety. But she'd also felt bad about her silence, like she was betraying her ancestors.

Nadia studies him. His eyes are wide. His body slumps, but his arms and legs are open, away from his torso—honest, revealing body language. His face is dreadfully pale.

She tucks her gun into her waistband.

Libby breathes a heavy sigh and rushes to Alan. "Hand me that water," she orders Nadia. She holds the bottle for Alan to drink. "So you believe him?"

Nadia nods.

"Then apologize," Libby demands. "You could'a killed him."

"For the record, I lied. I don't have bullets. I have tranqs."

"That was not an apology," Libby says.

"I'm sorry I pointed my gun at you."

"What about thinking he's a traitor? Shame on you."

"No, I'm not sorry for that," Nadia says. "Someone shot at us."

"If I was the traitor, why would they be shooting at me?"

"Maybe *they* don't like working with you, either." Nadia smiles.

"Not the time, honey," Libby says.

Alan leans against Libby for support. The fight weakened him. He licks his lips. "I think it was Jack. He is the only one who was not there."

"It wasn't Jack." Nadia crouches next to Alan and wipes the cold sweat from his face. Now that she's cleared him, she feels guilty for kicking him awake.

"How do you know? Because he is your boyfriend and you do not want it to be him?"

"I'm relieved to see your wound hasn't affected your sharp

tongue. I already checked his gun. It was my first thought too."
She moves toward the mouth of the cave.

"You cannot tell Jack," Alan calls after her. "Nadia, promise
me. Please!"

Nadia looks back. Libby holds Alan's weight against her body
and strokes his hair. She shakes her head almost imperceptibly.
Just what I need—another secret. "I won't say anything. Yet."

Alan opens his mouth, probably to protest.

"That's the best I can do right now." *Am I the only one in the
world with nothing to hide?*

Jack finally staggers into view as the sky lightens. Nadia considers apologizing for checking his gun, but she's still mad. *After
everything he did to me—all the lies. And he's offended I don't trust
him?*

He throws his arms around her before she can stop him. "You
were right to suspect me, and to check my gun. I'm sorry for my
reaction. I would've done the same thing. That's a good way to
keep yourself alive, and I'm really proud of you."

This isn't what she expects to hear, but she likes the compliment. At the same time, she's annoyed with herself for wanting
his praise.

"But you need to know," Jack lifts her chin to look in her
eyes. "I would never do anything to hurt you."

She actually believes him. He risked his future with the CIA
to tell her the truth about Wolfe's ongoing suspicions. Everything
that's important to him—he risked it all. To help her. She smiles
a little.

Libby emerges from the cave with Alan draped over her shoulder. "Is Damon with you?"

Jack shakes his head. "I haven't seen him since I left you
guys."

"He got up in the middle of the night to use the bathroom and
take a shift," Nadia says. "Do you think he hiked out for help?"

"I think he would've told someone." Libby's knees give a little
under Alan's weight; she eases him onto a rock.

Jack kneels to check Alan's wound. "We'll give Damon half an hour, but that's it. We were due back last night and Alan needs a doctor before his leg gets infected."

Nadia looks toward the sky as a hawk swoops into the canyon. She's trapped in a red-rock coffin, and straight up is the only way out.

Jack waits for forty-five minutes, constantly scanning the rocky walls for movement, a color aberration, any sign of the enemy sniper.

Damon doesn't return.

Nadia joins him, sitting as far away as possible on his rock. "What happened? Do you think he's in trouble? I mean, like captured or something?"

He shakes his head. "I don't know." They sit in silence for a few minutes before Jack asks, "Did you hear what he called me in the van?"

Nadia nods. "Boy scout." Her face pales.

"I think it might be him."

"It kind of looks that way."

"I can't figure out why he took off. He didn't really blow his cover," he says.

"Maybe it's not him. Maybe he was kidnapped."

"I'm pretty sure it's him. But how did the shooter make such a colossal mistake, hitting Alan instead of you?" Jack stands and reaches for Nadia's hand to help her up. Distracts her with a question. "You were nowhere near the guys, right?"

She takes his hand. "Not even close. Like, ten feet away."

He doesn't want to let go. She gently frees herself and turns away.

They find Alan and Libby resting near the mouth of the cave. "It's time to go," Jack says. "We're a day overdue, so I assume someone's looking for us, but I don't know for a fact. We need to get Alan to a doctor. Everyone, keep your eyes open and stay alert." He hesitates a moment before adding, "And make sure your weapons are readily available."

"What about Damon?" Libby asks.

"We can't wait any longer."

"We're not leaving him," she says.

"This is not a debate. And I'm not sure he's with us anymore."

"You think he's dead?"

"That's not what I mean."

"Well, what do you mean?" Libby presses for an answer.

"You know what? I don't even know. But we need to take care of Alan." Jack turns away.

"You think he's the double, don't you?"

He looks at Nadia. "You told them?"

"I didn't say anything. Everyone already knew. Alan mentioned it months ago."

Yeah, if I overheard it, I'm sure others did too. "I don't want to talk about it anymore, Libby. We have other priorities." Jack nods toward Alan.

Jack and Nadia take the first shift with Alan, supporting his weight as he limps along. They rotate every thirty minutes so that no one carries him more than an hour without a break. Their pace is agonizingly slow. Late in the afternoon, they find a steep incline leading out. They climb the hill on hands and knees.

The sun dips behind the mountains before they reach the highway. "We need to split up. You'll have better luck hitching a ride if it's just you two," Jack tells Libby. He kneels on the asphalt and rips open the side seam of his first aid kit. He flips through the plastic cards and hands her a small stack. Two Arizona State University student IDs, a health insurance card and a credit card.

Libby reads the names. "Libby Brown and Alan Cross. You have a set of these for all four of us?"

"Five of us," Jack corrects her. "Hide your weapons. Memorize your birth dates. You're freshmen at ASU. You were camping and Alan fell on some rocks. Don't report in. It's time to go dark. I'll have Wolfe find you."

"Got it," Libby says. She hoists Alan's arm over her shoulder.

The fear has not left Alan's face. Jack smiles, trying to reassure him. "You'll be fine. It's smooth sailing from here." He gently punches Alan's shoulder. "Hey, I told you one day your life would depend on her."

Alan glances at Libby and gives Jack a half-smile. "I guess you were right."

"Almost always."

Libby and Alan head southeast as Jack and Nadia go west, straight toward the setting sun. The sky burns orange before them.

"How far are we from school?" Nadia asks.

She's struggling to keep up, but Jack can't afford to slow his pace. "I think it's about seventeen-thirty. If we're lucky, we'll get back by twenty-three-hundred."

"Do you think it's safe? I mean, do you think the shooter is on campus?"

"I can't imagine he would stick around. Missing your target is generally frowned upon in our line of work."

"Do you think they'll try again?" She looks over her shoulder.

"No, I think you're okay. If they really wanted you dead, Damon could've slit your throat before he left." Jack stops and grabs Nadia's arm. "I'm so sorry I left you with him. If anything had happened to you . . ."

"It's okay. You didn't know."

"But I should have. After he called me boy scout?" They continue walking. "Dean Wolfe will know how to proceed. I don't know if he'll heighten security or what, but he'll do something. No worries, Nadia. It'll be okay." He has no idea if this is true, but she looks concerned and he wants to reassure her. "It's almost over. We'll explain it all to Wolfe and clear your name. You'll be exonerated."

He envisions the scene: relief will wash over Dean Wolfe. Jack might get a formal commendation. Maybe a letter signed by the President—or a dinner at the White House, followed by an awards ceremony, like they do for Navy SEALs. Not televised, of course, but still. And Nadia—he can patch things up with her. They can go on an actual date. Who knows? They might have a future together yet.

"Where do you think he went? Damon, I mean."

"I don't know. We had no reason to suspect him. He could've stayed with us. And I don't know why they took a shot at you. I guess if you'd died, they could claim you were the double. You wouldn't be around to disprove it. But then again, the gunfire might've been a distraction."

"What do you mean?"

"Maybe this was Damon's extraction. You know, they wanted to pull their agent out of the field, but still provide reasonable doubt. Like maybe we're supposed to think he was kidnapped, instead of believing he's the double."

"But if it is Damon, why didn't he kill me? It doesn't make any sense." They walk in silence for a few minutes. "Unless—maybe he couldn't. Maybe he got too close to me."

Jack nods. *I know I did.*

"Over Thanksgiving we talked about his brother."

Jack knows about Damon's brother; he read the police report. As team leader he's privy to any information involving past trauma.

"I know he's trained to deceive," Nadia continues, "but I felt a real connection with him."

Jack glances at Nadia. *Even better that he's gone. It'll be hard enough to win her back without competition from him.*

They walk along the deserted highway for an eternity. The land turns dark before the sky. The sliver of moon offers little light. They almost miss the dirt road leading to school.

"Thank God," Jack says, as they finally reach the gate.

The night guard greets them. "We were worried about you. Where's the rest of your team?"

"Long story," Jack says.

"Dean Wolfe is here. He wants to see you immediately."

"Right now? It has to be at least twenty-three-hundred," Jack protests.

"It's closer to two, and I'm just delivering the message." The guard pulls the gate closed behind them. With a solid *clunk*, it locks in place.

"I'll come with you. We can talk to him together," Nadia says.

Jack had left his team alone while he searched for Noah, then again when he looked for the shooter. If he'd stayed with them, if he'd been by Nadia's side, maybe none of this would've happened.

"No, go ahead to your room. I'd rather see him alone. I'll tell him about Damon. I can fill you in tomorrow."

"Thanks," Nadia says, and rests her hand on his arm. Her warmth feels like fire against his chilled skin. He grabs her quickly and pulls her against him. Her body tenses for a second, then she exhales and returns his hug.

"I'm crazy about you," he says, not letting go. "The only reason I even . . . Nadia, I take my duty to my country very seriously. I know you aren't from a military family, so maybe you don't understand the personal sacrifices I'm prepared to make, but I hoped you were innocent from the first time I met you."

He releases her and she smiles. For a second he thinks, *Everything is gonna be okay.*

"Thank you for telling me." She looks down, then back into his eyes. "I think I need a little time."

Jack nods and brushes a lock of hair from her cheek. *At least it's not a no.*

"Good luck with the dean. I'll see you tomorrow, okay?"

He waits as she crosses the lawn, then he goes inside.

The Exit sign casts a red glow through the foyer. *Just be honest with him.* Jack walks the darkened hallway to the sitting room. *This isn't my fault.* He knocks gently.

Wolfe throws the door open and Jack jumps.

"Finally. Come in. Sit down, son. What happened?" A deep crease is etched between Wolfe's eyebrows.

He must've been worried sick. Jack sinks into the chair. "We experienced enemy fire from an unknown assailant."

"Is everyone all right?" Dean Wolfe perches on the edge of his desk. He leans toward Jack, his concern evident.

"One of the bullets grazed Alan's leg. Libby took him to the hospital. We invoked Sunstroke Protocol."

"Alan Cohen was *shot*?"

"Yes sir."

"But he's not dead."

"No sir. It's not bad. He should be fine."

Wolfe whistles softly. He looks away and rubs his face with both hands. "And the others?"

"Nadia returned with me; she's in her room. Sir, I'm sorry to tell you this, but Damon's gone."

"Damon's dead?" Dean Wolfe's eyes widen.

"No, not dead. Missing. Disappeared. We have no idea what happened to him. But I believe he's the double. I'm confident it's not Nadia."

"Really."

"Dean Wolfe, I'm so sorry. I know I'm responsible for the safety of my group but I couldn't have prevented the attack. I may have made some bad choices, but they didn't lead to the assault."

"Jack, your dedication and commitment are unquestioned. I'm certain you had good reason to leave your group."

"Yes sir, I did. I thought Noah's team had prepared an ambush. Then later, Damon vanished while I searched for the gunman. Maybe I should've stayed with them, but I was concerned that the shooter would fire again at daybreak. I couldn't give him six hours to find a better sniper's nest." Tears sting his eyes. He squints, hoping the Dean won't notice.

"Son, it's okay." Dean Wolfe stands to touch Jack's shoulder. His brow pulls together as he offers reassuring words. "It's a miracle you weren't all killed with someone shooting down into the canyon. The bullets could've ricocheted off the rock—who knows what might have happened. I know you did what you could. I'm grateful you're all right."

Jack exhales. "Thank you for understanding." Exhausted, he leans back against the chair. He closes his eyes.

"I need to get Nadia's statement while it's fresh in her mind. Why don't you give her a call and have her come on in?"

The words sound overly casual. Jack opens his eyes. The Dean's face has changed slightly, from concern to . . . what is it? A guarded expression Jack can't quite read. Wolfe hands him the cordless phone from his desk.

Shots fired down into the canyon. Did I say where the shots were fired? Jack's heartbeat quickens.

"I'm certain you had good reason to leave your group, Jack"—that's what Wolfe said. A warm sensation floods his body. *I hadn't told him I left my team.* The warm turns to numbness as the blood rushes to his feet. Jack can't feel his legs. *How could he possibly know we weren't together—unless he's already been briefed?*

Jack's hands shake as he dials the girls' dorm. The phone rings five, six, seven times. He's sure Dean Wolfe will hear the panic in his voice as he whispers, "There's no answer."

"Give it a few more rings. Someone will pick up."

A moment later, Nadia's breathless voice, "Hello?"

"Nadia. It's Jack." His voice sounds strange and far away. His tongue feels thick. "I'm at the dean's office. He needs you to come in. He wants to get your report. Tonight."

"Are you kidding me?" She makes a groaning noise in the back of her throat. "All right. I'll be right there."

"I'm going to stay here," Jack says.

"Okay."

"And Nadia?"

"What?"

"Don't forget your sweater."

She pauses for a beat. "What did you say?"

"It's cold out."

Nadia is silent for a moment. Finally she answers in a tiny voice, "Okay, Jack. Thank you."

Jack hands the phone to Dean Wolfe. He doesn't think to hang up.

Wolfe nestles the receiver onto its charger. He sighs, very softly, and shakes his head. He looks up at Jack, into his eyes, and whispers, "I just realized what I said."

"What's that, sir?" Jack's voice cracks.

Wolfe is up now, pacing the floor in front of Jack. He stops and leans into Jack's seat, holding the arms of the wingback chair. Pinning Jack in place. "I'm sorry, son. You would have made a fine agent."

Jack feels a sharp blow to the side of his head and then . . . darkness.

69 NADIA
TUESDAY, DECEMBER 13
2:13 AM

Nadia lowers the phone onto its cradle. The hair on her arms stands on end.

Jack used their code.

What did he say to do if he used the code? Run, save yourself. That's what he'd said.

Her first instinct is to not trust him. *But why would he lie?*

Maybe Jack is the double. He's setting me up. He wants me to run so I look guilty.

No. If he wanted to frame me, he would've killed me on the way back to school. He'd call it self-defense—tell everyone I attacked him. That's what I would've done.

Maybe someone else is in the dean's office. Maybe Jack was ambushed. Maybe Wolfe is dead.

Or maybe it's Wolfe.

What if it's Wolfe?

Oh my God. It's Dean Wolfe. It's been him from the start. Assigning Jack to spy on me; arguing with Sloan about recruiting me; insisting I didn't need protection.

Adrenaline floods her body—fight or flight. She doesn't go back to her room. Her tranq gun is still in its harness, her knife clipped to her back. She can run.

If she can get out the back gate.

It'll be locked. She can't get past the guard at the front entrance. She can't call the police. She doesn't know the day's code to dial off campus. And even if she did—what would she say? Who would believe her word over the dean's? Especially after someone planted evidence in her room. Maybe more "evidence" has accrued.

She's out of her dorm, sprinting to the back wall before her next breath. She doesn't feel the ground under her. She doesn't feel her legs. She doesn't feel the cold air or the branches of the bushes that scrape her arms.

What about Jack? Am I just gonna leave him there?

He brought it on himself. Lying to me. Spying on me.

Nadia stops running before she reaches the gate. She moves into the shadow of the Navajo Building.

Where am I going to go?

She stands in the black night, listening to her pounding heart. It fills her head. And a rushing sound, like a hard wind.

It's her breath.

Frantic thinking will get me killed. She forces herself to breathe slowly, in for five, out for ten.

Can I really take off and leave Jack? Is that who I want to be?

She can't lie to herself. *I know how I feel about him. And he risked everything for me.*

It only takes a second to decide. Nadia turns around and runs to the dojo.

The shoji screens silently slide open and she bows out of habit as she enters the lobby. She races down the north hall, across the mats and up the south hallway to the covert-ops room. She strains to read the keypad in the darkened corridor.

Oh, what is the word! She realizes she never got around to looking up the meaning of Sensei's code. *Abunai.*

Nadia enters the password and the metal door clicks open.

From the first cabinet she takes a pencil, which conceals a tiny recording device. She pulls her ponytail into a bun and sticks the pencil through her hair.

Across the room, she opens the weapons cabinet. She takes

two CIA deer guns, which easily hide in her pockets. Almost as an afterthought, Nadia grabs the poisoned pen. She clips it inside her sleeve.

Halfway down the hall, she decides to leave a message for Sensei, just in case. Her heart lurches as she finishes the thought. *Just in case I don't make it out of there.*

In the front room she uses the pen to scribble on the rice paper covering the wall: *Sute Inu.*

She takes the long route to the dean's office, following the path instead of cutting across the dark, open lawn. She climbs the steps two at a time and eases open the front door. Inside, she draws her tranq gun and moves down the hall.

She reaches the sitting room. Her shallow breathing roars like an ocean in her head. *Control your breath. Four in, hold for four, eight out. Combat breathing.*

She stays against the wall as she approaches Wolfe's office. Her heart pounds so forcefully she's sure it will explode.

A sliver of light shines through the crack in his door. Nadia peeks inside. She sees his desk and one of the navy chairs, but the door obstructs the remaining view. She doesn't see Jack or Dean Wolfe.

She holds the gun in her right hand, finger on the trigger, muzzle pointed at the ceiling. With her left hand she pushes the door.

Shadows cloak the corners of the room. The light from Dean Wolfe's small desk lamp casts a tiny, motionless, yellow pool.

She moves inside. Along the wall, well behind the second chair, a man-sized lump lays on the Dean's Persian rug. Nadia approaches slowly, her weapon pointed at the dark pile. As she advances, the shape becomes clear: Jack's body crumpled on the floor.

Three steps into the room the door slams shut behind her.

Nadia spins, her gun pointed toward the door. Dean Wolfe, also armed, looks back at her. She loses feeling in her legs.

"Miss Riley," Dean Wolfe says. "If you would be good enough to drop your weapon."

Noise thunders in her head. She doesn't move. She can't breathe.

"Nadia, my gun is not equipped with tranquilizer darts. I strongly encourage you to drop your weapon," the dean says.

She drops the gun at her feet.

"Kick it."

Her foot moves toward the gun but she misses.

"Kick it!"

She tries again, this time making contact.

"And your knife."

She pulls her knife from her waistband and tosses it down.

"Sit down," he instructs, waving his gun toward the chairs.

Nadia sits. As the dean circles his desk, she reaches into her hair and clicks on the recorder in the pencil.

Dean Wolfe picks up the telephone and dials an on-campus extension. "Get down here. I need some help." He hangs up the phone.

"What happened to Jack?" She has trouble forming the words.

"It's a shame about Jack. He had the potential to be a fine agent. That is, until you came along." Dean Wolfe raises an eyebrow and shakes his head.

"I don't understand." *Stall him. Make a plan.*

"Jack possessed a single-minded determination regarding his career goals. That's why I chose him to investigate you. He was the perfect recruit: eager, intelligent—but malleable. Not like you. From the moment I read your profile I knew you'd be trouble. But Jack . . ." He sighs. "Jack disappointed me. We supplied all the evidence he needed, but his feelings for you interfered with his job. He told you, didn't he? That I still suspected you." Nadia doesn't answer. "I knew I'd lost him."

Past tense. Jack was malleable. Jack's already dead. "How will you explain two student murders?" she asks. She hears Hashimoto

Sensei's voice in her head: *Be smart, Nadia-san. Keep him talking. You are stronger than this.*

"Won't everyone be surprised when they find out you and Jack were *both* working as double agents. We'll plant the gun that shot Alan between your mattress and box spring. We'll throw in a couple one-way plane tickets to Afghanistan. Imagine, terrorists right here on our own campus."

"But Libby and Alan know it wasn't me. We were together when Alan was shot. Are you going to kill them too?"

"No one will doubt you were working with someone. Your accomplice has been apprehended already." The dean points to Jack's body on the carpet. "I understand he was not with his team when the shots were fired. Trust me, Nadia. I'm doing you a favor, taking care of this situation in-house. If Alan's grandfather gets a hold of the people he thinks shot his grandson, things will take an ugly, ugly turn. You would be *praying* for death."

So he does know. "What do you mean?"

"Never you mind."

The noise in her head begins to quiet. "Who are you working for?"

"You're full of questions tonight, aren't you?"

"You're going to kill me anyway; why not indulge my curiosity?" The steadiness of her voice shocks her.

Dean Wolfe smiles. "I work for America."

"You're not CIA."

"No." He shakes his head. "The CIA can't do what we do. The CIA merely identifies problems. My organization eradicates them. We are called the Nighthawks. We're not bound by the rules of the United Nations. We do what the president is incapable of—we protect the citizens of the United States of America by any means necessary."

Nadia slips her hand in her pocket. She wraps her fingers around the deer gun. *He won't kill me here if he doesn't have to— too messy. But if he takes me to the desert, my body may never be found.*

"We are a small assembly of men and women who *know* what goes on out there. We have no red tape to cut through; we do what needs to be done. If that means we eliminate an enemy of the state, we do so, regardless of his—or her," the dean pauses to glare at Nadia, "international standing. It is absurd that known enemies of this great nation are allowed to create and maintain nuclear, chemical and biological weapons. I don't care what the Geneva Convention states. Anti-American organizations must be abolished."

"And Damon is part of this?" Nadia guesses.

"Damon's done all he can for us. He isn't a team player. He went over his contact's head, refused a direct order—to kill *you*, by the way—and jeopardized our entire operation. A man who won't follow orders makes for a useless agent. I knew he'd fail us eventually. Damon has no ideology. He is motivated by his need for vengeance. Once he completes his revenge fantasy, he will have no loyalty to us whatsoever. The shot in the canyon was meant for Damon, not Alan. It's a shame too. We put a lot of time and money into that boy. Maybe too much time, as it turns out. He's smarter than we knew."

"How so?"

"Damon has amassed evidence against us. But his time is limited; we know how to find him. Sadly, if he'd died in the canyon, you wouldn't be here. We would've handed his body to the CIA. With Damon's death they'd have their double, you would be exonerated, everybody goes home happy. But our shooter missed."

She doesn't bother pleading—swearing to keep his secrets. Wolfe is not stupid. "Your cause sounds just," Nadia lies.

"Don't bother, Miss Riley. I have no thoughts of recruiting you. I didn't want you here, and I don't want you there." Wolfe strolls to the door. "Where is he?" He looks into the sitting room.

As he turns his back, Nadia leaps from the chair and rolls across his desk, firing at him as she launches herself over the wood. Her head hits the lamp and it shatters on the floor, leaving the room in darkness. Wolfe responds faster than she expects. He drops behind the abandoned chair and fires back. A searing pain pierces her side, like she's been stabbed with a hot poker. She slides off the back of the desk and falls to the floor.

Her ears ring from the closeness of the short-barrel shot. She can't remember if the deer gun is a single-use weapon. To be safe, she tosses it aside and withdraws the second gun from her pocket. Her eyes rapidly adjust to the darkness. She pulls herself into the empty space under his desk. Wolfe's heavy breathing surrounds her. The heaving sound closes in from all around—both sides, above her.

She realizes she's making the noise.

I can't stay here. I'm trapped. Nadia holds her breath and listens. The ringing continues. It's all she can hear. She crawls to the side of the desk. With her back against the wood, she pokes her head around the corner.

Wolfe has left his position behind the chair. She scans the room, looking for a dark shape or movement.

Can I make it to the door? Is he still in the room? He'll shoot me in the back when I run. Maybe he left—is he in the sitting room waiting for me?

Nadia creeps around to the front of the desk. She crouches on her knees and peers through his doorway into the sitting room.

She hears a whisper on the carpet near the broken glass. *He's on the other side of the desk.* She's a moment too late.

"Drop it," he says from behind.

He'll kill her. She has no doubt. These are her last moments on earth. Death closes around them, watching, waiting.

"Drop it!" he yells.

She rolls onto her back and fires. She hits his right shoulder. The force of her shot knocks his arm back as his weapon discharges. His bullet screams past her ear. It lodges into the floor beside her head.

Wolfe drops his gun as he cries out. He touches his shoulder. He stares at the blood on his fingers. His face reddens and twists in anger. He drops to his knees, grabs at her neck. She pushes her gun into his abdomen and fires again. The feeble *click, click* of an empty gun responds.

"Single-use, Nadia," the dean grunts through gritted teeth, squeezing her throat. Flecks of spit fly from his mouth and land on her face. His breath is heavy and sour. "You should've paid closer attention to your training."

His grip tightens around her neck. She claws at his hands but they're like steel. She tries to force her arms between his, to push his hands apart, but his elbows are locked. No oxygen finds her lungs—no blood pumps to her brain. She doesn't have much time.

Sensei's voice in her head: *Seven seconds.*

"Less mess," he whispers, "but such an ugly way to go."

Six seconds.

Nadia's face grows hot. The pressure behind her eyes builds to an unbearable level. Darkness swallows her peripheral vision; all she sees is his sneer. *Five.* The room quiets. *Four.* Her body weakens. *Three.* She remembers the poisoned pen. *Two.*

She slips the pen from her sleeve and clicks out the tip. With her last second of consciousness, she jabs the sharp, poisoned needle between his ribs.

Wolfe releases his grip and grabs at the pen. Nadia rolls onto her side, retching. Each inhalation feels like knives in her trachea. The dean leans forward. His shallow breathing rasps through his mouth in quick, tiny breaths.

He falls face down and lays motionless beside her.

She feels weak, and very tired. Nadia touches her stomach. The burning continues and she doesn't know why. Her hand is wet, the color of dark wine. The blood still seeps. Her shirt clings to her; a warm, sticky wetness.

The urge to drift off is overpowering. She always thought at the moment of death she'd find the will to fight, to live. But she doesn't have the strength. She doesn't care anymore. She just wants to sleep.

This isn't so bad. Nadia closes her eyes to succumb to the ocean of peace.

Someone shakes her. "Leave me alone," she whispers, her voice inaudible.

"Hold on!" The voice is too loud, intrusive in her silent space. "Please, hold on! An ambulance is on the way!"

Summoning all her strength, Nadia opens her eyes. The last thing she sees before her heart stops beating is Hashimoto Sensei leaning over her.

70 DAMON
TUESDAY, DECEMBER 13
7:24 AM

Damon tries to control the rage building in his chest. His thoughts wander back to the canyon and his blood pressure spikes, squeezing his heart. The cold air whipping across his face doesn't cool him—it infuriates him. Reminds him of a drill back in Baltimore. His trainers filled a hot tub with ice water in the dead of winter and made him stay in till he passed out. Then they'd warm him up and do it again.

Tortured and starved him in the name of education. He'd only been fourteen.

Deep breaths, man. You'll get yours.

He hadn't chosen this line of work. He'd been recruited by the director of the public library—the man who'd greeted him and his little brother every week. The director had been impressed with Damon's book choices: organic chemistry, evolution, the art of warfare, true stories written by ex-military. Occasionally he and Damon would grab a sandwich after the library closed. Then one night Roberts joined them.

Damon refused their first few offers. Yeah, the money tempted him, but risking his life to serve his country wasn't how he planned to make a buck. Plus, he was responsible for Gabriel: picking him up at school, dropping him at the rec center. He told Roberts, "Even if I wanted to join you—which, no offense, I don't—I've got my little brother."

But after Gabriel's death, they got through.

The pickup truck driving him from Phoenix to the small border town of Nogales, Arizona, skids to a dusty stop. He jumps down from the bed. *"¡Gracias!"* he calls to the driver, tapping on the tailgate. He waits in the shadows, watching the empty intersection, thinking about his little brother. If Damon hadn't been so self-involved, if he'd joined the Nighthawks the first time they asked, Gabriel would still be alive. Damon would've known what he was seeing, known what to do.

He'd identified the vehicle. Picked the driver out of a lineup. And because of some stupid technicality, that son of a bitch walked right out of the police station with his high-priced lawyer. The police couldn't do anything.

Agent Roberts came back to him a few months after Gabriel died. Didn't say a word, just touched his shoulder and handed him a Polaroid. The man who killed his baby brother, face up on the pavement, eyes open wide. His blood filling the cracks in the concrete. A bullet hole in the middle of his head. He'd seen that shot coming.

The next day, Damon Moore began his training.

He considers heading back to Phoenix straight away to seek his revenge, but common sense outweighs his anger. He'll get even with Hayden. If he goes now, it'll be like showing up late to the party. And he makes a point of never being the last man to arrive.

Anyway, it'll be a lot more fun if Hayden doesn't see it coming. Damon pictures him now, scared, pacing the floor. Every noise shooting fear through his body.

He better hope I get to him before Granddaddy Cohen figures out what went down.

A block away, on the corner of Mariposa and Grant, Damon finds the pay phone with the false bottom. The trap door is hidden under the heavy metal box that collects the coins. He slides his knife along the edge to loosen the seal. These phone booths are scattered across the country in case an agent needs to bolt.

At the start of his training Damon spent hours memorizing the locations, four to a state. Every weekend for two years, while his mother thought he was stocking shelves in a warehouse, Damon studied the ins and outs of clandestine operations. He pored over the manuals: lock-picking, cover and concealment, basic code-breaking, escape and evasion. And a never-ending list of Black-Ops case files.

The box is stuck. Damon jams his knife inside, up to the hilt, and then sharply twists. Basic physics. He pries the metal. Inside, he finds the plastic-wrapped package. A truck drives by his corner and slows. Damon slips the parcel under his arm and bends down to tie his shoe. The truck moves on.

The weight of the thick envelope feels good in his hands. He slices it open: tucked inside is a passport with no photo and a unisex name, a loaded gun, a prepaid Visa card and three thousand dollars cash. He's sure his former employers don't mean for him to benefit from the stash, but they haven't had time to clear out the boxes.

Damon waits until the Shop-Mart opens. He's tired, but alert—on the lookout for irregular activity. He watches the first wave of staff and customers as they enter the store. Everything looks cool, so he goes in.

He buys new clothes and clean shoes—a half-size too big in case anyone tries to track him, a roll of double-wide clear packing tape with a matte finish, and an iron. A pack of razor blades, and he's good to go.

He stops by the photo shop to request a passport picture.

In the bathroom he uses the baby-changing station as an ironing board. He cuts a piece of tape the length of a passport page. With steady hands, he smoothes the tape over the photo. He irons the page to heat-seal the edges and trims the excess with a razor blade.

Within the hour he's Jordan Phelps.

He studies himself in the mirror. *I wish it hadn't gone down like this.*

Damon's long-range mission was, of course, to score a spot in the CIA. He'd enter at ground level, but his handlers were confident he'd quickly climb the ranks. The Nighthawks wanted access to Project Genesis, currently in development at the CIA. Scientists would be working on it for at least another ten years. They'd finish right around the time Damon would receive full clearance.

According to Agent Roberts, "Project Genesis will catapult the security of the United States to an impenetrable level." The technology was insane. With Genesis, a satellite orbiting earth had the power to locate any person on the globe, provided the government had a speck of their genetic material. One microscopic flake of skin or a tiny hair from a razor.

Genesis analyzed the material, transmitted the information to the satellite and based on the individual's unique genetic code, located the host within a half-mile radius. After tracking the subject, a deployed guided missile finished the job.

A GPS for DNA.

The Nighthawks were pissed because America hadn't nuked the entire Middle East after 9/11. A bunch of guys in the CIA had resigned right after that and started their own agency, with an insurance business as their cover. Damon didn't care about their ideology then, and he doesn't care now. Roberts did what no one else could—but he only found the driver. Damon saw three men in the SUV that killed his brother. And he means to ferret out the rest.

Roberts promised that every available Nighthawk resource would be at Damon's disposal, in exchange for his service. And the pay was outstanding—his mom needed financial help and he knew it. He'd created letterhead, designed a webpage and opened a bank account: The Littlest Angels, a fake charity that offered financial assistance to single mothers who'd lost a child. Every month, he cashed his paychecks and sent her a check.

She never said the actual words, but she will always blame Damon for Gabriel's death. She'd told him a thousand times, *You are your brother's keeper.* And he takes that weight—it is absolutely his fault. He will spend the rest of his life hunting down the men responsible for his brother's death.

The Nighthawks were his way in.

"Guess I'm gonna need a new plan," he mumbles. He changes his shirt so it doesn't match the passport photo.

The parking lot is mostly empty when Damon steps outside. Employees park in the back, so that's where he'll boost a car. No one will notice for hours, and by then he'll be halfway to Baltimore. Like Nadia, Damon happens to be especially suited to this line of work. He's smart and strong. He knows people—deep down and right away. Knows how they think, what they feel. And his flexible moral compass could only have helped his future as an agent.

He throws his old clothes and the leftover tape, along with the iron and razors, into the dumpster. His shoes go in a second dumpster across the street. He selects a white, late-model sedan. Inconspicuous, no flash. He jimmies the door and climbs inside.

Five minutes later, he's on his way to Tucson. He eases the car onto the expressway and cracks the window. The cool breeze chills the sweat on his skull. Against his will, pictures of that morning fill his head, as they have so many times. The memories come in flashes, like photographs tossed onto a coffee table, one by one. Gabriel, his sweet baby brother, with his quick laugh and his tiny teeth. His little hands. His fat cheeks. He followed Damon everywhere.

He sighs as his adrenaline dips; fatigue will soon follow. *Not much longer.* He turns on the radio and takes a few deep breaths to wake up. In three hours he'll be on a plane, racing toward Baltimore-Washington International Airport.

Five hours later, somewhere over Kansas, Damon realizes his new passport has probably been flagged.

71 NADIA

Nadia wakes in a hospital, in a dimly lit room that smells of anti-septic and bandages. She hears her mother's voice in the hallway. "Mom?" she whispers.

A nurse leans in to adjust the pillows. Quietly she says, "You had appendicitis. We operated; you're going to be fine."

"Appendicitis? No, that's not—"

"Your cover story is that we removed your appendix. Which we did, just in case. Do you understand what I'm telling you?"

Nadia nods as her mother enters the room.

"Nadia! Are you all right?"

"Mom, what are you doing here?"

"You're in the hospital. Of course I'm here. Are you okay?" She turns to the nurse. "Maybe you should get the doctor."

"I'll let him know she's awake." The nurse leaves.

Nadia offers her mother a weak smile. Her lips feel like plastic, dry and cracked. A bitter metallic taste lingers in her mouth. She tries to remember her last moments awake, in the dean's office—it's like a dream.

"Your friends are here. I met Libby—she's a *doll*. And Jack, who also seems very nice. And quite taken with you, I might add. He brought me coffee."

"Jack's okay?" Nadia's eyes tear.

"Yes, dear, of course. Why wouldn't he be? And who's the other boy? Alan?"

Nadia grins and tries not to cry. She nods.

"He's a character, hobbling around on that cane. He says you kicked him during jujutsu!"

"Is that what he said?" Nadia laughs as tears drip down her cheeks.

"You've always been a firecracker. Are you crying? What's wrong?"

"I'm so happy to see you."

"Oh, you are so sweet! I've missed you too. Where is the doctor? If you want something done right, I guess you have to do it yourself. I'll go find him. Should I send in your friends?"

Nadia nods again. "And maybe some water?"

Jack, Libby and Alan enter the room as her mom leaves.

"Nadia, thank God you're all right!" Libby leans in to give her a gentle hug. "We've been worried sick about you!"

"How are you feeling?" Alan asks. He leans on a cane. "You look *awful*."

"You lied to my mother," she whispers. "Good for you."

"It was harder than getting shot," Alan whispers back.

Nadia looks at Jack. "I thought you were dead." She fights back her tears.

"No such luck." He leans in and kisses her forehead. "You'll have to try a lot harder if you want to get rid of me."

She struggles to keep her eyes open. She has a million questions but she can't stay awake. "Water?" she whispers.

"Okay, everyone, that's it for now," the doctor says as he shuffles her friends out of the room. "Nurse, can you get her some ice chips?"

"I'll see you soon," Jack promises.

Sunlight pushes through the cracks in the blinds when Nadia next opens her eyes. Hashimoto Sensei stands at the window, his back straight, arms crossed.

"Sensei."

"Ah, Nadia-san, welcome back." He pulls a chair next to her bed.

"What happened?"

"Dean Wolfe tried to kill you." He smiles. "He failed."

"He called *you*?" She remembers the dean calling someone, asking for help.

"No. When we discovered you recorded the incident, we checked his phone records. He called Professor Hayden."

"But Hayden never came." Nadia tries to scratch her nose but her arms are connected to many tubes. She roots her face into her shoulder.

"No, he did not." Sensei chuckles. "Hayden-san made a hasty departure. He disappeared."

"You saved my life." Nadia smiles at him.

"*Hai.*"

"You deciphered my message. I knew you would." She closes her eyes.

"Well done, Nadia-san. Get some sleep. We will talk later."

Over the next twenty-four hours Nadia pieces together what happened. Jack and Sensei explain what she's missed.

"I thought you were dead," she says again to Jack. She's able to sit up in bed. Her abdomen aches from the operation—they cut through her stomach muscles to dig out the bullet. By some miracle, no major organs were damaged.

"No, apparently not. I was unconscious, however. Wolfe knocked me out cold, but I guess since you were on your way in, he didn't want to risk the noise of a gunshot."

Nadia nods. "He didn't have a silencer."

Jack looks away. "I can't believe it was him this whole time. I should've seen—"

"Don't do that. You couldn't have known."

"Nadia-san is correct."

"I know. It's just embarrassing. I really looked up to him."

Jack clears his throat. He turns to Hashimoto Sensei. "I still don't understand how you got there."

Sensei smiles. "Nadia-san left a message when she broke into the covert-operations room at the dojo. When the door opens, it triggers a silent alarm that sounds only in my room."

"Sorry about breaking in." Nadia blushes and looks down at her hands.

"Nadia-san, it is no accident you saw my password. I knew you were suspected as the double agent. I also knew you were innocent. I thought the day might come when you would need access to that room." Sensei turns to Jack. "She scribbled her message on the wall—in *pen*, no less."

"I was afraid someone would see it and erase it. I would've carved it with my knife if I'd had time." A nurse comes in to check Nadia's vitals and they fall silent.

As she leaves, Jack looks from Sensei to Nadia. "So what was the message?"

Sensei leans back and laughs. "*Sute inu*. Well done, Nadia-san."

"What does that mean?" Jack asks.

"I was afraid if I wrote *ookami*, it would be too easy for someone else to figure it out and destroy my note," she interrupts. "And I thought you would be investigating my death, not saving my life."

"But what does *sute inu* mean?" Jack pleads.

Nadia grins. "It means: a dog with no master."

"What?" Jack furrows his eyebrows.

"A wild dog, Jack-san," Sensei answers. "A wolf."

72 DAMON

TUESDAY, DECEMBER 13
2:55 PM

Damon suspects agents will be at the gate when he disembarks. He spends the last two hours of the plane ride making friends. He trades places with a college student who is clearly annoyed by the screaming children beside him. He even moves the guy's carry-on bag—after attaching a luggage tag that reads *Jordan Phelps*. Then he goes to work on the young mother as she desperately tries to soothe her children.

When they land, he carries one of her kids off the plane. He keeps his head down, eyes on the sleeping toddler. Damon looks like part of their family. They're staying at the Airport Express Holiday Inn. What a coincidence; that's where he's meeting his Aunt Sarah. And he's more than happy to help her onto the complimentary shuttle. The kid in the University of Maryland sweatshirt gets tackled before he reaches the escalator.

Damon expects the Nighthawks to stake out his house, so he waits at the hotel until nightfall. At the gift shop he buys an Orioles ball cap, a red scarf and a puffy coat. Light disguise, but enough to change his shape and cast doubt if anyone's looking. The hardest part is adjusting his gait. He sticks a pebble in the corner of his shoe to establish a consistent limp.

After dark, he calls for a cab. He dozes in the back. The driver wakes him when they reach the address. A convenience store three blocks from his house. He'll walk the rest of the way.

It's cold enough to see his breath. The street smells like the woods after a campfire. A half-block from home he cuts through the neighbor's yard, coming up on his place from behind. He pushes through the screen of junipers that runs along the property line. The yard smolders.

His house is gone.

For a second, he's confused. A black pile of smoking debris has replaced his home. His mouth falls open as he stumbles toward the street.

"Damon? Is that you?" Mrs. Williams, the next-door neighbor, waddles up the pavement toward him in her slippers and housecoat.

"Mrs. Williams, where's my mom?"

"Don't worry, baby, she's fine. The man from the insurance company came by and took her to a hotel. He left this for you."

Damon's heart skips a beat. "What insurance company?"

"I'm not sure. It's right here on the envelope." Mrs. Williams holds the message at arm's length, struggling to read the return address. "I don't have my glasses. Looks like . . . Harkins—no, Hawkins Insurance." She hands it to him.

His hands shake as he tears the envelope. The note inside reads: *Welcome home. I'm willing to make a trade. You have my number.*

Damon's legs give out. He drops to his knees on the pavement. The acrid taste of bile burns the back of his throat as he vomits on the sidewalk.

"Oh, Damon. It'll be okay." Mrs. Williams puts her hand on his forehead. "Come next door. I'll get you a ginger ale." She starts down the walk.

He can't breathe. A vice crushes his chest. He grabs onto the grass to keep from falling over.

They took his mother. Then they took her house.

Damon looks up at the charred remains. Every last memory of her husband, her baby boy, gone. Burned to the ground. Roberts spared nothing.

And neither will I.

Rage chokes his heart. He gazes into the starless city sky. *I'll get her back.*

Quietly, much too low for Mrs. Williams to hear, he swears a solemn oath.

"And then I'll annihilate the Nighthawks."

73 NADIA
SATURDAY, DECEMBER 17

Nadia is released from the hospital just in time to pack her bags for winter break. And not a moment too soon. She's bored out of her mind lounging around in bed.

Her mom stayed in town, declaring it would be best if they flew home together. She drives Nadia back to school to collect her things. The guard at the gate is expecting them; he greets Mrs. Riley by name.

"Isn't he nice," Nadia's mom says. "How did he know me?"

Nadia shrugs. "It's a small school. Maybe Sensei told him you'd be coming."

"I'm glad to see security is so tight. It makes me feel a little better about your being here."

Nadia smiles at her mother as they pull into the parking lot. "Don't worry, Mom. No one gets in—or out—without permission."

"I'll pack up your clothes. You can say your good-byes," she offers.

Nadia limps next door to the dojo. She leans forward in the doorway as best she can, but bending over really hurts her incision. Hashimoto Sensei comes to the lobby as she's gasping her way out of the bow.

He rushes to help her straighten. "Nadia-san, today we will make an exception to the rule of etiquette."

"It's only pain. It will either kill me or go away, right?"

He smiles. "You are off for the holidays?"

"Yes. I wanted to come by and say thank you again. For everything."

"As soon as possible, I expect you to resume your exercise program. Do not push yourself now; you might cause internal bleeding. But if you do nothing for the next month you will find yourself at a disadvantage when you return to school, and I know how you feel about doing your best."

"*Hai*, Sensei." Nadia turns to leave.

"I will see you soon. Be careful."

His warning stops her. "Be careful of what?"

He frowns. "Nadia-san, the sparrow who flies behind the hawk believes the hawk is fleeing. It is not so. Dean Wolfe is in a coma with an armed guard watching his room, but Damon-san and Professor Hayden are both missing in action. Since we have no one to question, we do not know how many others were working with them."

Nadia nods and moves toward the door. Once more she stops and faces Sensei. "Can I ask you something?"

"No."

She ignores him. "You said I was the second student to be shown the covert-ops room. Who was the first?"

Sensei smiles as he answers, "Albert Vincent."

"The director of the CIA?"

"*Hai.*"

Nadia tries to suppress her smile. "What does *abunai* mean?"

Sensei laughs. "Ah, my password. It is a warning. It means *dangerous,* or *watch out!*"

"That seems about right."

Nadia leaves the dojo and hobbles up the path to the dining hall, hoping to see her friends before it's time to go. She finds Alan and Libby at their regular table. It seems strange that Damon isn't with them.

Nadia suddenly remembers what Dean Wolfe told her that night. Damon refused a direct order. *He couldn't kill me.* Somehow, she can't wrap her brain around the fact that Damon isn't really Damon. She's torn between the sadness of losing her friend and the anger accompanying her realization she never really knew him at all. Not to mention he was framing her as the double. *I guess that's bound to put a strain on any relationship.*

"Hey, guys," she greets her friends.

"Nadia, how are you feeling?" Alan stands and pulls out a chair.

"Look at you, getting me a chair!"

"People can change. You did. You were *useless* when you got here."

"That's more like it." Nadia eases herself onto the seat. "Anyway, I'm okay, thanks for asking. How about you?"

He nods. "A little sore, but not too bad. Libby is taking excellent care of me." He smiles at Libby and Nadia senses something more than gratitude.

Libby doesn't seem to notice. "Nadia, I took the liberty of stashing our textbooks in the back of my closet," she says. "I figured your momma might come by."

"Thanks, I didn't even think of that."

"Listen," Alan says. "I have been wanting to say something. When we first got here, I thought you two were dead weight. Libby, your Southern drawl makes you sound profoundly uneducated. And Nadia, where do I start? You were not good at *anything*."

"What is the matter with you?" Nadia asks.

Alan seems surprised by her reaction. "I am trying to say thank you." He holds up a finger and smiles. "*I'm* trying to say thank you."

Libby narrows her eyes. "Is that supposed to be a joke? I may be too *profoundly uneducated* to understand the delicate nuances of Yankee-talk, but let me tell *you* something: this is not gratitude."

"I am admitting I was wrong. I *do* need you. I would not have made it out of the canyon without you. I am very glad we are on a team. This is all I'm saying."

"Well, that was one God-awful thank you." Libby sits back and crosses her arms.

"You want to help me out, please?" Alan asks Nadia.

"Not even a little. Oh—but here's something interesting." Nadia glances around. "When I was in Wolfe's office, he said something to me about your grandfather. He knows."

A look of understanding crosses Alan's face. "Oh, of course! *That* is what he was talking about."

"Who? What?" Libby asks.

"Damon," he whispers. "He made a big point of telling me what close friends we were after I got shot."

"Why?" asked Libby.

"So no one would go looking for him," Nadia says. Alan nods. She drops her voice. "Have you trained with your grandfather? That's how you learned to shoot, isn't it?"

Alan's neck turns a splotchy red. "I cannot talk about him. Please do not ask me anything."

Libby jumps in. "That's fine. You'll tell us when you're good and ready. I accept that, because we Southerners are far more well-mannered than you New Yorkers."

They sit in silence for a few moments. Nadia can't let it go. "It's just—I've heard amazing things about Mossad. Can you teach us anything?"

Welts appear on Alan's throat. "Nadia. Please."

"Have you spoken to your grandfather yet? About how you feel?" she asks.

Libby changes the subject. "Think you'll be getting a new roommate?"

"I had not thought about it. It's weird, the whole thing with Damon—how someone so close to us could be so different from what he claimed to be, and we never knew."

"It certainly is," Libby agrees. "I mean, I'm not shocked you didn't know, but Nadia and me? I thought we were sound judges of character."

"Thanks a lot," Alan says.

"Sometimes the truth hurts. Hey, Nadia, Alan and I might get together over break, maybe meet in DC for New Year's Eve?" Libby pats Alan's hand. "Shall we call you?"

"No, we have to do New Year's Eve in Times Square," Alan says.

"Honey, not everyone can make it to New York."

"Your parents will get you a ticket."

"I didn't mean me." Libby's eyes flicker toward Nadia.

"Oh. Well, she does not have to come."

"Alan. Be nice," Libby says.

Nadia grins. Libby is walking right into this, and she has no idea. "Give me a call when you finalize your plans. Listen, you guys, I have to get going." She pulls herself out of the chair. "I hope you both have a great holiday." Libby stands to hug her. "It will be strange waking up without you. I'll miss you."

"I know. Same here," Libby says.

Nadia looks at Alan one last time. "The conversation with your grandfather is non-negotiable."

"I understand," Alan answers.

"We'll see you soon," Libby says. "Tell your momma we said hi."

On the way back to her dorm, Jack calls her name. She waits while he sprints across the lawn.

"Thank God. I've been looking all over for you." He leans over and rests his hands on his knees, trying to catch his breath.

Her eyes widen. Maybe they've found Damon. "What's the matter?"

"Nothing—I was afraid you left without saying good-bye." He smiles his brilliant, beautiful smile.

"I wouldn't do that." She smiles back.

He pulls her close, gathering her in his arms. "Why'd you go to the dean's office that night? After I warned you, why didn't you run? You saved my life, you know."

Nadia feels his heart beating through his sweater. "You would've done the same for me."

"True enough. Am I squeezing too tight?"

She shakes her head and leans further into him. They stand for a moment in silence, Nadia enjoying the warm sun on her back.

"Nadia, when we get back from break, do you think we could start over? Maybe go on a real date? I understand if it's too soon—if you need more time. But I'd never forgive myself if I didn't ask." He pulls away to look at her.

She thinks back to what Dean Wolfe said about Jack. *His feelings for you interfered with his job.* She smiles and says, "I'd like that."

Jack's eyes shine as he weaves his hand through her hair. He rests his head on hers. She feels him take a deep breath, inhaling her. He looks into her eyes and then kisses her on the lips, as soft as the sun rising over the desert.

ACKNOWLEDGMENTS

I would like to thank:

Terry, whose love and support made this writing possible.

Morgan and Elizabeth, for your comments (criticisms), encouragement (mockery) and ideas ("You're not going to say it like *that*, are you?").

My parents: for dragging me around the world and denying me cool toys, leaving me no choice but to entertain myself with—*gasp*—my imagination and creative writing; for letting me fingerprint you when I started my own detective agency at age eight; for always speaking in complete, grammatically correct sentences. Dad: for the mushroom story idea. Mom: for copyediting my manuscript a dozen times (and telling me for decades that I should be a writer. *Okay.* I get it).

My sister, Rachel Smith, for completely ignoring me until the age of thirty. I'm certain this contributed to the building of my rich inner world. More recently, your constant cheerleading (badgering) finally paid off. It is no exaggeration to say this book would not have seen the light of day without your help.

My dear friend, Anna Kline, for teaching me not to be stingy with my words. Anna, you know my characters better than I do. Thank you for not letting me move on.

Anna and Rachel, for reading twelve thousand slightly different drafts. I am forever in your debt. Or for the next twelve months or so. (These words of gratitude in no way constitute a legally binding contract.)

Deniese Hardesty, for your faith and vision. Writing is the easy part. Thank you for helping me with everything else.

My clever and imaginative agent, Logan Garrison, and her fabulous coworkers at the Gernert Company. Logan, you really should write a book of your own.

My infinitely patient editor, Sally Morgridge, and the wonderful team at Holiday House. I apologize for my obsession with the Oxford comma.

My very talented jacket artist, Kerry Martin. You can't judge a book by its cover, but I usually do anyway. Thanks for making me look good.

My sensei, Michael Cerpok, for your teaching and guidance.

Lonna Salter, for being a fan from the start.